# *Awakening*

## Cate Tiernan

**PUFFIN**

*To GC and EF, with many thanks*

PUFFIN BOOKS

Published by the Penguin Group
Penguin Books Ltd, 80 Strand, London WC2R 0RL, England
Penguin Group (USA) Inc., 375 Hudson Street, New York, New York 10014, USA
Penguin Group (Canada), 90 Eglinton Avenue East, Suite 700, Toronto, Ontario, Canada M4P 2Y3
(a division of Pearson Penguin Canada Inc.)
Penguin Ireland, 25 St Stephen's Green, Dublin 2, Ireland (a division of Penguin Books Ltd)
Penguin Group (Australia), 250 Camberwell Road, Camberwell, Victoria 3124, Australia
(a division of Pearson Australia Group Pty Ltd)
Penguin Books India Pvt Ltd, 11 Community Centre, Panchsheel Park, New Delhi – 110 017, India
Penguin Group (NZ), 67 Apollo Drive, Rosedale, North Shore 0632, New Zealand
(a division of Pearson New Zealand Ltd)
Penguin Books (South Africa) (Pty) Ltd, 24 Sturdee Avenue, Rosebank, Johannesburg 2196, South Africa

Penguin Books Ltd, Registered Offices: 80 Strand, London WC2R 0RL, England

puffinbooks.com

First published as separate editions in the USA in Puffin Books, a division of Penguin Group (USA) inc.,
as *Sweep: Awakening* and *Sweep: Spellbound* 2001
Published as separate editions in Great Britain in Puffin Books 2002
First published in one volume 2009

2

Copyright © 17th Street Productions, an Alloy Online, Inc. company, 2001
All rights reserved

17th Street Productions and associated logos
are trademarks and/ or registered trademarks of Alloy Online, Inc

Made and printed in England by Clays Ltd, St Ives plc

A C

future

# 1.
# Embers

*They fled tonight, the lot of them. Selene Belltower, Cal Blaire, Alicia Woodwind, Edwitha of Cair Dal, and more—all slipped through my fingers. They knew I was closing in on them. It's my fault. I was too cautious, too worried about proving the case against them beyond all doubt, and so I left it too long. I've failed, and badly. And worse, Morgan nearly died because I didn't stop them.*

*I've got to break the warding spells and get into Selene's house. She can't have had time to pack up all her things. Maybe I can find some clue, something to tell me where she went or what her group is planning.*

*Damn, damn, damn!*

*—Giomanach*

I stood with Bree Warren and Robbie Gurevitch, my two oldest friends, on the lawn in back of Cal Blaire's house. Together we stared at the flames that leapt hungrily up from the pool house and cast a smoky pall over the stark November moon. Somewhere in the inferno there was a crash as a section of the roof caved in. A fountain of white-hot sparks flew skyward.

"My God," Bree said.

Robbie shook his head. "You got out of there just in time."

Sirens wailed in the distance. Though it was the last night of November and snow lay inches deep on the ground, the night air felt hot and dry as I gulped in a deep breath. "You guys saved my life," I managed to choke out. Then I doubled over, coughing. It hurt just to breathe. My throat was raw and my chest ached and every cell in my body craved oxygen.

"Barely," Robbie murmured. He tucked an arm under my elbow, supporting me.

I shuddered. I didn't need Robbie to tell me how close I had come to dying, trapped in the tiny, spell-wrapped room that had been hidden in the pool house. Trapped by Cal Blaire, my boyfriend. My eyes, already stinging from the smoke, blurred again with tears.

Charismatic, confident, inhumanly beautiful, Cal had woken something that had been sleeping inside me for sixteen years. It was Cal who had first loved me, as no boy ever had. It was Cal who had helped me to the realization that I was a blood witch, with powers I'd never even known could exist in the real world. It was Cal who had shown me how love and magick could twine together until it seemed that all the energy in the universe was enfolding me, streaming through me, there for the taking.

And it was Cal who had lied to me, used me. Cal who, less than an hour ago, had tried to kill me by setting the pool house on fire.

The wailing sirens of the fire trucks sounded closer now, and I could see the reflection of their whirling lights faintly in the dense clouds of smoke. The red made a hellish glow against the roiling gray. I turned to see where the trucks were, then gasped as two dark, faceless silhouettes loomed up in front of me.

They resolved into Hunter Niall and his cousin, Sky Eventide, two English witches who'd arrived in our little town a few weeks ago. Oh, right, I realized foggily. I'd sent them a witch message, too, begging them to help me. I'd forgotten.

"Morgan, are you all right?" Hunter asked in his crisp, accented voice. "Do you need a doctor?"

I shook my head. "I think I'm okay." Now that I could breathe, my body was starting to thrum with adrenaline, and I was getting a weird, disconnected feeling.

"There'll be an ambulance coming with the fire trucks," Bree pointed out. "You should let them check you out, Morgan. You inhaled a lot of smoke."

"Actually, if Morgan's up to it, it would be better if we left now." Hunter cast a glance over his shoulder. The first of the fire trucks was turning into the curved gravel driveway in front of the big house where Cal and his mother, Selene Belltower, lived. "I don't think we want to talk to anyone official. Too many awkward questions. Sky, if you wouldn't mind delaying them for a moment so we can make our getaway . . ."

Sky nodded and set off across the lawn at a smooth lope. Stopping a few yards from the house, she held up her hands.

I watched, puzzled, as she moved her fingers in a complicated dance in the air.

"What's she doing?" Robbie asked.

"Casting a glamor," Hunter explained. "She's making the firemen believe the fire has spread to the house. The illusion won't last more than a few moments, but it'll keep them from noticing our cars while we're driving away." He nodded his approval to Sky as she hurried back toward us. "Let's get going. No time to waste. Robbie, if you'll drive Morgan's car, we can all meet down at the end of the block."

I was dimly amazed by the swift way he took charge of the situation. No exclaiming over what had happened. No expressions of shock or horror. Just business. Normally that would have irritated me. But at that moment I felt reassured; safe, almost.

Robbie hurried toward my car. I started to follow him, but Bree took my arm. "Come on, you can ride with me," she said.

My gaze met hers. Even at the scene of a fire, her glossy, shoulder-length hair looked perfect. But the shock of what had happened showed in her dark eyes.

Once we'd been so close that we'd finished each other's sentences. That was before she'd fallen for Cal, before he'd chosen me. This morning Bree and I had been enemies. But tonight I had called her, sent her a witch message with my mind, when I was facing my darkest hour. I had called out to *her*. And she had heard me and had come to my aid. Maybe there was hope for us yet.

"Come on," Bree repeated, and led me toward her BMW. She helped me into the passenger seat, then went around to the driver's side. As we drove down the narrow, winding back driveway, she glanced anxiously in her rearview mirror.

"They're still running around the main house. No one's even gone into the backyard yet," she said. A smile tugged at her lips. "Sky's spell really worked, I guess. All this witchcraft stuff really blows my mind."

She gave me a sideways look. "It was wild hearing your voice so clearly in my mind," she added after a moment. "I thought I was going nuts. But then I figured, enough bizarre things have happened lately that I probably should take this seriously."

"I'm glad you did. You saved me," I replied. My voice was hoarse, and the act of speaking triggered another coughing fit.

"Are you sure you're okay?" Bree asked when I straightened up. "No burns or anything?"

Not on the outside, I thought bleakly. I shook my head. "I'm alive," I said. "Thanks to you." It wasn't exactly a reconciliation, but it was all I could manage at the moment.

At the end of the dark, quiet block we pulled up to the curb behind Sky's green Ford. Robbie was already there, leaning against the door of my car, Das Boot. I winced as I looked at the battered '71 Valiant. It was already dented and missing a headlight from a minor accident I'd had a week ago. Then, moments ago, Robbie had used Das Boot to ram through the wall of the pool house where I was trapped. Now the hood was badly dented, too.

"Right, then," Hunter said. He spoke briskly, but I felt like I was hearing him through a layer of heavy cloth. Somehow I just couldn't focus. "People are going to be asking a lot of questions about what happened here tonight; how the fire started, and so forth. We need to get our stories straight. Robbie, Bree, I think it's best if you simply pretend you weren't here. That way no one will question you."

Robbie folded his arms. "I'm going to tell our friends in Cirrus the truth," he said. "They have a right to know." Cirrus was the coven Cal had started. Robbie and I were members, along with four other people.

"Cirrus," Hunter said. He rubbed his chin thoughtfully. "You're right, they should know. But please, ask them to keep it to themselves." He turned to me. "Morgan, if you can bear it, I need to talk to you. I'll drive you home in your car afterward."

I cringed. Talk? Now?

"Can't it wait until tomorrow?" Bree asked sharply.

"Yeah," Robbie agreed. "Morgan's a mess. No offense, Morgan."

"I'm afraid it can't," Hunter said. His voice was quiet, but there was a final tone in it.

Robbie looked like he was about to argue, but then he simply handed Hunter my car keys.

Sky turned to Hunter. "I'll try to find out where they've gone, as we discussed," she said.

"Right," Hunter agreed. "I'll see you at home later."

"Where who's gone?" I asked. This was all moving too fast for me.

"Cal and Selene," Sky told me. She pushed a hand through her short, silver-blond hair. "Their house is sealed with warding spells, and both their cars are gone."

I swallowed hard. The thought that they were out there,

who knew where, was terrifying. I had a sudden, irrational conviction that they were hiding behind a tree or something equally melodramatic, spying on me at this very moment.

"They're not in Widow's Vale anymore," Hunter said, as if he'd read my mind. "I'm sure of it. I'd be able to tell if they were."

Though the logical part of my brain told me that nothing is ever certain, something in the way Hunter spoke made me believe him. I felt a burst of relief, followed by a wash of intense pain. Cal was gone. I'd never see him again.

Hunter put one hand under my elbow and steered me over to my car. He opened the passenger door, and I slid in. The inside of the car was frigid and that, combined with the adrenaline still pumping through my body, made me shake so hard, my muscles started to ache. Hunter cranked the engine, flipped on the one remaining headlight, then pulled out onto the quiet, tree-lined street.

He didn't say anything, and I was grateful. Usually Hunter and I were like sparks and gunpowder. He was a Seeker, sent by the International Council of Witches to investigate Cal and Selene for misuse of magick. He'd told me they were evil. Before I'd learned, to my horror and shock, that he was right, Cal and I had almost killed him. That was just one of the things that made me intensely uneasy around him.

In one of those weird connections that seemed common among blood witches, Hunter was Cal's half brother. But where Cal was dark, Hunter was fair, with sunlight-colored hair, clear green eyes, and sculpted cheekbones. He was beautiful, but in an entirely different way than Cal. Hunter was cool, like air or water. Cal smoldered. He was earth and fire.

Cal. Every thought led back to him. I stared out my window, trying to blink back tears and not succeeding. I wiped them away with the back of my hand.

Gradually it dawned on me that I didn't recognize the road we were on. "Where are we going?" I asked. "This isn't the way to my house."

"It's the way to *my* house. I thought it would be better if you washed up first, got the smell of smoke out of your hair and so forth, before you faced your parents."

I nodded, relieved that once again he'd thought it out. My parents—my adoptive parents, really—weren't comfortable with my powers or with me practicing witchcraft. Besides the fact that they're Catholic, they were frightened by what had happened to my birth mother, Maeve Riordan. Sixteen years ago Maeve and my biological father, Angus Bramson, had burned to death. No one knew exactly how it had happened, but it seemed pretty clear that the fact that they were witches had had everything to do with it.

I pressed my hand against my mouth, trying desperately to make sense of the last few weeks. Just a month ago I'd discovered that I was adopted and that by birth I was a descendent of one of the Seven Great Wiccan Clans—a blood witch. My birth parents had died when I was only a baby. Tonight I had almost shared their fate.

And it had been at Cal's hands. At the hands of the guy with whom I'd hoped to share the rest of my life.

Ahead of us, a fat brown rabbit sat frozen in the middle of the icy road, paralyzed by my car's headlight. Hunter brought the car to a stop, and we waited.

"Can you tell me what happened tonight?" he asked, surprisingly gently.

"No." My hand was still pressed against my mouth, and I had to take it away to explain. "Not right now." My voice cracked with a sob. "It hurts too much."

The rabbit came out of its paralysis and scampered to safety on the other side of the road. Hunter pressed the gas pedal, and Das Boot surged forward again. "Right, then," he said. "Later."

Hunter and Sky's house was on a quiet street somewhere near the edge of Widow's Vale. I didn't really pay attention to the route. Now that the adrenaline of escaping the fire was leaking away, I felt exhausted, groggy.

The car pulled to a stop. We were in a driveway beneath a canopy of trees. We got out to the night's chill and walked up a narrow path. I followed Hunter into a living room where a fire burned in a small fireplace. A worn sofa covered in dark blue velvet stood against one wall. One of its legs had broken off, and it listed at a drunken angle. There were two mismatched armchairs across from it, and a wide plank balanced on two wooden crates served as a coffee table.

"You'll need a shower and clean clothes," Hunter told me.

I glanced at a small clock on the mantel. It was nearly nine. I was more than late for dinner. "I've got to call my folks first," I said. "They've probably called the police by now."

Hunter handed me a cordless phone. "Should I tell them about the fire?" I asked him, feeling lost.

He hesitated. "The choice is yours, of course," he said at

last. "But if you do, you'll have a lot of explaining to do."

I nodded. He was right. One more thing I couldn't share with my family.

Nervously I dialed my home number.

My dad answered, and I heard the relief in his voice as I greeted him. "Morgan, where on earth are you?" he asked. "We were about to call the state troopers!"

"I'm at a friend's house," I said, trying to be as honest as I could.

"Are you all right? You sound hoarse."

"I'm okay. But Cal and I . . . we had a fight." I fought to keep my voice steady. "I'm—I'm kind of upset. That's why I didn't call earlier. I'm sorry," I added lamely.

"Well, we were very worried," my dad said. "But I'm glad you're all right. Are you coming home now?"

The front door opened, and Sky walked in. She glanced at me, then looked at Hunter and shook her head. "Not a trace," she said in a low voice.

Ice trickled down my spine. "In a little while, Dad," I said into the phone. "I'll be home in a little while."

Dad sighed. "Don't forget that tomorrow is a school day."

I said good-bye and hung up. "You didn't find them?" I asked Sky anxiously.

"They're gone. They hid their tracks with so many concealing spells that I can't even tell which direction they went," Sky said. "But they're definitely nowhere nearby."

I stood there, feeling my heart beat, not knowing how to process that information. After a moment, Sky took my arm and gently led me upstairs. I was too out of it to notice much more than that there were two doors up there that were closed. The third, in between them, opened into a narrow bathroom.

Sky disappeared through one of the doorways, then reappeared a moment later holding a bathrobe. "You can wear this when you come out," she said. "Leave your clothes outside the door, and I'll throw them in the washer."

I took the robe and closed the door, feeling suddenly self-conscious. I turned and dared a look in the mirror. My nose was red and swollen, my eyes puffy, and my long dark hair matted and flecked with ash. Soot streaked my face and clothes.

I'm hideous, I thought, as Cal's face rose in my mind again. He'd been so incredibly beautiful. How could I ever have believed he could really love someone like me? How could I have been so blind? I was such an idiot.

Clenching my jaw, I stripped down. I opened the door a crack and dropped my clothes in a heap on the hall floor. Then I got into the shower and scrubbed my body and my hair hard, as if the water could wash away more than dirt and smoke, as if it could take my sorrow and terror and rage and sluice them down the drain.

Afterward I dried off and put on the robe. Sky was taller than I was, and the robe bunched at my feet, looking shapeless and drab. I pulled a comb through my wet hair and went back downstairs.

Sky was sitting in one of the armchairs, but as I came down, she rose gracefully to her feet and went up to her room. As she passed me, she let her hand rest briefly on my shoulder.

Hunter stood at the fireplace, feeding a log to the fire. A

small ceramic teapot and two mugs sat on the coffee table. He turned to face me, and I was keenly aware of how good-looking he was.

I settled myself on the sofa, and Hunter sat in a worn armchair. "Better?" he asked.

"A little." My chest and throat weren't quite as sore, and my eyes had stopped stinging.

Hunter's green eyes were locked on me. "I need you to tell me what happened."

I took a deep breath; then I told him how Sky and I had scryed together. How she'd helped me to spy on Cal and his mother in their spell-guarded house as they talked to their coconspirators about killing me if I refused to join them. How I saw that Cal had been assigned to seduce me, to get me onto their side so that my power could be joined with theirs. How I'd learned that they were also after my birth mother's coven tools, objects of enormous power that they wanted to add to their arsenal of magickal weapons. How I'd gone to talk to Cal, how he'd overpowered me with magick and taken me back to his house.

"He put me in a seòmar in the back of the pool house," I said, a vivid picture of the horrible little secret room rising in my mind. "The walls were covered with dark runes. He must have knocked me unconscious. When I came to, I heard Selene arguing with him outside. She was telling him not to do it, not to set it on fire. But Cal said"—my voice broke again—"he said he was solving the problem. He meant me. I was the p-p-problem."

"Shhh," Hunter said softly. Reaching out, he laid his palm flat against my forehead. I felt a tingling warmth spread outward from the spot, like a thousand little bubbles. His eyes held mine as the sensation washed over me, dulling the edge of my pain to the point where I could just bear it.

"Thanks," I said, awed.

He smiled briefly, his face transforming for a moment. Then he said, "Morgan, I'm sorry to press you, but this is important. Did they get your birth mother's tools?"

Maeve had fled her native Ireland after her coven, Belwicket, had been decimated. I had recently found her tools, the ancient tools of her coven. Selene had wanted them badly. "No," I told Hunter. "They're safe. I'd know if they weren't—they're bound to me. Anyway, I hid them."

Hunter poured us each a cup of tea. "Where?"

"Um—under Bree's house. I put them there right before I went to see Cal," I said. It sounded so lame as I said it that I cringed, waiting for Hunter to yell at me.

But he just nodded. "All right. I suppose they'll be safe enough for now, since Cal and Selene have fled. But get them back as soon as you can."

"What can they do with them?" I asked. "Why are they so dangerous?"

"I'm not sure exactly what they could do," Hunter said. "But Selene is very powerful and very skilled in magick, as you know. And some of the tools, the athame and the wand in particular, were made long ago, back before Belwicket renounced the blackness. They've since been purified, of course, but they were made to channel and focus dark energies. I'm sure Selene could find a way to return them to their original state. I imagine, for example, that Maeve's wand in

Selene's hands could be used to magnify the power of the dark wave."

The dark wave. I felt a coldness in the pit of my stomach. The dark wave was the thing that had wiped out Maeve's coven. It had also destroyed Hunter's parents' coven and had forced his mother and father into hiding ten years ago. They were still missing.

No one seemed to know exactly what the dark wave was—whether it was an entity with a will of its own or a force of mindless destruction, like a tornado. All we did know was that where it passed, it left death and horror behind it, entire towns turned to ash. Hunter believed that Selene was somehow connected to the dark wave. But he didn't know how.

I put my head in my hands. "Is all of this happening because Cal and Selene are Woodbane?" I asked in a small voice. Woodbane was the family name of one of the Seven Great Clans of Wicca. To be Woodbane meant, traditionally, to be without a moral compass. Woodbanes throughout history had used any means at their disposal, including calling on dark spirits or dark energy, to become more powerful. Supposedly this had all changed when the International Council of Witches had come into being and made laws to govern the use of magick. But as I was learning, the world of Wicca was as fractured and divided as the everyday world I'd known for the first sixteen years of my life. And there were many Woodbanes who didn't live by the council's laws.

I happened to be Woodbane, too. I hadn't wanted to believe it when I first found out, but the small, red, dagger-shaped birthmark on the inside of my arm was proof of it.

Many, if not most, Woodbanes had one somewhere. It was known as the Woodbane athame, because it looked like the ceremonial dagger that was part of any witch's set of tools.

Hunter sighed, and I was reminded that he was half Woodbane himself. "That's the question, isn't it? I don't honestly know what it means to be Woodbane. I don't know what's nature and what's nurture."

He set down his mug and rose. "I'll see if your clothes are dry. Then I'll run you home."

Sky followed us to my house in her car so that she could drive Hunter home. He and I didn't talk on the way. Whatever calming effect his touch had had on me was entirely gone now, and my mind kept replaying Cal lying to me, shouting at me, using his magick to nearly kill me. How could something that had been so sweet, that felt so good, have turned into this? How could I have been so blind? And why, even now, was some shameful part of me wanting to call to him? Cal, don't leave me. Cal, come back. Oh, God. I swallowed as bile rushed up into my throat.

"Morgan," Hunter said as he pulled up in front of my house. "You do understand, don't you, that you can't let your guard down? Cal may be gone, but it's likely he'll come back."

Come back? Hope, fear, rage, confusion swept over me. "Oh, God." I doubled over in my seat, hugging myself. "Oh, God. I loved him. I feel so *stupid*."

"Don't," Hunter said quietly. I looked up. His face was turned away from me. I saw the plane of his cheek, pale and smooth in the milky starlight that filtered in through Das Boot's windshield.

"I know how much you loved Cal," Hunter said. "And I understand why. There's a lot in him that's truly beautiful. And—and I believe that he loved you, too, in his own way. You didn't imagine that. Even though I was one of the ones telling you otherwise."

He turned to face me then, and we stared at each other. "Look. I know you feel like you'll never get past this. But you will. It won't ever go away, but it *will* stop hurting quite so much. Trust me. I know what I'm talking about."

I was reminded of the time he and I had joined our minds, and I'd seen that he had lost not only his parents but also his brother to dark magick. He'd suffered so much that I felt I could believe him.

He made a movement as if he were going to touch my face with his hand. But he seemed to stop himself and pulled his hand back. "You'd better go in before your parents come out here," he said.

I bit the inside of my cheek so I wouldn't start crying all over again. "Okay," I whispered. I sniffed and looked at my house. The lights were on in the living room.

I felt suddenly awkward. After that moment of connection, should I shake Hunter's hand? Kiss his cheek? In the end I just said, "Thanks for everything."

We both got out of the car. Hunter gave me my keys and headed down the dark street to where Sky waited in her car. I walked up the drive, my body on autopilot. I hesitated at the door. How was I going to act normal around my parents when I felt like I'd been ripped apart?

I opened the front door. The living room was empty, and the house smelled of chocolate chip cookies and wood smoke. There were still embers in the fireplace, and I could smell a faint tinge of the lemon oil that my mom used on the furniture. I heard my parents' voices in the kitchen and the sound of the dishwasher being unloaded.

"Mom? Dad?" I called nervously.

My parents, Sean and Mary Grace Rowlands, came into the living room. "Morgan, you look like you've been crying," my mom said when she caught sight of me. "Was the fight with Cal very bad?"

"I—I broke up with Cal." It wasn't exactly true, but it wasn't the falsehood that shocked me as much as the truth of my situation. Cal and I were no longer together. We were not a couple. We were not going to love each other forever. We were not going to be together again. Ever.

"Oh, honey," said my mom. The sympathy in her voice made me want to cry for the hundredth time that awful night.

"That's too bad," my dad chimed in.

"Um, I also had a little accident in Das Boot," I said. The lie slipped out before I'd even fully formulated it. I just knew I had to explain the crumpled hood of my car somehow.

"An accident?" my dad exclaimed. "What happened? Are you all right? Was anyone else hurt?"

"No one got hurt. I was pulling out of Cal's driveway and I hit a light pole. I kind of messed up the hood of my car." I swallowed. "I guess I was pretty upset."

"Oh my God," Mom said. "That sounds serious! Are you sure you're all right? Maybe we should run you over to the ER and have them take a look at you."

"Mom, I didn't hit my head or anything." I smothered a cough.

"But—" my dad began.

"I'm fine." I cut him off. I had to get to my room before I had a nervous breakdown right in front of them. "I'm just beat, that's all. I really just want to go to bed."

Then, before they could ask any more questions, I fled up the stairs. I was relieved to see that the door to my sister's room was closed. I couldn't handle another explanation. Or even another syllable.

In my room I paused briefly to pet Dagda, my little gray kitten, who was curled up on my desk chair. He mewed a sleepy hello. I went over to my dresser to get out my softest flannel pajamas. But I paused, staring at a tiny gift box on top of my dresser. It was one of the birthday gifts Cal had given me last week: a pair of earrings, golden tigereyes set in silver. I couldn't stop myself from opening the box to look at them again. They were as beautiful as I remembered: the silver swirling in delicate Celtic knots and the stones that were the same color as Cal's eyes. I could still see him, his dark, raggedly shorn hair, his sensual mouth, the golden eyes that seemed to see right into me. The way he used to laugh. The way he had felt like a soul mate from the start.

I laid the earrings on my palm. They gave off a little pool of heat. They're spelled, I realized with a rush of nausea. Goddess, they're just another tool to control me, to spy on me. I remembered thinking, when he gave them to me, that these gifts were wrapped in his love. But the fact was, they were wrapped in his magick.

I couldn't keep them anywhere near me, I realized. I would have to find a safe way to dispose of everything Cal had given me. But not tonight. I stashed the earrings in the back of my closet, together with his other gifts. Then I put on my pajamas.

As I was pulling back my covers, there was a soft knock at my door. A moment later my mom stepped in. "Are you going to be all right?" she asked. Her voice was quiet.

And then the tears were flooding down my cheeks, my defenses completely overwhelmed. I sobbed so hard, my whole body shook.

I felt my mom beside me, her arms encircling me, and I clung to her as I hadn't in years. "My darling," she said into my hair. "My daughter. I'm so sorry. I know how much you must be hurting. Do you want to talk about it?"

I raised my head and met her eyes. "I can't . . . ," I whispered, gasping. "I can't. . . ."

She nodded. "All right," she said. "When you're ready."

When I'd crawled into bed, she pulled the comforter up to my chin and kissed my forehead as if I were six. Reaching over, she turned off my light. "I'm here," she murmured, taking my hand in hers. "It'll be all right."

And so, clutching her hand tightly, I fell asleep.

# 2.
# Changes

I went back to Selene's house tonight after I drove Morgan home. I waited until the police and firefighters were all gone, and then I spent an hour trying to get in, but I couldn't break through the thicket of spells she put round the place. It's bloody frustrating. I felt like chucking a rock through one of those big plate glass windows.

I wonder if Morgan could do it? I know she got into Selene's hidden library without even trying. She is incredibly strong, though incredibly untutored, too.

No. I can't ask her. Not after what she went through at that place. Goddess, the pain in her face tonight—and all over that bastard Cal. It made me sick to see it.

—Giomanach

I drifted awake on Monday, aware that the house was awfully quiet. Was I actually up before my parents or my sister?

It didn't seem possible. They were all morning people, insanely perky long before noon, a trait I could not fathom. It should have been the great tip-off that I was adopted.

I squinted at my clock. Nine forty-eight?

I bolted upright. "Mary K.!" I yelled.

No answer from my sister's room. I cast my senses out and realized I was alone in the house. What is going on? I wondered, sitting up.

A cough tore at my throat. Within the next instant everything that had happened last night came back to me. The enormity of it overwhelmed me. I dropped back against my pillows again and took a deep breath.

Nine forty-eight. Calculus would be starting soon. It suddenly hit me that I would never share my calculus and physics classes with Cal again, and anguish clawed at me. How stupid are you? I asked myself in disgust.

I staggered to my feet and padded downstairs. A note from my mom lay on the kitchen counter.

> Sweetie,
>     I think you need to rest today. Dad gave Mary K. a ride to school, and she'll go to Jaycee's later. There's leftover chili in the fridge for lunch. Give me a call and let me know how you're feeling.
>                               Love, Mom
> P.S. I know you won't believe me yet, but I promise you will get over this.

I blinked, feeling both grateful and guilty. There was so much they didn't know; so much I could never tell them.

I stuck a Pop-Tart in the toaster and got a Diet Coke from the fridge. The first sip, though, convinced me it was a mistake. The bubbles of carbonation stung like little pin-pricks as they went down my throat. I made some tea instead and skimmed through the newspapers. The local paper only came out twice a month, and of course there was nothing in *The New York Times* or the *Albany Times Union* about a minor fire in Widow's Vale, two hours away from either city. I could watch the local news later on TV. I wondered if my school would have some kind of explanation for Cal's disappearance.

By the time I'd finished breakfast, it was after ten. For a moment I debated crawling back under the covers with Dagda. But I needed to deal with Cal's gifts right away, so a trip to Practical Magick was in order. I figured the people who ran the shop, Alyce and David, would know what to do.

Then a horrible thought occurred to me: David and Alyce were part of Starlocket, Selene's coven. Could they have had anything to do with what happened to me?

I sank back into the chair, resting my elbows on the kitchen table, my forehead in my hands. My stomach roiled. Had everyone I'd trusted betrayed me? Practical Magick was almost a sanctuary to me; Alyce, in particular, a kind of guide. Even David, who had initially made me feel uncomfortable, was turning out to be someone whose friendship I valued.

Think, I told myself. I'd felt awkward with David but never threatened. I hadn't heard their voices while I was trapped in the pool house. And Hunter had explained to me that Selene created covens wherever she went—and then destroyed the non-Woodbane members. Neither David nor

Alyce was Woodbane. They would have been in danger from Selene as well—wouldn't they?

It's okay, I told myself. David and Alyce are my friends.

I called my mom at her office and thanked her for letting me stay home.

"Well, I know that you share some classes with Cal," Mom said. "I thought it might be hard to see him today."

Her words reminded me: she didn't even know he was gone. My stomach knotted up again. My mom thought all I was suffering from was my very first broken heart. That was certainly true, but it was also so much more than that, Cal's betrayal so much deeper.

"I'm sorry, sweetie, but I've got to run," she said. "I've got an appointment to show a house in Taunton. Will you be all right? Want me to come home at lunch?"

"No, I'm okay," I said. "I think I'll go out and run some errands."

"Staying busy is a good idea," she said. "And if you feel like calling later, just to talk, I'll be here most of the after-noon."

"Thanks." I hung up and went upstairs. I changed into jeans and a heavy ski sweater that my Aunt Maureen had given me last Christmas. I don't ski, and the sweater was kind of snowflaky for my taste, but I was cold, and it was the warmest thing I owned.

I went into my closet, where I had shoved Cal's gifts. My hands shook as I put them in my backpack. I set my jaw and willed myself not to grieve over them, over him. Then I grabbed my parka and hurried out of the house.

I drove north in my battered, rattly car, beneath bleak,

wintry skies that seemed leached of all color. Despite the salt on the roads, a thin sheet of ice covered the ground. All the cars were moving slowly. I switched on the radio, hoping for the local news, but instead got a weather report stating that the temperature was currently eighteen degrees and would drop to ten by evening. With the wind chill, it was even more brutal.

I pulled into a parking spot right in front of Practical Magick; for a change, parking was easy, as the block was practically empty. Only after I had climbed out of my car did I remember that there was one more gift from Cal, the one I'd loved best of all: the pentacle that he had worn around his neck. It was somewhere on the floor of my car, where I'd let it fall the day before when it had hit me that Cal was using it to enhance his control over me. I leaned down, searched the damp floor mats, and found the little silver circle with its five-pointed star. Without looking at it, I slipped it into the outer pocket of my pack.

I pushed through the heavy glass doors into Practical Magick. The shop was dark and cozy; half of it given to books on every aspect of Wicca, the occult, and New Age spiritual practices; the other half filled with a huge variety of supplies: candles, herbs, powders, crystals, ritual tools like athames, pentacles, robes, even cauldrons. The warm air was scented with herbs and incense. It all felt familiar, reassuring, safe—all feelings I had in very short supply at the moment.

I was surprised to see a customer in the shop, since there weren't any cars out front. Alyce was talking to a young woman who wore a sling with a baby in it and was holding the hand of a boy who looked to be about four years old.

As the woman spoke to her, Alyce nodded, dislodging several strands of gray hair from her long braid. She tucked them back in without ever taking her blue eyes from the young woman's face. It looked like a serious conversation. I wandered along the rows of books, waiting until they were done. I wanted to be able to talk to Alyce and David privately.

Then I heard more voices and saw an elderly couple emerge from behind the curtain that blocked off the tiny back room that David used as an office. They looked upset, as the woman talking with Alyce did. I wondered what was going on. Were there all kinds of magickal emergencies requiring Alyce and David's help today?

The elderly couple spoke with Alyce and the young woman. From the way they were behaving, they all seemed to know one another. They must be the people who lived upstairs, I realized. Practical Magick was on the ground floor of a three-story building. There were apartments above it, but I had never seen any of the tenants before. That would explain why there were no cars outside and why the elderly couple wore only sweaters.

They all left together. Alyce watched them for a moment, shook her head sadly, and then went back behind the counter.

I studied her quietly. Could she have had any part in what had happened to me?

Sensing my gaze, Alyce glanced up. "Morgan," she said, and I could see nothing but concern in her face. She came out from around the counter and took both my hands. "Hunter came by this morning and told us what happened. Are you all right?"

I nodded, looking at her. I let my senses seek for danger from her. I sensed nothing.

"Let's go in the back and talk," Alyce said. "I'll put the teakettle on."

I followed her behind the counter to the small back room, where David, the other clerk, sat at the square, battered table he used as a desk. An open ledger, its columns filled with numbers, lay in front of him. David, who was in his early thirties, was prematurely gray, a trait that he said was typical of his clan, the Burnhides. Today his face looked drawn and weary, as if he were aging to match his hair.

"Morgan, " he said, "I was horrified to hear what happened to you. Please, sit down."

He closed the ledger as Alyce put a mixture of dried herbs into a metal tea ball. Then she turned to face me. "We owe you an apology," she said. David nodded his agreement.

I waited nervously. An apology for what?

"We were too slow to see what Selene was really after," David said. "Too slow to stop her."

I could feel truth, and sorrow, in his statement. My nerves began to unwind.

"It wasn't your fault," I said. It felt strange to have these adult witches apologizing to me. "I should have seen through Selene and . . . and the rest of them." I couldn't bring myself to say Cal's name.

The kettle on the hot plate began to steam, and Alyce poured the boiling water into a teapot. She set it on a trivet to let the tea steep.

"Selene is a very seductive woman," David said. "All of Starlocket was taken in by her, even those of us who should have been wary. Cal might have been the only one who truly knew her nature."

"She's pure evil," I said angrily. The force of my words surprised me.

David raised one silver eyebrow. "It's more complex than that, I think. Very few things are purely black or white."

"Plotting to kidnap or kill me?" I demanded. "To steal my mother's coven's tools? Doesn't that count as evil?"

"Yes, of course," David said. He wasn't flustered by my outburst. In fact, it occurred to me that I'd never seen him flustered about anything. "Her actions *were* evil. But her intentions may have been more complicated than that."

"Her intentions aren't at issue," Alyce said, and I heard a note of steel in her voice.

David looked thoughtful but didn't say anything.

Alyce poured the tea. "Mint, motherwort, lemongrass, and a pinch of catnip. It's a very soothing brew," she announced, as if she wanted to change the subject. She sat down and took my hand. "This must be so awful for you," she said.

All I could do was nod. I took a deep breath. "Did you know they were both Woodbane?" I blurted. I hadn't realized how much that troubled me until this moment.

Alyce and David exchanged glances. "Yes," said David. "But that name doesn't mean what it used to."

"Morgan," Alyce said, closing her hand over mine, "you know that being Woodbane doesn't make you evil. A person chooses his or her own way."

"I guess," I mumbled. In a way I wanted to believe that Cal had had no choice but to be evil because of his Woodbane blood. But that would mean that I didn't either. I sighed. Wicca had seemed such a beautiful thing at first. How had it all become so complicated and frightening?

"If you need anything," David said, "If you have a question, need someone to talk to . . ."

"A shoulder to cry on," Alyce added. "Please, come to us. We are so sorry we weren't able to protect you from Selene. You are so new to this world, so vulnerable."

"Maybe you can help me now," I said, pulling my pack up into my lap. I removed the things I'd packed. "I got some birthday gifts from . . . from Cal." There, I'd said it. "Plus his pentacle. They're all spelled. What should I do with them?"

"Burn them," David advised. "Cast a purification spell so that even the ashes will be free of his magick."

"I agree," said Alyce. "You have to break their powers. They could still be acting on you, influencing you, as long as they exist."

"Okay." As I gazed at the pile of gifts, the enormity of Cal's betrayal rose up and threatened to drown me again. I swallowed, fighting back a sob as I put them back into my pack.

"It will be hard, but it's something only you can do for yourself," Alyce said. "If you'd like, you can come back here after the ritual."

"Maybe I will," I said. I took another sip of tea.

The bells over the front door jangled, indicating that someone had come into the store. "I'd better go and see who that is," Alyce said, standing up.

The phone rang, and David looked at it, frowning. "Here we go again. Would you two excuse me, please?"

A shadow seemed to pass over Alyce's face. "Come on,

Morgan," she said. "Let me take care of this customer. Then I'll help you find a purification spell. A really strong one."

In the main room I skimmed the bookcases, looking for purification spells, while I waited for Alyce.

Suddenly I heard David's voice raised from the back room. It was so unusual to hear him excited that I glanced up, startled. "Look, it's not just me. Two families will lose their homes!" he shouted. "I need more time." Then he said something else, but his voice had dropped to its normal, quiet pitch, which put an end to my eavesdropping.

I glanced at Alyce. Her face wore its usual air of calm, but I saw that her shoulders had tightened. They only relaxed once David's voice returned to normal.

After her customer paid for his purchase, she joined me. She scanned the shelves, then took down a slender book titled *Rituals for Purification and Protection*. "Try page forty-three. I think you'll find what you need for dealing with Cal's gifts."

As I read through the spell, David's voice rose again, and of course I listened. I couldn't help it. "I can't afford that, and you know it!" he shouted.

Alyce gave me a quick glance. She knew I had heard David, so I figured, why not just ask? "Alyce, what's going on?" I asked bluntly. "Who is David talking to?"

Alyce took a deep breath. "It sounds like he's talking to Stuart Afton or, more likely, Afton's lawyers."

"But why?" I asked. "Is something wrong? And who's Stuart Afton?"

"It's a long story," Alyce said. "David's Aunt Rosaline, who owned the store—this entire building, actually—died last week."

"I'm sorry to hear that." So much for my witch senses. I

hadn't even detected David's grief. My own problems had overwhelmed me. "Is he okay?"

Alyce bit her lip as if she was trying to decide how much to say. "Well, Rosaline's death wasn't unexpected. She'd been ill for a while. But that's only the beginning, I'm afraid. David had always assumed that, as her only living relative, he'd inherit the shop. But Rosaline died without a will and, unbeknownst to David, heavily in debt to a local real estate developer named Stuart Afton."

Now I realized why the name had sounded familiar. "Afton as in Afton Enterprises?" I'd seen the sign on a gravel pit just down the road from Unser's Auto Repair, where I always took Das Boot for service.

Alyce nodded. "Rosaline had been borrowing for years to keep the store afloat, using the building itself as collateral. The store barely makes any money, and Rosaline couldn't bear to raise the rent on the Winstons and the Romerios."

"Who are the Winstons and the Romerios?" I asked.

"They were all here when you arrived, actually," Alyce replied. "Lisa Winston is the woman I was talking to; she lives with her two boys on the top floor. The Romerios were that sweet old couple that came out of David's office. They were living on the second floor when Rosaline bought the building, years ago—that's how far back they go. They never had any children; they live on social security." She shook her head. "It would be impossible for them to move. And it would be a struggle for Lisa Winston. Her husband left her with those two little boys and nothing else."

I shook my head, confused. "But what's the problem? Why would they have to move?"

"Well, Rosaline didn't borrow from a bank; she borrowed from Afton. I'm not sure why—maybe the bank wouldn't give her a loan. Anyway, Afton essentially took over her mortgage. He doesn't have to follow the same rules as a bank. And now he wants the loan repaid in full at once, or the building is his." Alyce sighed. "Unless David can raise the money to repay him or Afton forgives the debt, this building will go to Afton. That was obviously his plan all along. He owns the buildings on either side already. Apparently he's been soliciting buyers, and rumor has it one of the big bookstore chains is interested in buying the whole block of properties and converting it into one big superstore."

"So Afton's just going to throw the tenants out?" I asked.

"More or less," Alyce agreed. "He can't flat out evict them, but he can raise their rents to market value, which comes to the same thing. If they lose those apartments, they'll never find anything else they can afford in this area."

"And Afton doesn't care?"

Alyce shrugged. "He's a businessman. He doesn't like losing money. Believe me, David and I have spent this entire week on the phone, trying everything we could think of to raise the money, but without much success."

My stomach dropped as the implication hit me. "What will happen to the store?"

Alyce looked at me with a steady gaze. "We'll sell off the stock and close. We can't afford rent in this area, either."

I looked at her in dismay. "Oh, no. You can't close. We all need you here, as a resource." Panic made my breath come faster. Having lost the anchor of Cal in my life, the idea of losing Practical Magick, my haven, threatened to push me over the edge.

"I know, my dear. It's a shame. But some things are out of our hands," Alyce said.

"No," I said. "We can't just accept this." I was stunned that she seemed so calm.

"Everything in life has its own cycle," Alyce said gently. "And the cycle always includes a death of sorts. It's the only way you get to a new cycle, to regeneration. If it's time for Practical Magick to come to an end, it will end."

"It's awful," I said in dismay. "I can't believe Afton can do this. Why can't someone get through to him, show him what he's doing?"

"Because he doesn't want to see," Alyce replied. Her brow furrowed. "I'm worried more about David than myself. I can always go back to teaching. But I'm not sure what he'll do. This store has been more or less his home since he got out of college. It will be much harder for him than for me."

I clenched my teeth in frustration, wondering if there was anything at all I could do. Organize a protest? A petition? A sit-in? Surely there must be some spell that could be done? But I wasn't supposed to do spells. That was the one thing all the more experienced witches agreed upon—that I didn't have enough knowledge yet. Besides, I told myself, if there were spells, well, David and Alyce would surely have already done them.

"All right, enough gloom," said Alyce briskly. "Tell me, do you have Maeve's cauldron?" Alyce knew I'd found my birth mother's tools.

"No."

"Well, pick out a nice cauldron, then," she said.

"Do I need one?" I asked.

"It's something every witch should have as part of her tools," she explained. "And you need it to make the fire to burn Cal's gifts. You want the fire contained in something round that you can circle with protection spells."

I went and chose a small cauldron from the ones on display and brought it back to the counter. Alyce nodded her approval. "Do you have all the herbs you need?" she asked.

I checked my spell, and Alyce filled a small paper bag with the ingredients I needed. "Make sure that before you start, you purify the cauldron with salt water," she said. "And then purify it again when you're done to ensure that none of Cal's magick lingers."

"I will," I promised. "Thanks, Alyce. And please tell David how sorry I am about his aunt and the store. If there's anything I can do to help . . ."

"Don't worry about us," she replied. "This is a time to heal yourself, Morgan."

After I'd paid and left Practical Magick, depression settled on me again. Cal had been not only my first love, but my first teacher as well. I hadn't realized this before, but right up until the moment Alyce told me the store might close, some part of me had already assumed that even without Cal, I'd have a place to learn about Wicca. Now it looked like I was going to lose that, too.

# 3.
# Purified

December, 1982

A year ago I had no children. Now I have two—and I can't be a father to either of them.

Cal, the elder, was born in June. I love him; how could I help it? He's so beautiful, so sweet and trusting. But I can't bear it when he looks at me with his mother's golden eyes. I can't bear the growing fear that he is Selene's creation, that she'll mold him to follow her in her madness and that nothing I do can stop it.

Yet still, I feel bound to stay. Bound to try to save him.

Giomanach, my younger son, was born just three nights ago. I felt, across an ocean and a continent, Fiona's pain and joy as he came out of her body. I ache to be with her, with my dearest love, my soul mate—and I ache to see my newborn son. But I don't dare go to them for fear that Selene will take some terrible vengeance on them.

*Goddess. I'm being ripped in two. How much longer can I bear this?*

*—Maghach*

I made one quick detour on the way home, pulling into Bree's driveway. I climbed out and glanced around to see if anyone was watching me. Even though it was noon on Monday in a residential neighborhood and not many people were around, I whispered, "You see me not: I am but a shadow," as I hurried around to the side of Bree's house.

I knelt next to a big, winter-bare lilac that grew outside the dining-room window and reached deep into the crawl space hidden by the cluster of woody stems. Tucked behind a piling was a rusted metal box. I'd hidden it there less than twenty-four hours earlier, on my way to see Cal.

I pulled the box out carefully. It contained my most precious possessions—the tools that Cal, Selene, and the people with them had almost killed me for. Tucking the box and its contents under my coat, I hurried back to my car.

When I got home, I glanced at the kitchen clock. I had a few hours before anyone got home. It was time to get rid of Cal's gifts.

I read over the spell Alyce had recommended. As she'd advised, I purified the cauldron first with boiling, salted water, then with plain salt rubbed over the interior and exterior. In my room I opened the metal box and looked through Maeve's tools. I took out the athame. Since I was planning to perform the ritual in our yard, I decided against using Maeve's green silk robe. You never know when a meter reader will show up or a neighbor will traipse into the yard, chasing after a dog. It wasn't a good idea to risk being seen in full witch regalia.

I was about to close the box when my fingertips brushed against my mother's wand. It was made of black wood, inlaid with thin lines of silver and gold. Four small rubies studded its tip. I'd never used it before, but now I closed one hand around it and instinctively knew it would focus my energy, concentrate and store my power.

The ground was covered with a thick, crunchy sheet of snow. The temperature must have been close to the promised ten degrees; it was bitterly cold. The wind was battering sky, trees, and ground as if determined to whip the warmth from the earth.

Carrying the cauldron and the rest of my supplies, I crossed the yard to a big oak in the back. In a book of Celtic lore, I'd read that the oak was considered a guardian. I stared up into its bare branches, realizing that I actually did feel safer beneath it. I knew that the tree would lend its energy and protection to my ritual.

I set down the cauldron and began to collect fallen branches, shaking off the snow. Giving thanks to the oak for its kindling, I broke the branches and arranged them in the cauldron. Then, using Maeve's athame, I traced a circle in the snow. I sprinkled salt over the line traced by the athame, and I started to feel the earth's power moving through me. I drew the symbols for the four directions and for fire, water, earth, and sky, invoking the Goddess with each one.

I brushed the snow off a boulder and sat down, trying to ignore the cold wind. Closing my eyes, I began to follow my breath, aware of the rise and fall of my chest, the rhythm of my heartbeat, the blood coursing through my veins.

Gradually my awareness deepened. I felt the roots of the oak tree stretching through the frozen ground beneath the circle, reaching toward me. I felt the earth itself echoing with all the years that our family had lived in this house. It was as if all the love in my adoptive family had penetrated the earth, become part of it, and was now surging up to steady me.

I was ready. Opening my eyes, I put the herbs that Alyce had given me into the cauldron. Most of them I recognized: a lump of myrrh, its scent unmistakable, dried patchouli leaves, and wood betony. Two of them I didn't recognize, but as I added them, their names came to me: olibanum tears and small pieces of a root called ague. Finally I added a few drops of pine and rue oil and mixed the ingredients until I felt their essences swirl together.

I concentrated on the cauldron. Fire, I thought. A moment later a spark flickered, and I heard the sound of flames crackling. A thin line of smoke rose from the cauldron.

"Goddess, I ask your help," I began. I glanced at the spell book. "These gifts were given to bind me. Take them into your fire, cleanse them of their dark magick, and render them harmless."

Then, swallowing hard, I took Cal's gifts and one by one dropped them into the cauldron. The beautiful batik blouse whose colors reminded me of a storm at sunset, the book of herbal magick, the earrings, the pentacle, even the blood-stone he'd given me at our last circle. The flames crackled, licked at the rim of the cauldron. I watched the pages of the book curl into glowing whorls of ash. The burning ink gave off a faint, acrid smell. Wisps of glowing thread drifted upward as the batik blouse was consumed by the fire.

It burned hotter, hotter, until it gave off an incandescence that was almost too much for my eyes. The flames leapt to meet the wind high above the cauldron. I gasped, my heart aching with sadness. There, in the center of the white-hot flames, I saw Cal exactly as he had been when he gave me my gifts, a look of pure tenderness on his face. I felt myself falling deeper then, my heart opening to him the way a flower opens to the sun. Tears blurred my vision.

"No," I said, suddenly furious that here, in *my circle,* Cal's magick was still rising up to control me. I reached for Maeve's wand and aimed it at the cauldron. I felt my power pour into it and intensify. Beyond that I felt the power of Maeve and her mother, Mackenna, high priestesses both. I began to move deasil, chanting the words from the book aloud:

> *"Earth and air, flame and ice,*
> *Take darkness from me.*
> *Cleanse these things of ill intent.*
> *Let this spell cause no harm nor return any on me."*

On the last words of the spell the flames crackled, as if in answer to me, then died out completely. A white, nearly transparent smoke rose. The wand in my hand felt weightless. I gently laid it on the ground.

After a moment I gathered my courage and peered into the cauldron. The blouse was gone entirely, as was the book. There were a few darkened lumps of metal, which I took to be the earrings and the pentagram. The tigereyes seemed to be gone. I could still see the shape of the bloodstone, though, covered in a fine ash. I touched the edge of the cauldron. It was already cool, despite the white-hot flames that had blazed there just moments earlier.

I reached in for the bloodstone. White ash fell from it; it was cool to the touch. I gingerly extended my senses, examining it for any trace of Cal's magick. I couldn't find any.

My fist tightened around it, and something deep inside me snapped. It was a crackling, heartrending release, as if the ritual had broken not only Cal's magickal bonds on me, but my own bonds on my reined-in pain and anger. I flung the bloodstone away as hard as I could. "You bastard, Cal!" I screamed into the bitter wind. "You bastard!"

Then I dropped to my knees, sobbing. How could he have done this to me? How could he have taken something as precious as love and corrupted it so horribly? I crouched, praying to the Goddess to heal my heart.

It was a long time before I straightened up again. When I did, I felt that magick had left the circle. Things were back to normal—whatever normal was.

I opened the circle, grabbed my tools, and took them back into the house. I returned the tools to their old hiding place in the HVAC vent in the upstairs hallway. I made a mental note to find a new hiding place soon. I repurified the cauldron with salt water before stuffing it in the back of my closet. Then I took a hot shower and finally did what I'd wanted to do since that morning.

I got Dagda, crawled into bed, and went back to sleep.

# 4.
# Celebration

August, 1984

I've made my choice, if you can call it a choice. I'm with Fiona now, back home in England. Our second son will be born in a week, and I simply could not stay away any longer. She is my mùirn beatha dàn, my soul's true mate.

I think—I hope—that Selene has at last accepted this. When I left this time, she didn't plead. She said only, "Remember the threefold law. All that you do comes back to you." She turned away, and I watched Cal carefully copy her. I've lost him. He is wholly Selene's now.

Giomanach is so changed from the last time I saw him. He's nearly two years old now, no longer a baby but a wiry little boy with hair like bleached corn silk and Fiona's dancing green eyes. He's a happy child but still shy and a little fearful around me. I try not to let him see how it hurts me.

*I try, too, not to think too often of Cal, and of the battle that I lost.*
*—Maghach*

"Morgan." My sister was sitting on the edge of the bed, shaking my shoulder. "Mom asked me to wake you up."

I opened my eyes and realized it was dark outside. I felt like I'd been asleep for days. "What time is it?" I asked groggily.

"Five-thirty." Mary K. turned on the light on my night table, and I saw the concern in her warm brown eyes. "Aunt Eileen and Paula are on their way over for dinner. They should be here any minute. Hey, Mom told me about you and Cal. And I saw Das Boot. Are you okay?"

I drew in a shaky breath, then nodded. Something had shifted during the purification ceremony. Though I still felt deeply wounded, I didn't have quite the same sense of hopelessness I'd had this morning. "I've been better, but I'll live."

"Cal wasn't in school today," Mary K. said. She hesitated. "There's a rumor going around that he and his mom left town over the weekend. That there was some kind of suspicious fire on their property and now they've disappeared."

"They did leave, it's true," I said. I sighed. "Look, I can't talk about this right now. I'll tell you the whole story soon. But you have to promise to keep it to yourself."

"Okay." She looked solemnly at me, then went through the connecting door to her room.

I pulled on a pair of sweats and a red thermal top and brushed my long hair into a ponytail. Then I went downstairs. In the front hall I heard the doorbell, then a babble of excited voices. "What's going on?" I asked as I went out to greet them. They all sounded cheerful and happy.

"We made an offer on a house today, and it was accepted!" Aunt Eileen told me. When my aunt Eileen and her girlfriend, Paula Steen, decided to move in together, my mom had made it her personal mission to find them the house of their dreams.

Moments later we were all gathered around the dining-room table. Mary K. set out silverware and plates, my dad set out wineglasses, and Mom, Aunt Eileen, and Paula opened container after container of takeout food.

I sniffed the air, not recognizing the smells of either Chinese or Indian food, the two usual choices. "Wow. Smells great. What'd you bring?"

"We splurged at Fortunato's," Paula told me. Fortunato's was a trendy gourmet place that had opened a couple of years ago in Widow's Vale. Our family didn't shop there much, due to their insane prices.

"What's your pleasure?" Aunt Eileen asked. "We've got filet mignon with wild mushrooms, herb potatoes, cold salmon, asparagus vinaigrette, spinach salad, clam fritters, and chicken dijonnaise."

"And save room for chocolate-hazelnut cake," Paula added.

"Oh my God, I'm never going to be able to move again," Mary K. moaned.

Paula popped the cork on a champagne bottle and poured it into glasses as we all took our seats. She even gave Mary K. and me about a swallow each, though I noticed my mom raise her eyebrows as Aunt Eileen handed the glasses to us.

"A toast!" Paula said, and lifted her own glass high. "To our new, absolutely perfect home and the absolutely brilliant real estate agent who found it for us!"

My mom laughed. "May you always be happy there!"

We began passing around the food. It felt good to see everyone so cheerful, even Mary K., who had been looking pretty down since she and her boyfriend, Bakker, had broken up. I was glad to be able to focus on someone's good news. I felt myself start to relax, felt my anxiety recede a bit.

"So tell me all about this perfect house," I said to Eileen.

"It's in Taunton," Eileen began, naming a town about ten miles north of us. "It's a little house with bay windows, set back from the street, with a beautiful garden out back. Wood-burning stove downstairs and a fireplace in the master bedroom. The only bad part is, it's covered with ugly green vinyl siding."

"Which is old and needs to be replaced, anyway," Mom stuck in. "Apart from that, it oozes charm."

"Yeah." Paula grinned. "Just ask the realtor."

"When do you think you'll move in?" Mary K. asked Aunt Eileen.

Aunt Eileen had just taken a huge bite of spinach salad, so Mom answered for her. "The closing is scheduled for next week, after the inspection," she said.

"That's fantastic!" Mary K. said. "You could actually be in by next weekend."

Aunt Eileen took Paula's hand and with her other hand crossed her fingers. "That's what we're hoping," she said.

The rest of dinner went by quickly, with talk of moving plans, house plans, and a heated discussion about how many pets they would adopt once they were settled. Paula was a veterinarian, so Aunt Eileen thought they should have a good menagerie, including several cats and dogs and a rabbit or two. By the time we got to dessert, everyone was laughing.

All at once my smile froze into place as I felt Hunter on our front walk outside. His presence always had a weird effect on me. The doorbell rang a moment later, and I stood quickly. "I'll get it," I said.

I went to the front hall and opened the door. Hunter stood there in a thick green sweater that perfectly matched his eyes. His hands were shoved into the pockets of a worn brown leather jacket that emphasized his broad shoulders.

"You weren't in school today," he stated.

"Hello to you, too," I said dryly.

He ducked his head and kicked snow off his boot. "Uh, right. Hello. How are you feeling?"

"Better, thanks."

He brought his gaze back up to mine, his eyes glinting in the reflection from the little light over the door. "As I was saying—you weren't in school."

My forehead crinkled. Had he gone to my school to check up on me? Was Hunter actually concerned about me?

I must have been staring at him because I noticed the tips of his ears begin to turn pink. Was he blushing? Surely not. Not Hunter. He must really be cold.

"Morgan, who is it?" my mom called.

"Um—it's my friend Hunter," I called back. "I'll just be a second."

"Well, invite him in and shut the door. You're letting in cold air."

Silently I held the door, and Hunter stepped inside. "We need to talk," he said.

I knew he was right, but I wasn't ready yet. "It's not a good time."

"I don't mean about Cal," he said. "I mean about Cirrus." Cirrus was the coven that Cal had started. I was a member, along with Robbie, Jenna Ruiz, Sharon Goodfine, Ethan Sharp, and Matt Adler. Bree had originally been part of Cirrus, too, but when she and I split up over Cal, she and Raven Meltzer had formed Kithic, a coven that was now led by Hunter's cousin Sky.

"Cirrus?" I repeated, confused. "What about it?"

"With Cal gone, you need someone else to lead it. An initiated witch."

I hadn't even thought about that. With Cirrus, Cal had opened up the world of Wicca to me, permanently altering my world. His betrayal had left a deep black hole in my life, and my few new support systems were now being sucked away into it.

I didn't want to lose the coven. "I could ask Alyce or David if they'll take over."

"Alyce and David are already part of Starlocket. I hear Alyce has been asked to lead it now that Selene is gone," Hunter said.

I was silent, thinking, and then Hunter broke in.

"I want to lead Cirrus," he said.

Now I was seriously at sea. "Why?" I asked. "You don't know any of us. You don't even live here. Not permanently, anyway."

"I'll probably be here for a while. I've asked the council

to give me time to come up with new leads on Cal and Selene. I want to see if I can track them down."

"But you don't know how long that will take," I argued. "Anyway, there are five other people in our coven. They might have something to say about who leads us."

"I already discussed it with them," Hunter said. "I went to your school today. That's how I know you weren't there."

So he hadn't gone there out of concern for me. To my surprise, I felt a stab of disappointment. Then my anger rose. How could he be so presumptuous? "So you talked to them and they said yes? You're it?"

"We're going to see how it goes," he said cautiously. "There's a circle tomorrow night at my house at seven. I hope you'll be there. I think it would be good for . . . everyone."

"A circle on a Tuesday night?"

"We can't wait until Saturday," Hunter said. "It's important that Cirrus re-form quickly. When a circle is broken in this way, it can be devastating to the members. Besides, we don't know what magick Cal might have used on the members. I've asked everyone to bring the stones Cal gave them so we can purify them. You should bring yours, too, along with anything else he gave you."

"I already purified everything," I said, and felt a childish triumph when I saw the surprise in his eyes. Now maybe he'd stop being so superior, so remote, making me feel like he was ten years older than me rather than two.

Even as the thoughts formed, I knew I wasn't being fair to him. He really was trying to help. But his very competence irked me, made me feel clumsy, naïve.

He must have sensed a change in my attitude and figured the circle issue was a done deal, because he moved on. "Now, the second thing," he said, "is you. You've come into quite a birthright—far more power than most blood witches ever experience, and Belwicket's tools besides. But you know only the most rudimentary things about how to focus and control your power. And you know even less about how to protect yourself."

I took it as an accusation and felt anger flare again. "I've only known I was a blood witch for a month. I know I have a long way to go."

Hunter sighed. "All I'm saying is that you've got a hell of a lot of catching up to do. Most blood witches are initiated at age fourteen, after studying for years. Witches need to know the history of Wicca and the Seven Great Clans; the rituals of the Goddess and the God and the eight great Sabbats; herbalism; the basics of numerology; the proper use of talismans and runes; the properties of minerals, metals, and stones and how they interact with the cycles of the celestial bodies. The full correspondences; reading auras; spells of protection, healing, binding, and banishment. And though it's more advanced, you really ought to learn about the Guardians of the Watchtowers—"

A sudden burst of laughter came from the kitchen, where Aunt Eileen and Paula and my family were lingering over coffee. It sounded so safe and comforting in there, a world I was not fully part of anymore, a world I had taken for granted. An awful thought occurred to me. "Is my family in danger?" I blurted out.

Hunter ran a hand through his pale blond hair. Tiny crystals of ice had beaded up in it, so now bits of it stuck up in spiky tufts, making him look about eight years old.

"I don't think so," he said. "At least, not now. With Selene's plan exposed, I suspect she and her cronies will lie low for a while. You have a window of safety here, which is why it's vital that you don't waste it. You need to begin studying."

I gnawed my thumbnail. He was right.

"I have some books that I bought at Practical Magick," I told him. "I haven't read them cover to cover, but I've skimmed them." I told him the titles. "And of course I've read most of Maeve's Book of Shadows."

He nodded approvingly. "Those are all good. Keep working with them and we'll talk in a few days. Write down any questions you have. I'll give you a reading list after I have a better sense of what you know."

"Hey." Mary K. came out into the hall. "Hunter, right? How are you?"

"Fine, thanks," he said, flashing her a surprisingly warm smile. "You?"

"Good." Mary K. twisted a strand of auburn hair around her finger.

Was she *flirting* with him? "Hunter's got to go now," I said.

He looked at me, then nodded. "Good night," he called to my sister. To me he said, "You look tired. Get some sleep."

"What a hottie," Mary K. said as the door clicked shut behind him.

"Oh, please," I groaned, then went back to the kitchen to join the group.

# 5.
# Darkness

With Athar's help, I broke the warding spells today. It took the two of us the better part of the day—Athar was annoyed because I made her take a day off from her job.

But I found nothing useful inside. If Selene did leave anything, it's locked in that library of hers, and I can't get at it. The council is sending a fellow down from Boston next week to help me bind the house in spells. Perhaps he'll be able to help me get in. I will not ask Morgan for her help. It's clear that she dislikes me enough already.

I wish she didn't. There's something in her eyes, in the way she holds her head, that somehow draws me to her.

—Giomanach

Something was after me, I could feel it. Deep darkness was surrounding me, trying to find me, to envelop me. I tried to make the rune signs for protection, but I couldn't lift my hands: my fingers weren't working. I'd been bound, just as Cal had bound me to entrap me.

Smoke and flames burned in the back of my throat, and I heard a voice screaming, "Not again!" Somehow I knew the voice belonged to my birth mother, Maeve.

Then faces rose up out of the smothering darkness: Selene and Cal. I begged them to leave me alone. I pushed my lips together tightly, knowing, somehow, that they wanted me to breathe in the darkness, wanted it to become a part of me.

Just as I felt myself about to suffocate, I saw a tiny sliver of light. The faces of Cal and Selene dissolved as the light approached. And then I began to see a new face in its midst.

Hunter.

I woke up, sweaty and gasping for breath. My heart raced, pounding hard in my chest. I pushed my hair away from my damp forehead and looked around the room. I was in my own bedroom. I was alone. Dagda was sleeping on a pillow that had fallen to the floor. It was still pitch dark outside my window.

I shuddered. The dream had been so intense, it felt like it was still with me. I pulled at the sheets. They were completely wrapped around my body. I let out a shaky laugh. No wonder I'd thought I was being smothered. Those sheets were wound as tightly as a straitjacket. I struggled free, then reached over to my bedside table and flicked on the lamp. Not so good. The lamp cast spooky shadows all around my room. I got up and turned on my overhead light. Dagda stretched and blinked sleepily. I picked him up and brought him back into bed with me.

"It was just a nightmare," I told my purring kitten. "It's just my brain trying to process all that I've been through."

I pulled the comforter up around my shoulders. I'd gone from sweaty to freezing. Was my window open? I glanced over, but no, it was shut. I still felt anxious, unsettled. My heart started its syncopated beat again. Was it just the aftermath of the dream, or was I picking up something with my witch senses?

Cradling Dagda close to my body, I got up and went to the window. I took in deep breaths, trying to calm my mind. Dagda squirmed, so I put him down. I didn't want to be distracted.

Willing myself to breathe evenly, I opened myself to the night. I could feel the sting of frosty air on my face as my senses moved out of my cozy bedroom and into the backyard. The world was quiet under its blanket of snow, and the trees themselves seemed to be asleep. The houses were filled with sleeping bodies; a car drove slowly along the road. Beyond that, I didn't get much sensation, just vague cold.

Then a wave of nausea hit me. My veins felt like they were filled with cold sludge. The only other time I'd felt anything like this horrible sensation was when Cal had used magick to bind me.

There was dark magick in Widow's Vale tonight. I knew that with certainty.

Stay clear, stay calm, a voice said in my head. Was it my own? Don't fight the sensation, the voice told me. Examine it.

As I stopped fighting the nausea, it seemed to dissipate. I realized that I wasn't being acted upon. This wasn't an attack—it felt oddly impersonal. The energy, whatever it was, wasn't directed at me. It was as if I'd gotten a whiff of something really foul but hadn't actually come into contact with it.

But what was it? And where was it coming from?

Suddenly I could see the field where Cal had brought us for our very first circle. I couldn't make out what was happening there, but I was certain that I was seeing the place where the magick was being worked.

I gasped. It could only mean one thing. Cal and Selene were back. Who else would go to that particular field? They were there, working their dark spells. Whatever they were doing right now wasn't aimed at me. But it was only a matter of time before they came for me.

# 6.
# A New Circle

Kennet Muir, my council mentor, rang from London to say he'd got a new assignment for me. There was a cat found in a suburb of Montreal with its throat cut, and the council fears a rogue coven may have resurrected the blood rituals that were banned in the nineteenth century.

On the strength of one dead cat! It's ridiculous: it's a fool's errand, and I told Kennet so. I told him I needed to stay here, that I had many things to finish. He finally agreed, but only after warning me not to allow myself to become too emotionally wrapped up in my work.

Athar laughed when I told her that. "Too late," she said.

I had the feeling she was not referring only to finding Cal and Selene.

—Giomanach

I didn't sleep at all during the rest of the night. Whenever I shut my eyes, images of Selene and Cal rose up, unbidden. By dawn I gave up and used my nervous energy to do the next week's math problems. The only thing that kept me from jumping out of my skin was the knowledge that the dark magick hadn't been focused on me.

I knew I had to tell Hunter about what I had experienced, and I didn't want to wait until the circle that night. I went out to the hall phone.

Mary K. walked by on her way to the bathroom. Her eyes widened when she saw me. "You're up early," she said. "You even have time to eat breakfast sitting down."

"I may be up, but I'm not awake," I warned her. I dialed Hunter's number, hoping he and Sky were early risers.

No answer. And no voicemail. I banged the phone down in frustration. Where the hell were they at this ridiculous hour?

Luckily Mary K. misinterpreted my mood as my usual morning crabbiness, so she didn't ask any questions. Stay calm, I ordered myself. Selene and Cal may be back, but you'll find some way to be ready for them.

Since I was already up, Mary K. and I set out for school early. She was stunned since she usually had to nag me into my car. I figured I'd use the opportunity to find out what the other members of Cirrus really thought about Hunter taking over.

I could feel Mary K.'s eyes on me while I drove. Did she sense my tension?

"Do you want to talk about it now?" she asked hesitantly.

I sighed. I felt bad for not telling her the full story. But I just wasn't up to it yet. I squeezed Das Boot into a snug parking space. "Soon, I promise. It's really . . . really hard.

Cal—he wasn't who I thought he was." Understatement of the year.

She sighed. "Is it the Rowlands's curse to have bad judgment when it comes to guys?" Mary K.'s ex-boyfriend, Bakker, had tried to force himself on her. I had been so furious that I'd shot witch fire at him without even realizing what I was doing. Still, that didn't stop her from taking him back. Or him from trying it again. Luckily she'd been stronger the second time. He was out of her life for good. I hoped.

"Mom did okay," I said.

"She wasn't a Rowlands," Mary K. pointed out darkly.

"True!" I said, and unbelievably, I giggled. Then we were hugging in the front seat of my demolition-derby car. "I'm glad you're my sister," I whispered.

"Back atcha," Mary K. said, and then her friend Jaycee ran up to the car, bundled in a Day-Glo-pink ski jacket.

"Mary K.," she cried excitedly, tapping the window. "You are *not* going to believe who Diane D'Alessio is going out with!"

"Just a sec," Mary K. told her. She turned back to me. "I'll talk to you later, okay?"

"Yep," I told her.

Mary K. and Jaycee hurried across the icy parking lot toward school. I grabbed my backpack and followed them.

Inside the redbrick building, I headed to the basement stairs, where our coven usually hung out on cold mornings. Jenna and Sharon were already there, along with Ethan. Matt, Jenna's ex, was nowhere to be seen, and neither was Robbie.

"Hey," I said.

Sharon looked up at me, relief evident in her expression. "Morgan! Are you all right? Robbie told us about Sunday night."

I sat down on the step beside Jenna. "Yeah, I'm okay. I guess."

Ethan shook his head. "That totally blew me away. I can't believe I missed all the signs that Cal was lethal."

"We all missed them," Sharon said, shuddering. Ethan put his arm around her shoulders.

Jenna tucked a strand of her pale blond hair behind her ear. "I feel so stupid. Like we were all taken in by a con artist or something. That the whole thing was just part of a plot to get at you."

"It's strange, but I can't help feeling that a lot of what he was doing was sincere," I said thoughtfully. Then I caught myself, wondering if I had a total victim personality or what. "Of course, he seemed pretty sincere about trying to kill me, too," I added briskly. "So now we know. Wicca definitely has a dark side, and Cal and Selene were practicing it."

Ethan stood up and shoved his hands into the pockets of his jeans. "You know, I like the part of Wicca that's about connecting with nature, understanding yourself. But this dark stuff scares me."

"I don't think any of us realized what we might be getting into when Cal started Cirrus," I said. "Now I guess we have to decide whether we want to go on with it."

"Did you hear that Hunter wants to lead the coven?" Jenna asked.

I nodded. "He told me last night. How do you all feel about it?"

"Weird," Jenna said. "I mean, we started with Cal. Being in the coven is so much connected with him for me. I don't know what it will be like. Plus it seems weird that Hunter would even want to lead us. He doesn't know us."

"He's worried about us being exposed to dark magick, and

he wants to make sure no one gets hurt. That's what he said, anyway," Sharon said. She smiled. "In his sexy English accent."

"Hey!" Ethan protested. "What about *my* sexy accent?"

"He does seem to know what he's talking about," Matt said. "He's been doing this a lot longer than we have. I know he's not much older than we are, but he seems . . . I don't know . . . more grown-up or something."

"It's just the accent," Ethan said, poking Sharon in the ribs. "It makes him seem older."

"Cut it out." Sharon wiggled away, laughing.

"You're right," I admitted. Hunter did seem older than his years. It probably had to do with all he'd been through. He'd had to grow up fast.

"I loved Cal's circles," Sharon said wistfully. "He was totally laid-back but at the same time encouraging."

"That last circle with him, I felt real magick," Jenna agreed. "Still, it might be interesting to see how Hunter handles things. For variety." The first bell rang, and she got to her feet. "All I know is, I'm not joining Sky's coven," she said. We all knew what she meant. Along with Bree, Raven Meltzer also belonged to Sky's coven. Raven had tried to seduce Matt, and Matt had pretty much gone for it. Hence the end of the four-year romance between Matt and Jenna.

Sharon said, "I think we ought to give him a chance."

"Yeah," Ethan said. "If we hate it, we can just quit."

For a moment, I envied them. If they didn't enjoy Wicca, they could drop it, the way you drop a boring after-school activity. I didn't have that option. Wicca had chosen me as much as I'd chosen it.

\*     \*     \*

I'd hoped to get to Hunter and Sky's place early so that I could talk to Hunter about what I'd sensed the night before, but in the dark I missed the turn to his street and was out of Widow's Vale completely before I figured it out. By the time I pulled up in front of the house, it was already after seven, and everybody else's cars were parked against the curb. I wedged Das Boot in between Robbie's Beetle and Jenna's Corolla and started up the narrow path.

Hunter must have sensed me coming before I reached the porch. The front door opened, framing him in warm golden light. I caught my breath—it was so similar to the image of him in my dream, bathed in light, pushing back the darkness. I blinked to shake off the image. He watched me from the doorway, looking like one of those ads for an après-ski drink, and I suddenly felt self-conscious, as if I were about to slip and fall facedown on the walk.

"Welcome," he said.

"Morganita." Robbie came up behind him. "You've got to check this place out. It's very cool."

"I've been here before," I mumbled, oddly flustered.

Hunter stood aside to let me pass, and I walked into the living room. Sharon and Ethan were sharing an ottoman, leaning companionably against each other's backs. Jenna and Matt were in the armchairs, not looking at each other. Robbie sat down at one end of the blue velvet sofa and waved a hand at the seat next to him. I could sense that everyone was unsure about Hunter leading us, and I knew that Hunter sensed it, too.

"You know what's strange about this living room?" Robbie said. "There's no TV."

Hunter arched one blond eyebrow. "We don't have time

for it," he said. The implication was that neither should we. Not a great way to start.

"Is Sky here?" Jenna asked.

"No. She's out this evening," Hunter replied. He was wearing a deep-blue denim shirt, and worn black jeans hung loosely on his hips. I suddenly had a vivid flashback to the moment he'd almost kissed me, standing in the dark outside my house. That had been only three nights ago, but until this minute I'd forgotten about it.

I felt my cheeks burn. Where had that stray thought come from?

Hunter moved to stand in front of the hearth. "Welcome, everyone. I appreciate your showing up on a weeknight. I know this change is difficult. And I understand that despite the way things turned out with Cal, you liked the way he led Cirrus.

"My approach will inevitably be different," he went on. "But I'll try to see that Cirrus remains a coven where you feel comfortable, where you can be open with one another, where you can learn to safely draw on the power that lies within you, and where you will enter into a true connection with your magick."

Sharon smiled at that. But all I could think about was how with Cal the circles had seemed natural and comfortable. With Hunter it felt like we were getting the Wicca version of a Rotary Club speech.

"So," Hunter said, "let's begin. If you'll follow me, please . . ."

We followed him from the living room through a short hallway that I hadn't noticed when I'd been there before. It was lined with bookshelves that held a small collection of clothbound volumes. Through an arched doorway I could see into a small kitchen, where dried herbs and flowers hung from the ceiling.

At the end of the hall was a set of double wooden doors. Hunter opened them into a long, narrow room that was lit by candles and the glow of a wood-burning stove. The room ran the length of the house. Its back wall was covered with windows. A door led out to what seemed to be a deck. The windows rattled slightly, and I could hear the wind sighing through the trees.

An altar sat at one end of the room, holding more candles, a stick of burning incense, a shell, a dish of water in which purple blossoms floated, a pale blue crystal, and a stone sculpture of a woman. The sculpture was rough, the face barely defined, yet it was completely sensuous, a vision of the Goddess. You had only to look at it to know that it was made with love. I looked at Hunter. Had he sculpted it?

"Will you form a circle, please?" Hunter began. He sounded terribly proper and polite, very British. Once again I missed Cal with a pang and once again felt stupid and angry at myself for missing someone who had hurt me so badly.

I joined the others as Hunter drew a circle with white chalk around us. It was reassuring to feel Robbie on one side of me and Sharon on the other. I felt uneasy, though. I wondered if it was the threat of Selene and Cal or if it was Hunter. His presence always unsettled me, and being in a circle was so intimate. I wondered what it would be like to share this experience with him.

With the chalk Hunter traced four runes on each of the directional points. "I've chosen these runes specifically for our first circle together," he said. "Thorn is for new beginnings and opening gateways," he said, pointing to the rune at the east. "Beorc is a rune of growth. Ur is to create change and healing and strengthen all magick. Eolh is for protection."

I tried to quell the flutters in my stomach. What was my problem? Hunter hadn't done anything unusual so far.

"Did everyone bring the stones Cal gave out?" Hunter asked. When people nodded, he added, "Toss them into the middle of the circle, please."

Everyone but me pulled their stones out of their pockets. When they were all in a heap in the center of the chalk ring, Hunter drew a pentagram around them. At each of the five points he drew a symbol I didn't recognize.

"These sigils are from an older runic alphabet than the one we usually work with," he explained. "They're for protection and purification and will help strengthen our spell. We're going to use the circle itself to purify these stones. Now, have you all done the basic breathing exercises?"

Matt spoke up. "Cal taught us that."

"Then let's begin there," Hunter said. "May the circle of Cirrus always be strong."

We all joined hands, and I heard the familiar sound of Sharon's bracelets jingling against each other. I began to concentrate on my breathing, on pulling each inhalation deep into my stomach and then releasing it. Gradually I felt myself relax and become aware of the pattern of breathing within the circle. Hunter had the deepest, slowest breaths. Jenna, who was asthmatic, had the shallowest.

Hunter began to sing in a low voice. It was a simple chant in English, praising moon and sun, Goddess and God, asking them to be with us in our circle, to protect us from all evil intent and to guide us through the cycle of the seasons, the cycle of life. His voice was lilting, smooth and soft, yet with a core of strength. It resonated beautifully in the space. I never would have imagined that he could sing with such passion and simplicity. But for some reason, I couldn't hold on to the words. The others did, though, and as they sang together and we all moved widdershins, I saw their faces change. They were feeling something that I wasn't. A connection. Their voices gained power as some kind of energy surged through them. And I, the blood witch, the prodigy of Cirrus coven, felt nothing.

I became aware of Hunter's gaze on me. I closed my eyes, trying futilely to deepen my concentration, to snatch at the ethereal thread of magick that seemed to dance just out of reach. But I couldn't touch it, and finally, when I was almost weeping with frustration, Hunter slowed the circle and brought the song to an end. "Don't break the circle," he told us. "But everyone sit down."

We sat in place, our legs crossed.

"That was really good, everyone," Hunter said. His face glowed, his features relaxed in a way that I rarely saw, as if the circle was the place he felt most comfortable. It upset me that he could feel so at ease here in my coven while I, for the first time, felt like an outsider. He looked at each one of us in turn and then asked, "Do you want to share your thoughts?"

Ethan said, "That was . . . intense. The Wicca books talk about the Wheel of the Year. This time I felt like I could sort of . . . feel all of us traveling on it, our whole lives."

"Yeah," Matt said. "It was like I was both in this room and out there in the ravine."

"Me too." Robbie looked awestruck. "I felt like I was the wind in the trees."

Hunter looked at Sharon. "I didn't get anything cosmic," she admitted, sounding embarrassed. "I just felt how much my family cares about me. It was like I got this blast of mother-father love that I haven't been paying attention to lately."

Hunter smiled. "What makes you think that isn't cosmic?"

Robbie said, "What about you, Jenna?"

Jenna laughed softly. "I had a vision of myself being really *strong*."

It was my turn next, and I was dreading it. What had gone wrong? I wondered. Maybe Hunter was just the wrong person for me to be working with. Now I was going to have to say I hadn't felt anything, and everyone was going to wonder what was wrong with me, if I could only reach my power with Cal. I took a deep breath, trying to calm down.

"All right, then." Hunter got to his feet. "That was good work, everyone. Let's call it a night and meet again on Saturday."

I looked up, startled. He had skipped me!

When he walked over to blow out the altar candles, I followed him. "Do I not count?" I asked in a low voice. "Doesn't it matter what I felt?"

He glanced at me in surprise. "I could tell you didn't connect," he replied softly. "I thought you'd rather not talk about it. I'm sorry if I made the wrong assumption."

I couldn't think of a reply to that. It was the right assumption, in fact. It just bothered me, the way he could read me. I found it incredibly disconcerting.

He turned back to the others. "On Saturday we'll work

with the pentagram," he said. "Read up on it and spend some time visualizing it. See what it tells you."

I thought of Cal's pentacle necklace, and a shudder went through me.

"We can meet at my house," Jenna volunteered.

"Perfect," Hunter said. "Thank you all."

I knew I should seize the moment and tell him I needed to speak to him privately, but I just couldn't do it. I felt too off balance, too out of sorts. Before I'd made up my mind to do anything, Robbie came up and handed me my coat.

"So do you have a good book about pentagrams?" he asked as we walked out toward the cars.

"No," I said tiredly. "I don't seem to have anything right now."

# 7.
# Intruder

April, 1986

Today I found Giomanach, all of three-and-a-half years old, hunched over a bowl of water, staring into it so intently that his eyes were almost crossing. When I asked him what he was doing, he told me he was scrying for his sister. Goddess, I was startled. We'd not told him that Fiona is carrying another child, yet he knew. He's amazingly quick.

I asked him if he'd seen anything, expecting him to say he hadn't. He's too young to scry. But he said he'd seen a little girl with dark hair and eyes. I smiled and told him we'd have to wait and see. But my leug told me our Alwyn will have red hair and green eyes like Fiona's, so I'm afraid the water lied to my boy. Unless it showed him its own riddling truth.

Then Giomanach smacked his hand down so the water spilled out of the bowl. I opened my mouth to scold him, but he *looked up at me with that little mischievous smile, and I hadn't the heart. He's like sunshine to me. After looking over my shoulder for two years, I'm finally beginning to accept that nothing is going to happen, that life can actually be this good.*

*—Maghach*

I sat in Das Boot on Wednesday morning, thinking again about last night's circle. The truth was, part of me loved being the star pupil, the one who had off-the-charts power. In our coven, right from the start, I'd been the gifted one. It had made me feel special for the first time in my life. Was that over, too?

"Morgan?" a muffled voice called. "Morgan!"

I blinked and glanced up. My friend Tamara Pritchett was tapping on the window, her breath coming out in white puffs. "You're going to be late," she said as I rolled down the window. "Didn't you hear the bell?"

"Um . . . ," I mumbled. "Sorry. I was just thinking."

We walked to class together, and all the way there I was aware of the curious looks Tamara kept giving me. By now everyone knew that Cal was gone, that there had been a fire at his house. I'd told everyone who asked the standard story: that we'd broken up and I didn't know anything about the fire or where he was. But the people I'd been good friends with before Wicca came into my life, people like Tamara and Janice Yutoh, could tell there was a lot I wasn't saying.

I got through my morning classes, and then at lunch period I left school. I had an appointment for Das Boot at the body shop to get an estimate for the repairs. Unser's Auto Repair was off the highway on the outskirts of Widow's Vale. It was a big fenced lot, filled with cars, with a garage in the middle of it. With the exception of the Afton Enterprises gravel pit, which I passed about a quarter of a mile before Unser's, the road stretched out bleak and empty. I gave the gravel pit a glare as I drove past it, thinking of Practical Magick.

I pulled into the garage. Bob Unser, a gruff, gray-haired man in coveralls, wiped his hands on a rag and came over to the car as I got out. His big German shepherd, Max, bounded over, shoved his wet nose into my palm and licked it, then bounded away again. Max was technically a guard dog, but he was a total sweetheart. He and Bob both knew me pretty well. Being a genuine antique, Das Boot had had its share of problems, though nothing as major as this before.

Bob squinted at Das Boot's crumpled, scorched nose and smashed headlight. "What happened?"

"It kind of . . . collided with a building that was on fire."

He grunted. "That's original."

I huddled in my coat while he looked over Das Boot and made notes on a clipboard. "Let me call and get an estimate on the parts," he said. "Then I'll give you a total."

"Great." I had a feeling this repair was going to cost a fortune, and I wasn't sure how I was going to pay for it. I didn't want to put it on my parents' insurance and risk raising their rates.

Bob went into the little office, and I stayed in the garage. Max trotted back to my side, and I ran my hand through his thick coat. Then I felt the fur near his neck start to rise, and a low, rumbling growl filled the garage. I let go of him at once, wondering what was wrong.

Max swung his head toward the entrance of the garage. His growl deepened, and he loped outside. Then my own senses prickled. Something was out there. Something magickal.

My pulse rate picked up. I stood still, trying to get a better sense of the presence. It didn't feel human. Cautiously I stepped outside. Max stood on an icy patch of gravel a short distance from the garage, fur bristling and teeth bared. Then he began to race around the perimeter of the lot, barking furiously.

I cast out my senses and got feelings of stealth, concealment, malevolent power. Cold fear coursed through me, and my breath came fast as I traced the shape of Peorth in the air, the rune for revealing what is hidden. I visualized the rune, tracing it in my mind in bright red light until I felt its shape become a three-dimensional entity. Instinctively I began saying my power chant. "An di allaigh . . ."

There was a weird, whooshing noise, as if a whole flock of birds had started up from the ground at once. Something that felt like an ill wind brushed past me, making the tiny hairs on my arms stand up. I gasped. Max raced over to me, barking frantically. I saw nothing, but the air felt lighter, and I knew that the intruder was gone.

Bob walked out of the shop. "What's going on out here?" He frowned at Max, then at me. "What was all that noise about?"

I leaned against the car so he wouldn't see how I was shaking. "I guess Max heard something."

Max sat down in front of Bob and elaborated with short, eloquent barks.

"Okay, boy, okay." Bob was petting him now, comforting him. "We'll lock up good tonight."

We went back inside, and he handed me a written estimate for $750. That made me gasp again. "I'll have to special-order you a bumper and hood," he explained. "They don't make parts for this model anymore. I'll have to get them from a used-parts dealer in Pennsylvania. You call me and let me know when you're ready to go ahead."

I thanked him, barely even listening. Before I left I traced the rune Eolh on Max's forehead for protection. What had that mysterious presence been? Was it after me? Was it connected to the dark force I had felt the other night? Was it Cal or Selene?

Though the sun was shining brightly, I felt like a black veil had been pulled across the sky. Shivering, I got into my car and drove back to school.

Mary K. went to Jaycee's house after school, as she often did, so I drove straight home. I was still shaken up from the incident at the garage. I had no idea what it had been, but I didn't want to take any chances. I had felt something evil. If it was after me, I'd better start protecting myself fast.

In the empty house I went upstairs and took my birth mother's athame from its hiding place in the HVAC vent. Then I walked around the outside of my house, running the athame lightly over the clapboard siding. Hunter and Sky had placed runes of protection all around the house about two weeks ago. The athame revealed the magick signs to me, and I breathed a sigh of relief. They were still there and still glowing with potency.

Next I went up to my room and closed the door. I'd been planning to make an altar for some time, but now it seemed doubly urgent. If there really was someone or something after me, I needed to be as strong and sure in my magick as possible.

The problem was, the altar had to be somewhere my family wouldn't notice. Although my parents now seemed to realize that they couldn't prevent me from being a witch, there was no point in setting up an altar where they would see it and get upset.

I looked around my room. It wasn't big. There was no obvious place to set up an altar—certainly none that wouldn't be totally noticeable. I thought a moment and opened the door to my closet. It was a deep walk-in, with a long hanging rod running the length of it. I began taking clothes off the rod, laying shirts, dresses, jackets, and skirts on my bed. "Yuck," I said as a sundress with an enormous tropical flower print surfaced. It was time to give some things away.

When the closet was empty, I stared at the back of it. A small footlocker from when I went to summer camp sat on the floor. It had potential.

I rummaged in my dresser drawer for the length of plum-colored Irish linen that Aunt Eileen had brought back from her trip to Ireland. It covered the trunk perfectly, as if that's exactly what it had been woven for. Voilà. One altar.

Next I opened the junk drawer of my desk. I sorted through the crap until I found a small, perfect, pink-and-white scallop shell. I set it on one corner of the altar to represent water. On another I put a chunk of amethyst that had been among the crystals in Maeve's box of tools. That was for earth. On the remaining corners I set a candle for fire and a stick of incense for air. Of course, I wouldn't actually be able to light the candle or incense inside the closet. For that the altar would have to come out into my room. But I liked having all four elements in place.

I sat before my altar. It was pretty simple, as basic as you can get. Yet it felt right.

Something soft nudged me. Dagda. I ran my hand down his silky little back. "This is where we're going to invoke the Goddess," I explained. He purred as if in approval.

May I work strong, pure magick here, I said silently, spells of healing and wholeness.

And may they keep me safe, I couldn't help adding.

# 8.
# Potential

*Litha, 1991*

Goddess, help us. How can we go on from here? We've lost everything—our home, our coven, our children. Our children.

It all came so suddenly. We'd both been feeling ill and out of sorts for weeks, but I didn't think much of it. Then, late yesterday evening, I was working in my study when I heard Fiona scream. I raced to her workroom and found her lying on the floor, her leug clutched in her hand. She had been scrying to find the source of her illness and had seen something hideous in the stone. She described it as a wave of darkness, like a swarm of black insects or a pall of smoke, sweeping over the land. "It was evil," she whispered. "It wants us. It's . . . searching for us. We've got to warn the others, and then we've got to go. Now. Tonight."

"Tonight? But—the children. Giomanach's got an herbology lesson tomorrow," I objected stupidly.

*The look she gave me broke my heart. "We can't take them,"
she said. "It wouldn't be safe. Not for them or for us. We've
got to leave them."*

*I argued, but in the end she convinced me that she was
right. The only hope for any of us was for Fiona and me to
disappear, to try somehow to draw the evil away from our
children.*

*Fiona left a frantic message for her brother Beck, who lives
in Somerset. Then we laid the strongest protections we could on
our house. I kissed my children as they slept, smoothing Alwyn's
tangled red curls, pulling the covers back up over Linden. Last
of all I stood by Giomanach, watching the rise and fall of his
chest. I tucked my leug under his pillow, where he'd find it in
the morning.*

*And then, once again, I abandoned my children.*

*—Maghach*

I left a note for my mom saying that I'd be back for dinner, then drove over to Hunter's house. As much as being
around him upset me, I realized Hunter needed to know
about the dark presence I'd sensed at Unser's and the dark
magick I had felt on Monday night. He might be able to tell
me what it was, where it had come from, how I could protect myself from it effectively.

I started up the narrow path. Even in daylight it was hard
to be sure that there was a house tucked away behind all the
trees. The porch was even ricketier than it had seemed at

night. A post was missing from the railing, and the stairs had a split tread.

I reached the door and hesitated. Should I knock? I suddenly felt reluctant to bring my troubles to this particular door.

I chickened out. I'd turned and started off the porch when I heard the door open behind me. "Morgan," Hunter's voice said.

Caught. I turned to face him and felt myself blush. "I should have called first. Maybe this isn't a good time."

"It's fine," he said. "Come in."

Inside there was no sign of Sky. I settled myself in one of the living-room armchairs. The house was as cold as it had been last night, the fire in the little fireplace giving off hardly any warmth at all. I was shivering, growing more uncomfortable by the second. This had been a bad idea.

"So," Hunter said as he sat across from me. "Why are you here?"

To my surprise, I blurted, "I didn't feel anything at our circle last night. I'm the one who always gets swept away, but . . . Everyone else was transported, but I didn't get anything. I don't know if Cirrus is right for me anymore."

"Wicca isn't about getting things," Hunter said.

"I know that," I said defensively. "It's just—it's just that it doesn't usually happen to me." I studied his face, wondering how much to confide in him. "It scared me," I admitted. "Like my powers would be gone forever." A thought occurred to me. "Did you do something to damp down my power during the circle in any way?"

He raised his eyebrows. "If I were trying to control your

power, you'd have known it. And it's not something I would do unless it were an extreme emergency."

"Oh." I sank back into the chair.

He crossed a booted foot over his knee. He tapped it a few times. "Perhaps . . . my style doesn't bring out your potential."

He sounded disappointed. In me, I wondered, or in himself? "Everyone else, it worked for them," I said grudgingly. "They really liked how you did things."

His face brightened, making him look more like an ordinary teenager. Extraordinarily handsome, maybe, but less intense. "They did? I'm glad. I haven't been that nervous since . . . well, never mind." He pressed his lips together as if he wanted to make sure he didn't say anything else. He looked almost startled—as if he hadn't meant to say those words aloud.

"You were nervous?" I couldn't help enjoying that. "The mighty Hunter?"

Hunter leaned forward, gazing into the hearth. "Don't you think I know how highly you all thought of Cal? Especially you. I knew no one really wanted me taking over. And a part of me thought: Well, maybe they're right. Maybe I can't lead a circle as well as he did. God knows he's more at ease with people than I'll ever be."

I stared at him, stunned to hear him admit to so much vulnerability. I thought back to times when I'd watched Cal move from one clique at school to another, fitting in wherever he went. It was part of what had made him so good at manipulating people—he could present them with what they wanted to see. And what made it so powerful was that at some level, it was real. Hunter, on the other hand, could only be himself.

He and I had that in common.

A sadness clouded his clear green eyes. "I always thought my father would be there when I took over as a coven leader. It feels strange to take the step without him."

I nodded, aware of another connection we had. "Like my trying to learn about my birthright without my birth parents. I feel like something is missing."

"Yes," Hunter agreed. "Without Dad, being coven leader is all that more daunting."

"What made you decide to do it, then?" I asked.

He gave me a sudden, lopsided grin, gazing up at me from under a shock of pale hair. "The thought that *you* might try to lead them. I couldn't risk that."

If that was a joke, I didn't find it particularly funny. "Hey, I didn't come here to be insulted."

"Oh, stop." He laughed. "I didn't mean it as an insult. I only meant that you're a bit of a loose cannon because you've got all this power and no training. It's not an incurable condition."

"Glad to know it's not terminal," I muttered.

He looked at me more seriously now. "Morgan, listen to me. You have so much potential—it's very exciting, I know. But you've got to learn how to rein in and focus your power. For your own good as much as anything else. All that power makes you like a beacon. You're a walking target."

Abruptly I remembered the real reason I'd come here. I sat forward in my chair.

"There's something I need to tell you about," I said. I

described the dark force I'd felt after my dream and then again at the garage. "I tried to get it to reveal itself by drawing Peorth, but it just sort of evaporated," I said. "Do you have any idea what it was?"

He was frowning. "This is not good. It could have been another witch, cloaking him or herself. It sounds more like some sort of a taibhs, a dark spirit, though."

"The first time, when I sensed it in the middle of the night, I had the impression that whatever it was, it wasn't aimed at me," I said. "But after what happened at the garage, I'm not so sure. Do you think it's been following me?"

"You would have sensed that, I think." Hunter got to his feet, went to the window, and peered out into the trees that surrounded the house. "But we've got to assume that it wasn't coincidence, either. It was looking for you. And it found you."

"Did Selene send it? Or . . . Cal?" I asked in a low voice, not really wanting to know the answer.

"More likely Selene," Hunter said. "To her your power is an irresistible lure, almost as much as Belwicket's tools are. If she can't coerce you to join her group, she wants to absorb your power. It would increase her own to the point where she'd be practically invincible."

My skin crawled. I thought of David, saying that we had to take Selene's intentions into account as well as her actions. Maybe he was right, but her intentions sounded pretty awful in themselves. "They're really evil, aren't they?" I asked. "Selene and . . . and Cal?"

He took some branches from the box of kindling, snapped them in half, and added them to the fire. "Cal . . . is his mother's creation. I don't know if I'd call him evil." Glancing up, he gave me that quick grin again. "Besides, that's not a nice thing to say about one's own kin, is it?"

I grinned back. Hunter did have a sense of humor, I realized. It was just an offbeat one.

"As for Selene," Hunter went on, getting serious again. "She's ambitious and ruthless. She studied with Clyda Rockpel."

I shook my head, indicating that I didn't know the name.

"Clyda Rockpel was a Welsh Woodbane who was legendarily vicious. She's said to have murdered her own daughter to enhance her power. And it's certainly true that wherever Selene goes, witches tend to disappear or die. Destruction seems to follow in her wake. Yes, I would agree that she is truly evil."

I felt a wave of pity for Cal. With a mother like that, he'd never really had a choice. Or a chance.

As if he'd read my mind, Hunter said in a quiet voice, "Poor Cal." His eyes met mine, and I was startled by the depth of compassion in them.

We stared at each other, and then we were both suspended in a strange, timeless moment. I felt like I was falling into Hunter's gaze, and again I remembered the night when he'd almost kissed me. Of the profound connection I'd felt with him, the lightness I'd experienced when he and I had done tàth meànma, the intense sharing of minds I thought of as the Wiccan mind meld.

I wanted to feel Hunter's mouth on mine, his arms around me. I wanted to kiss away that sadness, all that had happened to him before we'd met. To tell him that his father would be proud of him if only he could be here. I could feel him wanting to do the same for me; I could sense him aching to stroke my face until he had wiped away all the tears I'd shed over Cal.

Then I blinked. What was I *thinking?* Here I was, talking to my ex-boyfriend's half brother and fantasizing about making out with him. Was I insane?

"I—I've got to go home," I said.

A faint flush had risen under Hunter's clear, pale skin. "Right," he said, standing up. He cleared his throat. "Wait just a moment. I've got some books for you."

He strode into the hallway and began pulling books off the shelves. "Here," he said, his voice back to its usually proper tone. "An advanced compendium of runic alphabets, Hope Whitelaw's critique of Erland Erlandsson's numerological system, and a guide to the properties of stones, minerals, and metals. Start with these, and when you've finished them, we'll talk about them. Then I'll give you more."

I nodded, not trusting myself to speak. When I took Hunter's books, I was careful to not allow our hands to touch.

Outside, the late afternoon sky was a harsh, glaring white. I drove home in a daze, my mind whirling, barely noticing the cold at all.

# 9.
# Almost Normal

*It happened again this afternoon. Just the way it did that other night. We were talking—talking about how to protect her, actually—and then, suddenly, I looked at her and it was as if I'd found an entire universe within her eyes. And I wanted so badly just to touch her, to kiss her mouth . . . I can't stop thinking about her. She moves me so strongly, so strangely. I've never felt like this before.*

*I'm an idiot. She can barely stand me.*

*—Giomanach*

Thursday and Friday, I worked really hard on keeping things normal. I went to school. I talked to my friends. I worked at my mom's office—I'd made a deal with my parents in which they'd front me the money for my car repairs in exchange for me getting all my mom's real estate listings entered into the computer. I cheered when the news came that Aunt Eileen and Paula had closed on their house and that they would start moving in over the weekend. I tried not to think about Cal. Or Hunter. Or the bad news about Practical Magick. Or dark forces that might be out to get me. I made it through the days like other teenage girls.

On Saturday, Robbie picked me up in his red Beetle. By now everyone in the coven had heard about Practical Magick closing, and Robbie had suggested a trip over there to see if there was anything we could do to help. I didn't think there was, but I was glad to go, anyway.

"So, how'd it go last night?" I asked as I buckled my seat belt. I knew that Robbie had gone out with Bree. It was a new direction for their age-old friendship.

Robbie shook his head, gazing through the windshield. "Same as before. We hung out, watched a video. Then we made out, and it was great. Fantastic. But the second I tried to talk about how I felt, she got all squirrelly." He grinned. "But this time I had the sense to shut up and kiss her again before she kicked me out of her house."

I laughed. "Quick thinking."

The fact was, Robbie had been in love with Bree for years. But Bree was gorgeous, while Robbie . . . well, he'd been a pizza face. It had made him afraid to approach her. Then, in trying out my newfound power, I'd made a potion to clear up the acne that for years had obliterated his looks. The potion had worked and kept on working in an almost frightening way. The scars had disappeared completely, and then his poor vision had improved, to the point where he no longer wore the thick glasses that he'd had ever since I'd known him. Without the acne or the glasses, he turned out to be amazingly good-looking and was now considered a major hottie at school.

With his new looks, Robbie had found the courage to go after Bree. But the results so far were uneven. They weren't exactly seeing each other but were definitely more than friends. On Robbie's side, it was love. For Bree . . . it was impossible to tell. Even back when we told each other everything, she'd always been hard to figure out when it came to relationships.

Thinking about Bree, I felt another pang of loss. With all that had happened to me in such a short amount of time, it was painful to not be able to confide in her. But the wounds were still too fresh. Maybe, just maybe, with Cal gone, we could begin to be friends again. I hoped so.

Robbie and I talked about Practical Magick's problems for the rest of the drive. Robbie's brow creased as he hunted for a parking space in front of the store. "There's something I don't get," he said. "I mean, we've got you, David, Alyce, Hunter, and Sky—that's five blood witches. And I assume you'd all like Practical Magick to stay open. Why can't you just all do a spell together so David hits the lottery or something?"

"I'm sure that kind of thing isn't allowed under Wiccan law," I said gloomily. "Otherwise David and Alyce would have done it already."

"That's a drag," Robbie said. He squeezed into a space behind a minivan, and we started for the store.

I nodded, but I couldn't help thinking—there must be some kind of spell to increase wealth. After all, going by the listings I'd seen in my mom's office, Selene Belltower's property must be worth at least a million dollars. And although

Cal had told me that Selene's employers had transferred her to Widow's Vale, I never had found out what she supposedly did for a living. I had a feeling her money didn't come through any of the usual channels.

Robbie pushed open the door, and I followed him into the store. I was stunned by Alyce's reception.

"Morgan!" she called. Her eyes were sparkling, her cheeks were pink, and she sounded almost giddy. "Robbie! I'm so glad to see you. I have excellent news!"

"What happened?" I asked.

"It's almost unbelievable. Stuart Afton has forgiven Rosaline's debt!" Alyce said.

"What?" I practically shrieked. "How did that happen?"

"Do rich people really do that?" Robbie asked.

"Apparently this one does," Alyce said, laughing. "Afton called David late last night to say he'd made a sudden windfall on the stock market and he'd decided to pass on some of his good fortune. I suppose it's the Yule spirit."

David stepped out from the little back room. "Have you heard?"

"Alyce was just telling us," I answered. "It's too good to be true."

David gave a faint smile. "It is rather surprising," he said.

"So the deal with the bookstore chain is off?" Robbie asked.

"That's right," David said. "And the upstairs tenants can stay, with their same rent."

"Best of all, Practical Magick stays," Alyce added. "We're throwing a party here tonight to celebrate. I was just going to start making calls to invite all of you, in fact. We want everyone to come—Wiccans, Catholics, Buddhists, atheists, you name it."

This was such great news. Even the idea of dark forces around couldn't keep me from a celebratory mood. "We'll be here," I promised.

"Uh, Morgan." Robbie elbowed me. "Hunter scheduled a circle tonight, remember?"

I'd forgotten, in fact. My stomach did a flip-flop at the thought of seeing Hunter again.

"I already spoke to Hunter. He's going to reschedule," Alyce said. She was practically giggling. "You don't get a gift like this every day, and we must give it a proper welcome. I've already arranged for The Fianna to play. It was the first thing I did when I heard the news." The Fianna was a hot Celtic pop band. Mary K. and I had tried to get tickets to one of their concerts last spring, and they had been totally sold out.

I glanced at David, who was methodically counting Tarot decks. Compared to Alyce's high-energy happiness, he seemed subdued. Then I remembered that this positive outcome came from a loss—the death of David's aunt. Perhaps now that the immediate crisis about the building was over, he had more time to actually feel his grief. Well, as Wicca teaches, everything is cyclical. Life leads to death leads to rebirth.

I wondered what kind of cycle I was in with Hunter. Annoyance leads to dreaming of kissing him to . . . irritation again?

"So what non-Wiccans are going to be at this party?" Mary K. asked as we waited for Das Boot's windshield to defrost. I'd come home that afternoon to find her so down about her breakup with Bakker that I'd talked her into coming with me to the Practical Magick party. Mary K. felt pretty much the same way that my parents did about Wicca, so she'd been reluctant—until I mentioned that The Fianna was going to play.

"The Fianna?" she'd gasped. "For real?"

After that she couldn't say no.

I wasn't just being nice by inviting her; I needed her support. I've never been the most comfortable person at a party. And knowing that Hunter would be there made me even more nervous.

I blew on my fingers to warm them up. "I'm not sure who'll be there," I said. "Probably the people who live above the shop. Plus you'll know Robbie and Bree and the other kids from school. They're Wiccans, but they're still people you've known forever."

I glanced at Mary K. She was wearing a short brown wool skirt and a russet-colored sweater. Citrine earrings sparkled against her auburn hair. As usual she looked perfect—neither too casual nor too dressy, just undeniably pretty.

"Well, you look great," she said, sounding uncharacteristically nervous.

On her advice, I had worn a lavender sweater, a long forest green skirt, an amethyst necklace, and brown lace-up boots. Did I really look good? Except when I was making magick, I usually felt depressingly plain. I'm five-foot-six, completely flat chested, with boring, medium-brown hair and what my mother calls "a strong nose." I mean, I'm not revolting or anything, but I'm not pretty.

At least, I was never pretty until Cal. Cal himself was so beautiful, he could have had any girl he wanted—and he chose me. Of course, he had chosen me for awful reasons, but in spite of that I didn't believe he'd totally faked the way he looked at me, touched me, kissed me. It seemed like I'd become beautiful. Now, without him, I felt plain again.

Mary K. fiddled with her seat belt and turned to me. "So . . . what happened with you and Cal? I mean, the real story."

My fingers tightened on the steering wheel. I took a deep breath. Then I finally told her everything that had happened the day of the fire. Everything I hadn't told my parents.

"Oh my God," was all she could say when I was done. "Oh my God, Morgan."

"You know, I owe you an apology for being so judgmental about you and Bakker," I told her. "I guess I expected you to handle the whole situation according to a simple, rational formula: Bakker hurts Mary K.; Mary K. dumps Bakker."

"That's how it should have been." Mary K.'s voice was so quiet, I could barely hear her. "I can't believe I gave him another chance."

"Two weeks ago I couldn't understand that," I said slowly, my thoughts forming my words. "But feelings don't work rationally. I did the same thing. All last week I knew things were wrong with Cal. But I didn't want to believe he could hurt me, even after he used his magick against me."

"He'd done it before?"

"The night before my birthday." The night we almost killed Hunter, I thought. Mary K. didn't need to know that part. I swallowed hard. "Cal—put a binding spell on me. I couldn't move. It was like I was drugged."

"Oh, great. All these things you're telling me really make me want to walk into a room full of witches." Mary K. peered out through her window as I pulled into a parking spot down the block from Practical Magick. "Is it too late to turn around and go home?"

"Yes. It's too late." I smiled and shut off the engine, but Mary K. just sat there, tugging her glove off and then on again. When she spoke, she sounded young and vulnerable.

"I appreciate what you said about me and Bakker. And I know that Wicca and your—your birth mother mean a lot to you. But all this witch stuff—it scares me. Especially when you tell me what's happened to you because of it."

I sighed. Maybe I'd told her too much.

"That's why it's so important to me that you come to this party," I tried to explain. "I want you to meet these people, to see that they're not all weird or scary or evil. I don't want to have to hide what I am. Please, Mary K. If you're really uncomfortable, we won't stay. I promise."

She looked down at her lap. After a moment she nodded.

"Okay," I said, trying to sound cheery. "Let's party."

# 10.
# The Party

July, 1991

We are in Bordeaux, staying with Leandre, a Wyndenkell cousin of Fiona's. Fiona is not well. She says it's only a chill she caught during the channel crossing, but I'm afraid it's something more serious. For a week now she's had a fever every night, and none of the usual remedies seem to help it. I'm almost ready to suggest that she go to a doctor of western medicine.

I went out today and hunted through the fields until I found a chunk of quartz the size of my fist. It's not as good as obsidian, but I think it will serve. I'm going to scry for our children, our town, our coven. I feel heavy with dread at the thought of what I might see.

—Maghach

Mary K. wasn't the only one who was nervous. I felt flutters in my stomach as we walked up the block toward the store. It had occurred to me that I was going to have to walk into a room full of people who all probably knew exactly what had happened with me and Cal. I pictured the talk stopping and all eyes turning toward me and Mary K. the minute we opened the door. My pace slowed to a halt.

Mary K. looked at my face. "Want to go home?" she asked shrewdly.

I swallowed. "No. Come on."

As it turned out, our entrance hardly attracted any notice at all. I stood by the glass doors, peeling off my gloves and gathering my courage. The party was already in full swing. Practical Magick was lit with candles and tiny white Christmas lights, and fragrant pine boughs decked the molding. Shelves had been moved into the nonbook half of the store so a platform stage could be set up. A cloth printed with Celtic knots was draped over the counter and covered with platters of food.

Alyce, wearing a long blue velvet dress, was the first to greet us. "Morgan," she said, folding me into a hug. "You look wonderful. I'm so glad you made it. And this is . . . ?"

"My sister, Mary K."

"Welcome," she said, clasping both of Mary K.'s hands in hers. "What a pleasure to meet you." Mary K. smiled; it was impossible not to respond to Alyce's warmth.

Alyce waved us in. "It's crowded already," she warned. "There's a coatrack set up against the back wall, cold drinks by the stockroom door, and hot apple cider on the little table by the Books of Shadows."

"Are The Fianna really playing?" asked Mary K.

"They are. They're in the back room, going over their set list."

"How did you ever get them?" Mary K. was clearly awestruck.

"Connections," Alyce told her. "The lead guitarist is my nephew. Would you like to meet them?"

My sister's eyes widened. "Are you serious?"

"Now's your chance." Alyce slipped an arm through Mary K.'s and led her behind the counter and into the back room.

I surveyed the other guests. It *was* crowded. I spotted the elderly couple from upstairs holding hands and beaming happily. Even from across the room, I could sense their relief. I felt a rush of pleasure, knowing that some problems had quick and happy solutions.

Sharon and Ethan were standing near an aluminum tub filled with ice and canned drinks, their heads bent toward each other. Jenna, wearing a silky slip dress with a cropped cardigan, was chatting animatedly to a guy who'd been in the shop the other day. He was laughing at something she said, and I noticed her ex, Matt, watching them. From the way Jenna cast a subtle glance in Matt's direction, I could tell she enjoyed knowing that Matt was watching her flirt.

Things are getting more and more complicated, I thought. I glanced around, looking for Hunter. I almost missed him because he was kneeling down in deep conversation with a little boy I recognized as the four-year-old son of the other tenant, Lisa Winston. The little boy seemed to be explaining something very important to Hunter, and Hunter was nodding seriously. Then Hunter said something, and the boy laughed with delight. Hunter must have felt my eyes on him because he suddenly glanced my way. I felt my heart catch; was it nerves?

Hunter went back to talking to the boy, and I was wondering if I should go join them when I heard someone say my name behind me.

"Morgan, isn't it?" I turned to see a middle-aged woman with salt-and-pepper hair in a thick French braid. She looked familiar, yet I couldn't place her.

"I'm Riva. I met you once at Selene's. I'm part of Starlocket," she explained. "I heard about what Selene and Cal tried to do to you," she added, staring at me.

"Oh," I said. This was just what I'd been afraid of. I felt like a zoo exhibit and wished desperately that she'd just go away and leave me alone.

"I couldn't believe it," she went on. "I had no idea Selene was mixed up with dark magick. I promise you, if any of us had known, we wouldn't have let her lead us."

"Thanks," I said awkwardly. "That's good to know."

She nodded and moved on to talk with another woman I recognized from Starlocket.

The mention of dark magick made me think again of the presence I'd felt at home and at the garage. I had checked to be sure that the protective sigils that Sky and Hunter had left at the house were still there, and it was reassuring that they were. Knowing that I had my altar set up also gave me something approaching peace of mind. Maybe I should find a book on altar magick, I thought. At least it would give me something to do besides standing here like a dork.

As I moved to the book section of the store, I felt a cold draft and turned to see the front door open.

"We're here!" Raven Meltzer announced from the open doorway. "The party can start now!" She strode into the store, Bree and Sky following her.

Raven took the prize for most outrageous outfit—no surprise there. She hadn't even bothered to wear a coat; she probably didn't want anything to spoil her dramatic entrance. Her black leather bustier showed off both the circle of flames tattooed around her belly button and a generous amount of cleavage. She wore tight black leather hip huggers, heavy-soled biker boots, hematite bracelets on her wrists, silver chains around her throat, and glittery eye shadow that went clear out to her temples. She'd put blue highlights in her dyed black hair. Catching sight of Matt, she gave him a smile and then ran her tongue over her lips in a slow, deliberate way. He flushed heavily.

As Bree shrugged off her heavy coat, Robbie stepped up to take it from her. But he was too late; a guy I knew from English class had already grabbed it, and Bree was thanking him sweetly, touching his arm. She was looking even more glamorous than usual in a slim coppery sheath of a dress.

Sky was as beautiful as Bree and Raven but in a completely different way. She was more subdued, more contained, in a pair of black jeans and a midnight blue camisole that set off her pale complexion and dark eyes. Those eyes never left Raven. She watched her in fascination, with yearning. I had been shocked to discover that Sky had a serious thing for Raven; they were so different. Maybe for Sky that was part of the attraction.

I sighed. Matt wanted Raven but sort of still wanted Jenna, too. Raven wanted to tease Matt and maybe Sky as well. Sky wanted Raven. Robbie wanted Bree, who only wanted boys she didn't have to take seriously. And I still wanted Cal, who had tried to kill me. Except when I wanted Hunter, whom I couldn't stand . . . Suddenly the idea of joining a convent sounded very appealing.

I snorted a laugh. Could witches even join convents? Well, this was one mess that I couldn't blame on Wicca, I realized. Wicca might have brought us together and intensified our feelings, but this little soap opera had high school hormones written all over it. In a weird way, the normalcy of these huge problems felt comforting.

And here I was, back to feeling my normal wallflower self.

Bree caught my eye and gave me a cautious little grin. She knew how uncomfortable I was in social situations. I had always counted on her to get me through them. I smiled back.

To my surprise, she walked over to me. "Hey, Morgan. That skirt looks great on you."

"Mary K. put this outfit together for me," I confessed.

Bree laughed, not meanly. "I figured." We stood side by side for a moment, looking out at the crowd. Then she asked quietly, "Is it hard for you, being here without Cal?"

I glanced at her, startled. I hadn't expected anything that direct. But as I met her gaze, I wanted so badly to reconnect with her.

"Everything feels hard with him gone," I said. My words tumbled out. "I miss him all the time. I feel like such a moron. It's like something out of a tabloid: High School Witch Grieves for Would-be Murderer."

"You're not a moron," she said. "You really cared about him. And—and maybe in some twisted way, he really cared about you, too."

I nodded numbly. I knew that it had been hard for her to say that. She had wanted Cal for herself. And it made me feel less like an idiot to think that he did care for me, even just a little.

Bree hesitated. "You know, I've been thinking about the way he played us."

I froze. Bree was treading on dangerous ground here.

"What I'm saying is . . ." She looked massively uncomfortable, then plunged ahead. "I think Cal deliberately slept with me, knowing it would set us against each other."

I gaped at her. "What?"

"He wanted to isolate you," she explained. "Come on, Morgan. You and I were best friends. We talked about everything. We trusted each other." Bree's voice started to quaver, and I could see her fighting to steady it. "Cal was trying to take you over, to control you completely. It would make sense for him to make sure he was the only one you talked to, the only one you really trusted. If he split us up, you'd be more dependent on him."

In a flash of sickening clarity, I realized she was right. I felt like I'd just been punched in the stomach. Every time I thought I'd faced the worst about Cal, I found more—new and deeper layers of deception on his part, blindness on mine.

"He pitted us against each other. He used us both," Bree said.

I nodded, unable to speak, seeing more layers falling away. But as I stood there, trying to process it all, it occurred to me that even if Bree was right about Cal, no one had forced her to do the cruel things she'd done to me. Maybe things were mending between us, but they could never go back to what they had once been. We'd never trust each other the way we used to. I felt incredibly sad.

"What happened to David?" Bree said, pulling my attention back to the room.

"What?" I asked.

She nodded toward the counter. David was dipping a carrot stick into some hummus. His left hand was wrapped in a white gauze bandage.

"I don't know," I said. "Let's go find out."

Before I could move, Mary K. emerged from the back room and, to my astonishment walked up onto the platform and took the mike. "Excuse me. Could I have everyone's attention, please?" she said. When the room was quiet, she announced with a huge grin, "I'm pleased to introduce The Fianna!"

Practical Magick erupted into applause as The Fianna made their way onto the stage. They were four skinny young guys and a wisp of a girl with short red hair. She launched into an a cappella verse in a voice that was positively haunting. It reminded me of Hunter's voice when he sang the chant in our circle, a voice drawn out of the world of our ancestors, a pure, shimmering thread that connected us to the past.

I jumped when I heard Hunter's voice behind me. "I need to talk to you," he said quietly.

Bree gave me a questioning look and then moved to rejoin Sky across the room.

"Not here," Hunter said. Taking my elbow, he led me through the crowded room and out the door.

"It's freezing out here," I complained, crossing my arms over my nonexistent chest. "And I want to hear The Fianna."

"Morbid Irish ballads later," he said. "Believe me, there are plenty more where those came from." He opened the door to Sky's green car. "Get in."

I ducked into the passenger seat, muttering, "Do you always have to order me around?"

He grinned. "It's the cold," he said. "Don't have time for the niceties. Don't want you freezing in that pretty outfit." He shut my door, then climbed into the driver's seat.

Flustered at hearing the word *pretty* come out of his mouth in reference to me, I sat there in silence.

He turned on the heat, then rubbed his hands to warm them up. "I went to that field. Where you thought the first dark presence might have been."

"Wh-what did you find out?" I wasn't sure if I wanted to hear his answer.

He shook his head. "I don't think it was Selene."

"Really?" My heart returned to its normal rhythm. But then it sped up again as I asked, "But then who? What?" Hunter let out a sigh. "That's just it. I'm not entirely sure. There was a dark ritual performed there—you were right about that." He gave me a quick glance. I knew my abilities as a beginning witch still surprised him. "But the traces I found of the ritual suggested to me that whoever performed it was someone who had to work quite hard to conjure power."

"What kind of traces?" I was fascinated in spite of myself.

"Blood, among other things," Hunter said, and I gasped. "One of the ways to summon a dark spirit is with a blood offering. But that isn't something Selene would need to do."

I shut my eyes. "Do you think it was Cal?" I asked in a low voice.

"It could be. But why he'd do work like that without Selene . . . well, it just doesn't add up."

I felt a tiny flicker of hope. Maybe Cal had left Selene. Maybe he was on his own because he'd come back to be with me. I doused that flame by reminding myself that it had been dark magick that I had felt, which would mean that Cal would still be incredibly dangerous.

I shivered, and it wasn't with cold. "If it's not Cal and Selene, who could it be? Who would perform a dark magick ritual?" I asked. I glanced at the door to Practical Magick, wondering if the wayward witch was inside. Among us. And what he or she would do next.

Hunter didn't respond. He looked straight ahead.

"What?" I demanded, a prickle of foreboding making the hairs on my arms stand up. "What aren't you telling me?" I was so sick of secrets and lies that my voice was louder than I had planned.

Hunter's jaw tightened, then he turned to face me. "You won't like this. I don't, either. But hasn't it occurred to you that Practical Magick was saved just in the nick of time? Don't you find it convenient that Stuart Afton has forgiven this huge debt, out of the blue?"

I stared at him. "Alyce said the guy had a windfall," I explained. "If I suddenly came into lots of money, I'd be generous, too."

Hunter smirked at me. "You, clearly, are not a business-man."

"It's not possible," I snapped. "Are you really suggesting that David and Alyce used some kind of dark magick to get Stuart Afton to cancel the debt?"

"Not necessarily Alyce," Hunter said. "But David, yes—I think it's possible. Did you notice the bandage on his hand?"

"What about it?" I asked, nonplussed.

"Remember the blood I found in the field?"

"Huh?" At first I didn't understand what he was trying to say. But then I got it, and it was so absurd, I let out a sharp laugh. "Oh, please. Are you saying David hurt his hand making a blood offering to a dark spirit? Come on! There are a dozen other ways he could have hurt himself. Did you even ask him about it?"

"Not yet," Hunter admitted.

"I can't believe you're thinking this way," I said. "I mean, we *know* Cal and Selene use dark magick, and we know the magick was done in a place Cal used to go to. Why are you even bringing David into it? Why do you have to be suspicious about *everything*?" I was starting to get worked up again. "Why can't good news just be good news?"

Hunter was silent. The door to Practical Magick opened as a couple entered, and the singer's voice drifted into the night. She was singing a joyful song of coming spring, and I was suddenly impatient to share in that pleasure, not sit out here listening to Hunter's ridiculous theories. I flung open the car door and hurried back inside.

The Fianna played for almost an hour, and practically everyone in the room danced. Mary K. even tugged me out onto the floor for a song. I ignored Hunter as best I could and noticed he left early.

After another hour or so, people began to filter out. Mary K. and I got our coats. As she went to say good night to the band, David joined me at the cider table.

"Did you enjoy yourself?" he asked.

I nodded and gave him a smile. "What happened to your hand?" I asked.

David shrugged. "My knife slipped as I was trimming pine boughs."

Ha, I thought. Wait until I tell Hunter. So much for his suspicions.

Mary K. returned, proudly displaying her autographed Fianna CD. "I can't wait until Jaycee gets a load of this," she declared as we headed for the car.

"So now do you believe that all Wiccans aren't evil and weird?" I asked Mary K.

"I'll say one thing for them," she answered. "They know how to throw a party. I still can't believe I met The Fianna!" She clutched the CD to her chest.

As I kicked Das Boot into gear, she went on. "It's just that . . . well, Wicca isn't my way. And the fact that the church is against it doesn't help," she added more quietly. Mary K. wasn't as religious as Mom or our aunt Maureen, but she did basically believe in what Catholicism taught. "I have to say I was never totally comfortable in there."

I nodded. I'd already pretty much known that my sister felt like this. But to hear it confirmed so baldly was painful. So that was it, I thought. The essence of my identity, the core of who I was, was the very thing that created an unbridgeable gap between me and my family.

We drove the rest of the way home in silence.

# 11
# Hunted

July, 1991

In Milan now. A close escape. It was my scrying, I think, that alerted the evil to our presence in Bordeaux.

First I sought our children and found them, as I had prayed they would be, safe with Beck. Then I asked my quartz to help me see our coven, and I saw. Oh, Goddess.

I saw the utter devastation of our town, the swathe of burnt houses, charred cars, blackened tree trunks whose branches seemed to claw at the sky in their agony. . . . Nothing, it seemed, was spared. Nothing except our house. It stood there, the mellow brick darkened by a pall of ash but otherwise untouched.

Then, from our bedroom, I heard Fiona screaming. I ran in and found her sitting upright in bed, her eyes wild.

*"It's coming,"* she cried. *"It's found us. We have to go!"*
*She's calling me. More later.*
—*Maghach*

My dad was in the kitchen when I came down the next morning, wearing his usual winter outfit of khakis, button-down shirt, and knit vest. He was peeling potatoes for dinner, then dropping them into a bowl of ice water. My dad has a thing about preparing far in advance.

"Your cat would like you to feed him," my dad greeted me.

Sure enough, Dagda was sitting on the floor next to his bowl, looking up with a hopeful expression. He wound himself around my ankles, arching his little back against my hand. I bent and picked up the dish.

"How was the party?" my dad asked as I spooned canned food into Dagda's bowl.

"Okay," I replied. Disturbing, I added silently. I went to the fridge and scanned for food.

"Morgan, don't just stand there with the door open," he admonished me.

"Sorry," I said. I grabbed a box of waffles and shut the fridge. As I crossed to the toaster, I noticed the local newspaper on one of the kitchen chairs. It was open to the business section, which my father reads religiously.

"Dad," I said, "have you ever heard of a guy named Stuart Afton?"

"You mean the cement-and-gravel tycoon?" Dad asked.

"He's a tycoon?"

Dad paused. "Maybe not exactly. But he is a big player in

the local building supplies industry. I've heard he's kind of ruthless, like a strong-arm guy."

"Hmmm." I had to admit that Afton didn't sound like the kind of person to forgive a debt. No, I told myself, rummaging for syrup, people can surprise you. Maybe Afton is tough on the outside but a softie on the inside. I pushed aside the thought that came after that: that David could also surprise me and that Hunter could be right.

Get your mind off it, I ordered myself. "Where are Mom and Mary K.?" I asked Dad.

"They went to church early to help with the Christmas clothing drive." He wiped his hand on a dish towel. "We're meeting them there for mass."

I brought my waffle over to the table and fiddled with my fork. "Um, I have a lot of studying to do," I said at last. "Is it all right if I skip church?"

Behind his tortoiseshell glasses, Dad's eyes were troubled. "I suppose so," he said after a moment.

"Thanks." I put a big bite of waffle into my mouth so I didn't have to say anything else. Since discovering Wicca, my relationship to Catholicism was changing, like everything else in my life. Though I still found the services beautiful, they didn't speak to me in the way they once had. I was pleased, though, that my parents were at a point where they accepted my ambivalence, despite the worry it caused them.

I spent most of the rest of the day tucked away in my room, studying the books Hunter had lent me. I copied spells and lessons into my Book of Shadows and even, feeling a little silly, made myself a set of rune flash cards. I wasn't going to leave Hunter any room to reprimand me for being lax in my studies.

As if he'd heard me thinking, Hunter called to suggest that I come over Tuesday afternoon for some more lessons. I couldn't think of a legitimate excuse, so I agreed.

That night I had trouble sleeping again. I was troubled by Hunter's suggestion that dark magick had anything to do with Stuart Afton's change of heart regarding Practical Magick. I couldn't believe that David would be involved in anything like that. How would I know for sure? It wasn't as if I could just go up to him and ask him.

I could scry, I realized. Maybe I'd find the proof I needed for Hunter to back off on this crazy idea. I hated that he could make me suspicious of my friends.

I peered out into the hallway. The light in my parents' room was out and so was Mary K.'s. Quietly I took the candle from the altar in my closet, set it on my desk, and lit it.

I stared into the flame, burning bright yellow with streaks of orange and blue. It seemed so insignificant. One breath could annihilate it. When I'd scryed before, I'd done it with a full, blazing fire, but in theory there was no reason why a candle shouldn't work just as well. Fire was fire, wasn't it? And right now the thought of any fire greater than this one made me shudder.

I closed my eyes and began to clear my mind. Breathe in, breathe out. In, out. I was aware of my pulse slowing, my muscles relaxing, the tiny fibers smoothing themselves into shining ribbons.

Fire, help me to see the truth. I am ready to see what you know, I thought, and opened my eyes.

The small flame of the candle had blazed up into a molten, white-hot teardrop. From its brilliant center, a face gazed back at me: a familiar nose and mouth, smooth skin, dark, thick hair, and golden eyes. That isn't David, I thought stupidly.

I stared, frozen, as Cal's image floated before me. His lips moved, and then I heard his voice.

"Morgan, I'm sorry. I love you. I'll love you forever. We're soul mates."

"No," I breathed, feeling my heart implode. It wasn't true. We weren't destined to be together. I knew that now.

"Morgan, forgive me. I love you. Please, Morgan . . ."

The last word was a whisper, and I struck out blindly with my hand and brought it down on the candle flame. There was a hiss and a faint, charring smell. And I was alone in the darkness.

# 12
# Ugly

*July. 1991*

I thought Fiona was delirious from the fever. but her terror was so intense that I ended up bundling her up and putting her into Leandre's car. I chose a direction at random: east. We had driven for less than an hour when Fiona let out a cry. "Leandre!" She grasped my arm. "I can *feel* him. He's dying."

I pulled up at the first little village bistro I could find and rushed in to phone Leandre. but I couldn't get through. Not until late that night did we find out that his farm had been consumed by a mysterious wildfire. He and all his family had been trapped in their house.

"It was the dark wave." Fiona whispered, shuddering. "It's hunting for us."

Without discussing it. we got back into the car and continued east. fleeing across France. As I drove through the *clear summer night, I kept remembering something Selene had said shortly before I left her the first time. She'd come back from a meeting with her Woodbane friends, the ones I feared, and once again she'd been in an oddly frenetic state, as if she had so much energy within her that she must keep moving or catch fire. I asked her what they'd done. "Watched the wave," she said with a strange, sharp laugh. Of course, I though she meant <u>waves</u>: we lived on the Pacific coast. But now, as I drove, I wondered if she'd meant something else altogether.*

*Did Selene have something to do with sending the dark wave? Is she taking her revenge at last?*

*—Maghach*

I don't know how long I sat there, shaking, too shocked even to cry. Goddess, help me, I thought desperately.

Cal. Oh, Cal. Tears began to rain down my cheeks, scalding and salty. I wrapped my arms around myself and rocked back and forth, keening quietly, trying to smother the sound. My palm throbbed where I'd crushed the candle flame, and as I sat there, the pain seemed to spread until my whole body was one pulsing, raw wound.

After a while Dagda mewed and tapped me tentatively with one paw. I looked at him numbly.

At some point my brain began to work again. How had that happened? How had Cal gotten into my vision? Was it his dark magick? Or had I summoned him somehow—had my own subconscious betrayed me?

He'd said he still loved me. He'd said he'd love me forever. Wasn't that truth I'd heard in his voice?

I gasped and squeezed my head between my hands. "Stop it. Stop it!" I muttered.

I sat there for another few minutes. Then I forced myself to climb into bed. Dagda sprang up and curled himself into a ball on my stomach. I lay there, staring blindly at the ceiling as tears ran down the sides of my face to soak my pillow.

I went through school the next day like an automaton. The burn on my palm had swelled into a shiny blister that burst halfway through the day. It hurt to write, so I just sat in class, not bothering to take notes. Not that my notes would have been much good, anyway. For all I got, my teachers might as well have been speaking Swahili. All I could think was: Cal. He had spoken to me.

What did it mean? Did he still hope to convince me to join him and Selene? Or was this some cruel plan to make me go crazy? If that was it, it was working. I'd never experienced such a horrible mixture of longing and revulsion. I felt like I was going to split apart.

When I got home from school, I had a message from Bob Unser, saying that Das Boot's parts had come in and asking me to drop off the car tomorrow morning. I could pick it up again on Wednesday morning, he said. Perfect, I thought. I couldn't possibly go to Hunter's on Tuesday since I wouldn't have transportation. I knew I was being incredibly stupid, not telling him about seeing Cal, but I just couldn't do it. I couldn't share it, especially with him. Not yet, anyway.

I shot off an e-mail to Hunter, saying I had to cancel

tomorrow because I would be vehicularly challenged. I also told him what David had told me about how he hurt his hand.

Then I sat at the kitchen table, drumming my fingers on the Formica surface. I had to do something to distract myself. I knew Aunt Eileen and Paula were moving in all week; some manual labor would be just what the doctor ordered. So I set off for Taunton.

Taunton was a smaller town than either Widow's Vale or Red Kill. Both Widow's Vale and Red Kill had had their town centers "revitalized," but Taunton was more mainstream America. There were the usual strip malls with the predictable fast-food joints, auto supply places, megastores, and video and drugstore chains.

Eileen and Paula's neighborhood was older. Although each house was different, they fit together harmoniously. Huge old trees shaded the lawns and arched out over the center of the street. The neighborhood had a nice, settled feel to it.

Paula and Eileen's house was at the very end of the street. I wanted to surprise them, so I parked at the other end of the block. I started walking.

As I got closer to the end of the block, I saw three teenage boys standing in front of one of the houses. Two of them wore parkas with shiny reflective tape on the seams. The third wore a loose camouflage jacket over camouflage pants. At first I thought they were having a snowball fight with some other kids I couldn't see; then I realized that they were throwing *rocks* at Paula and Eileen's house. My mouth dropped open, and I froze in my tracks.

"Queer!" one of them shouted.

"We don't need dykes in this neighborhood!" called another.

In one instant I got it, and then I was running hard toward the house, anger coursing through my veins like alcohol.

"Come on out, bitch!" one of the boys yelled. "Meet your neighbors! We're the welcome wagon!"

I heard the sound of glass shattering as at least one of the rocks connected. The boy closest to me looked up, his alarm quickly replaced by naked aggression.

"What the hell are you doing?" I demanded, breathing hard. "Get out of here, and don't come back!"

The boy couldn't be older than me, I saw. He had a shaved head, a nose that was nearly flat, and pale blue eyes. "Who are you?" He sounded amused. "One of their dyke friends? You don't know what you're missing, baby."

"Get. Out. Of. Here," I said, my voice vibrating with only marginally controlled fury. I felt on fire with rage.

The guy with the shaved head advanced on me, and his two friends closed in behind him. "Or what?" he said nastily. "You'll hit me with your purse?" He turned around to his friends, and the three of them laughed. My hands were trembling, clenched into fists, and I felt almost ill.

"Leave," I said, eerily calm. My voice didn't sound like my own. "Don't make me hurt you."

He burst into laughter. "Baby, maybe what you need is a man. Like those other dykes." He opened his arms wide. "Let me show you how it's supposed to be."

One of his friends laughed.

"You don't know what you're doing," I almost whispered.

Grinning, Flat Nose reached out to grab my arm, but before he touched me, I shot out my hand and sent a burning, crackling ball of blue witch fire at his throat. I didn't even think about it—I just unleashed my fury. The fire hit him so quickly, he had no time to react. His hands went to his throat, and he dropped to his knees. He doubled over, making little whimpering sounds of pain.

I felt encased in ice, completely calm, ready to annihilate them all. I began to call on my power. "An di allaigh, re nith la," I murmured.

The two friends were staring at Flat Nose and then back at me as they tried to figure out what happened. Flat Nose was gagging and retching on the cold sidewalk. He glared up at me and tried to climb to his feet. I pushed the air and he sank, crumpled, to the cement. I used my power to pin him like a bug without even touching him. Adrenaline coursed through my veins, and I felt unbelievably powerful.

"Shit," said the second guy. He and the third guy stared fearfully at each other. Then they turned and pounded down the street, looking back over their shoulders.

I leaned over the worm who lay writhing and frightened on the sidewalk. He was getting just what he deserved, I gloated with satisfaction. I felt filled with power, and I liked it.

I took a deep breath and stepped back, smelling the acrid scent of his fear. "Go," I whispered, and released him with my mind.

Clumsily he scrambled to his feet and backed away from me. Then he spun around and ran off. It was over, and I had won.

I felt dizzy, a little nauseous, the way I sometimes felt in circles when power rushed through me. I took a few moments to ground myself, then I looked up at the house.

The bay window was smashed, as well as another one on the first floor. Where were Eileen and Paula? I wondered. Were they hurt? Or had they seen what I'd done?

Wondering how I would explain it, I walked up to the door and rang the bell. Winter-bare rosebushes in front of the house were sparkling with shards of glass.

No one answered. I cast my senses and felt both Eileen's and Paula's familiar energy inside the house. They were okay. They were just afraid to answer the door, and I felt angry all over again. Prisoners in their own house. It was disgusting!

"Aunt Eileen, it's me, Morgan!" I called through the broken window.

"Morgan?" A minute later the door opened, and my aunt swept me into her arms. "Are you okay? There were these idiot boys outside—"

She hadn't seen me. Relief.

"I saw them," I told her.

Paula gave me a hug, too. "Welcome to the neighborhood," she said shakily.

We all stepped in, and Aunt Eileen shut the front door, locking the dead bolt. She crossed her arms over her chest, rubbing her own shoulders as if for comfort. "I'm glad they left before you got here," she said. "But I'm sorry they didn't stick around long enough for the police to show up. I just called them."

"We probably shouldn't clean up the glass until the police have seen it." Paula ran a hand through her sandy blond hair. "I guess we're an official crime scene now."

I felt so sorry for them—and so furious at those small-minded idiots.

"It's just glass," Aunt Eileen said, putting an arm around her. "We can have new glass put in." She looked at me. "I'm sorry, Morgan. This isn't a good welcome for you. Come in, take off your coat, and we'll give you the grand tour of broken glass and packed boxes."

We walked through the empty rooms, and Paula and Aunt Eileen explained their plans for decorating and renovating to me. They were both doing their best to sound excited, but I could sense their tension. The thugs had shaken them badly.

When the doorbell rang, we all jumped. My senses told me it was safe, though, and when Aunt Eileen opened the door, we saw two cops. Officer Jordan was a tall man and black. His partner was a younger woman with short, curly blond hair, whose badge said Officer Klein. I stood by as Aunt Eileen and Paula gave their report and showed them the damage.

"Did you get a good look at these boys?" Officer Jordan asked.

"We know there were three of them," Aunt Eileen told him. "But we stayed in the house."

"I saw them as I came up," I said. "They were about my age, juniors or seniors in high school. One of them was wearing camouflage. Another was bald with a flat, broken nose and blue eyes."

Paula looked at me in surprise. "How did you get such a good look at them?"

"They, um, they ran right past me," I explained. "Another

guy was little, maybe five-five, with a brown crew cut. The third guy had blond hair, slicked back, and thick lips."

Officer Jordan took notes on all of that, then looked at my aunt. "It looks like you people just moved in. Any idea of why these kids went after you?"

"Because we're gay," Aunt Eileen said matter-of-factly. "They called us dykes."

I noticed Officer Klein's lips tighten. "Some people are just ignorant," she muttered.

"I hope you catch them," Paula said. "Before they actually hurt someone."

The police left, and I helped Aunt Eileen and Paula clean up the shattered glass and seal off the broken windows with cardboard and tape.

"God, that's ugly," Paula said, looking at our handiwork.

"It's temporary," Aunt Eileen assured her. "I'll call a glass company tomorrow."

I glanced at my watch. "Oh, wow, I'd better get home. It's after six."

Aunt Eileen and Paula both hugged me and told me to come back anytime.

As I walked down the front steps, I turned back to wave and saw the two of them hugging each other tightly. Paula's face was buried in Aunt Eileen's shoulder. I could feel their tension from where I stood. And I knew what they were worried about. I'd had the same thought.

This wasn't over. Those kids would talk themselves out of their fear at what I'd done. And then they'd be back.

# 13.
# Protection

*Litha, 1993*

We're in Prague now, but Fiona feels we'll have to leave again soon. A dubious legacy of the dark wave—ever since she saw it in her leug, she can sense it coming.

It's been two years now since we left our lives behind us. Two years of running, hiding, locking our magick away to keep it from betraying us. Two years of longing for news of our children, yet not daring to reach out to them. Two years of Fiona gradually withering, racked by ailment after ailment. We've come to believe it's the effect of the dark wave itself—that it crippled her somehow when she saw it in her leug. So far we've found no cure.

—Maghach

That night I blew off my homework. I went through every magick book I had, looking for something that would help me protect Aunt Eileen and Paula. I could put runes of protection around their house, I reasoned. That would be a start, at least.

Too bad I couldn't get them to wear talismans for personal safety. Somehow I couldn't picture either of them wearing Wicca paraphernalia, no matter how open-minded they might be.

"Ew," I said as I found the instructions for making an old protection called a Witch's Bottle. The Witch's Bottle was not only supposed to shield you from evil but also to send the evil back to its source. It called for filling a small glass bottle halfway to the top with sharp objects: old nails, pins, razor blades, needles, and so on. Then you filled the bottle the rest of the way with urine and, ideally, some blood, too. Then you sealed the jar and buried it twelve inches deep. The bottle and its protection was supposed to last until the bottle was dug up and smashed.

I put down the book, completely grossed out. Did I have the stomach to be a witch? This was disgusting. But if it would really protect Eileen and Paula . . . I read it through again. No, it wouldn't work. The Witch's Bottle was to protect against negative *magick*. The guys who'd attacked Aunt Eileen and Paula's house were negative, all right, but they weren't using magick.

I finally settled on a protection charm that I could place in their house without their noticing. It called for ingredients that I didn't have, and I decided to make a trip to Practical Magick as soon as I had my car back.

Robbie followed me and Mary K. out to Unser's on Tuesday morning, then drove us to school. My plan was to go to my mom's office after school and spend some time inputting listings, then get a ride home with her. Mary K. was going to Jaycee's house. Jaycee's mom would drop her at our house in time for dinner.

After school I set out alone on the long walk to Mom's office, shivering and hoping someone I knew would drive by and offer me a ride.

Be careful what you wish for. A familiar pale green Ford pulled up at the curb, and the passenger window rolled down. Sky Eventide leaned over from the driver's seat, her white-blond hair luminous. "Hop in," she said.

"Were you out looking for me?" I asked, perplexed. "Or is this just a coincidence?"

Sky raised an eyebrow. "Haven't you yet learned that there are no coincidences?"

I stood on the sidewalk, staring stupidly at her. Was she joking or not? I wasn't sure. Just like Hunter, Sky wasn't easy to read.

Seeing my confusion, she said, "Hunter asked me to come pick you up. I even left work early. You're supposed to come to our house for lessons."

I had heard that Sky worked at a used-record store. She was so ethereal, it was hard to picture her doing mundane things like working a cash register. "But I already told Hunter I couldn't come," I protested. "And my mom's expecting me."

Sky tapped a gloved finger on the steering wheel impatiently. "Call her from our place. This is important, Morgan."

She was right, I realized, though not for the reasons she thought. I couldn't keep putting off talking to Hunter. Biting my lip, I opened the passenger door and climbed in.

My stomach felt fluttery. I still didn't feel ready to talk about seeing Cal, but I knew I had to face it sooner or later. And sooner was probably safer.

Sky pulled out into traffic and accelerated. She drove fast and tended to stomp on the brakes harder than she needed to at red lights. "Sorry," she said as I jerked forward against my seat belt. "I'm not used to all this power-assisted driving."

I glanced at her as she made a right turn. Her profile was pure, almost childlike, with its perfect nose and arched brows, the smooth curve of cheek covered with the finest, faintest golden down. She and Hunter looked very much alike, but while Sky seemed deceptively fragile, Hunter's face had a masculine angularity that projected strength.

"Why is Hunter doing this?" I found myself asking. "Why is he so concerned about making sure that I become a proper witch?"

Sky smiled slightly. "Wicca isn't something you can learn in a correspondence course or figure out on your own. It's experiential. You need someone who's gone through it before you as a guide. Otherwise bad things can happen. Especially with the kind of power that you've inherited."

"That's not what I was asking," I said. "Why Hunter? Doesn't he have more important things to do than worry about me?"

"He's a Seeker," Sky replied. "It's his job to make sure witches don't misuse their magick. And—" She broke off. Then, after a moment's hesitation, she added, "And you're Woodbane."

I bristled. "So he's waiting for me to turn bad?"

"You might," Sky said bluntly. "He can't ignore the possibility."

I folded my arms and pressed my back against the cushioned seat. So Hunter was acting as my watchdog, making sure I stayed on the path of righteousness. I was his assignment, just as I had been Cal's assignment.

I remembered how much I had hated both Sky and Hunter when I'd first met them. With Sky it was mostly from jealousy—her beauty and poise were intimidating to me. But, I realized now, it was also that I'd sensed their suspicion. I could feel that Sky still didn't truly trust me; even though we'd scryed together, she continued to scrutinize me. Apparently Hunter was doing the same thing. The thought sent a sharp pain through me.

Hunter looked up when I walked in with Sky. "Thanks," he said to her.

"Ta," Sky said. She tossed her leather jacket on the sofa, then pointed to the phone. "Feel free," she said, then disappeared up the stairs.

"How long can you stay?" Hunter asked me. "We've got a lot to talk about."

"I'm not staying," I said. "Sorry Sky went to all that trouble, but I have work to do." I crossed to his phone. "If you won't drive me, I'll call a taxi."

Hunter rubbed a hand across his chin. "What is the matter with you?" he asked mildly.

"I don't appreciate you sending your cousin to practically kidnap me off the street," I snapped. "I told you I didn't have a ride, so I couldn't make it."

"I'm sorry." To my astonishment, he actually sounded abashed. "I—well, I thought I was doing you a favor."

"No, you didn't," I retorted. "You just wanted me to stick to your plan. What gives you the right to just waltz in out of nowhere and take charge? You think just because the International Council of Witches told you to keep an eye on me that gives you the right to run my life?"

"They—" Hunter began, but I cut him off.

"You know what? I'm really sick of being somebody's assignment." Tears filled my eyes. I blinked furiously, trying to keep them from falling. "No one seems to care about who I really am, or what I want! What about *me* in all of this?"

"Morgan—" Hunter began, but I cut him off again.

"No!" I cried. "Don't! It's my turn." My fingers curled into fists, and I felt pressure build in my chest. "You're so self-righteous about your mission and the council and all that crap, but really you want exactly the same thing as Cal and Selene did—to control me. To use me for your own purposes." To my humiliation, my voice broke. I turned my back on Hunter and stood there, biting down hard on my lower lip as I struggled to hold myself together.

He didn't say anything at first, and silence stretched between us. At last he spoke in a curiously subdued voice.

"You're not my assignment. The council didn't tell me to keep an eye on you, actually," he said.

I fought to regain my normal pattern of breathing so that I would be able to understand what he was telling me. I wanted so much to understand, to be wrong.

I heard Hunter take a deep breath, too. "I'm here of my own choice, Morgan. I did contact them about you, that's true. I told them you were a witch of exceptional power and that I wanted to see if I could help guide you. They said I could do that as long as it didn't interfere with my primary work as a Seeker—which is to track down Cal and Selene and others like them."

He paused, and I heard him take a step toward me. Then I felt a featherlight touch on my shoulder. "I don't want to control you, Morgan," he said. "That's the last thing I want."

His hand left my shoulder, his fingers lightly stroking my long hair. He was just inches behind me; I could feel the warmth of his body, and I held my breath.

"What I'm trying to do," he went on softly, "in my own clumsy way, is to give you the tools you need to understand the forces that you will inevitably come up against."

I turned to face him, searching his eyes, wondering what it was that he wanted, what I wanted. His eyes are so green, I found myself thinking, so gentle. I could feel his breath on my cheek, warm everywhere except on the wet trail of tears.

"I just want . . . ," he whispered, and trailed off.

We stood there, our gazes locked, and it seemed to me that once again the universe suspended its motion around us and the only warm, living things in it were the two of us.

Then Sky's voice called down from upstairs, "Hunter, did you remember to get cheese and biscuits?" and suddenly everything started moving again, and I stepped backward until the backs of my knees hit the worn ottoman and I sat down. I was trembling, and I found I couldn't look at Hunter.

"Um—yes, I got them," Hunter replied, his voice raspy and a little breathless.

"Right, then. I'm going to make a cheese-and-tomato

omelette. I'm starved." I heard Sky's boots clattering down the stairs. "Want some?"

"Sounds great," Hunter said. "Morgan, how about you?"

"Um—no thanks, my family will be expecting me for dinner at six-thirty," I said shakily. "In fact, I'd better give my mom a call right now and let her know where I am."

"Tell her I'll run you home by six," he said. Then he added, "If that's all right with you, I mean. If you want to stay."

"It's all right," I told him. I didn't feel ready to leave.

By the time I hung up, I felt more normal. Hunter led me to the back of the house, where the wood-burning stove filled the long room with warmth. The windows were fogged with condensation, but I rubbed one with my sweater and looked outside. Another rickety porch lined the back of the house, and beyond it I could see trees growing from the sides of the ravine: oak, maple, birch, hemlock, and pine. The woods around Widow's Vale tended to have a well-trod, gentle feel to them. But the land behind Hunter and Sky's house felt raw, wild, as though floodwaters had just swept through and carved out something new and highly charged.

"It feels different here," I said.

"It is. It's a place of power." Hunter lit the candle and incense stick on the altar. He gestured to the floor where we'd held the circle. A worn oriental carpet now covered the center of the floor. "Have a seat."

I settled myself on the carpet.

He didn't sit. "There's something we need to discuss," he said.

"What?" I asked, feeling wary again.

"I did some checking on David's story, yesterday and today.

That's why I couldn't come pick you up myself." Hunter paced toward the woodstove, then swung around to face me. "First of all, he lied about how he hurt his hand. I asked Alyce, and she told me he'd come in with it bandaged up two days *before* the party. He didn't do it trimming boughs for the party."

My heart lurched. David had lied to me?

Wait. I thought back. Not so fast. He never said he cut his hand trimming boughs *for the party*. He could have been trimming some other boughs. Couldn't he?

"Second, Stuart Afton didn't make any money on stocks last week," Hunter said.

I frowned. "I'm not following you."

Hunter made an impatient gesture with his hand. "David said Afton forgave his debt because he'd made a killing on the stock market last week," he reminded me. "But I checked, and it never happened."

"You checked? How?"

"If you must know," Hunter said, looking uncharacteristically self-conscious, "I chatted up his secretary. No man has secrets from his secretary. She knew nothing about any sudden windfall."

"And why is this your business?"

"Because I'm a Seeker," Hunter said. "It's my job to investigate misuses of magick."

"This doesn't have anything to do with magick," I said, standing up. "Maybe there was a stock split and Afton's secretary was at lunch when the call came in. Maybe he got the news by e-mail. Maybe there was no stock split but Afton forgave the debt anyway, out of the simple goodness of his heart. This isn't council business, Hunter."

"Open your eyes," Hunter said flatly. "There's magick involved here. Dark magick. We both know that."

I realized I had no choice. I had to tell him about seeing Cal.

I took a deep breath. "There's something I have to tell you."

I explained how I'd scryed for the truth two nights ago and how instead of seeing David, Cal had appeared. I didn't speak about the feelings seeing Cal's face had induced, nor did Hunter ask. But two white creases appeared on the outsides of his nostrils.

"The way I see it, this is the strongest proof we've had yet that Cal is behind the dark magick we've detected," I said. "It isn't David at all."

I could see Hunter weighing this new information. "You say you asked to see the truth?" he asked after a moment. "Were those the words you used? Did you mention David's name?"

"No," I answered, puzzled. "Why?"

"You weren't very specific. And fire can be a capricious scrying tool," Hunter replied.

"Are you trying to tell me the fire lied to me?" I asked. I was starting to get angry again.

"No," Hunter said. "Fire doesn't lie. But it reveals the truths *it* wants to reveal, especially if you're not specific with your questions."

I put my head in my hands, feeling suddenly weary. "I don't get it, Hunter," I said. "I keep giving you clues that point clearly to Cal and Selene, the witches you came here to investigate—the witches you're still trying to track down. I don't want it to be them—I don't want to even think about them. But it makes total sense that they're the ones whose presence I felt. Why do you keep trying to make this about David and Practical Magick?"

Hunter was silent for a moment. At last he said, "It's a feeling I have. I've got an instinct for darkness. It's what makes me so good at my job." The words weren't a boast. His voice was quiet. For the first time I began to really wonder. Was it possible that he was right?

"Enough of this," he said with a sigh. "We're not getting anywhere, and it's nearly six. I'd better run you home."

We walked out to his car without talking. I noticed with a shock that it was the same gray rental sedan he'd had the week before. Selene had hidden it in an abandoned barn when she thought Cal and I had killed Hunter.

"I tracked it down," Hunter remarked, eerily echoing what was on my mind. We climbed into the car, and he drove me home in silence, each lost in our own thoughts. He pulled into my driveway. Then, as I reached for the door handle, he put his hand on mine. "Morgan."

A jolt of sensation ran up my arm, and I turned to face him.

"Please think about what we discussed, about David. I'm almost certain Stuart Afton didn't forgive that debt out of kindness."

"I just don't believe David would mess with dark magick," I said. As he began to reply, I cut him off. "I know, I know, you have a special sense for evil. But you're wrong this time. You have to be."

I climbed out and hurried up the walk to my house, hoping I was right.

# 14.
# Old Wounds

*Beltane, 1996*

*We are in Vienna, where I have found work tutoring college students in English. Evenings, Fiona and I walk along the Danube or in the Stefansplatz. She has gained some much needed weight and is looking better. The other night we even went on the Ferris wheel in the Volksprater. But the amusement park made us think of the children. Have Beck and Shelagh ever taken them to such a place?*

*Giomanach is now thirteen, Linden almost twelve, and Alwyn, nine. I wonder what they look like.*

*—Maghach*

At dinner Mom reported that so far there had been no new incidents at Aunt Eileen and Paula's house. "They're hoping that those creeps saw the police show up at the house and have backed off."

"I hope so," I said. I reminded myself to get to Practical Magick for those ingredients soon.

Mom dished out some goulash and handed me the plate. "Will you be able to finish inputting our real estate listings this week?" she asked.

"I'm getting Das Boot back tomorrow afternoon," I said. "So I can stop by your office around three-thirty, after I drop Mary K. at home."

"I forgot to tell you. I'm not coming straight home tomorrow after school," said Mary K. "I'm going shopping with Olivia and Darcy."

Shopping. I wasn't ordinarily a big fan of shopping, but suddenly I felt a sharp pang of envy. How long had it been since I'd gone shopping with my friends or just hung out after school, doing nothing in particular?

Since you and Bree stopped being friends, I answered myself.

After dinner I went upstairs and tried to do my math homework, but my brain was too overloaded with thoughts of Hunter, Cal, David. I sighed. With its connection to the harmony of nature, Wicca was about balance, something I sorely needed. I had to bring balance back into my life, and the only way I could think of doing that was with a healthy dose of non-Wicca normalcy.

Surprising myself, I opened my door and padded out into the hall, where I picked up the phone. I took it back into my room and perched cross-legged on my bed.

My heart pounded as I dialed Bree's number. It had been so long since I'd done this. Would she want to talk to me?

Bree picked up on the third ring. "Hi, it's Morgan," I said quickly, before my nerve failed me.

"Hi." She sounded uneasy. "What's up?"

"Um—" I hadn't thought this through. "Not a whole lot. I just . . . you know, wanted to say hi. Catch up."

"Oh. Well, hi," she said.

Then we had one of those long, awkward silences, and I wondered if maybe it was crazy of me to have called her. Maybe she didn't want to be friends with me anymore. Maybe there was just too much water under the bridge.

I was about to mumble that I had to go when she spoke. "Morgan." She hesitated. "Some of things I did to you—I know they really hurt. I can't undo them. But I'm really sorry. I was a complete bitch."

"I—I was, too," I admitted.

Another silence. Clearly neither one of us wanted to go into the details. It was still too raw to bring all that up again.

"So," she said, "what's been happening in your life? Robbie told me—well, he told me about your being adopted. About being a blood witch."

"He did?" I tried to decide how I felt about Bree and Robbie discussing my personal life.

"Yeah. I've been wanting to talk to you about it. If you want to," she said.

"I've been wanting to talk to you about it, too," I confessed. "But when we're face-to-face. Not on the phone."

"Okay," she said. "I'd like that."

"Meanwhile Hunter's got me in a Wicca study intensive," I told her. "You know, he's taken over the leadership of Cirrus now that . . ." I trailed off. Now that Cal's gone, I thought. Quickly changing the subject, I asked, "How's Kithic? How is it having Sky lead a coven?"

"Challenging," Bree said in a thoughtful tone. "We've been doing visualization exercises. At our last circle we were outside under the moon, and Sky told us to visualize a pentagram. At first everyone was distracted by the cold and the noise of cars going by. Finally, though, we got it together. We all closed our eyes, visualizing away, and there was this moment of absolute silence, then Sky told us to open our eyes, and there was this perfect pentagram, etched in the snow. It was amazing."

"Cool," I said enviously. It sounded like her coven was really growing. I leaned back against my pillows.

Bree's voice went conspiratorial. "Sky and Raven are flirting, I think. Isn't that wild?"

"Very wild." It was so easy to fall back into gossiping with Bree again. "I never figured Raven would turn out to be gay."

"I don't think she really is. I think she just really likes Sky. It's an attraction of opposites," Bree said with a laugh. There was another pause, but this time it didn't feel awkward. It was just—natural.

"Speaking of attractions," I ventured, "how's your love life?"

"Robbie." I heard a guarded note in her voice.

"Yeah," I said, hoping I hadn't shattered our new, fragile bond.

But Bree just sighed. "Well, it's—it's kind of weird," she said slowly. "I don't know . . . we've been buddies forever, and now all of a sudden we're making out. I guess I'm just sort of taking it as it comes and seeing what happens." She gave a little laugh. "I have to say, though, we really click physically. It's very hot."

"Wow." I felt voyeuristic but also fascinated. It was strange to hear these two people I'd known since childhood talk about each other in these new, romantic terms.

"Listen, I've got to go," Bree said. "I've got a history paper due tomorrow, and I'm still on page one."

"You'll crank it out," I told her. "You always do."

"Yeah, I do, don't I," she replied. "I'll talk to you later, okay? And—Morgan?"

"What?"

"Thanks for calling," she said softly. "I know it couldn't have been easy to do."

"You're welcome," I said.

We hung up, and I replaced the phone on the hall table. I was smiling as I went back into my room, feeling happier than I had for days.

# 15.
# Threads

*Imbolc, 1997*

Imbolc is a day for light. Fiona reminds me that Imbolc means "in the belly," in the womb of the Goddess, and celebrates the seeds hidden in the earth that are just beginning to stir. Even though it's dark and cold here in Helsinki, it's a day of hope, and we must light the sacred fire.

In England, among the covens, there are great bonfires. Here we lit candles throughout our small rented house. Then the two of us did a quiet ceremony as we fed kindling into our woodstove.

The cold is hard on Fiona. She is always shivering and in pain. We can't live this far north for long. Where next, I wonder?

— Maghach

After my conversation with Bree the night before, I felt so much better able to face the next day. I knew she and I still had many, many fences to mend, but for the first time it actually seemed possible.

"You're in a good mood," Mary K. commented as we were getting ready for school. "Is that because you were talking to Hunter on the phone last night?" she added, wiggling her eyebrows at me.

She shrieked as I threw a damp dish towel at her.

"It wasn't Hunter. If you must know," I said, grabbing my backpack, "I was talking to Bree."

Mary K. beamed at me. "That's great!" She knew how much my friendship with Bree meant to me. "Maybe now things will get back to normal around here."

Robbie honked outside. He was giving us another lift to school. I'd pick up Das Boot later, and then things really *would* get back to normal!

Just as I was slipping into my coat, the phone rang. My witch senses tingled. What could Hunter want so early in the day? I picked up the phone. "Hi, Hunter."

"Good morning."

"I can't really talk," I told him. "I'm on my way to school, and Robbie and Mary K. are waiting for me."

"I'll make this quick," he said. "I just—I feel I need to prepare you. I know you're being loyal to David, and that's good. But I don't want you to be blind to dark forces just because you like him."

"I'm not," I said, stung. "Don't you think, after what Cal did to me, that I've learned my lesson? It just doesn't make sense to me, that's all. David's not like Selene or

Cal. He's not power hungry. He's not even Woodbane."

He drew a long breath. "Listen, I told you how my brother, Linden, died. How he called up a dark spirit and it overpowered him."

That wasn't the whole story, I knew. When we'd joined our minds, I had learned that Hunter had been accused of causing Linden's death and had stood trial before the International Council of Witches. He'd been found innocent, but he still carried the pain of his loss and the conviction of his own guilt.

"I remember," I said.

"What I didn't tell you is that Linden had called up dark spirits many times before," Hunter went on. "After that first time, when he did it with me—it was as if the door had been opened for him. He liked working dark magick. It spoke to him. But the first time, Morgan—the first time we did it for the purest of reasons."

"And you think David did the same thing," I said. "You think he opened the door."

"I think it's possible, yes."

Robbie honked again outside. "I have to go," I told Hunter. "They're waiting for me."

"We'll talk more later," Hunter said.

"Fine. Whatever." I hung up and stared at the phone for a minute. I remembered my own pleasure when I fought off those horrible guys at Aunt Eileen and Paula's. I had enjoyed it. Did that count as dark magick? No. Even if I had felt a rush from it, I was defending people I loved against an attack. That couldn't be bad.

As I walked out to the car, I made a decision. I was going

to prove that David was innocent. That Cal was the source of the evil energy Hunter was feeling. I'd go talk to Stuart Afton myself and get this all straightened out.

After school I called Stuart Afton's office to make an appointment. His secretary told me that he wasn't in the office.

"Is he sick?" I asked.

She hesitated. "He's . . . indisposed. He's been out since the middle of last week."

Something in her voice made me extend my witch senses. I picked up on strong confusion and unease. She didn't know what was wrong with her boss, I sensed, and that was very unusual.

It also occurred to me that I'd first sensed the dark presence in the middle of last week. Around the same time Afton had stopped coming into his office.

Coincidence, I told myself.

There are no coincidences, my inner witch voice said.

"Did Mr. Afton come into any large sums of money recently?" I asked on impulse.

"Not that I have any intention of answering a question like that—but you're the second person to ask it in the last few days," the secretary said, sounding amazed. "What is going on?"

"I'm not sure," I said. "Thanks for your help."

I hung up and looked up Afton's home address. He lived in a fancy section of town, but one I could get to by bus. I didn't want Robbie to know what I was doing. Somehow I felt I needed to do this alone. I'd just take the bus back to pick up Das Boot.

The bus let me off a few blocks from Afton's house. The

houses were enormous, with wide lawns. Even the snow looked more elegant in this neighborhood. I walked fast, trying to stay warm, my breath forming a little fog in front of me.

I rang the bell and stamped my booted feet on the welcome mat. Was I nuts coming here? Would Afton even see me? I heard footsteps on the other side of the door, and then it swung open. A thick woman in a maid's uniform looked at me. A wave of worry radiated from her.

"Yes?" she asked. "May I help you?"

"Uh," I said brilliantly. "I was wondering if I could talk to Mr. Afton?"

She pursed her lips, and I realized she looked pale. "Oh, dear, I'm sorry. Mr. Afton . . . Mr. Afton . . . was taken to the hospital earlier this morning."

"What?" I gasped.

She nodded. "The paramedics thought he'd had a stroke."

"I—I'm so sorry," I stammered. My heart thudded hard. It's just a coincidence. It has nothing to do with magick, I told myself.

A crumpled shopping bag sitting in the hallway behind her caught my eye. It seemed so out of place, just lying there, as if perhaps Mr. Afton had been holding it when he'd suffered from his stroke. The forest green color and silver handles looked familiar. I was about to ask the maid about it when my witch senses tingled. Hunter was coming up the walk.

What was he doing here? I whirled and stared at him.

"Is everything all right?" he asked as he reached the door.

"Stuart Afton is in the hospital," I blurted. "He had a stroke this morning."

Hunter's green eyes widened slightly. He glanced at the maid. "I'm sorry to hear that. Can you tell me what hospital he's in? I'd like to send over some flowers."

"Yes—Memorial. That's the closest." She shook her head. "He runs six miles a day, more on weekends. You've never met anyone who takes better care of their health than Mr. Afton. A stroke just doesn't make sense."

I didn't need to do a mind meld to know what Hunter was thinking. A stroke made sense if dark magick was involved.

"Thank you. We're sorry to have bothered you," I said to the maid. Then I grabbed Hunter's arm and pulled him down the porch steps. "What are you doing here?" I demanded.

"The same thing you are, I suppose," he replied. "Trying to get some answers."

I didn't want to think about the conclusions I knew he was jumping to.

"Where's your car?" he asked as we reached the curb.

"I have to go pick it up from the shop," I said.

"Hop in. I'll give you a lift."

I stood on the sidewalk. I wasn't sure if I wanted to get into the car with him, knowing the conversation we were about to have. My stomach felt knotted.

"Morgan, make up your mind. I'm freezing." Hunter walked around the car and slid in behind the steering wheel.

I was freezing, too. I climbed into the car and told him how to get to Unser's.

I didn't know what to think and was lost in my own thoughts while Hunter drove. True, sometimes people did have inexplicable strokes. Maybe he had some congenital defect.

"Someone like Stuart Afton is a very unusual candidate for a stroke," Hunter pointed out, and though it was exactly what I'd been thinking, I felt a flash of irritation. Hunter always had to be right.

"It happens," I said. "All kinds of freak things happen. Look at my life."

Hunter nodded. "Exactly. Your life was straight-on normal until magick kicked in. I could say the same for Afton, except magick has dealt with him far more harshly than it has with you."

"You don't know that this has anything to do with magick," I reminded him tightly. "You're jumping to conclusions."

"Am I?" he asked.

I took a deliberate breath and tried to keep my tone reasonable. "Okay, for the sake of argument, let's say David did have something to do with Afton erasing the debt. Well, Afton did it. David has the shop. So why would David hurt him now? He's grateful to Afton. Hurting him now doesn't make sense."

"Unless David made mistakes, got involved with forces he can't control, lost his power over what was supposed to happen," Hunter said. "The darkness is not predictable. It often has effects beyond the immediate, planned ones."

He sounded so self-righteous that I lost my temper and words shot out of my mouth. "You know what? I think being a Seeker makes you suspicious of everyone. I think you're furious because Cal and Selene escaped, so now you're determined to get someone else. David just happens to be a convenient target."

The brakes squealed as Hunter suddenly swerved and pulled off the road. I barely had time to brace myself before he cut off the engine and turned to face me, his eyes blazing with anger. "You have no idea what you're talking about! Do you think this a *game* for me, where I cut notches in my belt for every renegade witch I run in? Do you think I get off on going after other witches?"

My own temper caught fire. "You do it, though, don't you? You *chose* it."

The muscle in his jaw twitched, and one hand clenched the steering wheel, his knuckles white. Then Hunter relaxed suddenly, releasing the tension from his body on a deep breath. He rubbed his hand over his chin, the way he did when he was thinking. The car was filled with the vanishing traces of our anger, our quiet breathing. The air seemed alive and crackling, and it occurred to me that when I was with Hunter, I literally felt more alive. Probably because I was so often angry at him. But when I was with him, I didn't have time to be crushed with sorrow over Cal.

"Morgan, it's important to me that you understand that what you accused me of—is not true," Hunter said, his voice low. "That's not what being a Seeker is. If the council even suspected me of acting that way, they'd strip me of my powers in a heartbeat. I don't understand how you could think that of me."

His gentle answer made me ashamed. "Okay," I said. "Maybe I was wrong." I've always been a rotten apologizer. It was one of the things I wanted to work on.

"Maybe?" He shook his head and started the car again. Neither one of us spoke after that until we were almost at Unser's. We drove past the entrance to the Afton Enterprises gravel pit, and I saw him turn his head to read the sign. When he faced front again, he was frowning.

We pulled into Unser's yard. "Is this where you felt that dark energy?" Hunter asked me, his frown deepening. "Right here?"

"Yes," I said, puzzled.

"What day was it?" Hunter asked.

"Last Wednesday," I said, but then I saw Das Boot parked over to the side, and I forgot everything else. My beloved white car had a new hood and new bumper, but the hood was *blue.*

"Oh my God," I gasped. "My car!"

Bob Unser heard Hunter's car and came out of the garage, wiping his hands on a rag. Max, the German shepherd, loped out at his side, grinning amiably. Hunter and I climbed out of his car, and I walked slowly to my Valiant, feeling like I was about to cry.

Bob looked over Das Boot with pride. "Good fit, huh?" he asked. "That hood is perfect. We got lucky."

I was speechless. The two front sides of my car had been hammered out and covered with Bondo body filler to fix the crumpling. The Bondo was sanded and looked like steel-gray dusty spackle all over the front of my car. And the hood was *blue.* The bumper looked all right, but was unusually shiny and looked out of place. My beautiful, lifesaving car looked like crap.

"Uh . . . uh . . ." I began, wondering if I was going to hyperventilate. After losing my boyfriend, almost being killed, having my magick disappear on me in a circle, worrying about David Redstone; now, ridiculously, what was finally sending me over the edge was owing my parents almost a thousand dollars so my car could look like *crap.*

Hunter patted my shoulder. "It's just a car," he offered hesitantly.

I couldn't even respond. My mouth just hung open.

Bob gave me a look. "Course, it needs to be painted," he said.

"Painted?" I was amazed at how calm my voice was.

"I didn't want to do that without talking to you," he explained, scratching his head. "We can paint it white, to match the rest of the car, but to tell you the truth, the whole car needs a paint job. See those bits of rust under the door? We should really sand those out, give it a coat of rust protector, then paint the whole body. If we Bondo the other dings, this car could look brand-new." The idea seemed to fill him with enthusiasm.

"How much?" I whispered.

"Another four hundred, five hundred, max," he said.

I gulped and nodded. "Um, does it run okay?"

"Sure. I had to tighten the engine block a bit, knock a few hoses tighter. But this baby's a tank. It was mostly bodywork."

Max panted his agreement.

Silently I handed Bob Unser the check my mother had made out, and he dropped the keys into my hand. "Let me think about the paint job," I said.

"Sure thing. Take care of this car, now." He headed back into the warmth of the garage, and I turned to face Hunter. It was dark now, but I could still see Das Boot's tricolored nose, and it made me incredibly upset.

"I'm sorry about your car," Hunter said. "I'm sure it will be fine."

I closed my eyes and nodded. It was obvious he didn't understand at all.

# 16.
# Uncertain

The witch from Boston came today. We spent the morning purifying Selene Belltower's house. But we had no luck getting into her library. In fact, this time I couldn't even find the door.

Then, in the afternoon, I fought with Morgan. I pushed her too hard about David. She's resisting me all the way. And why not, when it seems I'm doing nothing but persecute the people she cares for? Am I trying to make her hate me?

No, it's not that simple. I need her to be able to face the truth, even when it's ugly or painful. I need her to believe in her own strength, the strength that I see every time I look at her.

I've never met anyone who affects me the way she does. We argued today, and the things she said were so wrong and hurtful that I wanted to shake her. But then, later, when she saw what the mechanic had done to that old wreck of a car she drives, she looked so shattered, so utterly forlorn, that it was all I could do not to take her in my arms and kiss away the tears.

—Giomanach

In my hideous, piebald car, I drove to a fabric shop to get gold cloth and crimson embroidery thread. I needed them for the protection charm I was going to make for Aunt Eileen and Paula. It would be a little pouch embroidered with the rune Eolh, containing herbs and a crystal.

After that I drove to my mom's realty office. Das Boot no longer made a grinding metallic noise; in fact, the engine sounded perfect. But I was ashamed of how my beloved car looked. I parked at an angle and tried not to look at the nose as I walked to Mom's office.

Widow's Vale Realty was in a small, white-shingled building. Inside, the look was deliberately cozy, with polished hardwood floors, lots of plants, and arts-and-crafts-style rugs and furniture.

"Oh, Morgan, honey. Hi. Did you get your car?" My mom peered out from a desk piled high with three-ring binders, file folders, and loose computer printouts. She looked overworked and overwhelmed. I sighed. I was glad I'd be able to help.

"Yes," I said. "It's fixed. But please don't make me talk about how it looks."

My mom tried unsuccessfully to bite back a smile. A non–car lover, like Hunter. What strange creatures they were.

Thursday and Friday were uneventful days at Widow's Vale High. I met with Cirrus on Friday morning before classes. Everyone was excited about having a circle the following night with Hunter.

"I've been reading this guy, Eliade, who's an expert in the history of religions, and Eliade talks about sacred space," Ethan said. "I'm thinking that's where Hunter took us. And that's exactly what ritual is supposed to do."

I tried not to gape. If anyone had told me two months ago that Ethan Sharp would be discoursing on ritual and sacred space, I'd have told them they were nuts.

"That never happened with Cal," Jenna pointed out. "We did feel magick that one time, but with Hunter it was different. It was just this incredible . . . connection."

"That first circle with Hunter changed me," Sharon stated. "I can never go back to thinking about anything the way I did before."

Suddenly I realized they were all feeling something similar to what I'd felt during our very first circle with Cal, when he'd opened me up to magick. It *had* changed everything. And I ought to be feeling glad instead of resenting the coven and Hunter because my own experience in the circle had been so frustrating.

Matt, whom I'd considered totally self-absorbed, caught me off guard. "But Morgan didn't like it," he said. "It's funny that Hunter has all this power and the one blood witch among us doesn't think he's so great."

Blood witch? I looked up.

"Robbie told us. It sort of came out when he was explaining about Cal," Jenna said gently. "It's okay. We pretty much knew, anyway."

"Uh," I started, flustered. "It's not that I don't like Hunter."

"What is it, then?" Sharon asked.

It was complicated. It was Cal, losing Cal. Hunter being a Seeker and the one who'd made me see the truth about Cal. Hunter suspecting David of dark magick. I shook my head. I couldn't even begin to explain it. So I just shrugged and said, "I don't know, exactly."

Fortunately the first bell rang then. I hurried away, mumbling about how I had to get to my locker. How could I explain my feelings about Hunter to them when I couldn't even explain them to myself?

Saturday dawned cold and bleak. I woke up just after sunrise—unusual for me—shaken by a dream I couldn't remember. Dagda was curled up against my chest. I kissed the top of his silky head and tried to fall back asleep, but it was useless. My thoughts were already roiling. Hunter's face kept rising in front of my eyes. I wondered how Stuart Afton was doing. I needed to get a start on my physics homework and also get back to the realty office to input listings.

That night I had a circle, and Hunter wanted to get together on Sunday for a lesson. I'd told Aunt Eileen and Paula that I'd help them unpack sometime during the weekend, but what I really needed to do was get the last ingredients for my protection charm so I could place it in their house. That meant I had to go to Practical Magick and face David. Would he be able to sense my uncertainty about him?

Already totally stressed, I gave up on sleep, got out of bed, and got dressed. Then I settled at my desk and opened my physics book. *Plot the trajectory of a baseball that's been struck by a batter at a 45-degree angle and is traveling at 100 mph (assuming no air resistance)*, read the first problem. "Why?" I muttered. It was hard to imagine anything more irrelevant to my life, but I started crunching numbers and kept at it until nine, which seemed a respectable hour for me to show up for breakfast on a Saturday morning.

My mom was already gone when I got downstairs, the weekends being prime workdays for realtors. My dad sat at the table, reading the paper. "Morning, sweetie," he said.

Mary K. was standing at the stove, stirring something in a pot. "Want some oatmeal?" she asked.

"No thanks." I started to prepare my own nutritious breakfast regimen of Pop-Tart and Diet Coke.

She scraped her oatmeal into a bowl. "I talked to Aunt Eileen last night, and I'm going over there after church tomorrow to help them unpack. Want to come?"

"Yes, I told them I would. But can we talk about it later?" I said. "I've got a million things to do this weekend, and I'm not sure how the timing's going to work out."

My father lowered the paper. "What do you have to do?"

I blew out a stream of breath as I carefully edited my answer. "Um . . . working at Mom's office, errands, school-work, and getting together with friends tonight." My parents knew that on Saturday nights I attended Wiccan circles, but I tried not to mention it directly too often.

My father studied me with concern. "I trust schoolwork isn't coming last on your list?"

"No," I assured him. "I already did my physics. I've still got a history paper to work on, though."

He smiled at me. "I know you've got a lot going on. I'm proud of you for keeping your grades up, too."

Just barely, I thought.

Twenty minutes later I was out the door.

The light scent of jasmine was in the air when I entered Practical Magick, and Alyce was dressed in an ivory knit dress with a pale pink tunic over it. A strand of rose quartz beads hung from her neck.

"You look ready for spring." I said. "Three months early."

"There's nothing wrong with wishful thinking," she told me with a smile. "How are you, Morgan?"

"Overwhelmed but okay." I couldn't help asking, "Did you hear about what happened to Stuart Afton?"

"Yes, poor man. It's awful." She shook her head, her blue eyes troubled. "I thought maybe we would try to send him healing energy at our next circle."

"So . . . how is your coven going?" I knew that Alyce had been asked to lead Starlocket now that Selene was gone.

Alyce tucked a strand of gray hair back into its twist. "Selene is a hard act to follow. I don't have nearly the power she had. Then again, I've never abused my power the way she did. Our coven has a great deal of healing to do, and since I've always loved healing work, that will be my focus, at least for the present."

"Morgan, good morning," David said, emerging from behind a bookshelf. I noticed his hand was still bandaged and that some blood had seeped through it, staining the gauze. "Nice to see you."

I hoped my voice sounded natural as I said, "You too. Um, I need some ingredients." I took my list out of my pocket.

If he noticed anything in my manner, he didn't mention it. He simply took the list and scanned it. "Oils of cajeput, pennyroyal, lavender, and rose geranium," he murmured, nodding. "We've just gotten in a fresh stock of pennyroyal, haven't we, Alyce?"

"Yes. I'll get the oils," Alyce said. To me she explained, "We keep the big bottles in the back, by the sink. They're rather messy to handle. I'll be back in a few minutes."

She bustled off, leaving me alone with David. He looked up from my list. "Burdock, frankincense, and a sprig of ash," he said in a neutral voice.

"Do you have them?" I asked. I couldn't read him at all, and it was making me nervous.

"We've got them," he replied. He added in a conversational tone, "These are the ingredients for a protection charm. So what are you protecting yourself against?"

"It's not for me," I told him. "It's for my aunt and her girlfriend. They just moved into a house in Taunton, and they're being harassed because they're gay."

"That's a shame. It's never easy to be different," David said thoughtfully. "But I guess you know that, being a witch."

"Yes," I agreed. "Do you think this charm will really help?"

"It's worth trying."

"I used my power to stop the guys who were scaring them," I admitted. "With witch fire." I wanted to see how he would react to this turn in the conversation.

David raised one silver eyebrow but said nothing.

"Even now I want to see them suffer. It makes me worry about myself," I added.

David pursed his lips. "You're being very hard on yourself.

You're a witch, but you're human, too, with human weaknesses. Anyway, dark energy is not in and of itself necessarily evil." He slid his hand into the display case beneath the counter and took out a necklace with the yin-yang circle worked in white and black onyx. "To me, the most interesting part of this symbol is that the white half contains a tiny spot of black and the black a tiny spot of white," he said. "You need both halves—bright and dark—to complete the circle. They're part of a whole, and each contains the seed of the other. So there's no such thing as dark magick without a bit of light in it or bright magick without a bit of dark."

Alyce, who'd returned with some vials of oil while he was speaking, shook her head. "That's fine as philosophy, David, but on a purely practical level, I think we'd all do well to shun the dark."

David smiled at me. "There you have it, the combined wisdom of Practical Magick. Make of it what you will."

A customer came in, and Alyce went over to help her.

David rang up my items. Then he reached down and pulled up a paper shopping bag and put it on the counter. He set the vials inside it. "Like it?" he asked, seeing my eyes on the bag. "We had them made as part of our celebration of Practical Magick's new lease on life, as it were."

"It's nice," I managed. Grabbing the bag, I mumbled a good-bye and hurried out of the store.

Outside, I held up the bag and stared at it. It was forest green, with silver handles. Just like the bag I had seen lying crumpled in Stuart Afton's hallway the day he'd had a stroke.

# 17.
# Breaking In

*August, 1999*

*Beck contacted us today. I knew as soon as I saw his face in my leug that the news was bad. But I didn't imagine it would be this bad.*

*Linden was killed, Beck told us, trying to summon the dark spirits. "He called on the dark side to ask how to reach you and Fiona," was what Beck said in his blunt way.*

*Goddess, what have I wrought? I've abandoned four children, and now one is dead because of me. I didn't know this kind of pain was possible.*

*—Maghach*

I sat in Das Boot, trying to take meditative breaths to calm down. It doesn't mean anything, I told myself. It's just a shopping bag.

Right. Afton was just the type to shop at Practical Magick.

Twenty minutes later I pulled up in front of Afton's sprawling home. What was I doing here? How was I going to prove anything?

I gazed gloomily out my car window. It must be garbage day, I realized, spotting the cans lining the curbs.

Could my proof be in those cans? I wondered. I scrambled out of the car and raced to the cans in front of Afton's house. I opened one, and the stink hit me. Ew. Was I really going to paw through someone else's trash?

I held a hand over the can, trying to get a sense of what I was looking for. I seek witch power, I thought. If there is an object that has been handled by a witch, lead me to it, please. The tips of my fingers tingled, and I ripped open one of the black plastic bags.

A green shopping bag with silver handles lay on top. The logo for Practical Magick was stamped on its side in silver. A gift card was tied to one of the handles. With shaking hands, I pulled it out of the garbage. I flipped open the card and gasped. *These are for you,* the card read. *You know why.*

The card was signed, *Blessed be, Alyce.*

I dropped the bag as if it had bitten me. Home-baked muffins tumbled out into the snow.

A car drove up and stopped behind me. Once again, I realized, Hunter had tracked me down.

"Morgan, what is it?" he asked.

I lifted my stricken face to him. "It can't be," I whispered.

If Alyce had used dark magick to cause Stuart Afton's stroke, then everything that I thought I knew or understood was wrong. And no one was to be trusted.

"Get in the car," Hunter ordered.

I simply obeyed. My mind whirled. Alyce? Then she was an amazing liar because she had seemed to be very certain that no one should mess with dark forces.

Hunter got out of the car and picked up the bag I had dropped. He gathered up the muffins, sniffed them, gazed at them. Then he dumped everything back into the garbage can. He climbed back into the car.

"They're not spelled," he said.

"Wh-what?" I asked.

"The muffins, the bag, the note," he explained. "None of it is spelled. Alyce had nothing to do with Afton's stroke."

I leaned back and let out a sigh of relief.

I felt Hunter's eyes on me. "You suspected David, though, didn't you? That's why you came back out here?"

"I—I don't know what I thought," I said.

"I went to Red Kill, to Memorial Hospital. I saw Stuart Afton," Hunter said.

I didn't bother to ask how he had been able to see Afton since he wasn't a relative or even a friend.

"I had heard he'd been acting strangely for days, which they believe may have been signaling the stroke, despite the fact that there was no medical reason for it to have happened. And he was sort of babbling while I was there."

"What did he say?" I asked apprehensively.

"He said, 'I did what they wanted. Why isn't it over?'"

"That doesn't mean anything," I felt compelled to say. "He could have been talking about work or something."

"There's more," Hunter said. "Remember the dark presence you felt at your garage? I hadn't realized until I drove you there that the garage is right down the road from the Afton gravel pit. But when I saw that, I realized that the dark presence might not have been looking for you at all."

I gaped at him. "You mean . . . ?"

Hunter nodded. "Maybe it was looking for Stuart Afton."

I put a hand to my forehead. I didn't know whether to be relieved or upset. If the dark presence had been after Afton instead of me, that meant I wasn't being stalked. But it also meant that Hunter was right and David had called on the dark side.

"Anyway, I was heading over to his office to do some more checking, then I got this sense that you needed me," Hunter said.

I bristled. "I was fine," I said. "It was just upsetting to think that Alyce might have been involved somehow."

"Well . . . good," Hunter said. "So I'll see you later."

I turned in my seat to face him. "I'm going with you."

"What?"

"I am part of this now," I said firmly. "If you're going to check out Afton's office, then I'm going, too."

For a moment it seemed like he was going to argue with me, but then he sighed. "Fine. You'd just follow me, anyway."

I managed a grin. "Gee. I guess you do know me after all."

I scrambled out of his car and into mine. Then I followed him to Stuart Afton Enterprises. Hunter took my arm, and we crossed the street to Afton's building. "I want to get into his office and search for signs of magick."

"You mean like breaking and entering?" My voice sounded strangled. I'd never even so much as shoplifted.

"Well, yes," Hunter said. "Not to put too fine a point on it."

"Don't tell me: You're a Seeker and have some sort of magickal permission that lets you break all kinds of human laws." I crossed my arms over my chest.

Hunter smiled, and I caught my breath at how boyish he suddenly looked. "That's right," he said. "You can back out anytime. I didn't invite you, remember?"

I rolled my eyes. "I'm in."

"Fine. Just so long as you remember who's in charge here."

I gritted my teeth in irritation as he murmured under his breath, quickly tracing runes and other sigils in the air. "This is a spell of illusion," he told me. "Anyone looking at us here will see something else—a cat, a banner, a tall plant—anything but us."

I was impressed and also envious of Hunter's ability. I realized again how much I had to learn.

"All right, now. Here's something for you to do," Hunter instructed. "There's an alarm wired into this door. It runs on electricity, which is just energy. Focus your own energy, then probe inside for the energy of the security system and do something with it."

I didn't want this responsibility. "What if I short-circuit the microwave by mistake?"

"You won't," he assured me.

I sent my energy inside the building. It was the first time I'd ever tried to focus on energy that wasn't attached to a person or somehow linked to the land. This was searching for electric currents that had no character or easily recognizable pattern; they were simply circuits, designed to register a response when they were opened or closed.

At first all I felt was a general emptiness within the rooms of the building. I probed again and this time felt a lower-level energy around the perimeter of the building, steady and unobtrusive, designed to be noticed only if it were broken. It ran across all the doors and through the glass of the windows. I went deeper into the building and picked up other kinds of energy—ultrasonic sound waves and, upstairs, a laser, both motion detectors. And something else on the ground floor: a passive infrared light, designed to pick up on the infrared energy given off by an intruder's body heat.

"Well?" Hunter asked.

"This is so cool," I murmured.

"Find the security system," he reminded me.

"Right." I cast my energy again, found the security control box in the basement, and let my mind examine it. I concentrated harder, sensing a pattern that had been punched in time and time again.

"Six-two-seven-three-zero," I said. "That's the code."

"Excellent." Hunter tapped the numbers into the keypad by the door, and we heard a quiet click. "Let's go."

Inside, Hunter headed for a big, windowed room at the back of the first floor: Stuart Afton's office. Inside the room he looked around, closed his eyes for a moment, and controlled his breathing. Then he reached into his jacket pocket and pulled out an athame. The hilt had a simple design, set with a single dark blue sapphire.

Hunter unsheathed the blade and pointed it at Afton's desk. A sigil flickered, lit with sapphire blue light. Magick had been done here.

Hunter pointed the blade at Afton's chair and I saw the rune Hagell, for disruption. The rune Neid, for constraint, flickered over the doorway. There were other signs that I didn't recognize.

"These are used to mark targets," Hunter explained, holding the athame at some of the unfamiliar figures. "Do you still doubt that magick has been used against Afton?"

"No." Seeing these sigils, knowing they had been wrought with dark intent, was deeply upsetting. "But we still don't know whose magick this is."

"Don't we?" His voice was soft, dangerous. He held the athame to the sigil once more. "From which clan do you arise?" he asked.

The shape of a crystal flickered above the sigil.

"What is that?" I asked.

"The sign of the Burnhides," Hunter said. He didn't sound triumphant, just sad.

"Oh, no," I said. I felt hollow inside.

"This isn't real proof," Hunter said. "There are probably other Burnhides in the area besides David. Making magick is like handwriting—if you know someone's work, you can recognize it. I need to learn David's magickal signature. Then I'll have the proof I need."

I swallowed. "Great."

Hunter and I split up after leaving Afton's offices. Needing a break from the strain, I went home.

I walked in to find Mary K. sitting at the kitchen table, white-faced.

"What's wrong?" I asked quickly, thinking, Bakker.

"Aunt Eileen just called."

"What happened? Are they all right?"

She nodded, looking stricken. "Nobody was hurt, but those guys—or some of their buddies—came back last night. This morning they found the front of the house covered with spray paint."

"What did it say?"

"Aunt Eileen wouldn't tell me," said Mary K. "So I guess it was bad. They just got back from the police station."

I felt a surge of irrational guilt. If I hadn't gone to Practical Magick and then been with Hunter . . .

"I've never heard Aunt Eileen sound so shaken up," Mary K. went on. "She called here looking for Mom, and I could tell she'd been crying. She wants to put the house on the market."

"What? Oh, no! She can't be serious!"

Mary K. shook her head, her perfect bell of auburn hair brushing her shoulders. "They're tired of the Northeast. They think that in California, people will be more tolerant." Her voice trembled. "Aunt Eileen wants Mom to relist their house."

"That's crazy!" I said. "It's just three high school kids! Three idiots, three losers. Every town has them."

"Tell that to Aunt Eileen and Paula," Mary K. said. She got up and began taking clean dishes out of the dishwasher. "God, they were so excited about that house. I hate it that anyone is doing this to them!"

"I do, too," I said. And I can do something about it, I thought.

I glanced at my watch. I had about four hours before I had to be at Jenna's house for our circle. That would give me time to finish the protection charm. And to find a spell to teach those thugs a lesson they'd never forget.

# 18.
# Lost and Found

Fiona is dying.

The news of Linden's death broke her, I think. She'd been in pain before, but she had a core of toughness that kept the illness at bay. But in the last two years she has been . . . fading. Her hair, once so bright, is entirely white now, and her green eyes are sunk deep in her gaunt face. I see her agony, but I can't bear the thought of losing her, my dearest love, the only precious thing I have left.

This morning I broke the silence and sent a message to Giomanach. I didn't contact him directly, but I cast a spell that would open a door to him, that would let him know that we're alive. Now I'm living in terror that I've exposed him to the dark wave.

—Maghach

I was the first one to show up at Jenna's house. "This isn't like me," I said. "I'm never early." The truth was, I'd driven faster than I usually did. I felt weirdly edgy. Maybe because I was nervous about my decision to deliberately work a dark spell on the jerks who'd been harassing my aunt. Or maybe just because I was worried about going through another circle without connecting to my power.

Jenna took my coat. "All the others are running late. Ethan convinced them to go to a lecture at the Red Kill library with him. It's on sacred space and mythic time. I think it's being given by someone who studied shamanism."

"You didn't want to go?" I asked, following her into the Ruizes' comfortably shabby living room.

"With Matt? No thanks. I mean, I'm stuck in the same coven with him, but if I have a chance to avoid him, I take it."

"It must be awful to break up with someone after four years of being together," I said inadequately. Considering how I was pining over Cal, whom I had known barely three months, I could hardly imagine what Jenna was going through.

Jenna removed a large basset hound from the couch. "Go sleep in your own bed," she said. "We're having company." The dog padded off placidly, and Jenna turned to me. "Yeah. At first I just didn't know how to get through the days. Raven Meltzer!" She wrinkled her nose in disgust. "Of anyone he could have picked. I was so humiliated."

We sat down on the couch, and a big gray-and-white-striped cat jumped onto Jenna's lap, purring. She petted it absentmindedly. "We've been together since I was thirteen. I didn't know what to do without him. And everyone knew.

But now—" She shrugged. "It's amazing. I'm getting over it. I'm finding out that I'm different without Matt." She shook her head, and her fine, pale blond hair swished in a shining wave. "When I was with Matt, I was always checking in with him. I don't even know how I got into that habit. But there was nothing I did that Matt didn't know about."

The doorbell rang then, and I waited while Ethan, Sharon, Matt, and Robbie came into the house, all talking at once. "Sorry we're late," Robbie said, giving Jenna a casual hug. "We got hung up in traffic in Red Kill."

"Yeah, the place was packed," Matt said. "I had no idea that so many people even knew where the Red Kill library was."

I felt Hunter coming up the walk, and an unexpected sense of anticipation made me sit up straighter.

"My apologies, everyone," he said as he unzipped his jacket a minute later. He looked around, seeming pleased that everyone was there. "Since we're running late, let's get started. Jenna, what do you have for forming a circle?"

"Chalk, candles, incense, water," she answered.

"Perfect. Then if you'll get them and if everyone else will form a circle . . ."

Hunter quickly drew the circle and chanted an invocation to the Goddess and the God.

"I want to concentrate on things that have been lost," he said when we'd raised the energy of the circle. It was flowing among us so strongly that I could almost see it—a ribbon of light, linking and encompassing us in its strength. This time I felt more connected to it.

"Each of you, think of something lost that you want to be found," Hunter went on. "Don't say it aloud, but silently ask the energy of the circle to open a way inside you to find what's been lost."

What had I lost? My heart, was my immediate answer. But even to me that sounded too melodramatic to ask the energy of the circle to act on it.

My mind wandered, my connection to the circle weaker. I glanced at Hunter, wondering if he knew. His eyes were open, but whatever he was seeing wasn't in the room. He looked aeons away.

I closed my eyes, trying to find my connection again. Suddenly I was filled with a rush of emotion, a deep sense of loss, a yearning that I knew wasn't my own. I saw a man I didn't recognize, tall, with brown eyes and graying hair.

Father, something said within me. Father.

My eyes flew open. Somehow I knew I'd just seen Hunter's father. I had somehow picked up the images that he was experiencing in the circle.

Startled, Hunter's head whipped toward me. I flushed. I hadn't meant to invade his privacy in that way. I hoped he'd know that.

I felt him refocus, connecting to the rest of the group, and then he began taking the circle down. Once again we sat in a circle on the floor. Hunter avoided my eyes. He gave the others an apologetic look. "Would you please excuse us?" he asked. "Morgan, may I speak to you?"

Before I had a chance to answer, he was on his feet and steering me by my elbow to Jenna's kitchen.

"That was an abuse of power," he hissed at me. "You had no right!"

My mouth dropped open. "I didn't do it on purpose!"

Hunter's nostrils flared as he breathed in and out rapidly, trying to calm down. I couldn't tell if the two bright spots on his cheeks were anger or embarrassment.

I thought about how much I hated it when I felt he'd read my thoughts. He must feel awful, I realized. "I'm sorry. I truly, really, and totally have no idea how that happened."

He stared down at the tile floor. His breathing was returning to normal. "All right," he said shakily. "All right. I believe you."

"How could that have happened?" I asked. "I had a stray thought about you, and then I just . . . received all these images."

He nodded a few times, still not lifting his head. "We . . . we had a connection. That's all."

"That was your father, wasn't it?" I asked.

He looked at me, his green eyes glinting. "It was incredible," he half whispered. "I suddenly *knew,* clear as daylight, that I could call to my father, and he would hear me."

"You mean, you think he's alive?" Hunter's parents had disappeared when he was eight—more victims of the dark wave, the evil force that had destroyed Belwicket and other covens. Hunter, his brother, Linden, and their sister, Alwyn, had been taken in by their Uncle Beck and Aunt Shelagh. It had been hard, not knowing what had happened to his mother and father. No wonder it was what he focused on when thinking of something lost.

When Hunter looked at me, his eyes were full of pain. "Yes."

"Will you call to him?"

"I don't know. It's been so long since I've seen him—I

don't even know who I'd be calling. And I'm not sure he'd want to see what I've become."

"A Seeker?" I felt confused.

Hunter nodded. "We're not exactly popular among witches."

"You're the youngest member of the council. Wouldn't any Wiccan father be proud of that?"

"He's Woodbane," Hunter reminded me. "For all I know, he calls on the dark side, too."

"Don't you ever get tired of looking at the world that way?" I asked, feeling suddenly almost sorry for him. "This is your father! You haven't seen him in more than ten years. My God, if I could see my birth mother just once—"

"Ethan, quit it!" The sounds of Sharon's giddy laughter came through the kitchen door. Hunter gazed at it, as if he'd forgotten where we were.

"We'd better go back out there," he said.

I was reluctant to end this conversation. We were really talking to each other, not fighting, not having a lesson. But the others were waiting.

We went back into the living room, where the others instantly gathered around Hunter.

"I've been reading that book you told me about," Matt began. "And I don't get the part about the Four Watchtowers."

I watched for a few minutes as Hunter patiently answered their questions, in spite of all I knew he was feeling. His breadth of knowledge was impressive, and I knew he had much to teach me, including his ability to reach out to others and help them learn, even when he must be feeling so distressed.

Then it was time to leave. I got into Das Boot and sat for

a few moments, letting the engine warm up. Christmas lights were already twinkling from most of the houses on Jenna's street. The house directly across from hers had a giant illuminated sleigh and reindeer spanning the width of the roof. I have got to start getting ready for Christmas, I reminded myself, resolving to talk to Mary K. tomorrow about possible gift ideas.

Das Boot was ready to roll, so I shifted into gear. Then I shifted back into park. I couldn't just drive off, I realized, not after Hunter had revealed himself to me that way. He'd been seriously shaken, and I didn't want to just leave him.

Shifting back into drive, I drove around the block so that the others wouldn't see me. I felt very protective of the conversation I was going to have with Hunter. It was private. I didn't want the high school gossip mill to start grinding.

*I want to talk with you,* I thought to Hunter. *Please come.*

Hunter walked up to my car a few moments later. I leaned over and opened the passenger door, and he got in. "What is it?" he asked.

"I think that if you know your father's alive, then you ought to contact him."

Hunter stared out through the windshield. "You think so?"

"Yes," I said firmly. "I know it's not quite the same thing, but I only found out that I was adopted a couple of months ago. I'm still trying to find out what the truth is. It drives me crazy not to know. And with your dad—if you don't contact him, it will just eat at you. You'll never stop wondering."

"I've wondered about him every day for the last ten years," Hunter said. "Wondering is nothing new."

"What are you scared of?" I asked.

He gave me an annoyed glance. "What is it with this country? Are all Americans amateur shrinks? You've got therapists on the radio and therapists on the telly, and every one of you speaks fluent psychobabble."

Then he shut his eyes and rubbed them with one hand. I wanted to hold his other hand.

"I'm sorry," he said. He blew out a breath. "I miss England," he said. "I never feel right here. Being a witch and a Seeker on top of that already make me an outsider, but here everything feels *off*. I'm never at home."

I hadn't realized that, and the insight made me feel a strange, new tenderness for him. "I'm sorry," I said. "That must be awful."

"I'm getting used to it. I've even gotten used to you, your forthrightness." He gave me a rueful smile. "You hit close to the bone, Morgan, more often than you realize." He sighed. "It's probably good for me."

"Probably," I agreed. "Now, what about your father?"

"I don't know," he said. "It's loaded. Both in an emotional way—I'm terrified that since the message I got was only from him, it means my mother is dead—and in the sense that I don't know what effect my contacting him will have on the dark wave. I could be opening a Pandora's box that I'll never be able to close. I have to think about it."

"I—I shouldn't be so pushy. I don't know how you feel. Not really."

His hand closed over mine. "You were being a friend, and I have precious few of those. Thank you."

I loved how his hand felt on mine, then wondered how I could feel that way so soon after Cal. And then I told myself

I didn't owe Cal anything. Finally I decided it was too much for me to figure out, and I should just take what delight I could from the moment. "You're welcome," I said.

"It's late. I shouldn't keep you." Hunter took his hand away, and I felt a pang.

"It's okay," I said. I wanted so strongly to take his hand again that I actually slid my own hand under my thigh to keep it still.

He sounded exhausted. "We're still scheduled to work together tomorrow afternoon, right?"

I nodded. "I'm going to my aunt's house after church. I'll call you when I get home."

He got out of the car. "Get home safe, then." Hunter traced the rune Eolh in the air. "And sweet dreams."

# 19.
# Pursuit

*I'm going to contact my father.*

*I'm terribly afraid. Not just of putting him and Mum in danger, nor of putting myself in danger. More than that, I'm afraid of how changed he'll look, how old. I'm afraid he'll tell me Mum is dead. I'm afraid he'll tell me that he's heard I'm a Seeker, and he's ashamed of me.*

*I want to ask Morgan if she'll stay with me while I do it.*

*— Giomanach*

I didn't sleep well that night. My mind was whirling with thoughts of Aunt Eileen and Paula, of finding the right spell to help them, of David, of Cal, of Hunter. I'd never been as confused about anyone as I was about Hunter. I bounced from thinking he was the most insufferable male on the planet to seeing, beneath all that arrogance, one of the most complex and fascinating people I'd ever met. There was no neat way to sum up Hunter Niall or my feelings about him.

The next morning I got up early again. I left a note for my family, saying I'd be back in time for church. Then I went for a drive. I needed to think, and I didn't want to be at home when I did. I bought myself coffee, then headed along the river to a small sailing marina.

The marina was dead quiet, since it was the middle of December. Most of the boats had been pulled into dry dock and rested on pilings in a fenced yard. I got out of the car with my cup of hot coffee and walked along the waterfront. The air was bitterly cold, but that was okay. It would force me to make my decision quickly.

What was I going to do about Aunt Eileen and Paula? Every instinct told me that I had the power to protect them, but I knew the charm I'd made wouldn't be enough. If I wanted to be sure that those thugs never bothered them again, I'd have to take more direct action. How dangerous was that?

The wind whipped off the river in an icy gust, and I decided on procrastination: I'd go visit Aunt Eileen and Paula and see if they were serious about leaving. If they were, then I'd try the spell I'd found last night on the Internet.

Shaking with cold, I got back into Das Boot.


I arrived at Aunt Eileen and Paula's just in time to see a police cruiser pulling away. Oh, no, I thought. I was too late. My heart racing with dread, I ran toward the house.

Aunt Eileen opened the door seconds after I rang the bell. "Morgan! What are you doing up this early on a Sunday? I thought you and Mary K. were coming by later."

"I—I was worried about you two," I said honestly. "I just saw the police car pulling away and—"

She smiled and put a comforting arm around me. "Come on in," she said. "Have some breakfast with us, and we'll tell you all about our undercover triumph."

"Your what?"

Paula was in the kitchen, cooking eggs, spinach, and mushrooms in a skillet. "Morgan!" she said. "Care for some breakfast?"

"Sure," I said, pulling up a chair. "Now, what happened?"

Aunt Eileen gave me a sheepish glance. "I felt like an idiot after I got off the phone with your sister yesterday. I was totally giving in to hysteria and fear."

"And to those jerks," Paula added. "For the record, I was equally hysterical."

"We decided we couldn't give in to them," Aunt Eileen continued.

Paula set down three plates containing eggs. "Short version: We drove to a security store in Kingston and rented a couple of surveillance cameras. Then we came home and put them up. At about two o'clock this morning, the camera at the back of the house caught our vandals on tape and sounded a little alarm in our bedroom. We called the cops. They were too late to catch the kids in the act, but they took the tape."

"The cruiser that just left," Eileen finished, "came to tell us that all three are now in custody, and one of them has confessed. The DA thinks she can charge them with at least two other local hate crimes. And two of them are old enough to be tried as adults. What's more, two of our neighbors on the block have offered to testify to what they saw. The community is being really supportive, I'm happy to say."

"Wow!" I exclaimed, amazed. "That's fabulous!" I nearly collapsed with relief. They had solved their own problem without my help, without magick. The choice had been taken out of my hands.

Aunt Eileen sighed. "I'm glad we caught those kids, but I have to say this whole incident has really shaken me. I mean, you hear about gay bashing all the time, but it's just not the same as when you're actually experiencing it. It's totally terrifying."

"I know," I agreed. Then I couldn't help asking anxiously, "But . . . you're not going to move?"

"Nope," Paula promised. "We've decided to tough it out here—at least for now. You can't solve this kind of problem by running away from it."

"That is the best news! I am so thrilled," I told them. I got up and opened the fridge. "Oh, no," I groaned.

"What?" Aunt Eileen sounded worried. "What's the matter?"

I turned from the fridge, which was full of disgustingly healthy foods. "Don't you guys have any Diet Coke?"

After breakfast with Paula and Aunt Eileen, I helped them rearrange living-room furniture; then I drove to church and met my family there. I made the effort because I wanted to make my parents happy—and because I felt badly in need of a nonmagickal, normal day.

After church the whole family opted out of our normal Widow's Vale Diner lunch so we could go back to Taunton for more unpacking. We got back to our house at three-thirty, and I decided to have a nice, long soak in the bathtub before calling Hunter.

The bath never happened. I'd just turned on the hot water faucet when I felt Hunter and Sky approaching. With a sigh I turned off the bathwater and went downstairs. Now what?

I opened the front door and waited. They both looked grim.

"Yes?" I demanded. "Aren't we scheduled to meet later?"

"This couldn't wait," he said.

"Come in." I led them into the den. After shutting the door I asked, "Is it Stuart Afton?"

"He's the same," Hunter answered. He looked at Sky. "Tell her."

"Last night," Sky began, "Bree and Raven and I were out studying the constellations by the old Methodist cemetery. We saw David. He was performing a ritual. A ritual I recognized."

"So what was it?" I asked.

Sky glanced at Hunter. Then she met my gaze steadily. "He was letting blood as a preliminary ritual to a larger sacrifice that will be performed once the moon moves into a different quarter."

"Bloodletting?" I said. I looked back and forth between Sky and Hunter.

"It's a payoff," Hunter said. "For services rendered. It fits with the ritual markings I found in the field where you had first felt a dark presence. He needs to offer his own blood to call in the taibhs, the dark spirit. Remember, that's how I knew it wasn't Selene. She has enough power to call a taibhs without performing that particular rite."

I felt sick. "Well, I guess that's the proof you were looking for, then," I said to Hunter.

"It's proof that he's using dark magick," Hunter said. "It

still doesn't connect him irrevocably to Stuart Afton. But that's just a formality now."

"David may not have bargained on or agreed to Stuart Afton having a stroke," Sky put in. "That's the kind of extra tithe that attaches itself when you deal with the blackness."

"In any case," Hunter said, "I've contacted the council, and they've told me to examine David formally."

There was something terrible in that sentence. "What does that mean?"

"It means that with the power vested in me by the council I am to ask David whether or not he's called on the dark energies," Hunter explained, not sounding like himself. "The procedure requires that two blood witches witness my examination of him."

I looked at him.

"It will be Sky and Alyce," he said, answering my unspoken question. "We're going to do it now, right away. There's no point in wasting any more time."

"I want to go, too," I said.

He shook his head, and Sky looked upset. "No. That's not necessary," he said. "I only came to tell you because I felt you needed to know."

"I'm coming," I said more strongly. "If David is innocent, that will come out in the examination. I want to be there to hear it. And if he's not . . ." I swallowed. "If he's not, I need to hear that, too."

Hunter and Sky looked at each other for a long moment, and I wondered if they were communicating telepathically. Finally Sky raised her eyebrows slightly. Hunter turned to me.

"You won't say anything, you won't do anything, you won't

interfere in any way," he said warningly. I raised my chin but didn't say a word. "If you do," he went on, "I'll put a binding spell on you that will make Cal's look like wet tissue paper."

"Let's go," I said.

We drove to Red Kill in Hunter's car. My stomach was tight with tension, and I kept swallowing. I felt cold and achy and full of dread. As much as I wanted Hunter to be wrong, all the evidence pointed to David.

When the three of us walked into Practical Magick, Alyce looked up. She looked tired and ill, her face drawn and almost gray. As soon as I saw her, I felt her pain over what was about to happen. She, too, believed David was guilty, I realized.

"We need David," Hunter said quietly.

David emerged from the back room. "I'm here," he said, his voice perfectly calm. "And I know why you're here."

"Will you come with us, then?" Hunter asked.

David glanced at Alyce and said, "Yes. Just let me get my jacket. Alyce, can you get the keys for the door?"

"Of course," she said.

David disappeared into the back room to get his jacket. And then didn't reappear. We waited maybe a minute and a half before Hunter tore behind the counter and into the back room. Sky and I followed. The door that led outside from the back room was ajar.

"Dammit!" Hunter swore, going through the door to a weedy, overgrown lot outside. "I didn't think he'd bolt. Stupid, stupid, stupid!"

I wasn't sure if he was referring to David or to himself, but I was too freaked out to ask. Sky was scanning the trees at the end of the lot. "He's in there," she told Hunter.

The two of them set off at a lope across the snow-patched ground, and I followed, sick at heart. Alyce, wrapped in a lavender shawl, bustled after us.

It was dark and shadowy inside the area of evergreens where David had disappeared. The trees were tall enough to block out most of the fading daylight, and we found ourselves in a murky gray light, peering around shadowy trunks for any sign of David. I cast my senses and felt Sky, Alyce, and Hunter doing the same. It was strange to feel my power joined to theirs in this way.

My senses picked up hibernating animals, a few birds. Was Sky wrong? Had David come in here? Or was he somehow masking himself?

Sky suddenly whirled. "There!" she cried as a ball of witch fire flew straight toward Hunter.

Hunter raised a hand and murmured something, and the witch fire was deflected, bouncing away from an invisible shield and landing in a snowbank with a sizzle.

It seemed the witch fire had come from behind a tall blue spruce. Hunter moved toward it with a predator's quiet intensity.

Another ball of witch fire sped toward him, which he brushed off, not even bothering with the charm this time. I realized something in Hunter had changed. It was as if he was drawing power into him, taking in energies far beyond his own considerable powers, linked to the life force all around us. But it was even more than that.

Hearing my silent question, Sky said, "When he acts as Seeker, he can draw on the power of others on the council."

God, how much else did I not know? "Will the extra power protect him?"

"Yes and no. The act of drawing power itself will wear him out if he tries to use it for too long. But it will help him fight certain kinds of attacks."

"David Redstone of Clan Burnhide, I summon you to answer to the International Council of Witches. Athar of Kithic and Alyce of Starlocket appear as witnesses," Hunter stated in a cold, relentless voice. "You will stand forth now."

I heard David make a strange sound, as if he were in pain, and I wondered about the power of Hunter's words.

"Stand forth now!" Hunter repeated.

David staggered forward from behind the spruce, his eyes wild, pure animal terror driving him now.

The sapphire in Hunter's athame glowed with power. I watched as he traced a rectangle of blue light around David's body. David screamed and doubled over, trapped in the blue light. Hunter moved in quickly, and I saw the deceptively delicate silver chain, the braigh, appear in his hand.

Alyce put her hand to her mouth, her eyes full of anguish.

I couldn't watch but buried my face in Sky's shoulder as Hunter wrapped the silver chain around David's wrists. I heard David screaming and remembered Cal writhing in agony as Hunter bound his wrists.

"Let me go!" David was shouting. "I did nothing wrong!"

I opened my eyes. David was on his knees in the snow, his wrists bound by the silver chain. The flesh around the chain was already raised in angry red welts. Tears streamed from his eyes.

Hunter stood over him, stern and unyielding. "Tell us the

truth," he said. "Did you summon a taibhs to get Stuart Afton to forgive your aunt's debt?"

"I did it for the people who lived above the store," David insisted. "They would have been homeless."

Hunter pulled on the braigh, and David screamed in agony.

"Yes," David sobbed. "I made offerings to the taibhs in exchange for its help."

"Did you offer it Stuart Afton's life?"

"No, never!" Hunter pulled on the braigh again, but David didn't change his answer. "I just asked the taibhs to make him change his mind," he said. "I never wanted harm to come to him. I deliberately asked that no harm be done to anyone when I cast the spell."

"That was foolish." Hunter's voice was surprisingly gentle. "Don't you know that's the one request the blackness will never grant? It feeds on destruction, and all who seek out the darkness are powerless to control it."

David was sobbing.

Hunter turned to look at us. "Alyce of Starlocket, do you need to hear more?"

"No," Alyce choked out, weeping silently.

"Athar of Kithic? Are you convinced?"

"Yes," Sky said in an almost whisper.

Hunter looked at me then, an unspoken question in his eyes. I didn't answer, but my own tears were answer enough.

Hunter nodded and knelt next to David. I was surprised to see him put a hand on David's back and help him stand. Hunter seemed sad, tired, and old beyond his years. "Sky and I will take David to our house for safekeeping," he said quietly. "The council will decide what to do."

# 20.
# Dark and Bright

*I put the braigh on David Redstone today. Morgan was there. She saw the whole thing. I doubt she'll ever forgive me.*

*But I have to make her try, because I need her. Goddess, how I need her.*

*I think I'm falling in love. And I'm frightened.*

*—Giomanach*

Seeing David standing there in the snowy woods, tortured and ashamed, seeing the pain in Hunter's face caused by doing his job, made something snap in me. Without realizing what I was doing, I bolted. As I ran, I stumbled in the snow. Branches caught at my clothes. A birch twig tangled itself in my hair. I ran on, feeling my hair pull, hearing the snap of the twig. The tree flashed a current of pain. Everything that was alive was hurting, and I was part of the web, hurting and in turn causing pain.

I broke out of the woods and found myself behind an office building, its windows dark. Practical Magick was nowhere in sight. I had no idea where I was, and I didn't care. I kept running, my toes numb in my boots as they hit the tarmac. I was panting, my breath short, my chest aching. Then there were footsteps and a familiar presence behind me. Sky.

"Morgan, please stop!" she shouted.

I wondered if I could outrun her and realized that I was too worn out to try. I slowed to a walk, my heart pounding, and let her catch up with me.

She was panting, too. She waited until her breathing slowed before saying, "A formal questioning by a Seeker is never easy to witness."

"Easy?" I nearly shrieked. "I would have settled for non-horrific. I can't believe that Hunter *chooses* to do that."

Sky's jaw literally dropped. "Do you think he enjoyed that?"

I was still repulsed and sickened by what I'd seen. "He chose it," I said. "Hunter became a Seeker, knowing what he would be required to do. He's *good* at it."

There was long beat of silence, and then Sky said, "I'd slap you silly if I thought you knew what you were talking about."

Before I knew what I was doing I had shot out my hand, spinning off a ball of witch fire. Instantly Sky held up a finger, and the fire fizzled out like a Fourth of July sparkler.

"You're not the only blood witch here," she told me in a low, angry voice. "And while you may have more innate power than any witch I've seen, I've had a great deal more practice working it. So don't turn this into a fight, because you won't win."

I hadn't meant to send the witch fire at her. I was just so

angry and sickened and exhausted that her threat was enough to make something inside me lash out. "I'm too tired to fight," I said.

"Fine, then get over yourself and listen for a minute. What Hunter does is harder on him that it is on anyone else."

"Then why does he do it?" I choked out the question. "Why?"

Sky thrust her hands into the pockets of her jacket. "In large part because of Linden's death. He still feels responsible. Being a Seeker is Hunter's atonement. He feels that if he can protect others from courting the dark, then maybe his brother's death won't be in vain. But it eats him alive whenever he has to do something like what he did to David."

The wind picked up, and I pulled my collar higher. "It sounds like he's punishing himself."

"I believe that's true," she admitted. "Even though the council acquitted him of all responsibility in Linden's death. Hunter's like a pit bull. He doesn't let go of anything—not the good or the bad. He'll be loyal to the death, but he'll also carry every grief with him to the grave."

We were drawing closer to another strip mall. There were neon lights, cars, people hurrying into stores. It seemed so strange that the normal world existed so close to the woods where David had been just bound by an ancient and terrible magick.

"I still don't see how Hunter can stand to be a Seeker," I said. "It's as if he's chosen to always be miserable."

Sky turned to face me. "There's another way to look at it, you know. Hunter's seen the destruction and grief caused by the dark side, and he's dedicated his life to fighting it. He's fighting the good fight, Morgan. How can you hate him for that?"

"I can't," I said quietly. "I don't."

"There's something else," she went on. "As the only surviving descendent of Belwicket, you must realize how vital it is that you help him in this fight. We can't let the dark wave win."

I shook my head, feeling dazed. "I thought I was finally okay with all of this—being a blood witch, being adopted, even dealing with Cal and what he did to me. Now there's this war against the dark side, too."

"Yes," Sky said. "And it's as dreadful and painful as any war ever fought. I'm sorry you're caught in it."

"My family doesn't even know the dark side exists."

"I wouldn't say that. They're Catholics, aren't they? The Church has a pretty well-defined notion of evil. They just give it different names than we do and use different means to deal with it. Darkness and evil have always been part of the world, Morgan."

"And I just lucked into getting close to it?"

Sky smiled. "Something like that. The only comfort is knowing you're not alone in the fight." She nodded toward a phone booth at the end of the strip mall. "I told Hunter to take David home. We'd better call someone if we're ever going to get home from here. How about Bree?"

I dug some change out of my pocket. "I'll call her."

Bree came and got us and drove us home. I went to sleep at once, and the next day I lay low at school. I avoided everyone in the coven, even avoided friends who weren't part of my Wiccan life. I was aching everywhere. I felt beaten, hurt, betrayed by my own birthright. I couldn't help thinking of that first circle with Cal. Wicca had been so beautiful to me. Now it was wound through with pain.

After school I drove Mary K. home and immediately shut myself in my room to do homework—calculus and history and English, all of it reassuringly mundane. I wanted nothing to do with magick. Mary K. poked her head in at one point, told me she was going out with her friend Darcy and that she'd be home in time for dinner.

It was my turn to cook, so at five-thirty I went down to the kitchen and started rummaging through the pantry and freezer. I found some ground beef, onions, canned tomatoes, garlic, a can of mild green chiles, and a box of cornbread mix.

I was putting diced onions into the cast-iron skillet when I sensed Hunter's presence. Dammit, I thought, what do you want now? Resigned, I turned off the flame beneath the pan.

Hunter was coming up the walk when I opened the door. He looked drained.

"I'm making dinner," I said. I turned around and went into the kitchen. I knew he was hurting, but I couldn't bring myself to even look at him. Despite what Sky had told me, despite what I knew in my own heart, all I could see right now was the Seeker.

He followed me into the kitchen. I turned the burner back on beneath the skillet and started chopping up the tomatoes.

"I came to see if you were all right," Hunter said. "I know yesterday was rough on you."

"It doesn't look like it was great for you, either." He moved as if he were badly beaten up.

"It's always hard," he said in a low voice. "And I didn't manage to deflect all the witch fire he shot at me."

I was surprised to realize how much the thought of him being hurt scared me. "Are you all right?" I asked.

"I'll heal."

I added the chilies and tomatoes to the pan and poured the cornbread mix into a bowl.

"I've got bad news," Hunter said. "I've heard from the council. They've passed sentence on David."

I dropped the wooden spoon I was holding. Hunter reached for it in the same instant that I did. He caught it and handed it to me.

"David must be bound and his magick stripped from him." Hunter's jaw trembled as he spoke, and I knew with certainty that this was harder on him than on anyone, except maybe, in this case, David. David had once told me that witches can lose their minds if they can't practice magick.

"So the council strips him?" I asked.

Hunter's face looked harsh beneath the kitchen's fluorescents. "I do. Tomorrow at sunset at my house. I'll need witnesses. Four of them—blood witches."

I stared at him, seeing the pain on his face, and knew what he wanted to ask me.

"No," I said, backing away from him. "You can't ask me to be part of that."

"Morgan," he said gently.

Suddenly I was crying, unable to hold it back anymore. "I hate this," I sobbed. "I hate it if having magick means I have to be part of this. I never asked for this. I'm tired and I hurt and I don't want to hurt anymore."

"I know," Hunter told me, his own voice breaking. His arms wrapped around me, and I let myself fall onto his chest. When I looked up, I saw that his eyes were wet with tears. "I'm so sorry, Morgan."

At that moment I remembered something Cal had told me: that there is beauty and darkness in everything. Sorrow in joy, life in death, thorns on the rose. I knew then that I could not escape pain and torment any more than I could give up joy and beauty.

I clung to Hunter, sobbing, in the middle of my kitchen. He murmured nonsense words and stroked my hair gently. Finally my sobs quieted, and I pulled away. Wiping my eyes, I turned the heat off under the frying pan before it all burned.

Hunter drew a deep breath and brushed a tear from my cheek. "Look at us. Two kick-ass witches falling to pieces."

I reached for a tissue on the counter and blew my nose. "I must look like hell."

"No. You look like someone who has the courage to face even what breaks your heart, and I find you . . . beautiful."

Then his mouth found mine and we were kissing. At first the kiss was gentle, reassuring, but then something in me took over, and I pressed against him with an urgency and intensity that shook us both. It was as though there was something in Hunter I wanted with a hunger I barely recognized—something in him I needed the way I needed air to breathe. And clearly he felt that way, too.

When we pulled back, my mouth felt swollen, my eyes huge. "Oh," I said.

"Oh, indeed," he said softly.

We stood there for a long moment, looking at each

other as if we were seeing each other for the first time. My heart was beating like crazy, and I was wondering what to say when I heard my dad's car pulling into the driveway.

"Well." Hunter ran a hand through his hair. "I'd better go."

"Yes."

I walked him to the door, and suddenly the reason for his visit came rushing back. "Tomorrow is going to be terrible, isn't it?" I said.

"Yes." He waited, not looking at me.

"All right." I leaned my head against the door frame. "I'll be there." I wanted to cry again, and I said, "Oh, Goddess, is anything ever going to feel good again?"

"Yes." Hunter kissed me again, quickly. "It will. I promise. But not until after tomorrow."


On Tuesday at sunset we gathered at Hunter and Sky's house for the ceremony. Sky and Hunter were there, of course, and so was a skinny teenage boy who looked familiar. "Where do I know you from?" I asked him.

"Probably from the party at Practical Magick. I play guitar with The Fianna. That was a sweet night," he said sadly.

"You're Alyce's nephew."

He nodded and held out his hand. "Diarmuid." He shifted uneasily. "Lousy occasion to be formally introduced."

"Will Alyce be here?" I asked.

"Already is," he said in a grim tone. "She started crying the moment we walked through the door. She's upstairs with Sky now. Auntie Alyce always wants to believe the best of everyone. She still can't quite believe it—that David called on the dark side. He's her dear friend, you know."

When everyone had assembled, there were five of us in the living room: Hunter, Sky, Alyce, Diarmuid, and me. Wordlessly Hunter led us to the room at the back of the house.

Candles flickered on the altar and in each of the four corners of the room. Outside, wind swept through the ravine, sending a high keening sound into the room.

David knelt in the very center of the room, inside a pentagram of glowing sapphire light. He wore a simple white shirt and white pants. He was barefoot. His hands were bound behind him with rope, his head bowed. He looked fragile and frightened. I ached to hold him, to comfort him somehow. But I knew I couldn't get past the light.

Hunter gestured, and we each stood on one point of the pentagram, with Hunter at the top of it. I noticed a drum on the floor behind Sky. Alyce stood quietly, her eyes locked on David and filled with grief.

Hunter surrounded the pentagram in a circle of salt, tracing signs for each of the four directions and invoking the Guardian of each.

"We call on the Goddess and the God," he began, "to be with us in this rite of justice. With the setting of the sun we take from David Redstone the magick that you gifted him.

"No more shall he wake a witch. No more shall he know your beauty or your power. No more shall he do harm. No more shall he be one of us.

"David Redstone, the International Council of Witches has met and passed judgment on you," Hunter went on in a still, neutral voice. "You called on a dark spirit, and as a result a man nearly died. For that you are to be punished by having your powers stripped from you. Do you understand?"

David lifted his head and nodded. His eyes were shut, as though he couldn't bear to keep them open.

"You must answer," Hunter said. "Do you understand the punishment that is now passed on you?"

"Yes." David's voice was barely audible.

Alyce bit back a cry of dismay, and I saw Diarmuid grasp her hand.

"Anger has no place here," Hunter cautioned us. "We are here for justice, not vengeance. Let us begin."

Sky began to beat a slow, solemn rhythm on the drum. The drumbeats seemed to go on forever. Gradually I noticed something shifting in the room. The drum was guiding us, subtly working on each one of us so that our breath aligned with it, our pulses followed it, and our energy joined and began to travel along the sapphire blue light of the pentagram as a line of blazing white.

I saw David hunch in on himself, as if trying to make himself small so that neither the blue light nor the white light could touch him.

The drum beat faster, more insistently, and the light intensified. The energy of five blood witches was fully intertwined now. The energy flowing around the pentagram crackled with power. We all held out our hands, drawing on the power, and I almost wept to feel my energy pouring out, familiar and strong.

Hunter stepped forward and touched the hilt of his athame to the pentagram. For a second the knife lit with blue and white light. The light continued to define the pentagram, but now Hunter walked around it, drawing his athame in a spiral around David, and the sapphire and white light blazed in a spiral as well.

I watched as our power flowed into the spiral and the spiral began to whirl around David. He whimpered as a transparent, smokelike image of a boy I recognized as himself appeared and vanished on the whirls of the spiral. Next came images of David in his robe, athame in hand, casting spells; David finding a wounded bird, making the sign of a healing rune over it and watching in delight as the bird flew from his hand; David charting the phases of the moon and its effect on the tides; David scrying with a crystal; David purifying Practical Magick with cedar and sage; David and another man facing each other in a circle and chanting in perfect harmony. All of it was leaving him, flying up the spiral like escaping spirits. And with each thing that left him, he sobbed with grief, a man watching everything he loved being destroyed. These were the experiences that had shaped him, that he used to define himself. They had formed the fabric of his life, and we were unraveling it.

When the very last of David's magick had vanished on the whirls of the spiral, Hunter held out the hilt of his athame, drawing the glowing spiral into it once again.

"David Redstone, witch of the Burnhides, is now ended," Hunter said gently. "The Goddess teaches us that every ending is also a beginning. May there be rebirth from this death."

The drumbeat finally stopped, and with it the sapphire light of the pentagram winked out. David lay collapsed on the floor, a hollow shell. I wanted to fall over, too, but I stayed upright, feeling if I moved, I would crack into a million brittle pieces.

Alyce bent down slowly and put her arms around David.

"Goddess be with you," she murmured; then Diarmuid had to lead her out because she was weeping uncontrollably.

Sky watched silent and stricken as Hunter cut the bonds on David's wrists and gently helped him to his feet. "I'm going to give you some herbs to help you sleep," Hunter told David. The stern Seeker was gone from Hunter now, and he seemed only tender and sad. "Come with me," he said, taking David by the hand.

David let himself be led, walking with halting steps, like a lost child in a man's body.

Sky ran her hand through her hair and blew out a breath. "Are you all right?" she asked me as they left the room.

"It wasn't what I expected," I said. "I thought it would be more like the braigh."

"You mean, physical torture?"

I nodded. "This was gentler. And yet, much worse." I thought of how Selene had wanted to take my power for herself. Goddess, what would that have been like? It was unthinkable.

"I never want to do anything like it again." Sky walked to each corner of the room and extinguished the candles there but left the two on the altar lit. "Let's get out of here," she said with a shudder. "I'll come back in and do a purification ceremony in the morning."

Moving in slow motion, I followed her into the living room.

"We found out what happened, you know," Sky said. "The taibhs terrified Afton so badly that he wanted nothing to do with the store. That's why he forgave the debt. Then, later, the continued stress of the encounter led to the stroke. Receiving Alyce's muffins was what pushed him over the edge."

"You mean Alyce . . ." It was unbelievable.

"She had sent them as a thank-you. But dark forces work in devious ways, and so her kindness resulted in a terrible event." Sky put a finger to her lips. "She doesn't know, and I hope you won't tell her. It would hurt her too much."

I nodded. Then a thought occurred to me. "What happens to the store now?"

"Hunter spoke with Afton. He's getting better, but he wants nothing to do with Practical Magick. And the bookstore deal fell through, so the building has lost its value." Sky shrugged. "I think Alyce will probably have to pay off the debt, but Afton seems willing to work with her on the timing. She'll be able to keep the store running." She touched my shoulder comfortingly, and left the room.

I heard Hunter coming down the stairs and turned to look at him. "Morgan," he said. "You're still here." He looked exhausted and so much older than he had earlier that day. He came to stand before me. "Thank you. I know how hard that was for you."

I looked at him. He wasn't a monster. He had done what he had to, and through it all there'd been an undercurrent of compassion streaming from him, from Hunter to all of us.

"I have something for you." He reached into his pocket and took out a clear, faceted crystal.

"Quartz?" I guessed.

He gave me a look that made it clear that was the wrong answer.

"Oh, Hunter, please, I'm too worn out for guessing games."

"Tell me what it is," he said softly.

So I tried, thinking of the stones I'd learned, trying to fit a name to it: Zircon? Danburite? Diamond? Albite? It couldn't be moonstone. Frustrated, I sent my energy into the stone, asking it to yield its name to me. The answer it gave made no sense.

I gazed up at Hunter, baffled. "What it tells me is beryl, but that can't be right. Beryl is either aquamarine or emerald, and this is—"

"Morganite," he told me. "Your name stone, another form of beryl."

"Morganite?"

"It changes colors with the sunlight. At different times of day it will be white, lavender, pink, even pale blue. It's a powerful healing stone. And there's something else it can do." His hand closed around the stone. He looked at me, and his green eyes were as fathomless as the sea. "If a blood witch holds it and sends energy into it, it will reveal what is deepest in his heart."

Hunter opened his hand, and in the very center of the crystal I saw myself.

# Spellbound

## Cate Tiernan

PUFFIN

# 1.
# Kithic

Beltane, 1962, San Francisco

Today I met my future, and I'm dancing on sunlight! This A.M. I celebrated Beltane in the park downtown, and all of us from Catspaw made beautiful magick right there in the open while people watched. The sun was shining, we wore flowers in our hair, and we wove our ribbons around the fertility pole and made music and raised a power that filled everything with light. We had elderflower wine, and everything was so open and beautiful. The Goddess was in me, her life force, and I was awed by my own power.

I knew then that I was ready to be with a man—I'm seventeen and a woman. And as soon as I had that thought, I looked up into someone's eyes. Stella Laban was giving him a paper cup of wine, and he took it and sipped, and my knees almost buckled at the sight of his lips.

*Stella introduced us. His name is Patrick, and he's from Seattle. His coven is Waterwind. So he's Woodbane, like me, like all of Catspaw.*

*I couldn't stop looking at him. I noticed that his chest-nut brown hair was shot through with gray, and he had laugh lines around his eyes. He was older than I thought, much older, maybe even fifty.*

*Then he smiled at me, and I felt my heart thud to a stop. Someone grabbed Stella around the waist, and she danced off, laughing. Patrick held out his hand, and without thinking I put mine in his and he led me away from the group. We sat on a boulder, the sun warm on my bare shoulders, and talked forever. When he stood up, I followed him to his car.*

*Now we're at his house, and he's sleeping, and I am so, so happy. When he wakes up, I'll say two things: I love you. Teach me everything.*

*—SB*

I had been to Sharon Goodfine's house once before, with Bree Warren, back when Bree and I were best friends. Tonight Sharon was hosting Cirrus's usual Saturday-night circle, and I was curious to see how it would feel different from other circles we'd had. Each place had its own feeling, its own atmosphere. Every circle was different.

"Nice pad," said Robbie Gurevitch, my other best friend from childhood. He squinted at the landscape lighting, the manicured shrubs with their caps of snow, the white-painted brick of the colonial house. The landscaping alone probably cost more than what my dad makes in a year at IBM. Sharon's dad was an orthodontist with a bunch of famous clients. I'd heard a rumor that he'd straightened Justin Timberlake's teeth.

"Yep," I answered, pushing my hands into my pockets and starting up the walk. I'd gotten a ride with Robbie in his red Beetle, and I saw other cars I recognized, parked along the wide street. Jenna Ruiz was here. Matt Adler had come in his own car, of course, since he and Jenna were broken up. Ethan Sharp was here. Hunter was here, I noticed. I shivered inside my coat with a blend of excitement and dread. More cars were parked nearby, but I didn't recognize them and figured one of the neighbors was having a party.

On the porch Robbie stopped me as I started to ring the doorbell. I looked at him questioningly.

"You okay?" he asked quietly, his gray-blue eyes dark.

I opened my mouth to indignantly say, "Of course," but then I shut it again. I'd known Robbie too long and had been through too much with him to fob him off with white lies. He had been one of the first people I'd told about being a blood witch, about being adopted, about being Woodbane. Of the seven Great Clans of Wicca, Woodbanes were the ones who sought power at all costs, the ones who worked with dark magick. When I'd found out about being a blood witch, I hadn't known my clan and had hoped that I was a Rowanwand, a Wyndenkell, a Brightendale, a Burnhide. Even a mischievous Leapvaughn or warlike Vikroth would have been fine. But no. I was Woodbane: tainted.

Robbie and Bree had saved my life three weeks ago, when

Cal, the guy I'd loved, had tried to kill me. And Robbie's friendship had helped give me the strength to continue searching for the truth about my birth parents. He could read me well, and he knew I was feeling fragile right now.

So I just said, "Well, I'm hoping the circle will help."

He nodded, satisfied, and I rang the doorbell.

"Hi!" Sharon said, opening the door wide and ushering us in, the perfect hostess. I caught sight of Jenna and Ethan standing behind her, talking. "Dump your coats in the living room. I've set up a space in the media room. Hunter told me we'd have a real crowd tonight, and he was right." She pointed to a doorway on the far side of the large living room. Her fine, dark hair swirled around her shoulders as she turned to answer a question from Jenna. Her trademark gold bracelets jangled.

I was standing there, wondering how small the room must be if the seven members of Cirrus would crowd it, when Robbie caught my eye. "Media room?" he mouthed silently, shrugging out of his coat. I couldn't help smiling.

Then I felt a prickle of awareness at the back of my neck, and knowing what it meant, I looked around to see Hunter Niall coming purposefully toward me. The rest of the room faded, and I suddenly heard my own heartbeat loud in my ears. I was only vaguely aware of Robbie walking away to greet someone.

"You've been avoiding me," Hunter said softly in his English accent.

"Yes," I admitted, looking into his sea green eyes. I knew he'd called my house at least twice since the last time we'd seen each other, but I hadn't returned his calls.

He leaned back against the door frame. I was five-six, and Hunter was a good seven inches taller than me. I hadn't seen him since a few days ago, when I'd had witnessed him stripping one of my friends of his magickal powers. He'd done it because it was his job. As a Seeker and the youngest member of the International Council of Witches, Hunter had been obligated to wrest David Redstone's power from him and to bind him magickally so that he couldn't use magick again for any reason. It had been like watching someone being tortured, and I'd had trouble sleeping since then.

But that wasn't all. Hunter and I had kissed the night before the ritual, and I'd felt a longing for him that astonished and disturbed me. Then, after the ritual, Hunter had given me a spelled crystal into which he'd put his own image, through the sheer power of his feelings. We both knew there was something between us, something that might be incredibly powerful, but we hadn't explored it yet. I both wanted to and didn't want to. I was drawn to him, but what he had done still frightened me. Unable to sort out my own feelings, I'd resorted to a tried-and-true tactic: avoidance.

"I'm glad you came tonight," he said, and his voice seemed to smooth away some of my tension. "Morgan," he added, sounding uncharacteristically hesitant. "It was a hard thing you saw. It's a hard thing to be part of. It was the third one I've done, and it only gets harder each time. But the council decreed it, and it was necessary. You know what happened to Stuart Afton."

"Yes," I said quietly. Stuart Afton, a local businessman, was still recovering from the stroke David Redstone had caused by working a dark spell. Now David was in Ireland, at a hospice run by a Brightendale coven. He would live there for a long time, learning how to exist without magick.

"You know, some people join Wicca or are born into it, and it's more or less smooth sailing," Hunter went on. Ethan passed us on the way to the media room, and I heard the fizzy pop of someone opening a soda can. Hunter lowered his voice, and the two of us were alone in our conversation. "They study for years, they work magick, and it's all just a calm acknowledgment of the cycle, the circle, the life wheel."

I heard a burst of laughter from the media room. I glanced over Hunter's shoulder, catching a glimpse of a boy I almost recognized. He wasn't part of our coven, and I wondered why he was here.

Hunter was making me nervous, jumpy, as he often did—he had always affected me strongly, and I didn't understand our connection any more than I understood the surprising, even frightening attraction I had to him.

"Yes?" I said, trying to follow his thought.

"With you," he went on, "it hasn't been a smooth ride. Wicca and everything associated with it has been one huge trauma after another. Your birth mother, Belwicket, the dark wave, Cal, Selene, now David . . . You haven't had much of a chance to revel in magick's beauty, to appreciate the joy that comes from working a perfect spell, to experience the excitement of learning, finding out more and more. . . ."

I nodded, looking at him. My feelings about him had changed so radically, so fast. I'd hated him when I met him. Now he seemed so compelling and attractive and in tune with me. What was that about? Had he changed, or had I?

Hunter straightened his shoulders. "All I'm saying is,

you've had a hard time, a hard autumn, and so far a hard winter. Magick can help you. I can help you—if you'll let me." Then he turned and went to the media room as I gazed after him, and a moment later the voices quieted, and I heard Hunter asking for attention.

I peeled off my coat, dropped it on a chair, and went to join the circle.

Sharon's plush media room was indeed crowded. Our coven, Cirrus, consisted of seven members: Hunter, our leader; me, Morgan Rowlands; Jenna; Matt; Sharon; Ethan; Robbie. But there were more than seven people in the room. Next to the big-screen TV, I caught sight of Robbie talking to Bree Warren. Bree—my ex–best friend, then for a while my enemy when we'd fought over Cal. What was she doing at Sharon's house, at our coven meeting? She was a member of Kithic, the rival coven that she'd formed with Raven Meltzer and Hunter's cousin, Sky Eventide.

"Morgan, have you met Simon?" a voice beside me said, and I turned to see Sky herself, motioning to the boy I'd thought I recognized. I realized I'd seen him at a party at Practical Magick, an occult store in the town of Red Kill. The store David Redstone had owned.

"Nice meeting you," Simon said to me.

I blinked. "You too." Turning to Sky, I asked, "What are you guys doing here?"

I was surprised to see a nervous look on Sky's face, which reminded me so much of Hunter's. They were both English; both tall, slender, incredibly blond, somewhat cool and standoffish. They were also both loyal, brave, dedicated

to doing what was right. Sky seemed more at ease with people than Hunter did. But Hunter seemed stronger to me.

"Hunter and I have a suggestion," Sky said. "Let's get
everyone together, and we'll fill you all in."

"Thank you all for coming," Hunter said, raising his
voice. He took a sip of his ginger ale. "We have here two
covens," he went on, gesturing around the room. "Cirrus,
which has seven members, and Kithic, which has six." He
pointed them out to us. "Kithic's leader, Sky Eventide. Bree
Warren, Raven Meltzer, Thalia Cutter, Simon Bakehouse, and
Alisa Soto."

There was a moment when we were all smiling and nodding at each other, all mystified.

"Hunter and I have been thinking about joining the two
covens," said Sky, and I felt my eyebrows raise. When had
this discussion happened? I wondered.

Across the room I caught Bree's eye, and she made an I-
didn't-know-about-this-either face. Once Bree had been part
of Cirrus. Once I had known all her thoughts as well as my
own. Well, we were making progress: now we were speaking
to each other without fighting, which was more than we'd
done for months.

"Each coven is quite small," Hunter explained. "It divides
our energy and our powers. If we join, Sky and I can share in
the leadership, which will make us stronger."

"And the new coven will have thirteen members," said
Sky. "In magick the number thirteen has special properties. A
thirteen-member coven will have strength and power. It will
make our magick more accessible, for lack of a better word."

"Join?" Jenna asked. Her light brown eyes flitted quickly

to Raven, and I remembered her saying she could never be in the same coven as the girl who had so blatantly stolen Matt away from her. Then her glance fell on Simon, and he looked back at her. I'd seen her talking to him at the Practical Magick party. Well, good for her, I thought. Maybe the lure of Simon would outweigh her feelings about Raven.

"Thirteen sounds really big," said Alisa, who looked young, maybe only fifteen. She had wavy golden brown hair, tan skin, and big dark eyes. "The smaller size is nicer because we know everyone and we can relax with them."

Hunter nodded. "I understand that," he said, and from the tone of his voice I knew he was about to flood her with logic, the way he had done with me so many times. "And I agree that part of a circle's appeal is its intimacy, the sense of closeness and support that we get from one another. But I assure you, after a couple months of working together, we'll appreciate the wider circle of support, the larger group of friends, the greater resource of strength."

Alisa nodded uncertainly.

"Do we get to vote on this?" asked Robbie.

"Yes," Sky said at once. "This is something Hunter and I have thought about a great deal. We share some of the same concerns that you might have. We do think it would be best for the two covens to merge, though, for us to join our energies and strengths. It's what we want to do, how we want to continue on our journey of discovery. But of course, we'd like to hear what the rest of you think."

We were all silent for a moment, everyone waiting for someone else to say something. Then I straightened up. "I think it's a good idea," I said. Until I spoke I wasn't sure what my reaction would be, but now I knew. "It makes sense for us to join together, to be allies, to be working together instead of working apart." Hunter's eyes sought mine, but I looked at the group. "Magick can be dark and dangerous sometimes," I added. "The more people we can count on, the better, in my opinion."

Twelve people looked at me. I had been shy and self-conscious for seventeen years, and I knew that my class-mates, people who knew me well, were surprised at my offering an opinion so openly. But in the last month so much had happened that, frankly, I didn't have a lot of energy left to be self-conscious anymore.

"I agree," Bree said into the silence. I saw the warmth in her brown eyes, and suddenly we smiled at each other, almost as if it were old times.

Everyone started speaking then, and after another twenty minutes of discussion we voted and it was agreed: the two covens would merge. We would be thirteen mem-bers strong, and we would call ourselves Kithic. I hoped the end of Cirrus would help me cope with the traumatic end of Cal's and my relationship. And I tried not to be over-whelmed by all the new beginnings in my life.

We had what I thought of as a "baby" circle: we didn't actually go through the whole ritual, but we did stand in a circle, holding hands, while Hunter and Sky led us through some breathing exercises.

Then Hunter said, "As some of you have already discov-ered, Wicca has its frightening side." He cast a swift look in my direction. "It's not so surprising, perhaps, when you think that all of us have within us the capacity for both bright and dark. Wicca is part of the world, and the world can be a dark place, too. But one of the things this coven can do for you is support you and help you to conquer your personal fears. The fewer unexplored places you have within you, the easier it will be to connect with your own magick."

"We're going to go around the circle," Sky said, picking up where Hunter left off, "and each of us is going to tell the group one of our great fears. Thalia, you start."

Thalia was tall and earth-mothery looking, with long, ringlety hair and a pretty Madonna face (the saint, not the singer).

"I'm afraid of boats," she said, her cheeks turning slightly pink. "Every time I get in a boat, I panic, and I think a whale is going to come up under it and knock me into the sea and I'll drown. Even if it's just a rowboat on a duck pond."

I heard Matt stifle a snicker, and felt a twinge of irritation.

Robbie was next. He looked at Bree, then said, "I'm afraid I won't be patient enough to wait for the things I really want." Robbie and Bree had recently begun seeing each other, in a very cautious, uncommitted way. He was in love with her and wanted a real relationship, but so far she had shied away from anything more than fooling around.

I watched as Bree's gaze dropped from his, and I also noticed the interested gleam in Thalia's eyes. Weeks ago I had heard gossip that Thalia was hot for Robbie. If Bree's not careful, Thalia will steal Robbie from her, I thought.

Ethan spoke next, with none of his usual joking around. "I'm afraid I'll be weak and lose a really great person in my life." I guessed he was talking about his pot smoking. Around the time he and Sharon had started seeing each other, he'd more or less given up pot, in part because he knew she didn't like it when he smoked.

Sharon, who held Ethan's left hand, looked at him with open affection. "I'm not," she said simply. Then she looked at the rest of us. "I'm terrified of dying," she said.

We kept going around the circle. Jenna was afraid she wouldn't be brave. Raven was afraid of being tied down. Matt was afraid no one would ever understand him. I thought of telling him he should start by trying to understand himself, but I realized this wasn't the right time or place.

"I'm afraid I'll never be able to have what I really want," Bree said in a small voice, looking at the floor.

"I'm afraid of unrequited love," Sky said, her dark eyes as enigmatic as ever.

"I'm afraid of fire," Simon said, and I jerked, startled. My birth parents had burned to death in a barn, and Cal had tried to kill me with fire when I'd refused to join the conspiracy he and his mother were part of. I, too, was afraid of fire.

"I'm afraid of my anger," Alisa said. That surprised me. She looked so sweet.

Then it was my turn. I opened my mouth, intending to say I was afraid of fire, but something stopped me. I felt Hunter's gaze on me, and it was as if he were shining a spotlight on the darkest recesses of my mind, urging me to dredge up my deepest fear.

"I'm afraid I'll never know who I am," I said, and as I said it, I knew it was true.

Hunter was last. In a clear voice he said, "I'm afraid of losing any more people I love."

My heart ached for him. His brother had died at the age

of fifteen, murdered by a dark spirit called a taibhs. And his father and mother had disappeared ten years ago, driven into hiding by the dark wave, a cloud of evil and destruction that had wiped out many covens, including my own birth parents'. He had a younger sister, I knew, and it occurred to me that he must worry about her all the time.

Then I looked at him and found his gaze locked on me, and my skin prickled as if the air were suddenly full of electricity.

A moment later we dropped hands and it was over. I guessed a lot of people would stay to hang out, but I felt oddly antisocial, and I went to snag my coat. The events of the last week had shaken me more than I had admitted to anyone. As of the day before, school was out officially for winter break, and it was a huge relief to finally have hours of free time in front of me so that I could try to begin processing the myriad ways my life had changed in the last three months.

"Robbie?" I said, interrupting his conversation with Bree. They were huddled close, and I thought I heard Robbie cajoling and Bree playfully resisting.

"Oh, hey, Morgan," Robbie said, looking up reluctantly, and then Hunter's voice was at my ear, sending a shiver down my spine as he said, "Can I give you a ride home?"

Seeing the relief on Robbie's face, I nodded and said, "Yeah. Thanks."

Hunter put on his leather jacket and his hat, and I followed him out into the darkness.

# 2.
# Spin

August 7, 1968 San, Francisco

I've been packing up Patrick's things. Last week we had his memorial service—all of Catspaw and some folks from Waterwind were there. I can't believe he's gone. Sometimes I'm sure he's not gone—that he's about to start up the stairs, he's about to call, he'll walk through the door, holding some new book, some new find.

My friend Nancy asked if it had bothered me that he was nearly forty years older than me. It never did. He was a beautiful man, no matter what his age. And even more important, he loved me, he shared his knowledge, he let me learn anything I could. My powers are ten times stronger now than they were when we first met.

Now Patrick's gone. The house is mine, all his things are mine. I'm looking through his books and finding so many I never knew he had. There are books hundreds of years old that I can't even decipher. Books written in code. Spelled books that I can't even open. I'm going to ask Stella for help with these. Since she became Catspaw's leader, I've trusted her more and more.

Without Patrick here to distract me, so many things are becoming clearer. I'm not sure, but I think he worked with dark magick sometimes. I think some of the people who came here worked with darkness. At the time I didn't pay much attention to them. Now I think Patrick often had me spelled so I wouldn't question things. I guess I understand, but I wish he'd trusted me to accept what he was doing and not automatically condemn it.

I managed to open one book, breaking through its privacy charm with a counterspell that took me almost two hours to weave. Inside were things that Patrick never showed me: spells about calling on animals, spells for transporting your energy somewhere, spells to effect change from far away. Not dark magick per se, but proscribed nonetheless; the council says spells to manipulate should never be used lightly. No one in Catspaw would touch a book like this, even though they're Woodbane. But I would. Why shouldn't I learn all there is to know? If the knowledge exists, why should I blind myself to it?

This book is mine now. And I will study it.

—SB

There's something about being with someone in a car at night that makes you feel like you're the only people in the world. I had felt that way three weeks ago, when Cal kidnapped me, spelled me so I couldn't move, and drove me to his house. That night, alone in the car with Cal, it had been unspeakably bad: pure panic, fear, anger, desperation.

I felt differently tonight, with Hunter by my side. Recently, when it became clear that he might have to stay in Widow's Vale for a while, he'd bought a tiny, battered Honda to replace the rental car he'd been driving. The small space inside felt cozy, intimate.

"Thanks for backing us up about joining the two covens," he said, breaking the silence.

"I think it's a good idea. I'd rather know where everyone is and what they're doing."

He gave a short laugh and shook his head. "That's harsh," he said. "I hope someday soon you'll be able to trust other people again."

I tried not to flinch at the thought. I had trusted Cal, and it had almost cost me my life. I had trusted David, and he'd turned out to have a dark side, too. What was it about me that blinded me to evil? Was it my Woodbane blood?

And yet . . . "I trust you," I said honestly, uncomfortable with the feeling of vulnerability those words awoke in me.

Hunter glanced at me, his eyes an unfathomable shade of gray in the darkness. Without speaking he reached across the seat and took my hand. His skin was cool, and my fingers brushed against a callus on his palm. Holding hands with him felt daring, strange. Holding hands with Cal had been so natural, so welcome.

I was seventeen and had had only one boyfriend. I'd known since that remarkable kiss that Hunter and I had a definite connection, but he wasn't my boyfriend, and we'd never been on an official date.

I breathed deeply, willing my pulse to slow down. "I know magick is all about achieving clarity," I said. "But I feel so confused."

"Magick itself is about clarity," Hunter agreed. "But people aren't. Magick is perfect; people are imperfect. When you put the two together, it's bound to get cloudy sometimes. When it's just you and magick, how does it feel?"

I thought back to when I had worked spells, had circles by myself, scryed in fire, used my birth mother's tools. "It feels like heaven," I said quietly. "Like perfection."

"Right," Hunter said, squeezing my hand and turning the steering wheel with the other. His headlights sliced through the night on this winding road toward downtown Widow's Vale. "That's pure magick and only you. But as soon as you add other people into the mix, especially if they aren't totally clear themselves, you get confusion."

"It's not just magick," I said, looking out the window, trying to ignore the exciting feeling of his hand on mine. I didn't know how to put it—despite my two months with Cal, I was still a relative newcomer to the guy-girl thing. I thought that Hunter liked me, and I thought I liked him. But it was so different. Cal had been obvious and persistent in his pursuit of me. What kind of a person was I, liking Hunter, finding him attractive, when until just a few weeks ago I'd thought I was madly in love with Cal? Yet here Hunter was, holding my hand, taking me home, possibly kissing me later. A little shiver went down my spine.

Hunter zoomed around a tight corner, making me lean toward him.

Then he pulled his hand from mine and put it on the steering wheel.

"Whoa," I said, covering my disappointment. "Going a little fast, huh?"

"I can't help it," he said in his crisp English accent. "The brakes don't seem to be working."

"What?" Confused, I glanced over to see his jaw set, his face tense with concentration.

"The brakes aren't working," he repeated, and my eyes widened as I understood the words.

In alarm I looked ahead—we were going downhill, toward the curviest parts of this road, where signs recommended going no more than twenty miles an hour. The speedometer said fifty.

My heart thudded hard, once. "Crap. Downshift?" I said faintly, not wanting to distract him.

"Yes. But I don't want to make us skid. I could turn off the engine."

"You'd lose the steering," I murmured.

"Yes," he said grimly.

Time slowed. The facts—that the road was icy, that we were wearing seat belts, that the car was small and would crumple like a tin can, that my heart was thudding against my ribs, that my blood was like ice water in my veins—all these things registered as Hunter downshifted forcefully, making the engine buck and groan. The whole car shuddered. I gripped the door handle tightly, my foot pressing a nonexist-ent brake pedal on the floor. I'm too young to die, I thought. I don't want to die.

We were in third gear, going about forty miles an hour downhill. The engine whined, straining uselessly against the gravity and inertia that pulled the car forward, and we began to pick up speed again. I glanced at Hunter, hardly breathing. His face looked bleached in the dim dashboard light, as if he were carved from bone. I heard the squeal of the wheels and felt the sickening lurch of the car as we skidded around another curve, then another.

Hunter downshifted once more, and the whole car jumped with an annoyed sound. My back hit my seat, and the car seemed to dance sideways, like a spooked horse. Hunter grabbed the parking brake and slowly eased it upward. I didn't feel any effect. Then with a hard jerk Hunter popped it into place, and the car jolted again and started skidding sideways, toward a tree-lined ditch. If the car rolled, we would be crushed. I quit breathing and sat frozen.

He shifted into first gear and simultaneously turned into the skid so we did an endless, semicontrolled fishtail right in the middle of Picketts Road. Hunter let us skid, and when we had slowed enough, he cut the engine. The steering wheel locked, but it was okay—we were still headed into the spin, and finally we scraped to a noisy halt at the side of the road, not six inches from a massive, gnarled sycamore that would have flattened us if we'd hit it.

After the grinding screeches of the tortured engine and tires, the silence of the night was broken only by our shallow panting. I swallowed hard, feeling like my seat belt was the only thing holding me upright. My eyes felt huge as I searched Hunter's face.

"Are you all right?" he asked, his voice slightly shaky.

I nodded. "You?"

"Yes. That could have been bad."

"You have a knack for understatement," I said weakly. "That *was* bad, and it could have been deadly. What happened to the brakes?"

"Good question," Hunter said. He peered through his window at the dark woods.

I looked around, too. "Oh. We're near Riverdale Road," I said, recognizing this bend in the road. "We're about a mile and a half from my house. This isn't far from where I put Das Boot into a ditch."

Hunter unsnapped his seat belt. "Can we walk to your house?"

"Yeah."

Hunter locked the car where it sat neatly and quietly by the side of the road, as if it hadn't almost killed us. We started walking, and I didn't speak because I could tell Hunter was sending out his senses, and I realized he was searching for other presences nearby. And then it hit me: he wasn't sure the failure of the brakes had been an accident.

Without stopping to think, I flung out my own senses like a net, letting them infiltrate the woods, the night air, the dead grass beneath the snow.

But I felt nothing out of the ordinary. Apparently Hunter didn't, either, because his shoulders relaxed inside his coat, and his stride slowed. He came to a stop and put his hands on my shoulders, looking down at me.

"Are you sure you're all right?" he asked, his voice quiet.

"Yes." I nodded. "It was just scary, that's all." I swallowed. "Do you think that part of the road is spelled? It's so close to where I had my wreck. And Selene—"

"Is nowhere around here. We check every day, and she's gone," said Hunter. Selene Belltower was Cal's mother and the one who'd urged him to pursue me. She'd wanted me and my Woodbane power and my Woodbane coven tools under her control. Failing that, she'd wanted me dead and out of the way. Though she'd fled Widow's Vale weeks ago, I still felt my pulse race whenever I thought of her.

"When you had your wreck, you thought you saw head-lights behind you, right?" Hunter went on. "And you felt mag-ick, didn't you?" He shook his head. "This felt simply mechanical—there just weren't any brakes. I'll call a tow truck from your house, if that's okay."

"Sure," I said, taking a deep breath and trying to unkink muscles still knotted with fear. "And I can give you a ride home."

"Thank you." He hesitated, and I wondered if he was going to kiss me. But he straightened again and took his hands away, and we began walking toward home.

The cold made us walk fast, and at some point Hunter took my hand in his and put them both in his pocket. The feeling of his skin against mine was wonderful, and I wished I could put my arms around him, under his coat. But I still felt unsure of myself with him—there was no way I could be that daring.

As if he'd read my thoughts, Hunter turned and caught

my gaze. I blushed, ducked my head, and walked even faster. I was relieved when we turned onto my street.

My parents and my fourteen-year-old sister, Mary K., were watching a movie in the family room when we got home. Hunter blandly told them he'd had "a little car trouble," and they clucked and fretted while he called the tow service. When he hung up, I looked at the clock—it was a few minutes after eleven.

"Mom, is it okay if I take Hunter to his car and then to his house?" I asked.

Mom and Dad did the usual silent parent-communication thing with each other, then Mom nodded. "I guess so. But please drive extra carefully. I don't know what it is with you and cars, Morgan, but I'm starting to worry about you on the road."

I nodded, feeling a little guilty. My parents didn't know the half of it. Three weeks ago Robbie had saved my life. Unfortunately he had saved it by driving my car through the stone wall of Cal's pool house, where I'd been trapped. My parents (who thought I'd hit a light pole) had lent me some of the money to have the front end repaired.

"Okay," I agreed, and Hunter and I got our coats again and went out to Das Boot, my giant, submarine-like '71 Plymouth Valiant. Automatically I winced as I saw its shiny new front bumper, slate blue hood, and gray-spotted sides. I had to get it painted and soon. This rainbow look was killing me.

Inside my car it was freezing, and its old-fashioned vinyl seats didn't help any. We didn't speak as I drove back to Hunter's car to wait for the tow truck. Hunter seemed lost in thought.

After only a minute Widow's Vale's one tow truck came into view. I'd seen John Mitchell a few weeks before, when I had put Das Boot into the ditch. He flicked a glance at me as he bent to hook up the chain to Hunter's car.

"We lost the brakes," Hunter explained as John began to crank the car onto the bed of the truck.

"Hmmm," John said, and bent beneath the car to take a quick look. When he came up again, he said, "I don't see anything offhand," and spat onto the side of the road. "Besides the fact you don't seem to have any brake fluid."

"Really," said Hunter. His brows rose.

"Yeah," John replied, sounding almost bored. He gave Hunter a clipboard with a paper to sign. "Anyway, I'll bring it to Unser's and he'll fix you up."

"Right," said Hunter, rubbing his chin.

We got back in Das Boot and watched the tow truck take Hunter's car away. I started the engine and headed toward the edge of town, toward the little house he shared with Sky. "No brake fluid," I said. "Can that happen by itself?"

"It can, but it seems unlikely. I had the car tuned up last week, when I bought it," Hunter said. "If there was a leak, the mechanic should have caught it."

I felt a prickle of fear. "So what are you thinking, then?" I asked.

"I'm thinking we need some answers," Hunter said, looking out his window thoughtfully.

Ten minutes later I pulled up in front of his shabby rented house and saw Raven's battered black Peugeot parked out front.

"Are Raven and Sky getting along?" I asked.

"I think so," Hunter answered. "They're spending a lot of time together. I know Sky's a big girl, but I worry about her getting hurt."

I liked seeing this caring side of Hunter, and I turned to face him. "I didn't even know Sky was gay until she and I did our tàth meànma." Weeks ago Sky and I had done what I think of as a Wiccan mind meld. When our thoughts had been joined, I had been surprised to see that she felt such a strong desire for Raven, our resident gothy bad girl.

"I don't know that Sky *is* gay," Hunter said thoughtfully. "She's had relationships with guys before. I think she just likes who she likes, if you know what I mean."

I nodded. I had barely dipped my toes into plain vanilla heterosexual relationships—any variation seemed too mind-boggling to contemplate.

"Anyway," said Hunter, opening his car door and letting in the cold night air, "drive very carefully on your way home. Do you have a cell phone?"

"No."

"Then send me a witch message," he instructed. "If anything the slightest bit out of the ordinary happens, send me a message and I'll come right away. Promise?"

"Okay."

Hunter paused. "Maybe I should borrow Sky's car and follow you home."

I rolled my eyes, refusing to admit I was worried about the lonely drive home. "I'll be fine."

His eyes narrowed. "No, let me get Sky's keys."

"Would you stop? I've driven these roads a million times. I'll call you if I need you, but I'm sure I won't."

He sat back and pulled the door closed. The dome light blinked off.

"You are incredibly stubborn," he remarked conversationally.

I knew he meant well, so I swallowed my tart response. "It's just—I'm very self-reliant," I said self-consciously. "I've always been that way. I don't like owing other people."

He looked at me. "Because you're afraid they'll let you down?"

I shrugged. "Partly, I guess. I don't know." I looked out the window, not enjoying this conversation.

"Look," he said calmly, "I don't know what happened with the car. We don't think Cal and Selene are around, but in fact we don't know where they are or what they're doing. You could be in real danger."

What he said was true, but I felt reluctant to concede the point. "I'll be okay," I said, knowing I was being pointlessly stubborn and unable to stop myself.

Hunter sighed impatiently. "Morgan, I—"

"Look, I'll be fine. Now stop fussing and let me go home." Had I ever been so forthright with Cal? I had wanted so badly for Cal to find me attractive, felt I had fallen so far short of the kind of girl he would want. I had tried to be a more appealing Morgan for him, as stupid and clumsy as my attempts had been. With Hunter, I had never bothered. It felt very freeing to say whatever came to my lips because I wasn't worried about impressing him.

We stared at each other in a standoff. I couldn't help comparing his looks to Cal's. Cal had been golden, exotic, and astoundingly sexy. Hunter was more classical, like a

Greek statue, all shapes and planes. His beauty was cool. Yet as I looked at him, the desire to touch him, to kiss and hold him, grew in me until it was almost overpowering.

He shifted in his seat, and I almost flinched when he brought a cool hand up to stroke my cheek. With that one touch I was mesmerized, and I sat very still.

"I'm sorry," he said, his voice low. "I'm afraid for you. I want you to be safe." He smiled wryly. "I can't apologize for worrying about you."

Slowly he leaned closer, his head blotting out the moonlight streaming through the windshield. Ever so gently his warm lips touched mine, and then we were kissing, kissing hard, and I felt completely exhilarated. When he pulled back, we were both breathing fast. He opened the door again, and I blinked in the glare from the dome light. He shook his head, as if to clear it, and seemed at a loss for words. I licked my lips and looked out the windshield, unable to meet his eyes.

"I'll talk to you tomorrow," he said softly. "Drive carefully."

"Okay," I managed. I watched him walk up to the front porch and wanted to call him back, to throw my arms around him and press against him. He turned then, and I wondered with embarrassment if he had picked up on my feelings. I stepped on the gas and sped off.

With witches, you never know.

# 3.
# Sharing

November 5, 1968

My mind is still reeling from all that I've seen in the past week.

It started when I found Patrick's Turneval Book of Shadows. That's when I discovered that Waterwind was only one of the covens that he'd belonged to. It was the one he had grown up with, back in Seattle, and it was just like Catspaw: Woodbanes who had renounced everything to do with the dark side. But since I started going through his Turneval stuff, I've seen a whole new side of him. What a waste: oh, Patrick, if only you had shared this with me, the way you shared everything else!

I wonder if he thought Turneval would horrify me. How could he not know I'd be open to anything, anything he wanted to show me, teach me, any kind of power? He must have known. Maybe he was biding his time. Maybe he wanted to show me but died too soon.

I'll never know. I only know that I would've loved being in Turneval with him, loved for him to teach me all that it meant to be Woodbane.

On Samhain, instead of going to Catspaw's festivities, I went to a Turneval circle. We started by making circles of power and invoking the Goddess, just like at Catspaw. Then everything changed. The Turneval witches knew spells that opened us to the deepest magick, the magick contained in all the creatures and lives that are no longer part of this earth. For the first time I was aware of a universe of untapped resources, whole strata of energy and power and connection that I had never been taught. It was frightening and unbearably exciting. I'm too much of a novice to use this power, of course—I don't even fully know how to tap into it. But Hendrick Samuels, one of Turneval's elders, gave himself over to it, and he actually shape-shifted in front of us. Goddess, he shape-shifted! Covens talk about shape-shifting like it's the story of Goldilocks—but it's real, it's possible. Before my eyes I saw Hendrick assume the form of a mountain lion, and he was glorious. I have to get close to him so he'll share the secret with me.

This is what Patrick spent his life studying, what he

*hid from me. It's what I was meant to do, what I should
have been born to but wasn't. I see that now.*

*—SB*

"Your folks don't mind you skipping church?" Bree's dark
eyes were dimmed by the ribbon of steam coming from her
coffee mug. We were in a coffee emporium in a strip mall off
the main road. It was popular on Sunday mornings, and people surrounded us, drinking coffee, eating pastry, reading sec-
tions of newspaper.

I made a face and loaded my currant scone with butter.
"They mind. Somehow they would be more comfortable
about my being Wiccan if I also remained a good Catholic."

"And that's not possible?" Bree asked around a mouthful
of bear claw.

I sighed. "It's hard."

Bree nodded, and we ate for a few minutes. I studied her
covertly. While she was very familiar to me, still, we were
both undeniably different people from who we had been
three months ago, when Wicca and Cal came into both our
lives. We were feeling our way back to being friends again.
Things were still awkward between us sometimes, but it felt
good to hang out and talk, anyway.

"I like a lot of things about Catholicism. I like the services
and the music and seeing everyone," I said. "Feeling like I
belong to something bigger than just my family. But it's hard
to wrap my mind around some of it. Wicca just feels so much
more natural to me." I shrugged. "Anyway, I just wanted to
skip it this week. It doesn't mean that I'm never going back."

Bree nodded again and tugged her black top into place.

As usual, she looked chic and beautiful, perfectly put together, though she was only wearing jeans and a sweater and no makeup. Usually I felt like a lumberjack around her, with my flat chest, strong nose, boring hair, and lame wardrobe. Today I was surprising myself by feeling strong beneath my looks, as if the witch inside might someday be attractive enough for the Morgan outside.

"How's Mary K.?" Bree asked.

I stirred my coffee. "She's been kind of down lately. Since the whole Bakker fiasco, it's like she's walking around waiting for a ton of bricks to fall on her." Bakker Blackburn, my sister's ex-boyfriend, had twice tried to use force to get her to have sex with him.

"That prick," said Bree. "You should put some awful spell on him. Give him Robbie's old acne." In October, in a fit of experimentation, I'd made a magick potion to clear up the terrible acne that had marred Robbie's looks for years. It had had some unexpected side effects, like correcting his bad vision so that he no longer needed his coke-bottle glasses. Without the glasses and the acne, he turned out to be startlingly good-looking.

I laughed. "Now, you know we're not supposed to do things like that."

"Oh, like that would stop you," she said, and I laughed some more. It was true that I had either bent or flat-out broken quite a few of the unwritten Wiccan guidelines for responsible use of magick since I had first discovered my powers. But I was trying to be good.

"Speaking of Robbie," I said leadingly, raising my eyebrows.

Bree looked down at her plate. "Oh, Robbie," she said vaguely.

"Are you going to break his heart?" My voice was light, but we both knew I was serious.

"I hope not," she said, and tapped her finger against her plate. "I don't want to. The thing is—he's just throwing himself at me, heart, soul, and body."

"And the body you want," I guessed.

"The body I'm dying for," she admitted.

"You don't want anything else from him?" I said. "You know Robbie's a really good guy. He'd be a great boyfriend."

Bree groaned and dropped her face onto her hands. "How can you tell? We've known him since we were babies! I know him *too* well. He's like a pal, a brother."

"Except you want to jump him."

"Yeah. I mean, he's gorgeous. He's . . . fabulous. He makes me crazy."

"I don't believe it's only physical," I said. "He wouldn't tie you up in knots if there weren't some emotion going on, too."

"I know, I know," Bree muttered. "I don't know what to do. I've never had this problem before. Usually I know exactly what I want and how to get it."

"Well, good luck," I said, sighing. "So, relationships are heating up all over," I added. "Raven and Sky, Jenna and Simon . . ."

"Yeah," Bree said, cheering up. "Sky and Raven are freaking me out. I mean, Raven's a boyfriend machine."

"Maybe what she was looking for all along was a girl," I said, and we made dorky oh-my-gosh faces at each other.

"Could be. And you think Jenna and Simon?" Bree asked, taking a sip of her coffee.

"I think so. They seem to be interested in each other," I reported. "I hope they do get together. Jenna deserves to be happy after Matt was such an ass to her." I stopped suddenly, remembering that Raven had tried to nail Matt primarily to get him to join her coven—the coven that Bree had also been a member of. The old Kithic.

For a moment Bree looked uncomfortable, as if she too were mulling over the convoluted events of the last month. "Everything changes, all the time," she finally said.

"Uh-huh."

"Anyway," Bree said, "what's with you and Hunter?"

I choked on my coffee and spent the next minute coughing gracelessly while Bree arched her perfect eyebrows at me.

"Uh," I finally said hoarsely. "Uh. I don't know, really."

She looked at me, and I shifted in my seat.

"It just seems that you guys set off sparks when you're together."

"Sometimes," I admitted.

"Do you still love Cal?"

Just hearing his name, especially spoken by Bree, made me wince. Bree had thought she was in love with him. They had slept together before Cal and I started going out, which, as I saw it now, Cal had done partly to drive a wedge between Bree and me so that I'd be all the more dependent on him. I still found it hard to stomach the fact that Cal and Bree had had sex, and he and I hadn't, despite how much I had loved him and thought he loved me.

"He tried to kill me," I said faintly, feeling like the coffee shop was too small.

Compassion crossed her face, and she reached across the table to touch my hand. "I know," she said softly. "But I also know you really loved him. How do you feel about him now?"

I still love him, I thought. I am filled with rage and hatred toward him. He said he loved me, he said I was beautiful, he said he wanted to make love to me. He hurt me more than I can say. I miss him, and I hate myself for being so weak.

"I don't know," I finally said.

As I was opening my car door in the parking lot, out of the corner of my eye I saw a guy come out of the video store next door to the coffee place. I glanced up, and my heart stopped beating. He was looking down at a piece of paper in his hand, but I didn't need to see his face. I'd run my fingers through that raggedly-shorn dark hair. . . . I'd kissed that wide, smooth chest. . . . I'd stared so many times at those long, powerful legs in their faded blue jeans. . . .

Then he looked up, and I saw that it wasn't Cal after all. It was a guy I'd never seen before, with pale blue eyes and bad skin. I stood there, stunned in the bright sunlight, while he gave me a funny look, then walked to his car and got in.

It felt like a full minute before my heartbeat returned to normal. I climbed into Das Boot and drove home. But the whole way, I couldn't help checking my rearview mirror to see if anyone was behind me.

Later that day the phone rang. I raced to answer it, knowing it was Hunter.

"Can I come over?" he asked when I picked up the receiver.

When I'd gotten back from seeing Bree, Mom, Dad, and my sister were already home from church. I felt guilty about not having gone with them, so since then I had been trying to do good-daughter-type stuff around the house—shoveling the front walk, picking up my crap from the living room, unloading the dishwasher. Having Hunter over would kind of wreck my attempts at scoring points with my family.

"Yes," I said quickly. My heart kicked up a beat in response to his voice. "How will you get here?"

Silence. I almost laughed as I realized he hadn't thought about that.

"I'll borrow Sky's car," he said finally.

"Do you want me to come get you?" I asked.

"No. Are your parents there? Can we talk alone?"

"Yes, my parents are here, and we can talk alone if you want to stand out on the front porch with my whole family inside wondering what we're talking about."

He sounded irked. "Why can't we just go to your room?"

What planet did he come from? "I'm sorry, Your Highness, but I don't live by myself," I said. "I'm seventeen, not nineteen, and I live with my parents. And my parents don't think it's a good idea for boys to be in my room, because there's a bed in there!" Then of course the image of Hunter on my bed made my cheeks burn, and I was sorry I had ever opened my big mouth. What was wrong with me?

"Oh, right. Sorry—I forgot," he said. "But I need to speak to you alone. Can you meet me at the little public park that's by that big grocery store on Route Eleven?"

I thought. "Yes. Ten minutes."

He hung up without saying good-bye.

When I got there, Hunter was standing by Sky's car, waiting for me. He opened Das Boot's door and climbed into the front seat. He was in a tense, angry mood, and the funny thing was, I picked up on that just from waves of sensory stuff I got from him, not from the look on his face or his body language. It was as if he was projecting those feelings and I could just sense them. My witch powers were developing every day, and it was wonderful and a bit scary at the same time.

I waited for him to speak, looking out the windshield, catching the faintest hint of his clean, fresh smell.

"I talked to Bob Unser this morning," he said. "There wasn't any brake fluid in the car, but more than that, the actual brake lines had been severed, right by the fluid reservoir."

I turned to stare at him. "Severed?"

He nodded. "Not cut exactly, not as smooth as that. He couldn't say for sure that someone had cut them. But he did say that it was unusual since both brake lines looked fine when he checked the car last week. It didn't seem like they could simply wear through so quickly."

"Did you check the car for spells, magick?" I asked.

"Yes, of course," he said. "There wasn't anything, apart from the spells of protection I'd put on it."

"So what does that mean? Was this an accident, a person, a witch, what?"

"I don't know," he admitted. "I think it was a person

rather than an accident. I think it was a witch because I just don't know that many nonwitches, and I certainly haven't got any nonwitch enemies."

"Could it have been Cal?" I forced myself to ask. "Or Selene?"

"They're the first ones I thought of, of course," he said matter-of-factly, and the hair on my arms rose. I remembered the guy I'd seen in the parking lot this morning—the one I'd thought was Cal.

"But I still don't think they're in the area," he added. "I run a sweep every day, checking this whole area for signs of them, and I haven't picked up on anything. Of course, I'm not as powerful as Selene," he said. "Just because I can't feel her doesn't mean she's truly gone. But I can't help thinking that I would pick up on something if they were still around."

"Like what?" I asked. My mouth felt suddenly dry.

"It's hard to say," Hunter said. "I mean, sometimes I do feel . . . something. But there are so many other things going on that I can't really delineate it." He frowned. "If you were stronger, we could work together, join our powers."

"I know," I said. I was too freaked to bristle at being called weak. "I'm just a newbie. But what about Sky?"

"Well, Sky and I have already joined our powers," he said. "But you have the potential to be stronger than either of us. That's why you must be studying and learning as much as you can. The faster we can get you up to speed, the faster you can help us, help the council. Maybe even join the council."

"Ha," I exclaimed. "There's no way I'm joining the council! Be a hall monitor for Wicca? No thanks!" Then I realized how that must have sounded to Hunter, who was a member of the council himself, and I wanted to take the words back. Too late.

Hunter pressed his lips together and stared out his window. No one else was around: it was a Sunday afternoon and not warm enough for kids to be on the playground. Silence filled my ears, and I sighed.

"I'm sorry," I said. "I didn't mean that. I know that what you do is more important than that. Much too important for me to contemplate doing it," I said honestly. "It's just I can hardly manage to dress myself these days, much less think about doing anything more. Everything is so . . . overwhelming right now."

"I understand," Hunter surprised me by saying. "You've been through a lot. And I know I'm putting a lot of pressure on you, and sometimes I forget how new this is to you. But a talent, a power like yours is rare—maybe once in a generation. I don't want to give you an inflated sense of your own importance, but you should realize that you are and will become an important person in the world of Wicca. There are two ways of dealing with it: You can become a hermit, shutting yourself away from people, studying and learning on your own. Or you can embrace your power and the responsibility it brings and accept the joys and heartbreaks associated with it."

I looked at my lap, feeling self-conscious.

"There's something I wanted to mention to you—a way of acquiring a lot of knowledge quickly. It's called a tàth meànma brach, and it's basically a supercharged tàth meànma."

"I don't understand," I said.

"You do a tàth meànma with a witch who knows a lot more than you, who's more learned and more experienced though not necessarily more powerful," Hunter explained. "The two of you join very deeply and openly and in essence give each other all your knowledge. It would be as if you suddenly had a whole lifetime's worth of learning in a couple of hours."

"It sounds incredible," I said eagerly. "Of course I want to do it."

He gave me a warning look. "It's not something you should decide lightly. It's a big thing, both for you and the other witch. It can be painful and even dangerous. If one witch isn't ready or the two personalities are too dissimilar, the damage can be severe. I heard of one case where one of the witches went blind afterward."

"But I would know so much," I said. "It would be worth the risk."

"Don't decide right now," he went on. "I just wanted to let you know about it. It would increase your ability to protect yourself—the more knowledge you have, the better you'll be able to access your power. And part of the reason I'm telling you this is because you've already attracted the attention of some very powerful people: Selene and the rest of her Woodbane organization. The sooner you can protect yourself, the better."

I nodded. "I wish I knew where they were," I said. "I'm afraid to look over my shoulder. I keep expecting to see Cal or Selene."

"I feel the same way sometimes. Not about them specifically, but I've made enough enemies in my job as a Seeker to have an assortment of witches who would love to see me dead. Which, by the way, is something I've been thinking about in regard to the cut brake line. I'd be stupid if I didn't take every possibility into account." He shifted in his seat. "Really, all I'm trying to say is that we both have to be extra careful from now on. We need to strengthen the protection spells on your car and your house, and my car and house, and Sky's car. We have to be vigilant and prudent. I don't want anything to happen to . . . either of us."

For several minutes we sat quietly, thinking things through. I was worried, but Hunter's presence made me feel safer. Knowing he was in Widow's Vale made me feel protected. How long would I have that feeling? How long before he would have to leave?

"I don't know how much time I'll have here," he said, unnerving me with the accuracy of his response to my thoughts. "It could be another month, or it could be a year or more."

I hated the thought of his leaving and didn't want to examine why. Then his strong hand was brushing back a tendril of hair off my cheek, and my breath caught in my throat. We were alone in my car, and when he leaned closer to me, I could feel the warmth of his breath. I closed my eyes and let my head rest against my seat.

"While I'm here," he said softly, "I'll help and protect you in any way I can. But you need to be strong with or without me. Promise me you'll work toward that."

I nodded slightly, my eyes still closed, thinking, *Just kiss me, kiss me.*

Then he did, and his lips were warm on mine and I coiled

my hand up to hold his neck. The barest wisp of Cal's image brushed across my consciousness and was gone, and I was drawn into Hunter's light, the pressure of his mouth, his breathing, the hard warmth of his chest as he pressed closer. I felt something else, too—a feathery touch deep inside me, like delicate wings brushing against my very heart. I knew without words, without doubt, that I was feeling Hunter's essence, that our souls were touching. And I thought, Oh, the beauty of Wicca.

# 4.
# Begin

May 2, 1969

My skin is shriveled, and my hair is sticky and stiff with salt. I soaked in the purifying bath for two hours, with handfuls of sea salt and surrounded by crystals and sage candles. But though I can dispel the negative energy from my body, I can't erase the images from my mind.

Last night I saw my first taibhs, and when I think of it, I start shaking. Every Catspaw child hears of them, of course, and we're told scary stories about evil taibhs that steal the souls of Wiccan children who don't listen to their parents and teachers. I never thought they really existed. I guess I thought they were just holdovers from the Dark Ages, along with witches riding brooms, black cats, warts on noses: nothing to do with us today, really.

But Turneval taught me differently last night. I had

dressed so carefully for the rite, wanting to outwitch, out-beauty, outpower every other woman there. They had prom-ised me something special, something I deserved after my months of training and apprenticeship. Something I need-ed to go through before I could join Turneval as a full member.

Now, thinking back, I'm ashamed at how naive I was. I strode in, secure in my beauty, my strength and ruthless-ness, only to find by the end of the evening that I was weak, untaught, and unworthy of Turneval's offering.

What happened wasn't my fault. I was just a witness. The ones leading the rite made mistakes in their limita-tions, in the writing of the spells, the circles of protection — it was the first time Timothy Cornell had called a taibhs, and he called it badly. And it killed him.

A taibhs! I still can't believe it. It was a being and not a being, a spirit and not a spirit: a dark gathering of power and hunger with a human face and hands and the appetite of a demon. I was standing there in the circle, all eager anticipation, and suddenly the room went cold, icy, like the North wind had joined us. Shivering, I looked around and saw the others had their heads bowed, their eyes closed. Then I saw it, taking form in the corner. It was like a miniature tornado, vapor and smoke boiling and coiling in on itself, becoming more solid. It wasn't supposed to do any-thing: we were just calling it for practice. But Timothy had done it wrong, and the thing turned on him, broke through our circles of protection, and there was nothing any of us could do.

Death by a taibhs is horrible to watch and sickening to remember. I just want to blank it all out: Tim's screams, the wrenching of his soul from his body. I'm shaking now, just thinking of it. That idiot! He wasn't worthy to wield the power he was offered.

For the first time I understand why my parents, limited and dull as they were, chose to work the gentle kind of magick they did. They couldn't have controlled the dark forces any more than a child can hold back a flood by stuffing a rag in a dike.

Now I'm curled up on my bed, my wet hair flowing down my back like rain, and wondering which way I will choose: the safe, gentle, boring way of my parents or the way of Turneval, with its power and its evil twined together like a cord. Which path holds more terror for me?

—SB

"Open a window. This smell is making me sick," Mary K. complained.

I put down my paint roller and flung open one of my bedroom windows. Instantly frigid air rolled in, dispelling the sour, chemical smell of the wall paint. I stepped back to admire what my sister and I had already done. Two walls of my room were now a pale coffee-with-cream color. The other two walls were still covered by the childish pink stripes I was trying to obliterate. I grinned, already pleased with the transformation. I was changing, and my room was changing to keep up.

"You're only going to live here for another year," Mary K. pointed out, carefully edging a line by the ceiling. A paint-spattered bandanna covered her hair, and though she was in sweatpants and a ratty old sweater, she looked like a fresh-faced teen singer. "Unless you go to Vassar or SUNY New Paltz or something and just commute."

"Well, I don't have to decide about that for a while," I said.

"But why worry about your room now?" Mary K. asked.

"I can't take this pink anymore," I said, rolling a swath of paint over the wallpaper.

"Remember when I asked you if you'd had sex?" Mary K. suddenly said, almost making me drop my roller. "With Cal?"

There it was, the familiar wince and stomach clench I felt whenever that name was mentioned.

"Yeah?" I said warily.

"So, did you guys ever do it? After we talked?"

I took a breath and slowly released it to the count of ten. I focused on rolling a smooth, broad line of paint across the wall, feathering the edges and rolling over any drips. "No," I managed to say calmly. "No, we never did." A bad thought occurred to me. "You and Bakker . . ."

"No," she said. "That was why he always got so mad."

She was only fourteen, though a mature and curvy four-teen. I felt incredibly thankful that Bakker hadn't managed to push her further than she was ready to go.

I, on the other hand, was seventeen. I'd always assumed

that Cal and I would make love someday, when I was ready—but the times he'd tried, I said no. I wasn't sure why, though now I wondered if my subconscious had picked up on the fact that I wasn't in a safe situation, that I couldn't trust Cal the way I would need to trust him to go to bed with him. Yet I had loved the other things we had done: the intense making out, how we had touched each other, the way magick had added a whole other dimension to our closeness. Now I would never know what it felt like to make love with Cal.

"How about Hunter?" Mary K. asked, looking down at me thoughtfully from her ladder.

"What about him?" I tried to sound careless, but I couldn't quite pull it off.

"Do you think you'll go to bed with him?"

"Mary K.," I said, feeling my cheeks heat up. "We're not even *dating*. Sometimes we don't even get along."

"That's the way it always starts," Mary K. said with fourteen-year-old wisdom.

We'd started early, so we finished the walls around lunchtime. While I cleaned up the painting equipment, Mary K. went down to the kitchen and made us some sandwiches. Recently she'd gotten into eating healthy food, so the sandwiches were peanut-butter and banana on seven-grain bread. Surprisingly, they were good.

I polished off my sandwich, then took a sip of Diet Coke. "Ah, that hits the spot," I said.

"All that artificial stuff is bad for you," Mary K. said, but her voice was listless. I regarded her with concern. It really was taking her a while to come out of her depression over Bakker.

"Hey. What are you doing this afternoon?" I asked, thinking maybe we could hit the mall, or go to a matinee movie, or do some other sisterly activity.

"Not much. I thought maybe I'd go to the three o'clock mass," she said.

I laughed, startled. "Church on a Monday? What's going on?" I asked. "You becoming a nun?"

Mary K. smiled slightly. "I just feel . . . you know, with everything going on—I just need extra help. Extra support. I can get that at church. I want to be more in touch with my faith."

I sipped my Diet Coke and couldn't think of anything constructive to say. In the silence I suddenly thought, Hunter, and then the phone rang.

I lunged for it. "Hey, Hunter," I said.

"I want to see you," Hunter said with his usual lack of greeting. "There's an antiques fair half an hour from here. I was wondering if you wanted to go."

Mary K. was looking at me, and I raised my eyebrows at her. "An antiques fair?" was my scintillating reply.

"Yes. It could be interesting. It's nearby, in Kaaterskill."

Mary K. was watching the expressions cross my face, and I pantomimed my jaw dropping. "Hunter, is this a date?" I asked for Mary K.'s benefit, and she sat up straighter, looking intrigued.

Silence. I smiled into the phone. "You know, this sort of sounds like a date," I pressed him. "I mean, are we meeting for business reasons?"

Mary K. started snickering quietly.

"We're two friends getting together," Hunter said, sounding very British. "I don't know why you feel compelled to label it."

"Anyone else coming?"

"Well, no."

"And you're not calling it a date?"

"Would you like to come or not?" he asked stiffly. I bit my lip to keep from laughing.

"I'll come," I said, and hung up. "I think Hunter just asked me out," I told Mary K.

"Wow," she said, grinning.

I skipped upstairs to take a shower, wondering how, when my life was so stressful and scary, I could feel so happy.

Hunter picked me up in Sky's car twenty minutes later. My wet hair hung in a long, heavy braid down my back. I offered him a Diet Coke and he shuddered; then we were on our way to Kaaterskill.

"Why did you care if this was a date or not?" he asked suddenly.

I was startled into an honest reply. "I wanted to know where we stand."

He glanced at me. He was really good-looking, and my brain was suddenly bombarded with images of how he had been when we were kissing, how intense and passionate he'd seemed. I looked out my window.

"And where do we stand?" he asked softly. "Do you want this to be a date?"

Now I was embarrassed. "Oh, I don't know."

Then Hunter took my hand in his and brought it to his mouth and kissed it, and my breathing went shallow.

"I want it to be what you want," he said, driving with one hand and not looking at me.

"I'll let you know when I figure it out," I said shakily.


The antiques fair took place in a huge warehouse-like barn in the middle of rural New York. There weren't many people there—it was the last day. Everything looked kind of picked through, but still, I enjoyed the time with Hunter, the time without magick involved. My mood got even better when I found a little carved box that would be perfect for my mom and an old brass barometer that my dad would love. Two Christmas gifts that I could cross off my list. I was woefully behind on my holiday shopping. Christmas was coming up fast, and I'd barely thought about it. Our coven was planning a Yule celebration, too, but fortunately that didn't involve any gift-giving.

I was engrossed in the contents of an old dentist's cabinet when Hunter called me over. "Look at these," he said, pointing to a selection of Amish-type quilts. I'd always liked Amish quilts, with their bright, solid colors and comforting geometry of design. The one Hunter was pointing to was unusual in that it had a circular motif.

"It's a pentacle," I said softly, touching the cotton with my fingertips. "A circle with a star inside." The background was black, with a nine-patch design in each corner in shades of teal, red, and purple. The large circle touched each of the four sides and was of purple cotton. A red five-pointed star filled the circle, and a nine-patch square was centered in the star. It was gorgeous.

I glanced at the middle-aged woman selling the quilts and cast my senses quickly to see if she was a witch. I picked up nothing. "Is it Wiccan?" I asked so only Hunter could hear.

He shook his head. "More likely just a Pennsylvania Dutch hex design. It's pretty, though."

"Beautiful." Again I ran my fingers gently across the cotton.

The next thing I knew, Hunter had pulled out his wallet and was counting out bills into the woman's hand, and she was smiling and thanking him. She took the small quilt, barely more than four feet square, and wrapped it in tissue before putting it into a brown paper bag.

We headed back to Hunter's car. "That's really beautiful," I said. "I'm glad you bought it. Where will you put it?"

We climbed into his car, and he turned to me and handed me the bag. "It's for you," he said. "I bought it because I wanted you to have it."

The air around us crackled, and I wondered if it was magick or attraction or something else. I took the bag and reached my hand inside to feel the cool folds of the quilt. "Are you sure?" I knew neither he nor Sky had much income—this quilt must have put a huge dent in his budget.

"Yes," he said. "I'm quite sure."

"Thank you," I said softly.

He started the car's engine, and we didn't say anything until he dropped me at my house. I climbed out of the car, feeling uncertain all over again. He got out, too, and coming around to the sidewalk, he kissed me, a soft, quick meeting of the lips. Then he climbed back in Sky's car and drove off before I could say good-bye.

# 5.
# Flicker

May 17, 1970

    Spring has finally sprung in Wales. Here in Albertswyth the hills are a new bright green. The women of the village are on their hands and knees, setting plants in their gardens. Clyda and I have been walking over the hills and among the rocks, and she's been teaching me the local herb lore and the properties of the local stone, earth, water, and air. I've been here six months now, on one of life's detours.

    Since I found out about Clyda Rockpel from one of Patrick's spelled books, I was determined to find her, to learn from her. It took two weeks of camping on her doorstep, eating bread and cheese, sleeping with my coat pulled over my head before she would speak to me. Now I'm her student, taking knowledge from her like a sea sponge absorbs ocean water.

*She's deep, dark, terrifying sometimes, yet the glimmers of her power, the breadth of her learning, her strength and guile in dealing with the dark forces fill me with a giddy exhilaration. I want to know what she knows, have the power to do what she does, have control over what she controls. I want to become her.*

*—SB*

On Tuesday, Mary K. and I once again spent the morning working on my room, touching up messy spots on the walls and painting the woodwork. In the afternoon I persuaded my sister to come shopping with Bree and me. The lure of hanging out with us had outweighed her disapproval of our destination: Practical Magick, an occult store up in Red Kill, ten miles north.

"The good thing about Christmas break," Bree said as she drove through downtown Widow's Vale, "is seeing all the poor saps who have to go to work."

"We're going to be poor working saps one day," I reminded her, watching people weaving in and out of the shops on Main Street. I picked at some speckles of paint on the back of my hand and adjusted the heater vent of Breezy, Bree's BMW.

"Not me," Bree said cheerfully. "I'm going to marry rich and be a lady who lunches."

"Gross!" Mary K. protested from the backseat.

Bree laughed. "Not PC enough for you?"

"Don't you want more than that?" Mary K. asked. "You could do anything you want."

"Well, I was kind of kidding," said Bree, not taking offense. "I mean, I haven't figured out what my life calling is yet. But it wouldn't be the worst thing to be a housewife."

"Bree, please," I said, feeling a shade of our old familiarity. "You would last about two weeks. Then you'd go crazy and become an ax murderer."

She laughed. "Maybe so. Neither of you wants to be a housewife? It's a noble profession, you know."

I snorted. I had no concrete idea what to do with my life—I'd always thought vaguely about doing something with math or science—but I knew now without a doubt that the majority of my life would center on Wicca and my own studies in magick. Everything else was optional.

"No," said my sister. "I never want to get married."

Something in her tone made me crane around from the front seat to look at her. Her face looked drawn, almost haunted, in the gray winter light, and her eyes were sad. I glanced across at Bree and was touched by the instant understanding that passed between us.

"I hear you dumped Bakker in a big way," Bree said, looking at Mary K. in the rearview mirror. "Good for you. He's an ass."

Mary K. didn't say anything.

"You know who's cute in your class?" Bree went on. "That Hales kid. What's his name? Randy?"

"Just plain Rand," said Mary K.

"Yeah, him," said Bree. "He's adorable."

I rolled my eyes. Trust Bree to have scoped out the freshman boys.

Mary K. shrugged, and Bree decided not to press it. Then

she pulled Breezy into a parking spot in front of Practical Magick, and we piled out into the chilly December air.

Mary K. looked at the storefront with only faintly disguised suspicion. Like my parents, she strongly disapproved of my involvement with Wicca, though I'd talked her into coming to a party here recently, and she'd enjoyed it.

"Relax," I said, taking her by the arm and pulling her into the store. "You're not going to have your soul sucked out just by looking at candles."

"What if Father Hotchkiss saw us?" she grumbled, naming our church's priest.

"Then we'd have to ask him what he was doing in a Wicca shop, wouldn't we?" I answered, grinning. Inside, I let go of my sister's arm and took a moment to get my bearings. I hadn't been to Practical Magick since I'd come with Hunter to confront David Redstone, the owner, about using dark magick. It had been profoundly horrible, and being in the store brought back the memories in a wave: Hunter questioning David; David's admission of guilt, wrenched from him against his will.

It hurt to associate those memories with this place, the place I had come to think of as my refuge, a lovely, scent-filled shop full of magickal books, essential oils, crystals, herbs, candles, and the deep, abiding peace of Wicca, permeating everything.

Looking up, I saw Alyce, a gentle sorrow still showing on her face. David had been a dear friend of hers. He had turned over the shop to her, a Brightendale blood witch, when he'd had his power stripped from him. She owned the shop now.

She walked toward me, and we embraced: I was taller than she, and I felt bony and immature next to her womanly roundness. We looked into each other's eyes for a moment, not needing to speak. Then I stepped back to include Bree and Mary K.

"Hi, Alyce," Bree said.

"Nice to see you, Bree," Alyce replied.

"You remember my sister, Mary K.?" I asked.

"Certainly," said Alyce, smiling warmly. "The one who was so taken with The Fianna." The Fianna was a Celtic band that Mary K. and I both loved. Alyce's nephew, Diarmuid, played in it. The only way I'd gotten Mary K. to come to the party here was by luring her with promises of The Fianna playing.

"Yes," said Mary K. shyly.

"We just got in a shipment of really interesting jewelry from a woman who works in Pennsylvania," Alyce said, leading Mary K. over to a glass case. "Come see."

I smiled as Mary K. was drawn to the jewelry. Bree moved down the aisle to examine a collection of altar cloths, and I was free to wander the side of the store that was floor-to-ceiling bookshelves. Soon Alyce joined me.

"How is Starlocket?" I asked. Starlocket was Selene Belltower's old coven. With her disappearance, Alyce had been asked to lead it.

"Going through transitions," Alyce said. "Some people have left, of course—those who'd been drawn to Selene's dark side. The rest of us are trying to heal and move forward. It's very challenging, leading a coven."

"I'm sure you're a wonderful leader," I said.

"Alyce?" I looked up as a man came toward us, holding up a box of black candles. "Do we put out all the stock at once or keep some in the back?" he asked.

"I usually put out as much as the shelves will hold," Alyce said. "Finn, come meet Morgan."

Finn looked like he was in his fifties; tall, and neither thin nor fat, but sturdy looking. He had short, thick hair that was a faded red shot through with white. His eyes were hazel, his skin was fair, and he had faded freckles across his nose and cheeks. I sent out my senses without even deciding to and ran a quick scan. Blood witch. Probably Leapvaughn, I thought. They often had red hair. Then I saw the surprise in his eyes and shut down my senses, vaguely embarrassed, as though I'd been caught in the Wiccan equivalent of seeing someone's underwear.

"Hmmm," Finn said thoughtfully, holding out his large hand. "Pleased to meet you, Morgan." He gave Alyce an odd glance, as if she had introduced him to a questionable character.

Alyce smiled. "Morgan, this is Finn Foster. He's helping me in the shop," she explained. To Finn she added, "Morgan is a dedicated customer." She offered no other explanation, and with Finn's eyes on me I felt even more strongly that I had committed a faux pas.

"Who do you study with?" Finn asked.

"Um, right now a lot by myself, and some with Hunter Niall."

Finn blinked. "The Seeker?"

"Yes."

"You're Morgan Rowlands," Finn said, as if he'd just made a connection.

"Yes." I glanced at Alyce uncertainly, but she just smiled reassuringly.

Finn hesitated, as if debating whether to say something more, but then he just smiled and nodded. "Nice meeting you," he said. "Hope to see you again soon." He gave Alyce a glance and took the box of candles to the other side of the store. A moment later I heard Bree asking him about some clover oil. I looked for Mary K. and saw that she was holding some silver earrings up, looking at them in a small mirror.

"What was that about?" I asked Alyce, and she chuckled softly.

"I'm afraid you're a bit notorious," she said. "I'm sorry if you feel like a performing seal, but lots of people have already heard of your power, your heritage—not to mention what happened with Cal and Selene—and they're curious."

Ugh. I shifted uncomfortably.

Alyce reached past me to straighten some books on a shelf. "Has Hunter talked to you about your studies? About tàth meànma brach?"

"Yes," I answered, surprised by the change of subject.

"What do you think of the idea?" Her clear, blue-violet eyes searched mine.

"It sounded exciting," I said slowly. "I want to do it. What do you think about it?"

"I think it might be a good idea," she said, looking thoughtful. "Hunter's right—you need to learn as much as you can as fast as you can. For almost any other witch I would advise against it. It's hard, and I'm sure Hunter told you it can be dangerous. But you're an exceptional case. Of course, it's your decision alone. But you should consider it carefully."

"Would you do it with me?" I asked.

She looked deeply into my eyes. I had no idea how old she was—in her fifties?—but I saw a wealth of knowledge in her gaze. What she knew could help me, and I suddenly wanted her knowledge with a surprising hunger that I tried not to show.

"I'll think about it, my dear," she said quietly. "I'll talk to Hunter, and we can decide."

"Thank you," I whispered.

"Are you about ready?" Bree called down the aisle. Finn had already rung up her purchases; she held a small green bag with silver handles.

"Yes," I called back. "Where's Mary K.?"

"Right here," my sister said, emerging from the other aisle.

"Did you want those earrings you were looking at?" I asked, and she shook her head, her shiny auburn hair swinging around her shoulders. I wondered if she thought buying those earrings would be like taking witchcraft into the house and resolved to try to put her fears to rest on that point. Maybe I could surprise her with them for Christmas.

It was late afternoon when we headed home in Breezy. I was quiet and full of thought about the possibility of doing the tàth meànma brach with Alyce.

"Why do you like that store so much?" Mary K. asked from the backseat.

"Don't you think it's cool?" Bree asked. "Even if I wasn't into Wicca, I would still be into the candles and jewelry and incense and stuff."

"I guess." My sister sounded subdued, and I knew she

was struggling with the conflict of liking anything that had to do with witchcraft while remaining true to her own religion and to my parents. She looked out her window, distant and withdrawn. None of us spoke for several miles, and I looked out my window at the rapidly darkening landscape, the rolling hills, the old farms, the snow clinging to everything. With a start I realized that Bree had taken her old route toward home and that we were in Cal's neighborhood. My heart sped up as we drew closer to the large stone house he had shared with his mother. I hadn't been past here since the night I'd almost died in the pool house, and my skin broke out in a clammy sweat at the memory.

"I'm sorry," Bree murmured as she realized where we were.

I swallowed and didn't say anything, my hand clenching the door handle tightly, my breathing fast and shallow. Relax, I told myself. Relax. They're gone. They're nowhere around. Hunter looks for them—scries for them every day—and he hasn't found them. They're gone. They won't hurt you.

As we passed, my eyes were irresistibly drawn to the house. It looked dark, abandoned, forbidding. I recalled the first floor, with its large kitchen, the huge living room with a fireplace where Cal and I had kissed on the sofa. Selene's hidden, spelled private library that I had found, where I had discovered Maeve's Book of Shadows. Cal's room that ran the length of the attic. His wide, low bed where we had kissed and touched each other. The pool house, where he had trapped me and tried to burn me to death . . .

I felt like I was choking and swallowed again, unable to move my eyes away. Then I stared hard as a flickering light, as if from a candle, passed in front of a dark window. Just one moment and it was gone, but I was sure I had seen it. Wildly I looked over at Bree for her reaction, but her eyes were on the road, her hands poised on the leather steering wheel. In the backseat Mary K. gazed out her window, unhappiness making her face seem younger, rounder.

"Did you—" I started to ask. I stopped. Was I sure I had seen it? I thought so. But what was the point of mentioning it? Mary K. would be upset and worried. Bree wouldn't know what to do, either. If only Hunter was here, I thought, and then grimaced as I realized what would be set in action if Hunter had seen it: a full-blown investigation, worry, trouble, fear.

And had I really seen it? A flickering candle in an abandoned house, at night, for just a moment? I leaned my head against the cold car window, my heart aching. Was this ordeal never going to be over? Would I ever relax again?

"Did we what?" Bree asked, glancing at me.

"Nothing," I mumbled. Surely it had been my imagination. Cal and Selene were gone. "Never mind."

# 6.
# The Lueg

*March 18, 1971*

At the age of twenty-seven, I have completed the Great Trial. It was four days ago, and I am only now able to hold a pen and sit up to write. Clyda thought I was ready, and I was so eager to do it that I didn't listen to the people who warned me not to.

The Great Trial. I have wondered how to describe it, and when my words get close, I want to cry. Twenty-seven is young—many people are never ready. Most people, when they do it, are older, have been preparing for years. But I insisted I was ready, and in the end Clyda agreed.

It took place on top of Windy Tor, past the Old Stones left by the Druids. Below me I could hear the waves crashing against rocks in a timeless rhythm. There was no moon, and it was as black as the end of the world. With me were

Clyda and another Welsh witch, Scott Mattox. I was naked, sky clad, and we cast the circle and started the rite. At midnight Clyda held out the goblet. I stared at it, knowing I was scared. It was the Wine of Shadows: where she had gotten it, I don't know. If I passed the Great Trial, I would live. If I didn't pass, this wine would kill me. I took the goblet with a shaking hand and drank it.

Clyda and Scott sat nearby, staying to keep me from going over the edge of the cliff. I sat down, my lips numb, muttering all the spells of power and strength that I knew. Then the first needlelike tingles of pain started in my fingertips, and I cried out.

It was a long, long night.

And here I am, alive, on the other side. I am wasted by fasting, by vomiting, by a sharp-edged sickness in my gut that makes me wonder if they fed me glass. This morning I saw myself in the mirror and screamed at the dull-haired, hollow-eyed, greatly aged woman I beheld. Clyda says not to worry: my beauty will come back with my strength. What is it to her? She was never beautiful and has no idea how it feels to lose it.

Yet hollowed out as I am, like a tree struck by lightning, I can tell the difference. I was strong before, but now I'm a force of nature. I feel like wind, like rain, like lava in my strength. I'm in tune with the universe, my heart beating to its primordial, deeply held thrum. I'm made of *magick, I'm walking magick, and I can cause death or life with a snap of my fingers.*

*Was the Great Trial worth this? The illness, the screaming agony, the clawed, ripped hands, the gouges in my thighs made when I was shrieking in terror and desperation and trying to feel anything normal, anything recognizable, even physical pain? My brain was split open and put on display, my body was turned inside out. Yet in the destruction is the resurrection, in the agony is the joy, in the terror is the hope. And now I've taken that terrible, mortal journey and I've come through it. And I'll be like a Goddess myself, and lesser beings will follow me. And I'll found a dynasty of witches that will amaze the world.*

*—SB*

"So if your mother comes home, what should I do?" Hunter asked. "I mean, is she going to hit me with a cooking pan?"

I grinned. "Only if she's in a bad mood." It was Wednesday, my parents were at work, Mary K. was upstairs, and we were getting ready to study. "Anyway, I told you I could come to your place," I reminded him.

"Sky and Raven are at my place," he said. "I assume they wanted privacy."

"Really?" I asked with interest. "Are they getting serious?"

"I didn't come here to gossip," he said primly, and I wanted to smack him. I was trying to think of a clever reply when he looked around the kitchen restlessly.

"Let's go up to your room," he said, and I blinked.

"Uh," I began. Boys were *so* not allowed upstairs in our house.

"You said you'd made an altar," he said. "I want to see it. Your room is where you do most of your magick, right?" He stood up, pushing his hand through his pale hair, and I tried to gather my thoughts.

"Um." The only time Cal had ever been in my room was just for a minute, after Bree had almost broken my nose during a volleyball game at school. Even then my mom had gotten twitchy, despite the fact that I was a total invalid and hardly feeling romantic.

"Come on, Morgan," he coaxed. "We're working. I'll try not to jump you, if that's what you're afraid of."

My face burned with embarrassment, and I wondered what he would do to me if I zapped him with witch fire. I was almost willing to find out.

"Sorry," he said. "Let's start over. Please, may I see the altar you made in your room? If your parents come home unexpectedly, I'll do a quick look-over-there spell and get the hell out of here, okay? I don't want to get you in trouble."

"It's just that it's my parents' house," I said stiffly, standing up and leading the way toward the foyer. "I try to respect their rules when I can. But let's go up quickly. I want you to see it." I plodded up the stairs, intensely aware of his quiet tread behind me.

I was thankful that my room was no longer pink and stripy. Sea grass window shades replaced my frilly curtains, complementing my new café-au-lait-colored walls. The old cream-colored carpet had been pulled up, and I had a simple jute area rug instead. I loved my new room but stood nervously by my desk as Hunter looked around, taking it all in. I went to the closet and pulled out the old camp footlocker that served as my altar, complete with violet linen cloth, candles, and four special objects that represented the four elements.

My single bed seemed to take on mythic proportions, almost filling the room, and I blushed furiously, trying to wipe the image of Hunter + bed out of my mind.

He looked at my altar.

"It's pretty basic," I muttered. "It's hard because I have to keep it hidden."

He nodded, then glanced up at me. "It's fine. Nice. Perfectly appropriate. I'm glad you made one." His voice was calm, reassuring. I pushed the altar back in my closet and artfully draped my bathrobe to cover it. Should we go back downstairs? I wondered, but as I came out of my closet, I saw that Hunter was sitting casually on my bed, his fingers playing with the smooth texture of my down comforter. With no warning I wanted to throw myself on him, press him down against the mattress, kiss him, be physically aggressive in a way I never had with Cal. And then of course as soon as that thought crossed my brain, I recoiled, knowing with certainty how attuned Hunter was to my every feeling. Oh, man.

But his face remained neutral, and he said, "Have you been memorizing the true names of things?"

"Sort of," I said, feeling guilty. I hadn't done much studying since the David incident, but before that I'd made a start on my memorization. I pulled out my desk chair and sat down in it, and at that moment Mary K. tapped lightly on the door and came in, not waiting for me to invite her. She stopped dead when she saw Hunter sitting on my bed, her mouth open in an almost comical O. She looked from him to me and back again, and even Hunter grinned at her expression, his normally serious face lighting up, making him look younger and lighthearted.

"We have to get a lock for that door," he said cheerfully, and I wanted to die. My sister's eyebrows rose, and she looked fascinated.

"I'm sorry," Mary K. said. "I just wanted to ask you about dinner—but I'll come back later."

"No, wait," I started to say, but she had already whirled out the door, closing it behind her with an audible click. I glanced back at Hunter to see him grinning again.

"I feel like a fox in a henhouse full of Catholic girls," he said, looking pleased. "This is doing wonders for my ego."

"Oh, like your ego needs help," I retorted, then wanted to bite my tongue.

But Hunter didn't take offense and instead said, "What names have you been studying?"

Huge, long freaking lists, I wanted to say. I took a deep breath and said, "Um, wildflowers and herbs of this geographic zone, ones that bloom in spring, summer, and fall and are dormant in winter. Ones that are poisonous. Plants that can counteract spells, either good or bad. Plants that neutralize energy." I named ten or eleven of them, starting with maroc dath—mayapple—then paused, hoping he was suitably impressed. Learning just the English or Latin names of hundreds of different plants would have been quite a feat, but I had also learned their true names, their magickal names, by which I could use them in spells, find them, increase or decrease their properties.

Hunter, however, looked underwhelmed. His green eyes were impassive. "And under what condition would you use maroc dath in a spell?"

I hesitated, something about his voice making me think carefully about his question. Maroc dath, maroc dath—I knew it as mayapple, a wild plant with a white flower that bloomed before the last frost of the year . . . used to clarify potions, to make a healing ointment, to . . .

Then I got it. Maroc dath wasn't mayapple. "I meant maroc *dant,*" I said with dignity. "Maroc dant. Mayapple." I tried to remember if maroc dath was something.

"So you're not studying spells in which you use menstrual blood," Hunter said, his eyes on mine. "Maroc dath. Menstrual blood, usually that of a virgin. Used primarily in dark rites, occasionally in fertility spells. That's not what you meant?"

Okay, now I wanted the earth to swallow me. I closed my eyes. "No," I said faintly. "That's not what I meant."

When I opened my eyes again, he was shaking his head. "What would happen if you did that in a spell?" he asked rhetorically. "What happens if you don't know all of this and therefore make errors in your spells?"

My first instinct was to throw a pillow at him. Then I remembered that he was trying to get me to learn so I would be protected. He was trying to help me. I remembered that I had told him I trusted him, and that it had been true.

With my next breath an awareness came over me, something unconnected to what Hunter and I were talking about, and my eyes widened and flew to his face.

"Do you feel it?" I whispered, and he nodded slightly, his whole body tense and still. I moved cautiously toward him, and he reached out his hand to clasp mine. Someone was scrying for me, someone was trying to find me. I sat next to Hunter on the bed, barely conscious of the warmth of his thigh against mine. As one, we closed our eyes and sent out our senses, dissolving the barriers between us and the world, reaching out toward our unseen spy as he or she reached out toward us.

I began to get a sense of a person, a person shape, an energy pattern—and in the next instant it was gone, snuffed as quickly as a candle, without even a wisp trail of smoke to lead me to it. I opened my eyes.

"Interesting," Hunter muttered. "Did you get an identity?"

I shook my head and untangled my fingers from his. He looked down at our hands as if he hadn't known they were joined.

"I have something to tell you," I said, and then I gave him the story of possibly seeing a candle in a window at Cal's house the day before.

"Why didn't you tell me immediately?" he asked, looking angry.

"It just happened last night," I began, defending myself. Then I stopped. He was right, of course. "I—I didn't know what to do," I offered awkwardly. "I figured I was making a big deal out of nothing, just being paranoid." I stood up, moved away from the bed, and pushed my hair over my shoulder.

"Morgan of course you should have told me," Hunter said. His jaw tensed. "Unless you have a good reason not to."

What was he trying to say? "Yes," I said sarcastically. "That's it. I'm in league with Cal and Selene, and I didn't want to tell you because when I *give* myself to the dark side, I *won't* want you to know about it."

Hunter looked like I had slapped him, and he stood quickly, so we were only inches apart and he was towering over me, bright spots of anger appearing on his fair cheeks. His hands gripped my shoulders, and my eyes widened. I jerked away from him, slapping his hands away, and we stared at each other.

"Don't ever joke about that again," he said in a low voice. "That isn't funny. How can you even say something like that after what you saw David Redstone go through?"

I gasped, remembering, and to my horror, hot tears welled in my eyes. It *had* been stupid and appalling to throw that at Hunter after seeing it in reality. What had I been thinking?

Deliberately Hunter stepped back, away from me, and pushed his hand through his hair. A muscle in his jaw twitched, and I knew he was trying hard to control himself.

"I never lose my temper," he muttered, not looking at me. "My whole job, my whole life is about being calm and objective and rational." Then he glanced up, and his eyes were like green water, cool and clear and beautiful, and I felt caught by them, the fire of my anger doused. "What is it about you that gets under my skin? Why do you get to me?" He shook his head.

"We just rub each other the wrong way sometimes," I said clumsily, sinking back down into my desk chair.

"Is that what you think it is?" he asked cryptically. He sat down on my bed again, and I had no idea how to answer him. "All right," he said, "back to the candle. I believe that you saw something. Selene's house has been spelled inside and out with ward-evil, confusion, barrier spells, you name it. A member of the council and I worked for hours after the fire, trying to seal the house and dispel the negative energy from it. Obviously we didn't do enough."

"Do you think it's Cal, or Selene, back inside?" I asked. Had that been Cal I saw in the window, Cal, so close?

"I don't know. I can't see how they could get in, after everything we did. But I can't dismiss the possibility. I'll have to check into it."

Of course he would. He was a Seeker. I realized then that I hadn't wanted to tell him in case it *had* been Cal I'd seen. Even after all that Cal had done, I didn't want Hunter to be seeking him. A vision of David Redstone, weeping and writhing as his power left him, rose up in my mind. I couldn't bear the thought of Cal suffering the same torment.

Hunter's face was serious and still. "Look," he said, standing up and reaching into his backpack. "Let's scry together, right now, joining our energy. Let's just see what happens." He took a purple silk bundle out of the backpack and unwrapped it. Inside was a large, dark, flattish stone. "This was my father's lueg," he said, his voice expressionless. "Have you scryed with a stone before?"

I shook my head. "Only with fire."

"Stones are as reliable as fire," he told me, sitting cross-legged on the floor. "Fire is harder to work with but offers more information. Come sit down."

I sat across from him, our knees touching, as if we were

about to do tàth meànma. Leaning forward, I looked into the flat, polished face of the stone, feeling the familiar excitement of exploring something new in Wicca. My hair draped forward, brushing the stone. Quickly I gathered it at the base of my neck and with practiced gestures twisted it into a braid. I didn't bother securing the end but let it hang behind me.

"It seems like not too many girls have long hair anymore," Hunter said absently. "They all have short, layery . . ." He motioned with his hands, unable to come up with the vocabulary to describe modern do's.

"I know," I said. "I think about cutting it sometimes. But I hate fussing with a style. This way I never have to think about it."

"It's beautiful," Hunter said. "Don't cut it." Then he blinked and became businesslike, while I once again tried to get my bearings on the peaks and valleys of our interaction. "Right. Now, this is just the same as scrying with fire. You open yourself to the world, accept what knowledge the universe offers you, and try to not think: just be. Just like with fire."

"Got it," I said, still processing the fact that Hunter liked my hair.

"Good. Now, we're looking for Cal or Selene," Hunter said, his voice softening and fading.

We leaned toward each other, our heads almost touching, our hands joined lightly on the lueg. It was like looking into a black pool in a woods, I thought. Like looking down a well. As my breathing shifted and slowed and my consciousness expanded gently into the space around me, the lueg began to seem like a hole in the universe, an opening into incomprehensible wonders, answers, possibilities.

I could no longer feel anything physically: I was suspended in time, in space, and only existed because of my thoughts and my energy. I felt Hunter's life force near mine, felt his warmth, his presence, his intelligence, and nothing startled me. Everything was fine.

In the face of the stone I began to see swirls of gray mist, like striated clouds, and I released any expectations I'd had and simply watched to see what they would become. Then it was like watching a video or a moving photograph: I saw a person, walking toward me, as if looking into a camera. It was a middle-aged man, a handsome man, and he looked both surprised and alarmed and intensely curious. I'd seen him before, but I couldn't think where.

"Goddess," Hunter muttered, his breath suddenly coming sharp and fast. I felt my consciousness flare.

"Gìomanach," said the man softly. His face was lined, his hair gray, his eyes brown. But there was something of Hunter in the shape of his jaw, the angle of his cheek.

"Dad," Hunter said, sounding strangled.

I gasped. Hunter hadn't seen either of his parents in ten years, and though we'd talked about the possibility of his trying to find them, as far as I knew, he'd done nothing about it yet. What was happening?

"Gìomanach," said the man again. "You're grown. My son . . ." He looked away. In the background I could barely make out a house, painted white. I heard a seagull cry faintly and wondered where Hunter's father had been all this time, where he was now.

"Dad," Hunter said. I felt the coiled tension of his emotions; it almost caused me pain. "Linden—"

"I know," said the man, looking older and sadder. "I know. Beck told us how your brother died. It wasn't your fault. It was his own fate. Listen, my son—your mother—"

Then the picture changed as a dark presence washed across the face of the lueg. It was like a cloud, a purple-black vapor roiling across the lueg, and Hunter and I watched unspeaking as the dark wave focused and concentrated, blotting out his father's face, the whitewashed window.

With a jolt Hunter snapped back, straightening, his eyes flicking open to stare widely at me, and I gazed at him, seeing his pale face as the grounding of my reality.

My temples were damp with sweat, and my hands were shaking. I rubbed my palms against my corduroys and tried to swallow but couldn't. I knew I had just seen the dark wave in the stone—the dark wave that had consumed my ancestors and almost every member of my ancestral coven almost twenty years before. The dark wave that we believed was somehow connected to Selene.

Hunter spoke first. "Do you think the dark wave took my father just then?" he asked, his voice hoarse.

"No!" I said strongly. He looked so lost. Without thinking I rose to my knees and clasped him in my arms, cradling his head against my chest. "I'm almost sure it didn't. It was more like it passed in front of the stone. Between us and him. I can't believe it, Hunter, that was your father. He's alive!"

"Yes," Hunter said. "I believe he is." He paused, then said. "I wonder what he was trying to tell me about Mum."

I was silent, unable to think of anything comforting to tell him.

"I've got to tell the council," he mumbled against my shirt.

After a few moments he pulled back slightly, and reached up to brush my damp hair away from my face. I looked in his eyes and couldn't read the emotions there. Cal's emotions had always seemed so transparent: desire, admiration, light-hearted flirtation. Hunter was still mostly unreadable to me.

Then I thought, To hell with it, and before either of us realized it, I bent down, put my hands on his shoulders, and pressed my lips against his, keeping my eyes open. I saw the flash of surprise, the sudden ignition of desire, and then his eyes drifted closed and he pulled me backward with him to the floor. I was on top of him, his chest against mine, our legs tangled together.

I don't know how long we lay against the hard floor, the unforgiving jute rug, kissing again and again, but finally I heard a furtive tap on my door and Mary K.'s quiet voice: "Mom just pulled up."

Flushed, breathing hard, I trotted downstairs and helped Mom unload groceries from her car, and ten minutes later when I went back to my room, Hunter was gone, and I had no idea how he had managed to leave without any of us noticing.

# 7.
# Circle of Three

November 8, 1973

Clyda fainted again yesterday. I found her at the bottom of the stairs. This is the third time in two weeks. Neither of us have mentioned it, but the fact is that she is old. She hasn't taken care of herself, she's worked too much magick with too few limitations, and she's dabbled too freely with the dark forces.

That's a mistake I never make. Yes, I'm part of Turneval, and yes, I call on the dark side. But never without protecting myself. Never without precautions. I don't drink from that cauldron without making sure it will be refilled.

At any rate, Clyda's health is Clyda's concern. She doesn't ask for or want my care, and now I need her less and less in my studies. Since the Great Trial, I can learn *anything easily; of course, the strength and the weakness of Wicca is that there's always more to be learned.*

*I just reread this entry and can't believe I'm yapping on about an old woman's health when just last night my life changed again. Clyda finally introduced me to some members of her coven, Amyranth. Even now my skin gets chilled, just writing the name. I won't lie: they terrify me, by reputation, by their very existence. And yet I'm so drawn to them and their mission. I have no doubt I was meant to be part of them. From birth I was marked to be in Amyranth, and to deny that would be lying to myself. Oh, I have to go — Clyda is calling.*

*—SB*

There were only four other cars in the parking lot of St. Mary's when I pulled in to drop off Mary K. Probably thirty years ago, weekday-morning services were more attended, but nowadays it seemed amazing that Father Hotchkiss bothered to have them at all.

"You sure you want to go?" I asked Mary K. "Wouldn't you rather just go get coffee instead?"

My sister shook her head but made no move to get out of the car.

"What's going on, Mary K.?" I asked. "You seem so unhappy lately. Is it because of Bakker?"

Again she shook her head, looking out her window. "Not just Bakker," she said finally. "All guys. I mean, look at you and Cal. And Bree and all her boy toys. Guys are just . . ."

"Losers?" I suggested. "Jerks? Imbeciles?"

She didn't smile. "I just don't get it," she said. "It's just—I feel like I never want to date again. Never want to be vulnerable again. And I hate that. I don't want to go through my whole life alone."

I closed my mouth hard before I could say something stupid like, You're only fourteen, don't worry about it.

Instead I said, "I know how you feel."

She looked at me, troubled, and I nodded.

"I feel the same way sometimes. I mean, Cal was my first boyfriend, and look what a mistake that turned out to be. After that, how can I ever be sure of any guy again?"

"You can be sure of Hunter," she said. "He's a good guy."

"I think so. But then I think, Cal seemed like a good guy, too." I grimaced. "You know what the really sick thing is?"

"What?"

"I miss Cal," I admitted. "I felt like I knew him, like I understood him. Now I know he was lying to me, using me, setting me up. But it didn't feel that way at the time, so I don't remember it that way. I'm drawn to Hunter, really drawn to him, but I feel like I don't know him and never will."

We sat in Das Boot, feeling depressed. Instead of cheering her up, I had only brought myself down. "I'm sorry," I said. "I didn't mean to go off on my own problems."

"Want to come to church with me?" Mary K. asked with a touch of humor.

"No." I gave a tiny laugh. "Want to come to Practical Magick with me?"

"No. Well, I'd better go in. I'll walk home after. Thanks for the ride."

"Sure."

"And thanks for talking, too." She gave me a sweet smile. "You're a good sister."

"You are, too," I said. I loved her so much. She got out and walked up the church steps, and I put Das Boot in gear and headed north, to Red Kill and Practical Magick.

I'd come to Practical Magick looking for Christmas gifts, but once I got there, I realized I really wasn't in the mood to shop. I've got time, I told myself. I'd get those silver earrings for Mary K., and then everyone in my immediate family would be accounted for. That left my aunt Eileen and her girlfriend Paula, my aunt Maureen and her husband and kids, and Robbie . . . and after that I was in a gray area. Should I give Hunter a gift? It seemed almost too intimate for whatever our relationship was—but on the other hand, he'd bought me my beautiful hex quilt. And then what about Bree? Were we exchanging gifts this year or not? I sighed. Why did it all have to be so confusing?

A comforting voice interrupted my thoughts. "You look like you need to take your mind off your troubles. Come up and see my new apartment," Alyce suggested. After David's departure, she'd moved into one of the apartments upstairs from the store; it had been David's aunt Rosaline's apartment. David had inherited the shop—and Rosaline's considerable debts—when she'd died not long ago. Trying to find a way out of the debts was what had led him into his disastrous experiment with dark magick. Now that Alyce owned Practical Magick, she was paying back the money Rosaline had owed, on a long-term schedule.

Alyce told Finn where we'd be, and then we went out the front doors. "Since I'm running the shop, it makes sense to live close by, and it saves on rent," Alyce explained. Outside were three other doors, all in a line to the right of the store's glass double entrance. Alyce unlocked the door in the middle, and we went up a steep, narrow wooden staircase.

At the top of the stairs were two small, narrow apartments. Alyce led me through the door on the left. The living room was small and bare but freshly painted a warm cream color. Sitting on a surprisingly modern couch was Sky Eventide, reading a leather-bound book.

"Hey," I said. I hadn't seen her since last Saturday's circle.

"Hi," she answered, searching my face. I wondered if Hunter had told her about our vision of his father and about the dark wave.

"Sky and I have been working together," Alyce explained, stepping into the tiny windowless kitchen to make tea. I sat down on a large pillow on the floor.

"When you came in today, I thought maybe the three of us could have a circle," Alyce went on, getting out cups and saucers. "It'll help center you, Morgan. Also, you and Sky are both working with unanswered questions, and it could be helpful."

I thought about the two circles I had been to recently where my powers had been nonexistent and dreaded the idea of feeling that again.

"Yeah, okay," I said, taking the cup of tea that Alyce offered me.

Our circle was small, just the three of us, and somehow intensely *Alyce:* open, receptive, nurturing, strong, very womanly.

We stood, hands linked, in the middle of the living room. Pale winter sun streamed through the windows. Closing our eyes, we each chanted our personal power calls.

"An di allaigh, ne ullah," I began.

Sky and Alyce each quietly chanted to themselves: Alyce's was in English, while Sky's sounded more like mine, Celtic, old, incomprehensible. Three times we walked deasil around our central candle. By the third cycle I felt power flowing from Sky's fingers to mine, from my fingers to Alyce's. The power had a distinct and different quality: eternal, life enhancing.

Then Alyce invoked the four elements, the Goddess and the God, and said, "Lady and Lord, we are each on a personal quest. Please help us to be open to the answers that the universe provides. Please help us open our minds to the world's wisdom.

"My quest is as leader of Starlocket," Alyce went on. "Help me open my consciousness to receive the wisdom I need to guide the women and men of my coven. Help me understand why I have been chosen as leader. Help me fulfill my duties with love."

Then her blue-violet eyes were on Sky, and she nodded. Sky looked thoughtful, then said, "My quest is . . . whether I'll live up to my parents' heritage. Whether my magick will be as strong, as pure as theirs."

I looked at her, surprised to hear her doubt her own power and ability. She'd always struck me as arrogant, even overconfident, and I knew she had much more knowledge and spellcraft than I did. Now I saw that she had weaknesses, too.

Alyce looked at me, and I felt unprepared. This wasn't what I had come here for, and I had no ready statement. Which quest should I mention? I had so many unanswered questions: about Cal, Selene, Maeve's tools, my natural father, Hunter, Bree. . . . Where to begin?

"No, dear," Alyce said softly. "It's more than that."

Oh. Then I thought of the circle we'd had at Sharon's house, and it came to me. "My personal quest is about my own nature," I said, knowing it was true as the words left my mouth. "Am I more likely to lean toward evil because of my Woodbane blood? Will I have to fight it twice as hard as anyone else? How can I learn to recognize evil when I see it? Am I . . . can I escape the darkness?"

I felt rather than saw Alyce's approval that I had found the right questions, and Sky's piqued interest and slight alarm. We held hands for a moment longer, just standing there, and I felt the power flowing among the three of us, almost like an electric current. I am strong, I thought. And I have good friends. Hunter, Robbie, Bree, Alyce, even Sky—they would all stand by me and help me to make the right choices. For a moment I held that sure knowledge in my mind, and it gave me a sense of comfort and peace.

Then we walked widdershins three times, Alyce disbanded our circle, and we snuffed the candle.

"Thank you both," Alyce said. She began to put away her ritual cups. "Now my apartment will be blessed with good energy. And we've each found a question in our hearts that must be answered before we move forward."

"How do we find the answer?" Sky asked, sounding frustrated.

Alyce laughed and said gently, "That's part of the question, I'm afraid."

We stayed in Alyce's apartment for another half hour or so, just talking, enjoying one another's company. Then Alyce had to go back to the shop, so Sky and I reluctantly left. "That was nice," Sky said as we came out onto the street.

"Yeah." I smiled, enjoying the moment of uncomplicated friendliness.

"Well, see you later." She walked down the street to where her car was parked.

As I started Das Boot, I thought about our circle. Oddly, I felt more afraid than I had before, now that I had openly acknowledged my greatest fear. I kept glancing over my shoulder the whole way home, as if expecting the dark wave to loom up in my rearview mirror.

Not really thinking, I started to take the road home that led past Cal's old house. At the last minute I realized what I was doing and swerved back into my lane, causing an angry honk from in back of me. I made an I'm-sorry kind of wave and took another route home. I didn't want to pass his house. Not today.

# 8.
# Attacked

Last night my two-year apprenticeship with Amyranth ended. So much has changed in my life in the past five years. When I think back to who and what I was, it's like looking back at a different lifetime, a different person. Who I am now is so much more intense and fulfilling.

We're in northern Scotland now, and it's as bleak and forbidding a place as there is. The land is wild here, and I love it, even though I know I wasn't meant to live here. But here we are, and my bones are soaking up the power that seeps from the very rocks in this place.

Two years ago, when I was inducted into Amyranth, I'd heard only vague rumors of dark waves. Since then there have been three events that I know of, but I wasn't allowed to participate in them or know the details. Last night that changed.

*The coven we took was Wyndenkell, and it was older than anyone knew. It had existed for at least 450 years. I can't imagine that. In America, most of our covens have existed for less than a hundred. The magick here is ancient and compelling, which is why we wanted it.*

*I'm bound not to describe the event, nor what we did to call the wave. But I will say that it was the most terrifying, exhilarating event I've ever witnessed. The sight of the huge, fierce wave, the purplish black color of a bruise, sweeping over the gathered circle—feeling its icy wind snatching the souls and power of the witches, feeling its energy being fused into me, like lightning—well, I'm a changed woman, a changed witch. I'm a daughter of Amyranth, and that fact alone gives my life meaning and joy.*

*Now the Wyndenkell coven's knowledge and magick are ours. As they should be.*

*—SB*

"Now, this is a nice car," Hunter said, running his hand over Breezy's leather seats. "German engineering, fuel efficient."

My eyes narrowed. Was that a dig against Das Boot? It wasn't my car's fault that it was made before fuel economy became a desired trait. I tried to glare at Hunter, but I couldn't hold a grudge. It was just too beautiful a Friday, sunny, perfectly clear, and almost forty degrees. To have even a little break from the hellish winter we'd been having was a treat.

"Yeah, I like it," Bree said from the front seat. She navigated the on-ramp smoothly, and then we were on the highway, headed toward the nearby town of Greenport. Its downtown area had lots of cute shops and restaurants, and Bree had talked Robbie and me into an outing. After which I'd taken my nerve in both hands and called to invite Hunter to come, too. It wasn't exactly a date, but I was starting to feel more and more like we were a couple.

"Did you speak to the council about what we saw in the scrying stone?" I asked Hunter in a low voice.

He nodded. "I told Kennet Muir, my mentor. He promised the council would look into it. He warned me not to scry again, that it would only lead the dark wave to Mum and Dad. I know he's right, but . . ." He trailed off. I heard the impatience and frustration in his voice. I knew exactly how he felt. Even to know they were dead would in some ways be better than this constant state of limbo. I reached over and took his hand.

He turned to me, and we shared a look that seemed to melt my very soul. When had I ever felt so in tune with anyone?

"I know," he whispered, and I understood that he was saying he shared my feelings. My heart soared, and the bright day suddenly seemed almost too brilliant to bear.

Robbie turned around to look at me and Hunter. "Chip?" he offered, holding out the bag.

It was only ten-thirty in the morning, but I took a handful of barbecue-flavor potato chips and crunched them. With a particularly English look, Hunter declined. I hid a smile.

"Can I have a chip?" Bree asked.

Robbie fed one to her, watching her with an endearing combination of adoration and lust.

I ate another handful of chips and popped open a Diet Coke. Hunter gazed at me steadily, and I tried very hard not to think about making out with him on the floor of my room. "Nature's perfect beverage," I said, holding up the can. He grimaced and looked away.

"What an amazing day," Bree said, stretching in her seat.

"Thanks to me and my weather charm," I said lightly.

Robbie and Hunter both looked at me in alarm. "You didn't," said Robbie.

"You didn't," said Hunter.

I was enjoying this. "Maybe I did, maybe I didn't."

Hunter looked upset. "You can't be serious!"

Cahn't, I thought. Cahn too.

"Have you learned nothing these past weeks?" he asked. "Weather-working is not something to be taken lightly. You have no idea of the consequences this could have. How could you possibly have toyed with improper magick in this way?"

I met Bree's eyes in the rearview mirror. Instantly a smile broke across her face; she alone could tell I was teasing. It felt so wonderful to be driving somewhere again with her. The last three months had been desolate without her. We had a long way to go toward rebuilding our relationship, but we were making progress, and it felt great.

"You don't understand what the council—" Hunter went on, really getting wound up.

"Relax, Hunter," I said, taking pity on him. "I was just kidding. I don't even know how to work weather magick."

"Wha—what?" he sputtered.

"I don't even know how to work weather magick," I

repeated. "And I certainly have learned my lesson about the improper use of magick. Yes, sir. You won't catch me doing *that* again." I took a deep, satisfying swig of Diet Coke.

Hunter drummed his fingers on his door handle and looked out the window. After a moment a reluctant grin crept across his face, and I felt a burst of delight.

"By the way," he said a few minutes later, "I went into Selene's house and checked it out, looking for the source of that candle you saw. I didn't find any trace of anything, neither a person nor any magick."

"What candle at Cal's?" Robbie asked.

"I thought I saw someone holding a flickering candle in the window of Cal's old house," I explained.

Robbie looked startled and alarmed. "Yikes."

"So you didn't see footprints or anything?" I asked Hunter.

"No. It's already dusty inside, and the dust was undisturbed," Hunter said. "I wanted to have another go at getting into Selene's hidden library, but once again I couldn't find the door." He shook his head in frustration. "She has incredibly strong magick, I'll say that for her."

"Hmmm," I said, thinking. I had been in that library only once, by accident, when I had found Maeve's Book of Shadows. I wondered if I could get into it again. The International Council of Witches would surely want to see what, if anything, was left in that room. But I just couldn't face it. I never wanted to go in that house again. I wanted to help Hunter but just couldn't bring myself to offer to do this.

"Hey, Bree, you'll be getting off at the next exit," said Robbie, who was navigating.

"Okay," said Bree.

We didn't talk much about magick after that. I started thinking about the circle I'd had with Sky and Alyce yesterday. I knew I needed to learn more about my heritage, my birth parents, but I was at a loss as to where to begin. They'd died more than fifteen years before, and they'd known no one, had no close friends that I knew of, in America.

When I'd first found out that I was adopted, I'd read every newspaper article I'd found about the fire that killed my birth parents. I'd also found Maeve's Book of Shadows hidden in Selene's library (which probably should have tipped me off that Selene wasn't as open and giving as she seemed), and in the last few weeks I'd read it cover to cover. I'd even found secret passages detailing Maeve's passionate and tragic love affair with a man other than Angus, my birth father. I had Maeve's magickal tools, which she'd helped me to find through a vision.

But all that knowledge wasn't enough. It didn't fill in the gaping holes in my understanding of Maeve and Angus as *people*—and as Woodbane witches.

As I thought, the miles flew by, and then suddenly we were in Greenport, and Robbie was saying he was ready for lunch.

It was a happy, carefree day. We walked around, shopped, ate, laughed. I found a beautiful necklace of glass beads and twisted wire in a craft shop, and bought it to give Bree for Christmas, deciding on the spot to take the initiative. Someone had to be bold if we were going to put our friendship back together.

We all went home in the afternoon, and my aunt Eileen and her girlfriend Paula came over for dinner. Aunt Eileen, my mom's younger sister, is my favorite aunt, and I was glad to see them. I was even gladder to hear that they were settling into their new home. They'd recently moved to a house in the nearby town of Taunton, and at first they'd been harassed by a bunch of gay-bashing teenagers. Happily, those kids had been arrested, and the rest of the neighbors seemed to be going out of their way to make Aunt Eileen and Paula feel welcome.

At about eight-thirty I said my goodnights to everyone and headed out to my car. Our coven was having its weekly circle a day early this week, because a couple of people had holiday obligations with their families on Saturday night. The circle would be at Hunter and Sky's house.

The beautiful day had flowed into an equally beautiful winter evening. I felt I hadn't seen the stars for ages, and I relished looking at them through Das Boot's windshield.

"Morgan."

In one second my heart stopped cold. I slammed on the brakes, and my car swerved to the right. When I recovered, I wheeled around and scanned the backseat frantically, then looked at the seat next to me, which was of course empty. That voice. Quickly I reached over and pushed down all the door locks and peered out into the darkness.

It had been Cal, Cal's voice, calling me, as he had done many times before. A witch message. *Where was he?* He was searching for me. Was he nearby? My heart pounded, and adrenaline flooded my body so that my hands were shaky on the steering wheel. Cal! Oh Goddess. Where was he? What did he want?

My next thought was that I had to get to Hunter. Hunter would know what to do.

I sat for a moment, willing my body to stop trembling. Then I put my car back in gear and pulled out again onto the road. I cast my senses out as strongly as I could. I drove carefully, trying to interpret the feelings and impressions I got, but there was no Cal anywhere in them: no voice, no image, no heartbeat.

Cal. The instantaneous tug of my heart horrified and angered me. For one moment, when I'd heard his voice, my heart had leaped in eager anticipation. How stupid *are* you? I asked myself furiously. How big an idiot?

With my senses still at their most alert, I turned down Hunter's street and parked along his dark, weedy curb. Still no inkling of Cal's presence. But could I be sure my senses were correct? I cast a fearful look around me, then ducked through the opening in the hedge and headed up the narrow path to Hunter and Sky's ramshackle house.

A few feet from the front stairs the sound of voices and laughter from around back stopped me, and I picked my way impatiently through the dead grass and clumps of old snow, down the sloping lawn to their back porch. Hunter, I thought. I need you. I had made a mistake in not telling Hunter about the candle in Cal's house. This I knew I had to tell him right away.

"Yo! Morganita," Robbie called, and I looked up to see him hanging over the side of the deck. The house had been built into the side of a steep hill, so in front there were only four steps to the porch, but in back the porch was on the second story, supported by long wood pilings. Dropping off sharply behind the house, the hill turned into a steep, rocky ravine that was wild and beautiful during the day, dark and ominous at night.

"Hey," I called. "Where's Hunter?" I heard Bree's voice, and Jenna's laugh, and smelled the spicy, comforting scent of clove and cinnamon and apples.

"Right here," Hunter called.

I looked up at him, sending him a message. I need to talk to you. I'm scared.

Frowning, he started down to meet me. I hurried up the stairs, comforted by the reality of his presence. How far could someone send a witch message? I wondered. Was it possible Cal had called me from, say, France? I wanted to believe it was.

The porch staircase was long and rickety, with two turns before the top. Hunter was halfway down, and when I was almost to him, our glances met: we were both feeling the first prickle of alarm, our senses processing the unnatural feelings of shakiness and sway in the staircase. Then Hunter was reaching out his hand to me in slow motion, and I reached back even as I heard the first, thundering crack of wood splitting and felt the steps fall away beneath my feet, leaving me to drop endlessly into darkness, away from the light and my friends.

I was unconscious barely a moment: when I opened my eyes, wood fragments were still settling around me, and dust tickled my nose. I hurt all over.

"Morgan! Morgan! Hunter!" It was hard to tell who was calling, but I sensed Hunter near me, trying to struggle into a sitting position beneath one of the porch's support beams.

"Here!" Hunter called back, sounding shaken. "Morgan?"

"Here," I said weakly, feeling like my chest had been crushed, like I would never have enough breath in my lungs again. I tried to turn my head to look at the porch, but I must have rolled far down into the ravine, because I couldn't see the top.

"Hang on—I'll come get you," said Hunter, and I saw that he was about eight feet above me. Then Robbie, Matt, and Sky were leaning over the edge of the ravine with flashlights and a long rope. Holding the rope, Hunter edged his way toward me, and I grabbed his hand. Together we climbed up the rocky slope, and by the time I reached the top and sat down on the edge, I was trembling all over. I saw that the porch was still attached to the house, but the corner where the stairs had been sagged frighteningly, and the stairs themselves were in pieces. Our coven members stood on the lawn in a frightened group. It looked as if only Hunter and I had fallen when the stairs collapsed.

"Are you guys all right?" Bree asked. I saw fear and concern in her eyes.

I nodded. "Nothing feels broken. I must have landed on something soft," I said.

"That was me, I think. But I'm all right, more or less," Hunter added. He put a hand to his side and winced. "Just a few scrapes and bruises."

Sky put her arm around my waist and helped me around to the front of the house and inside.

"What happened?" Matt asked, following us. "Was the wood rotten?"

The coven members gathered around, going over what had just happened. As soon as they'd seen the stairs collapsing, they had crowded back through the kitchen door. I was so glad no one else had been hurt.

Sky left the kitchen, and Bree led me to a chair. "That was terrifying," she said. "Seeing you and Hunter go down." She shook her head.

"Here. I found some kava kava tea," said Jenna, pressing a warm mug into my hand.

I nodded and took it from her. "Thanks." I sipped the herb tea, hoping it would take effect soon. What a night it had been already, between hearing Cal's voice and then having this accident.

A few minutes later Sky came back in. "Hunter's looking at the porch," she reported. "Now let's get you cleaned up." She fetched a small basket of supplies from the bathroom and started washing my cuts and bruises. "Arnica," she said, holding out a small vial. "Good for trauma."

I was letting the pills dissolve under my tongue when Hunter limped in, his face grim. He had scrapes on his cheek, and his sweater was ripped and bloody on one side. For myself, I knew I'd have bruises on my back and legs, but that was pretty much it.

"The posts were sawed," Hunter announced, throwing down the coil of rope.

"What?" Robbie exclaimed. He, Bree, and Jenna were hovering by my chair. Matt, Raven, Sharon, and Ethan were standing at the back door, looking out at what was left of the porch. Thalia, Alisa, and Simon hadn't arrived yet.

I stared at Hunter in alarm, and Cal's voice echoed in my

head again. "Sawed with a saw, or spelled to break?" I asked.

"Looked like a saw," Hunter said as Jenna gave him a mug of the same tea I was drinking. "I didn't sense any magick. I'll have a closer look tomorrow, in the daylight."

He looked at me: we needed to talk. This was the second time we had almost been killed when we were together. It couldn't be coincidence.

"Maybe we should call the police," said Jenna.

Hunter shook his head. "They'd think we're subversive Wiccan weirdos who are being persecuted by the neighbors," he said dryly. "I'd rather not bring them into this."

"Okay, everybody, I'm going to lead the circle tonight," Sky announced, getting everyone's attention. "We'll start in a few minutes. Why don't the rest of you come to the circle room and start getting settled in while Morgan and Hunter finish their tea?"

They all trooped out. Robbie cast a worried glance over his shoulder at me as he left.

Alone, Hunter and I sat in silence for a moment.

"Neither of these accidents looked like magick," Hunter said at last. He breathed in the steam from his mug. "But as I said, I just can't think of any enemies I might have who aren't witches."

"What about someone who used to be a witch?" I asked, thinking of how David had been stripped of his magick. David was in Ireland, but Hunter must know other witches whose magick was bound.

"That's a thought," Hunter agreed, "although I pretty much know the location of the ones I've had to work against, and none of them are anywhere nearby." He put down his mug. "I'd better get cleaned up," he said, wincing as he stretched his arm. Automatically I followed him to the downstairs bathroom.

He snapped on the light. The room was small, unrenovated, with old-fashioned white tiles. It was scrupulously clean, and he started rummaging in the medicine cabinet. I perched on the edge of the tub. "I have something to tell you," I said.

He turned to look at me. "That sounds ominous." With careful movements he stripped off his dark, ripped sweater and the torn T-shirt underneath. Then he was wearing only his jeans, and I was trying not to stare at his naked, muscled chest. He was much fairer than Cal, his skin a smooth ivory color, and he had more chest hair than Cal. It was a golden brown and stretched from beneath his collarbone down in a V to where it disappeared into his pants, at eye level to where I was sitting. My mouth went dry, and I tried to focus on the large scrapes that sullenly oozed blood along his side.

When I dragged my eyes up to his face, he was looking at me with an almost glittering awareness. Wordlessly he handed me a wet washcloth, then held his arm away from his side.

Oh, I thought, standing up and starting to wash away the blood and dirt. My fingers tingled where they touched him. He turned for me, and I saw his back had been scraped as well, though not as badly. His skin was smooth, and he had pale freckles across both shoulders. I remembered that he was half Woodbane. He and Cal had the same father.

"Do you have a Woodbane athame?" I asked. "The birthmark?"

"I do, actually," he said. "Do you?"

"Yes." I dropped the washcloth in the sink and reached for the antibiotic ointment.

"I'll show you mine if you show me yours," he said with a wolfish smile.

Mine was under my left arm, on my side. Since I couldn't see his, I could only assume it was somewhere under his pants. My mind couldn't even begin to go there, so I said nothing.

"Don't you want to know where mine is?" he asked teasingly, and I could feel my blush starting at my neck and working its way upward. He leaned over me and brushed my hair over my shoulder, then traced my jawline with one finger. I remembered the way he felt, pressed against me, and most of my coherent thoughts fled.

"No," I said unconvincingly, lost in his eyes.

"I want to know where yours is," he breathed, his mouth close to mine.

The idea of his hands under my shirt, roaming over my skin, almost made my knees buckle. "Uh," I said, trying to talk myself out of whipping off my shirt right there. Focus. Come on, Morgan.

"Cal called me tonight," I blurted.

His hand fell away from my cheek. "What?" His voice reverberated loudly off the tiles.

"On my way over here. He sent me a witch message. I heard it in my head."

Hunter stared at me. "Why didn't you tell me right away?"

I just looked at him, and then he realized what had happened as soon as I got here.

"Right. I'm sorry. Well, what did he say? Could you tell where he was? Do you know where he is? Tell me everything." Moments before he had been playful and flirtatious; now he was intense, all business.

"There's nothing much to say," I explained. "I was driving here, and suddenly I heard Cal say, 'Morgan.' That's all. I was totally freaked and sent my senses out to find him but didn't feel him anywhere. I mean, I didn't feel a thing. And that was all he said."

"Do you know where he is?" Hunter demanded, holding my shoulders. "Tell me the truth."

"What do you mean? I *am* telling you the truth! I don't know where he is." I stared at him in bafflement. How could he think I might lie about something so important to both of us?

"Cal! That bastard," Hunter snapped, letting go of me. His hands clenched into fists, and the bathroom seemed too small to hold his rage. "Are you sure he didn't say anything else?"

"I'm positive. I already told you." I returned his glare. "Why are you treating me like a criminal? I didn't do anything wrong."

A muscle in his jaw flickered. But he didn't reply directly. Instead he shot questions at me like bullets. "Did you feel at all different? Is there a period of time you don't remember? Anything that feels confusing or odd?"

I realized what he was getting at. "Wouldn't I know if he'd put a spell on me?"

"No," Hunter said disdainfully. "He's a piss-poor witch, but he knows more than you do." He looked deeply into my eyes, as if he would see the spell reflected there. Then he turned away. I felt embarrassed and angry. Hunter was hurting my feelings, and I felt myself closing off to him. Especially when he wheeled back to me and added, "You're not holding anything back from me, are you? You're not feeling some idiotic urge to protect him because he's such a bloody stud and you still want him even after he tried to kill you?"

My mouth fell open, and my hand had shot up to slap him when it hit me: he was jealous. Jealous of my past with Cal. I stood there with my hand in the air as I tried to process this.

"Goddess, that bastard!" Hunter said. "If he's here, if I find him . . ."

Then what? I wondered. You'll kill him? I couldn't believe Hunter, cool, reserved Hunter had turned into this furious person I barely recognized in a matter of seconds. It frightened me.

"Hey, are you lot almost done in there?" Sky called from the other room.

"Yes," I called back, wanting to get away from Hunter. I wondered why on earth I had thought telling him would make me feel better or safer.

"This is one of the most useful rituals there is," said Sky almost half an hour later. I was finding that Sky's circle was different from any circle I'd attended: the fact was that whoever was leading a circle naturally imbued it with their aura, their power, and their whole persona. It was fascinating to see how different leaders cast different circles. So far I liked Sky's circle.

"I'd like to teach you how to deflect negative energy,"

said Sky. "This isn't something to use if you're under attack or in real trouble. It's more like something gentle and constant to surround yourself with in order to reduce negativity in your life and increase your positive energy."

I glanced at Hunter, thinking, He could use some positive energy right about now. His anger seemed less intense, but I could tell he was still brooding.

"It uses runes as its base," Sky explained. She took a small red velvet pouch from her belt and knelt. "Everyone sit down and come closer." Opening the pouch, she dumped its contents onto the wooden floor. Rune tiles spilled out, really pretty ones, made of different-colored stones. I had a rune set at home that I'd bought at Practical Magick, but mine was only fired clay. "There are so many different tools a witch can use. Incense, herbs, oils, runes or other symbols, crystals and gems, metals, candles." She grinned up at us as we crowded around her like kindergartners. "Witches are very practical. We use whatever we can find. Today we're using runes."

With deft fingers she organized the runes into three rows, each tile in line according to its place in the elder futhark, the traditional runic alphabet. We all knew the runes by heart at this point, and I could hear the coven members quietly identifying them.

"First we need eolh, for protection," said Sky, pulling it out of line. "What's another name for eolh?"

"Algiz," I said automatically.

"And wynn," she said, placing the wynn tile next to eolh. "For happiness and harmony. Another name for it?"

Simon said, "Wunjo."

"Uine," said Robbie, and Sky nodded. I liked how she was

involving everyone—she wasn't just lecturing, but including what little knowledge we had.

"Sigel, for sun, life, energy," said Sky, placing it by the other to form a triangle.

"Sowilo," said Thalia, looking pleased that she knew.

"Sugil," Bree added.

Sky grinned. "You guys are good. One more. Ur, for strength." She placed the tile for ur so that the four symbols together made a diamond shape.

"Uruz or uraz," said Raven, and her eyes met Sky's for a moment of private communion.

"Right. Now," Sky went on. "You can write these runes on a piece of paper, scratch them into an old slate or stone, carve them into a candle, or what have you. But use *these* four runes in *this* order. Put the written runes in your personal space, your bedroom, your car, even your school locker. When you see them, tap them with a finger and repeat, "Eolh, wynn, sigel, ur. Come to me from where you are. Guide the things I do or say, and let your wisdom come this way."

She sat back. "You can also circle your hand, palm down, three times deasil over the runes to help increase their power." She showed us. "That's all there is to it. It's not big magick or especially beautiful magick, but it's very useful magick."

"I think it's beautiful," said Alisa, looking young and sincere. "All magick is beautiful."

"No," I said, sounding more abrupt than I had meant to. "It isn't."

People looked at me, and I felt self-conscious. Hunter

and Sky nodded, and I knew they understood. We three had seen magick that was dark and ugly. It existed; it was all around us.

That night I found myself driving behind Bree on the way home from Hunter and Sky's. I felt shaken and upset, not to mentioned bruised and achy: hearing Cal's voice, the frightening fall I'd had, Hunter's awful reaction to hearing about Cal. Was Cal nearby? Just thinking about it terrified me. It was all too much. I just wanted to go home and get in bed and hold my kitten, Dagda.

Bree had taken the short route home, down Gallows Road. There were lots of twists and turns, but it took less time than going on main streets. Bree had always been the more daring driver of the two of us, and despite my trying to keep up, within minutes I lost sight of her in the darkness. Suddenly I was overwhelmed with the feeling of being completely alone on a dark road.

Without warning, my headlights flashed on something on the road ahead. I caught a blurry glimpse of something—a deer?—barely in time to slam on my brakes. As Das Boot screeched heavily to a halt, my eyes focused, and my mouth opened in a wordless, "Oh." My headlights shone on a figure who was walking toward my car, hands upraised.

Cal.

# 9.
# Cal

Lammas, 1976

I'm fairly well settled into the house now that Clyda's gone. Her death three months ago was a surprise to everyone but me. She'd been sick, getting frailer and weaker. I think it was the dark wave in Madrid that really took it out of her. Really, she had no business traveling at her age. But it's difficult for some people to acknowledge their weaknesses.

I was in Ireland last week and met two interesting witches. One was a gorgeous boy, just old enough to shave, whose power is already frightening and strong and worth watching. I took Ciaran to bed for a night, and he was charmingly youthful, enthusiastic, and surprisingly skilled. I'm smiling even now, thinking about it.

But it's Daniel Niall who's haunting my thoughts,

*and the irony of this can't escape me. Daniel is a Woodbane from England who came to one of Amyranth's gatherings in Shannon. I could see he was uncomfortable, had come out of curiosity and found us not to his liking. For some reason that made him even more attractive to me. He doesn't have Ciaran's harsh, raw beauty, but he is good-looking, with strong, masculine features, and when he looked into my eyes and smiled shyly, my heart missed a beat. Sweet Daniel. He's deeply good, honest, from one of those Woodbane covens that renounced evil ages ago. It's oddly endearing and also a challenge: how much more satisfying to seduce an angel than a villain?*

— SB

At once I felt a wash of cold fear sweep over me from head to foot, and my hands clenched the steering wheel. Cal gestured with one hand, and Das Boot's engine died quietly and the headlights winked out. Automatically I began to use my magesight, the enhanced vision I'd been able to call on since shortly after I learned I was a blood witch.

Cal came closer, and I wrenched my door open and jumped out, determined to be standing during any meeting we had. When I saw his face, my breath left me, not in a whoosh but in a quiet trail, like a vine of smoke in the cold night air. Oh Goddess, had I forgotten his face? No—not when he haunted my dreams and my waking thoughts. But I had forgotten his impact on me, the sweet longing I felt when our eyes met, despite my fear.

Then of course came the remembered anger and a fierce rush of self-protective instinct.

"What are you doing here?" I demanded, trying to make my voice strong. But in the darkness I sounded harsh and afraid.

"Morgan," he said, and his voice crept along all my nerves, like honey. I had missed his voice. I hardened my heart and stared at him.

"Last time I saw you, you were trying to kill me," I said, striving for a flippancy I was too scared to pull off.

"I was trying to save you," he said earnestly, and came so close, I could see he wasn't an apparition, wasn't a ghost, but a real person in a real body that I had touched and kissed. "Believe me—if Selene had gotten her hands on you, death would have been far better. Morgan, I know now that I was wrong, but I was crazy with fear, and I did what I thought was best. Forgive me."

I couldn't speak. How did he do it? Even now, when I knew I should just jump in my car and drive away as fast as I could, my heart was whispering, Believe him.

"I love you more now than ever," Cal said. "I've come back to be with you. I told Selene I wouldn't help her anymore."

"You're telling me you've broken away from your mother?" I said. Emotion made my voice harsh, raw. "Give me one good reason I should believe you."

Wordlessly Cal opened his jacket. Underneath he wore a flannel shirt, and he unbuttoned the top three buttons and pulled it open so that I could see his chest. Instantly Hunter's naked chest flashed into my mind. Oh God, I thought with a tinge of hysteria.

Then I saw the blackened, burned-looking patch of skin directly over Cal's heart. I focused my magesight on it so that I could see clearly, despite the darkness. It was in the shape of a hand.

"Selene did that to me," Cal said, and remembered pain thrummed in his voice. "When I told her I chose you over her."

Goddess. I swallowed hard. And then, without allowing myself to think about what I was risking, I put out my hand and touched my fingers to his cheek. I had to know the truth.

His eyes flared open as he realized what I was doing, but he stood still. I pushed through the outer layers of his consciousness, feeling his resistance, feeling him will himself to accept my invasion. For the first time with Cal, I was controlling the joining of our minds. I would see what I wanted to see, not simply what he wanted to show me.

Then I was inside, and Cal was all around me. I saw my face, but the way he saw it, with a sort of glow around it that made me beautiful, unearthly. I was shaken to sense how much he wanted me.

I saw Hunter striding down the street in Red Kill, and felt an ugly burst of hatred and violence from Cal that rocked me.

I saw a steep hillside below me, dotted with small stucco houses with red roofs, that stretched down to a sparkling blue bay. I felt a breeze blowing against my cheeks. In the distance a red bridge stretched from one headland to another, and I realized I was seeing San Francisco, where I'd never been. It was beautiful, but it wasn't what I needed to see, so I kept searching.

Then I saw Selene.

She was looking directly at me, and I had to fight a strong impulse to hide my face, though I knew I was only seeing Cal's memory. She wasn't looking at me but at him. The expression in her eyes was cold fury.

"You can't go," she said. "I won't allow it."

"I am going," Cal said, and I felt his defiance, his fear, his resolve.

Selene's beautiful face twisted into a snarl of rage. "You idiot," she said. Then her hand was snaking toward him, so fast, it was just a blur, and I felt a searing pain as she touched Cal's flesh. Her hand felt deathly cold, as if it were made of liquid nitrogen, but then a wisp of smoke rose up in front of my eyes, and I smelled charred flesh. I cringed and gasped, twisting with Cal as he sought to escape the agony.

Then she took her hand away, and it was over, except for the memory of the pain.

"That was just the barest taste of what I can do," she said in a voice like iron. "I could have taken your heart as easily as plucking a cherry out of a bowl. I didn't because you are my son, and I know this foolishness will pass. But now you've experienced what I can do to those who cross me."

And she turned and strode away.

I let my hand drop, shaken, but Cal grabbed it. "Morgan, I need you. I need your love and your strength. Together we're strong enough to fight Selene, to win against her."

"No, we're not!" I cried. I snatched my hand away. "Are you insane? Selene could crush both of us and five other witches besides. I don't even know if she *can* be stopped."

"She can!" Cal said, coming closer still. He looked thinner than when I had seen him last, and his perpetual golden tan had faded slightly. I wondered if he had been eating, where he had been staying, and then told myself I didn't give a damn. "Selene can be stopped. The two of us, and your mother's coven tools, will be enough to stop her cold. I'm sure of it. Just tell me you'll work with me. Morgan, tell me you still love me." His voice dropped to a raspy whisper. "Tell me I haven't killed your love for me."

With a sense of shame I recognized that I cared for him, cared about him, that despite everything I didn't, couldn't hate him. But I couldn't say I still loved him, either, and there was no way I would agree to help him go up against Selene.

"There's no way we can be together now," I said, and the image of myself pressed against Hunter, kissing him fiercely, flashed into my mind.

"I know what I did to you was terrible," Cal said. "At first I was just trying to get next to your power. I admit that. But then I fell for you. Fell for your strength and beauty, your honesty and humility. Every time I saw you was a revelation, and now I can't live without you. I don't want to live without you. I want to be with you forever."

He looked so sincere, his face contorted with pain. I didn't know what to say: a thousand thoughts flew through my head like sparks flying upward from a fire. I recoiled from his presence even as part of me ached for his words to be true. I was scared of him and also afraid that what he was saying was real, that no one would ever love me so much again.

"All I ask is that you give me another chance," he pleaded in a tone that threatened to break my heart. "I was so horribly wrong—I thought I could have you and give

Selene what she wanted, too, but I couldn't. Please give me a chance to make it up to you, a chance to redeem myself. Morgan, please. I love you." He stepped closer still, and I could feel his breath, as cold as the night air, brushing against my cheek. "I don't want Selene to hurt you. Morgan, she wants to kill you. Now that she knows you'll never join her, she needs you dead so she can have your tools." He shook his head. "I can't let her do that."

"Where is she?" I asked shakily.

"I don't know," he said. "We were in San Francisco, but she's not there anymore. She's not far. I pick up on her sometimes. At least four members of her coven are with her. They're coming for you, Morgan. You have to let me protect you."

"Why should I trust you?" I demanded, trying to shut out the pain that seared my heart. "You tried to kill me once— why should I believe you won't just do it again?"

"Do you remember how good we were together?" Cal whispered, and I shivered. "Do you remember how we touched, how we kissed, how we joined our minds? It was so good, so right. You know it was real; you know I'm telling you the truth now. Please, Morgan . . ."

Part of me was no longer listening, my senses attuned to another vibration, another image. I looked down the road. "Hunter," I said before I thought.

Cal wheeled and looked down the road. I thought I could see the faintest stripe of light on the tree trunks. Headlights.

For an endless moment Cal and I looked at each other. He was just as breathtaking as he'd always been, with a new layer of vulnerability that he'd never had but that made him even more appealing. He was Cal, my first love, the one who'd opened new worlds to me.

"If you call me, I'll come," he said so softly, I could barely hear him.

"Wait!" I said. "Where are you staying? Where can I find you?"

He just smiled, and then he was running easily toward the woods that lined the road, and he faded between the trees like a wraith. I blinked, and he was completely gone, with no trace of ever having been there.

The headlights caught me in their glare, and I understood how a deer or rabbit could be pinned by them in terror. I stood by Das Boot, waiting for Hunter to stop.

"Morgan," he said, getting out of his car. Illogically, even after the scene in the bathroom, I felt almost like weeping with relief to see him. "Are you all right? Did something happen?"

My tongue pressed against my lips. Hunter was a Seeker. He had gone ballistic at the thought that Cal had even contacted me. If I told him I had just *seen* Cal, that Cal was nearby somewhere, Hunter wouldn't stop until he found Cal. And when he found him . . .

Hunter and Cal hated each other, had tried to kill each other. It was only luck that they *hadn't* killed each other. If Hunter found Cal now, one of them would die. That thought was completely unacceptable to me. I didn't know what to do about Cal, didn't know what to do about the knowledge that Selene was coming. All I knew was that I had to keep Hunter and Cal apart until I figured something out.

"I'm okay," I said, making my voice strong and sure. I chose my words carefully, knowing that he'd sense it if I lied outright. "I thought I almost hit a deer just now and stopped, but it's gone."

Hunter glanced at the woods, then he frowned slightly. "I sense something. . . ." he said, half to himself. He stood still for a moment, a listening expression on his face. Then he shook his head. "Whatever it was, it's gone now."

I kept my face blank.

He looked back at me. "I got an odd feeling about you," he said. "Like . . . panic."

I nodded, hoping he couldn't tell I was lying. "I thought I was going to crash. It's been kind of . . . an eventful day. I guess I freaked."

Hunter's frown cleared, and he looked contrite. "Are you sure you're okay?" he asked.

"Yeah." I started to get back in my car and prayed desperately that it would start, that Cal hadn't permanently disabled the engine. I couldn't believe I was lying so blithely to Hunter, Hunter who I had acknowledged was just about the only person I could trust. But I wasn't lying for me—I was trying to save Cal. And Hunter. I had to save them from each other.

Hunter leaned in the open doorway, bending to be at eye level with me. "Morgan—I'm sorry about the way I behaved earlier, in the bathroom. It's just—I'm upset about my father. I want to reach him and I can't. And I'm afraid for you. I feel that I need to protect you, and it kills me that I can't be with you all the time, making sure you're safe."

I nodded. "And that's why you want me to do the tàth meànma brach," I said.

"Yes." He paused. "Are you sore from the fall?"

"Yeah. I bet we'll both feel awful tomorrow. Especially you."

He laughed, and I turned my key. Das Boot's engine turned over at once.

"I'm going to get home now," I said unnecessarily. Quickly Hunter leaned in and kissed me, and then he stood back and shut my car door.

Had Cal seen that? I thought in panic. Oh Goddess, I hoped not. It would only infuriate him more. I drove off, looking back at Hunter in the mirror until I went around the next bend and I couldn't see him anymore. All I wanted to do was go home, curl up, and cry.

# 10.
# Open

*December 13, 1977*

The mysteries of Amyranth can't hold a candle to the mysteries of love. What is it about Daniel Niall that makes me so crazy? Has he spelled me to love him? No— that's ludicrous. Noble, honest Daniel would never do such a thing. No, I love him for himself, and it's so out of character for me that I can't stop questioning it.

Why is he so compelling? How is he different from other men I've had? Like every other man, he's given in to me—no one has ever told me no, and Daniel is no exception. Yet I sense an inner wall that I can't breach. There's something within him that my love, my power, my beauty hasn't touched. What is it?

I know he loves me, and I know he wishes he didn't. I enjoy making him realize how much he wants me. I take *pleasure in watching him try to resist and being unable to. And then I make his compliance worth his while. But what is he holding back?*

*At any rate, Daniel is here and there working on various studies—he's very academic; he wants to understand everything, know the history of everything. A real book witch. It takes him away from me often. Which is a good thing, because his presence severely curtails my Amyranth activities. I'm now doing more and more within the group and less with Turneval. The Unnamed Elders have begun teaching me the deeper magick of Amyranth, and it's more draining and exciting than anything I've imagined. I'm lost within it, drunk with it, immersed in it—and the only thing that pulls me out is the chance of spending time with Daniel. This makes me laugh.*

*—SB*

That night I dreamed that Selene took on the form of a giant bird and snatched me off the school playing field, where, ludicrously, I was playing hockey with Hunter and Bree and Robbie. They stood on the grass, waving their hockey sticks helplessly, and I watched them get smaller and smaller as Selene bore me away. She took me to a giant nest perched on top of a mountain, and I looked down and saw Cal in the nest, and before my eyes he turned into a baby bird and gazed up at me with his sharp predator's beak gaping wide to engulf me. Then I woke up, drenched with sweat, and it was morning.

I spent the morning trying not to think about Cal. Three times I found myself picking up the phone to call Hunter, and three times I put the cordless handset back in its cradle. I felt too conflicted about what I would say.

"What's the matter, Morgan?" my mom asked as I prowled through the kitchen for the fourth time. "You seem so restless."

I forced myself to smile. "I don't know. Maybe I just need to go for a drive or something."

I grabbed my coat and car keys and headed out to Das Boot, not sure what my destination was. Then my senses tingled, and I knew Hunter was nearby. I felt a surge of elation and alarm as I saw him pull up in front of the house.

I walked over to his car, willing myself to seem calm, normal. He rolled down his window and peered out at me.

"We need to talk. Can I drive you somewhere?" he asked.

"Uh—I was just going for a drive," I mumbled. "I'm not really sure where."

"How about Red Kill?" he suggested. "I need to pick up some essential oils at Practical Magick. And you need to talk to Alyce."

So I climbed into his car and off we went.

"This morning Sky and I examined the porch supports more carefully," Hunter said as he drove. "They'd definitely been sawed, and we couldn't find any trace of magick."

"So what are you thinking?" I asked.

"I don't know," he said, tapping his fingers against the steering wheel.

I thought: had it been Cal? Had he been trying to kill

both me and Hunter at the same time? Had he cut Hunter's brake line as well? But why would he do it mechanically instead of with magick? Was I being a complete and total idiot by not telling Hunter that I'd seen Cal? I was so confused.

Alyce fed us lunch in her small apartment. I hadn't realized I was hungry until I smelled the beef stew that was filling the rooms with its rich scent. Hunter and I fell on it, and Alyce watched us, smiling. She sat at the table with us, not eating but sipping from a mug of tea.

"I've been considering your request for a tàth meànma brach," she said as I took a second slice of bread. "It's a serious thing, and I've given it a great deal of thought."

I nodded, my heart sinking at her tone. She was going to say no. I saw a glance pass between her and Hunter and felt my appetite fade away.

"You know, it can be very difficult," Alyce went on. "It would be very draining, both physically and emotionally, for both of us."

I nodded. I had asked too much.

"But I understand why you want to do this, why you asked me, and why Hunter also thinks it's a good idea," Alyce said. "And I've come to agree. I think that you're a target of Selene's group, and I think you need more protection than others can provide for you. The best kind of protection comes from within, and by joining with me and learning what I know, you will be much stronger, much more capable of defending yourself."

I looked at her with hope. "Does that mean—"

"You'll need to free yourself of as many mental distractions as you can," Alyce said gently. "And there are some ritual preparations you'll need to make. Hunter and Sky can help you with them. Let's do it soon—the sooner the better. Tomorrow evening."

Back in Hunter's car, on our way to my house, I could hardly sit still. The idea of being able to absorb all of Alyce's considerable learning, all in one day, was exhilarating and nerve-racking.

"Thank you for speaking to Alyce for me," I said. "Encouraging her to do the tàth meànma brach."

"It was her decision." He sounded remote, and I felt a surge of frustration about our relationship. It struck me for the first time that Hunter and I were similar, and that was why we clashed so much. With Cal it had been clear, easy— he had been the pursuer and I the pursued, and that had worked well with my shyness and insecurity. But both Hunter and I would be more comfortable if the other person were taking charge. At this point I had to assume there was some reason why we had kissed each other, and not just once or twice. Hunter wasn't the kind of person who would do that lightly, and neither was I. So what were we doing? Were we falling in love?

I have to lay myself on the line, I realized with a flash of perfect clarity. If I want to go deeper with him, I have to open myself to him and trust that he doesn't want to hurt me. And I do want to go deeper with him.

But first . . . but first I had to tell him about Cal. It was too huge a secret between us. Nor was it my secret to keep.

Hunter was in danger from Cal as much, maybe even more than I was. I would have to tell him and hope that he wouldn't let his emotions overtake his good sense.

I swallowed hard. Do it, I told myself. Do it!

"I saw Cal last night," I said quietly.

Next to me Hunter went rigid, his hands clenching the steering wheel. He glanced quickly right and left, then swung the car onto a dirt road that I hadn't even seen. We bumped over rocks and frozen mud before coming to a halt about twenty feet off the main road.

"When?" Hunter demanded, turning off the engine and facing me. He unclipped his seat belt and leaned toward me. "When?" he repeated. "Was it when I saw you on the road?"

"Yes," I admitted. "It wasn't a deer I saw. It was Cal. He was standing in the road, and he held up his hand and my car went dead."

"What happened? What did he do to you?"

"Nothing. We just talked," I said. "He said he came back to Widow's Vale to be with me. He told me he's broken away from Selene."

"And you believed that load of crap?" Hunter exclaimed. His eyes blazed.

My chin came up. "Yes." His contemptuous tone made me feel small, hurt. "I did tàth meànma with him. He's telling the truth."

"Goddess." Hunter spat out the word. "How could you be so bloody stupid? You've done tàth meànma with him before, and he still managed to fool you."

"But I controlled it this time!" I cried.

"You *think* you did. Why did you lie to me?" His eyes narrowed. "He *has* put a spell on you!"

Remembering how it had felt when Cal had put a spell on me made me shiver. "No. I just—I had just told you about his witch message, and you freaked out, and I thought if I told you he was right there, you guys would—would fight, and it made me sick to think about."

"You're damn right I freaked out!" Hunter said, raising his voice. "Good God, Morgan, we've been looking for Cal and Selene for three weeks now! And all of a sudden you say, guess what? I know where he is! I mean, what the hell kind of game are you playing?"

I hated the way he was looking at me, as if he were questioning his trust of me—if he had ever trusted me at all, and to my horror, I started crying. I don't cry easily in front of people, and I would have given up a lot to have not cried then, but everything crashed down on me all at once, and I crumbled.

"I'm not playing games!" I said, dashing my tears away. "I'm just confused, just human! I loved Cal, and I don't want you two to kill each other!"

"You're not *just* human, Morgan," Hunter said. "You're a witch. You have to start living up to that fact. What do you mean, you loved Cal? What has that got to do with anything? He tried to kill you! Are you stupid? Are you blind?"

"It wasn't all his fault!" I yelled, seeing the blazing fury in Hunter's eyes. "You know that, Hunter. He grew up with Selene for eighteen years. What would you have been like in that situation?" I took a couple of quick, hard breaths, trying to get hold of myself. "I'm not blind. Maybe

I am stupid. Mostly I'm just confused and scared and tempted."

He narrowed his eyes, seizing on my words like a snake does a rat. "Tempted? Tempted by what? The dark side? Or by Cal? Is that it? Are you saying you still love him?"

"No! Yes! Stop twisting my words! All I'm saying is that I loved him, and I thought he loved me, and I haven't forgotten that!" I shouted. "He introduced me to magick. He made me feel beautiful!" I abruptly shut up, breathing hard.

Heavy silence filled the car. I sensed Hunter striving to rein in his anger. What am I doing? I thought miserably.

Then his face softened. I felt his hand at my neck, brushing my hair back, stroking my skin. My breath caught in my throat, and I turned to him.

"I'm sorry," I whispered. My skin felt like it was on fire where his fingers passed over it.

"What do you want? I know you were happy with Cal, and I want you to be happy with me. But I'm not Cal, and I never will be," he said, his face close to mine. His voice was soft. "If you want me, then tell me. I need you to tell me."

My eyes widened. Cal had always been almost forceful, the one who decided, cajoled, seduced. Why was Hunter asking me to make myself vulnerable?

As if reading my thoughts, he said, "Morgan, I can tell you and show you what I want. But if you don't know what you want, I don't want to go there. You need to know what you want, and you need to be able to tell me and show me." His eyes were wide, vulnerable, his lips were warm and close to mine.

Oh my God, I thought.

"It's not enough for you to let me want you," he went on. "I need you to actually want me back and to be able to show me that. I need to be wanted, too. Do you see what I mean?"

I nodded slowly, processing a hundred thoughts.

"Can you give me that?"

My eyes felt huge as I wondered if I could—if I was brave enough. I didn't speak.

"Right, then." He pulled back, my body saying, no, no, and then he started the car, carefully backed up, and we went back to Widow's Vale. In front of my house he stopped and turned to look at me again.

"I have to look for Cal," he said. "You know that, don't you?"

I nodded reluctantly. "Don't hurt him," I said in a near whisper.

"I can't promise that," he told me. "But I'll try. Will you think about what I said?"

I nodded again.

Hunter took my chin in his hand and kissed me hard and fast on the mouth, not once but again and again, hungrily, and I made a little sound and opened my mouth to him. Finally he pulled back, breathing hard, and we looked at each other. He put the car into gear again. I climbed out in a daze and headed up my front walk.

# 11.
# The Graveyard

Beltane, 1979

I've been married for less than twenty-four hours, and already my new husband is threatening to leave me—he thinks the ceremony was all my doing, it wasn't what he expected, I didn't respect his wishes, etc. He'll be all right. He needs to calm down, to relax, to get over his fears. Then we can talk, and he'll see that everything is all right, everything is fine, and we were meant to be together.

Why did I marry Daniel Niall? Because I couldn't help myself. Because I wanted him too much to let him go. Because I needed to be the one he wanted, the one he would live with and come home to. My mother would have approved of this match. Anyone who actually knows me thinks I'm crazy. At any rate, Daniel and I were married last night, and for me it was beautiful, powerful, primal.

*When we stood, sky clad, under the ripe, full moon, with Turneval chanting around us, the heady scent of herbs burning, the warmth of the bonfire toasting our skin—I felt like the Goddess herself, full of life, fertile. For me it was so natural that we embrace, open our mouths and kiss, that I press myself against him. And how could he not respond? We were naked, I was seducing him, it was a full moon. Of course he responded. But he found his physical response (so public, so witnessed) to be unbearable. For Daniel it was humiliation, abasement.*

*How will I reconcile these two areas of my life? How can I keep my work with Amyranth a secret? How can I protect Daniel from Amyranth?*

*I'll have to solve the problems as they come.*

*—SB*

On Sunday, I once again skipped church and tried to ignore my mother's disapproving looks. She and my dad tried to talk me into meeting them for lunch at the Widow's Vale Diner afterward, but I was fasting to purify my body for my upcoming tàth meànma brach with Alyce, so I declined. Instead, I stayed in my room, meditating. Alyce had recommended that I spend at least three hours meditating on the day of the ritual to cleanse my spirit and my psyche of negative patterns and clutter, for lack of a better word.

By eleven o'clock, I was starving. My stomach cried out for Diet Coke and a Pop-Tart, but I resisted, feeling virtuous.

At noon I'd just pulled out my altar when Hunter called.

He told me in a neutral way that he'd gone to Cal and Selene's old house and one or two other places to see if he could find Cal, but he'd had no luck. "I know he's been there—I can feel traces of him," Hunter said. "But everywhere I go, he's moved on, and I can't tell where he's gone. I didn't think he was skilled enough to hide his trail from me once I'd picked up a trace of him, but he seems to be."

I decided it was time to change the subject. "I can't believe the tàth meànma brach is tonight," I said. "I'm kind of nervous. Should I be?"

"Yes," Hunter said. "But come over to my house at three, and we'll help you get ready. You've got to drink the tea, then take the ritual bath so that you'll be fully cleansed. And you'll need to wear a green linen robe—Sky's got one. Tell your mum and dad you're having dinner with us and you won't be home until fairly late."

"Okay," I said, feeling scared and uncertain.

His voice softened. "You'll be all right, Morgan," he said. "You're strong. Stronger than you know."

After we said goodbye and hung up, I went back to my room. I opened a spell book that Alyce had loaned me and began to read through the purification spell she'd marked, but my stomach kept distracting me. All of a sudden, when I was trying so hard not to think about food, I had a realization: my brain was still incredibly cluttered with Cal. I thought about him, wondered about him, dreamed about him.

Then I realized I had to talk to him, find out once and for all where we stood. I had to put all my feelings toward him to rest or I would never be able to move forward, and I couldn't take part in the tàth meànma brach. I had to get closure somehow, put an end to all my confusion about him.

I knew I was doing something that could be dangerous. But I also knew I had to do it. Before I could change my mind, I drove over to the old Methodist cemetery, the place where my former coven, Cirrus, had celebrated Samhain. The place where Cal had kissed me for the first time.

It was another clear, cold day, sunny with a wintry brightness and almost no wind. Sitting on the old tombstone we had once used as our altar, I felt almost shaky with nervousness and adrenaline and lack of food. Would Cal come? Would he try to hurt me again? There was no way to know except by calling him. Closing my eyes, trying to ignore the rumbling of my stomach, I sent a witch message to him. *Cal. Come to me, Cal.* Then I sat back and waited.

Before, when I had called Cal, he had usually come within minutes. This time the wait seemed endless. My butt had turned numb on the cold stone before he appeared, gliding silently between the overgrown juniper trees. My eyes registered his appearance, and I was glad it was broad daylight and that I wasn't alone on a dark road.

"Morgan." His voice was soft as a breeze, and I felt it rather than heard it. He walked toward me with no sound, as if the dried leaves underfoot were silenced. I was drawn to his beautiful face, which was both guarded and hopeful.

"Thanks for coming," I said, and I suddenly knew without a doubt that he'd been waiting, scanning the area, making sure I was alone. The last time we were in this place, he had overpowered me and kidnapped me in my car. This time, despite some lingering fear, I felt stronger, more prepared. This time, too, I was ready to call Hunter at a moment's notice.

"I was so glad to hear from you," he said, coming to stand in front of me. He reached out and put his hands on my knees, and I drew back from the familiarity. "There's so much I need to talk to you about. So much I need to tell you, to share with you. But I didn't know how much Gìomanach had influenced you." He spat Hunter's coven name, and I frowned.

"Cal, I need to know," I said, getting to the point. "Have you really broken away from Selene? Do you really want to stop her?"

He again put his hands on my knees. They felt warm through my jeans, against my cold flesh. "Yes," he said, leaning close. "I'm finished with Selene. She's my mother, and I always had a son's loyalty to her. That's not hard to believe, is it? But now I see that what she does is wrong, that it's wrong for her to call on the dark side. I don't want any part of it. I choose you, Morgan. I love you."

I pushed his hands off my knees. His brow darkened.

"I remember when you didn't push me away," he said. "I remember when you couldn't get enough of me."

"Cal," I began, and then my anger pushed ahead of my compassion. "That was before you tried to kill me," I said, my voice strong.

"I was trying to save you!" he insisted.

"You were trying to control me!" I countered. "You put binding spells on me! If you had been honest about what Selene wanted, I could have made my own decision about what to do and how to protect myself. But you didn't give me that chance. You wanted all the power; you wanted to decide what was best." As soon as I said that, I realized it was true, and I realized that I had never absolutely trusted Cal, never.

"Morgan," he began, sounding infuriatingly reasonable, "you had just discovered Wicca. Of course I was trying to guide you, to teach you. It's one of the responsibilities of being an initiated witch. I know so much more than you— you saw what happened with Robbie's spell. You were a danger to yourself and others."

My mouth opened in fury, and he went on, "Which doesn't mean I don't love you more than you can imagine. I do, Morgan, I do. I love you so much. You complete me. You're my mùirn beatha dàn, my soul's other half. We're supposed to be together. We're supposed to make magick together. Our powers could be more awesome than anything anyone's ever seen. But we have to do it together."

I swallowed. This was so hard. Why did it still hurt so much, after all Cal had done to me? "No, Cal. We're not going to be together. We're not mùirn beatha dàns."

"That's what you think now," he said. "But you're wrong."

I looked deeply into his golden eyes and saw a spark of what looked like madness. Goddess! My blood turned to ice, and I felt incredibly stupid, meeting him here alone.

"Morgan, I love you," Cal said cajolingly. He stepped closer to me, his eyes hooded in the look that had never before failed to make me melt inside. "Please be mine."

My breath became more shallow as I wondered how to extricate myself from this. This Cal wasn't the Cal I had known. Had that person ever existed? I couldn't tell. All I knew was that now, here, I had to get away from him. He frightened me. He *repulsed* me.

Just like that, like extinguishing a candle with my fingertips, my leftover love for him died. I felt it in my heart, as if a dark shard of glass had been pulled out, leaving a bleeding wound. My throat closed and I wanted to cry, to mourn for the death of the naive Morgan who had once been so incredibly happy with this falsehood.

"No, Cal," I said. "I can't."

His face darkened, and he looked at me. "Morgan, you're not thinking clearly," he said, a tone of warning in his voice. "This is me. I love you. We're lovers."

"We were *never* lovers," I said. "And I don't love you."

"Morgan, listen to me," Cal said.

"You're too late, Sgàth," said Hunter's voice, cold and hard, and Cal and I both jumped. How had he come up without our feeling it?

"There's nothing for you to hunt here, Gìomanach," Cal spat. "No lives for you to destroy, no magick you can strip away."

I felt a wave of power welling up from Cal, and I scrambled off the tombstone. I had once been caught between Cal and Hunter during a battle. I didn't want to go through it again.

"Hunter, why are you here?" I asked.

"I felt something dark here. I came to investigate," he said tightly, not taking his eyes off Cal. "It's my job. It was you who cut the brakes in my car, wasn't it, Sgàth? You who sawed through the stair supports."

"That's right." Cal grinned at Hunter, a feral baring of teeth. "Don't you wonder what else is waiting for you?"

"Why didn't you use magick?" Hunter pressed. "Is it because without Selene, you have nothing of your own? No power? No will?"

Cal's eyes narrowed, and his hands clenched. "I didn't use magick because I didn't want to waste it on you. I am much stronger than you will ever be."

"Only when you're with Morgan," Hunter said coldly. "Not on your own. You're nothing on your own. Morgan knows that. That's why she's here."

I started to say it was *not,* but Cal turned on me. "You! You lured me here, to turn me in to him."

"I wanted to talk to you!" I cried. "I had no idea Hunter would be here."

Hunter turned his implacable gaze on me. "How could you go behind my back after all we've talked about?" he asked in a cold, measured voice. "How could you still love *him?*" He flung out his hand at Cal.

"I don't love him!" I screamed, and in the same instant Cal threw up his hands and began to chant a spell. The language he used was unfamiliar, ugly, full of guttural sounds.

Hunter let out a low growl. I sucked in my breath as I saw that his athame was in his hand, the single sapphire in its hilt flashing as it caught the late winter sun. Stepping back, I saw how he and Cal were facing each other, saw the violence ready to erupt. Damn them! I couldn't go through this again, not Cal and Hunter trying to kill each other, myself frozen, an athame leaving my hand and sailing through the intense cold. . . .

No. That was another time, another place. Another Morgan. I felt power rise inside me like a storm. I had to put an end to this. I had to.

"Clathna berrin, ne ith rah." The ancient Celtic words poured from my lips, and I spat them into the daylight. Hunter and Cal both spun to look at me, their eyes wide. "Clathna ter, ne fearth ullna stàth," I said, my voice growing stronger.

"Morach bis, mea cern, cern mea." I knew exactly what I was doing but couldn't tell where it was coming from or how I knew it. I snapped my arms open wide, to encompass both of them, and watched with a strange, fierce joy as their knees buckled and they sank, one at a time, to the ground. "Clathna berrin, ne ith rah!" I shouted, and then they were on their hands and knees, helpless against the force of my will.

Goddess, I thought. I felt like I was outside myself, watching this strange, frightening being who controlled the gravity of a world with her fingertips. My right hand outstretched to keep Cal in place, I slowly moved toward Hunter.

He didn't speak, but when I saw the blazing fury in his eyes, I knew I couldn't release him yet. I pointed at him. "Stand up," I commanded. When I raised my hand, he was able to stand, like a puppet. "Get in my car."

Stumbling like an automaton, Hunter headed for Das Boot. I walked backward, following him, keeping Cal under my power. Hunter climbed clumsily into the passenger seat, and I fished out my keys with my left hand. Then I drew some sigils in the sky, sigils I didn't remember learning, that would keep Cal in place until we were well away.

Then I leaped into the driver's seat, jammed the keys into the ignition, stomped on the gas, and got the hell out of there.

I released Hunter after I had parked in front of his house and felt the sudden tightening of his muscles as he took control of them again.

I was afraid to look at him, scared even to think about what I'd done. It was as if I'd been taken over by my power, as if the magick had controlled me instead of the other way around. Or was I just trying to make excuses for having done something unforgivable?

I felt the burning fury of Hunter's gaze on me. He slammed the car door and walked unsteadily up to his house. I felt weak and headachy from lack of food and too much magick, but I knew I needed to talk to Hunter. I got out of Das Boot and followed him into the house.

Inside, Sky looked up as I came in, and seeing my troubled expression, she pointed wordlessly up the stairs. I'd been upstairs once before but hadn't really taken in any details. Now I looked into one room: it was Sky's, or at least I hoped it was since there was a black bra draped across the bed. I walked past a small bathroom with black-and-white tile flooring and then came to the only other room and knew it must be Hunter's bedroom. The door was ajar, and I pushed it open without knocking: daring Morgan.

He lay across his bed, staring at the ceiling, still wearing his leather jacket and his boots.

"Get out," he said without looking at me.

I didn't know what to say. There was nothing I could say right now. Instead I dropped my coat onto the floor and walked to the bed, which was just a full-size mattress and box spring stacked on the floor, neatly made up with a threadbare down comforter.

Hunter tensed and looked at me in disbelief as I lowered myself next to him. I thought he was going to push me right off the bed onto the floor, but he didn't move, and hesitantly I edged closer to him till I was lying by his side. I put my head on his shoulder and curled myself up next to him, with my arm draped over his chest and my leg across his. His body was rigid. I closed my eyes and tried to sink into him. "I'm so sorry," I murmured, praying that he would let me stay long enough to really apologize. "I'm so sorry. I didn't know what else to do. I didn't know what was going to happen. I just couldn't bear to see you hurt each other—or worse. I'm sorry."

It was a long time before he relaxed at all and longer still before his hand came up to stroke my hair and hold me close to him. It was starting to get dark outside, it was late, and I hadn't yet drunk the special herb tea I was supposed to drink before my tàth meànma brach. But I lay there with Hunter slowly stroking my hair, feeling like I had found a special sort of refuge, a safe haven completely different from what I had experienced with Cal. I didn't know if Hunter would ever be able to forgive me; I had never been able to truly forgive Cal for doing the same thing to me. But I hoped that somehow Hunter was a bigger person than I was, a better person, and would find a way not to hold this against me forever.

It was then I realized how incredibly important his opinion of me was, how much his feelings mattered to me, how desperately I wanted him to care for me, admire me, the way I cared for and admired him.

Finally I took a deep breath and said, "I love you. I want you. This is right."

And Hunter said, "Yes," and he kissed me, and it was as if a universe unfolded within me. I felt infinite, timeless, and when I opened my eyes and looked at Hunter, he was outlined in a blaze of golden light, as if he were the sun itself.

Magick.

# 12.
# The Brach

Daniel is in England again. He's been gone two weeks, and I'm not sure when he'll be back. He always comes back, though. The temptation is strong to cast a summoning spell on him, pulling him to me sooner, but I have resisted, and there's a satisfaction in knowing that he always comes back because he can't help himself and not because I forced him to.

Is this marriage? This isn't my parents' marriage, quiet and sedate and tandem. When Daniel and I are together, we are shouting, arguing, fighting, and despising each other, and then we are grappling, falling to the bed, making love with intense passion that has as much to do with hate as it does with love. And then in the aftermath I see his beauty once again, not just his physical beauty, but *his inner sweetness, the goodness inside him. I love and appreciate that, even as it clashes so harshly with what is inside me.*

*We have moments of calm and gentleness, during which we're holding hands and kissing sweetly. Then Amyranth raises its head or his studies call him away, and we are again two angry cats tied in a burlap bag and thrown into a river: desperate, clawing, fighting, trying only to survive no matter the cost. And he goes away and I immerse myself in Amyranth, and I know I could never give it up. Then I miss Daniel and he comes back, and the cycle starts again.*

*Is this marriage? It is my marriage.*

*—SB*

I'm not sure how long I lay with Hunter. Eventually his even breathing told me he was asleep. I didn't think he had forgiven me just because I had told him I loved him and he had kissed me. Was I fickle, to love someone else so soon after Cal? Was I setting myself up for another heartbreak? Did Hunter love me? I felt he did. But I had no idea whether we had a future, where our relationship would lead us, how long it would last. These questions would have to wait: now it was time, past time, for me to prepare for the tàth meànma brach.

Moving quietly, I uncoiled myself and left the room. Holding my shoes in one hand, I went downstairs. Sky was in the kitchen, reading the newspaper and drinking something hot and steaming in a mug. She looked at me expectantly.

"I'll explain it all later," I told her, feeling very tired.

"It's late," she said after a moment. "Almost five o'clock. I'll fix you your special tea." She made me a huge pot of it, and I started drinking it obediently. It tasted like licorice and wood and chamomile and things I couldn't identify.

"What does this tea do?" I asked, finishing the mug.

"Well . . . ," said Sky.

I found out before she finished speaking. The secret of the herbal tea was that it was a system cleanser and basically finished off the effects of the fasting and the water drinking. I doubled over as I felt my stomach cramp. Sky, trying not to smirk, pointed to the downstairs bathroom.

In between bouts of, ahem, gut emptying, I meditated and talked to Sky. I told her what had happened with Cal, and she listened with surprising compassion. I wondered—hoped—that my binding spell had worn off and he wasn't still stuck in the cemetery in the cold. It must have. Where was he now? How angry was he? Had he felt my love for him die, the way I had?

Sky asked at some point, "How are you feeling?"

"Empty," I said bleakly, and she laughed.

"You'll be glad of it later," she said. "Trust me. I've seen people do a brach without cleaning out their systems and fasting, and they truly regretted it."

I sniffed the air. "What's that?"

"Lasagna," Sky admitted. "It's almost seven."

"Oh, Jesus," I moaned, feeling hollow and starving and exhausted.

"Here," Sky said briskly, holding out a bundle of pale

green linen. "This is for you. I've drawn you a bath upstairs and put in some purifying herbs and oils and things. Have a good soak in the tub, and you'll feel better. Afterward put this on, with nothing underneath. Also, no knickers, no jewelry, no nail polish, nothing in your hair. All right?"

I nodded and headed up the stairs. Hunter was in the upstairs bathroom, putting out a rough, unbleached towel. I had showered here once before, but now it felt bizarrely intimate, taking a bath in his house—especially so soon after we had been kissing on his bed. I felt myself blush, and he gave me an unreadable look and left the room, closing the door behind him.

The bathroom looked lovely, very romantic, with all the lights off and candles burning everywhere. Steam rose from the water in the claw-foot tub, and there were violet petals floating on it, and rosemary, and eucalyptus. I shimmied out of my clothes and sank blissfully into the hot water. I don't know how long I lay there, my eyes closed, inhaling the fragrant steam and feeling the tension draining away. There was a fine grit of salt lining the bottom of the tub, and I rubbed it into my skin, knowing it would help purify me and dispel negative energy.

I felt Sky coming closer, and then she tapped on the door and said, "Ten minutes. Alyce will be here soon."

Quickly I grabbed the homemade soap and a washcloth and scrubbed myself all over. Then I shampooed my hair. I ran fresh water and rinsed myself off well, then rubbed hard with the rough towel until I was dry. I felt like a goddess; clean, light, pure, almost ethereal. The horrible events of the day receded, and I felt ready for anything, as if I could wave my hand and rearrange the stars in the sky.

I untangled my long, damp hair with a wooden comb I found, then put on the green robe. At last I floated downstairs barefoot to find Alyce, Sky, and Hunter waiting for me in the circle room. I paused uncertainly in the doorway, and the first thought I had was, Hunter knows I'm naked under this. But nothing in his face betrayed that knowledge, and then Alyce was walking toward me, her hands outstretched, and we hugged. She was wearing a lavender robe very similar to mine, and her hair was down for once, silver and flowing halfway down her back. She looked serene, and I was so grateful to her for doing this.

Sky and Hunter both came forward and hugged each of us, and I was acutely aware of how his lean body felt against mine. I noticed that he had already started drawing circles of power on the floor. There were three: a white one of chalk, then one made of salt, and then an inner one of a golden powder that smelled spicy, like saffron. Thirteen white pillar candles ringed the outer circle, and Alyce and I walked through the circle openings. We sat cross-legged on the floor, facing each other, smiling into each other's eyes as Hunter closed the circles and chanted spells of protection.

"Morgan of Kithic and Alyce of Starlocket, do you agree to enter knowingly and willingly into a tàth meànma brach here tonight?" asked Sky formally.

"Yes," I said, and nervousness bubbled up inside me. Was I really ready? Could I accept Alyce's knowledge? Or would I end up going blind, like that witch Hunter had told about?

"Yes," Alyce said.

"Then let's begin," said Hunter. He and Sky drew back

from the circles and sat leaning against cushions by a far wall. I got the impression they were like spotters who would jump in and help us if anything weird happened.

Alyce reached out with her hands and put them on my shoulders, and I did the same to her. We leaned our heads over until our foreheads touched lightly, our eyes still open. Her shoulders felt warm and smooth and round under my hands; I wondered if I felt bony, raw, under hers.

Then, to my amazement, she started chanting my own personal power spell, the one that had come to me weeks ago.

*"An di allaigh an di aigh*
*An di allaigh an di ne ullah*
*An di ullah be nith rah*
*Cair di na ulla nith rah*
*Cair feal ti theo nith rah*
*An di allaigh an di aigh."*

My voice joined hers, and we sang it together, the ancient rhythm flowing through our blood like a heartbeat. My heart lifted as we sang, and I saw joy on Alyce's face, making her beautiful, her violet-blue eyes full of wisdom and comfort. We sang, two women, joined by power, by Wicca, by joy, by trust. And slowly, gently, I became aware that the barriers between our minds were dissolving.

The next thing I was aware of was that my eyes were closed—or if they weren't closed, I was no longer seeing things around me, was no longer conscious of where I was. For a moment I wondered with panic if I were blind, but then I lost myself in wonder. Alyce and I were floating, joined, in a sort of nether space where we could simultaneously see everything and nothing. In my mind Alyce held out her hands and smiled at me, saying, "Come."

My muscles tensed as I seemed to be drawn toward an electrified wormhole, and Alyce said, "Relax, let it come," and I tried to release every bit of resistance I had. And then . . . and then I was inside Alyce's mind: I was Alyce, and she was me, and we were joined. I took in a sharp breath as waves and waves of knowledge swept toward me, cresting and peaking and lapping against my brain.

"Let it come," Alyce murmured, and again I realized I had tensed up and again I tried to release the tension and the fear and open myself to receive whatever she gave. Reams of sigils and characters and signs and spells crashed into me, chants and ancient alphabets and books of learning. Plants and crystals and stones and metals and their properties. I heard a high-pitched whimpering sound and wondered if it was me. I knew I was in pain: I felt like I wore a helmet of metal spikes that were slowly driving into my skull. But stronger than the pain was my joy at the beauty around me.

Oh, oh, I thought, unable to form words. Flowers spun toward me through the darkness, flowers and spiked woody branches and the scents of bitter smoke, and suddenly it was all too intense, and bile rose in my throat, and I was glad I had nothing in me to throw up.

I saw a younger, brown-haired Alyce wearing a crown of laurel leaves as she danced around a maypole as a teenager. I saw the shame of failed spells, charms gone wrong, a panicked mind blanking before a teacher's stern rebuke. I felt flames of desire licking at her skin, but the man she desired faded away before I saw who he had been, and something in me knew he had died, and that Alyce had been with him when he had.

A cat passed me, a tortoiseshell cat she had loved profoundly, a cat who had comforted her in grief and calmed her in fear. Her deep affection for David Redstone, her anguish and disbelief at his betrayal swirled through me like a hurricane, leaving me gasping. Then more spells and more knowledge and more pages and pages of book learning: spells of protection, of ward evil, of illusion, of strength. Spells to stay awake, to heal, to help in learning, to help in childbirth, to comfort the ailing, the grieving, the ones left behind when someone dies.

And scents: throughout it all the scents roiled through me, making me gag and then inhale deeply, following a tantalizing scent of flowers and incense. There was smoke and burned flesh and oils gone bad; there was food offered to the Goddess, food shared with friends, food used in rituals. There was the metallic tang of blood, coppery and sharp, that made my stomach burn, and wretched odors of sickness, of unhealed flesh, of rot, and I was panting, wanting to run away.

"Let it come," Alyce whispered, and her voice cracked.

I wanted to say something, say it was too much, to slow it down, to give me time, that I was drowning, but no words came out that I could hear, and then more of Alyce's knowing came at me, swept toward me. Her deep, personal self-knowledge flowed over me like a warm river, and I let myself go into it, into the power that is itself a form of magick, the power of womanhood, of creation. I felt Alyce's deep ties to the earth, to the moon's cycles. I saw how strong women are, how much we can bear, how we can draw on the earth's deep power.

I felt a smile on my face, my eyes closed, joy welling up inside me. Alyce was me, and I was her, and we were together. It was beautiful magick, made more beautiful as I realized that as much as Alyce was sending toward me, she was also receiving from me. I saw her surprise, even her awe at my powers, the powers I was slowly discovering and becoming comfortable with. Eagerly she fed on my mind, and I was delighted by how exciting she found the breadth of my strength, the depth of my power, my magick that stretched back a thousand years within my clan. She shared my sorrow over Cal and rejoiced with me in the discovery of my love for Hunter. She saw all the questions I had about my birth parents, how I longed to have known them. Gladly I gave to her, opened myself to her thoughts, shared my heritage and my life

And it was in opening my mind to share with Alyce that I saw myself: saw how strong I could be if I realized my potential; saw the dangerously thin line between good and evil that I would walk my whole life; saw myself as a child, as I was now, as a woman in the future. My strength would be beautiful, awe-inspiring, if only I could find a way to make myself whole. I needed answers. Dimly I became aware of warm tears on my cheeks, their saltiness running into my mouth.

Slowly, gradually, we began to separate into two beings again, our one joined whole pulled into two, like mitosis. The separation was as jarring and uncomfortable as the joining had been, and I mourned the loss of Alyce in my consciousness and felt her mourn the loss of me. We pulled apart, our hands slipping from each other's shoulders. Then my spine straightened, and I frowned, my eyes snapping open.

I looked at Alyce and saw that she, too, was aware of a

third presence: there was Morgan, and Alyce, and some unnamed force that was intruding, reaching toward me, sending dark tendrils of influence into my mind.

"Selene," I gasped, and Alyce was already there, throwing up blocks against the dark magick that had crept around us like a bog wisp, like smoke, like a poisonous gas. The ward-evil spell came to me easily, remembered and retrieved, and without effort I said the words and drew the sigils and put up my own blocks against what I sensed coming toward me. Alyce and I knew each other, had each other's learning and essence, and I called on knowledge only minutes old to protect myself against Selene, scrying to find me, reaching out to control me.

She was gone in an instant.

When I opened my eyes again, the world had settled into relative normalcy: I was sitting on the wooden floor of Sky and Hunter's house, and they were kneeling close, outside the circles, watching us. Alyce was opposite me, opening her eyes and taking a deep breath.

"What was that?" Sky asked.

"Selene," I answered.

"Selene," Alyce said at the same time. "Looking for Morgan."

"Why would she need to look for me?" I asked.

"It's more getting in touch with your mind," Alyce explained. "Seeing where you are magickally. Even trying to control you from a great distance."

"But she's gone now, right?" said Hunter. When I nodded, he asked, "How did it go? How do you both feel?"

My eyes met Alyce's. I ran a mental inventory. "Uh, I feel strange," I said, and then I fainted.

# 13.
# Charred

November 12, 1980

Another day, another fight with Daniel. His constant antagonism is exhausting. He hates Amyranth and everything about it, and of course he only knows a tiny, tiny part of it. If he knew anything like the whole story, he would leave me forever. Which is completely unacceptable. I've been trying to come to terms with this dilemma since I met him, and I still don't have an answer. He refuses to see the beauty of Amyranth's cause. I've rejected his attempts to show me the beauty of goody-two-shoes scholarship and boiling up garlic-and-ginger tisanes to help clear up coughs.

Why am I unable to let him go? No man has ever held this much sway over me, not even Patrick. I want to give Daniel up, I've tried, but I get only as far as wishing him gone before I start aching desperately to have him back. I *simply love him, want him. The irony of this doesn't escape me. When we're good together, we're really, truly good, and we both feel a joy, a completeness that can't be matched or denied. Lately, though, it seems like the good times are fewer and farther between—we have truly irreconcilable differences.*

*If I bend Daniel's will to my own through magick, how much would he be diminished? How much would I?*

*—SB*

When I woke up on Monday, I felt awful. I had dim memories of Hunter driving me home in Das Boot, with Sky following in her car. He had whispered some quick words in my ear on my front porch, and I was able to walk and talk and look halfway normal for my parents before I stumbled upstairs into bed with all my clothes on. How did I get out of the robe and back into my clothes? Ugh. I'd think about that later.

"Morgan?" Mary K. poked her head around the bathroom door. "You okay? It's almost ten o'clock."

"Mpf," I mumbled. Dagda, my gray kitten, padded in after her and leaped up onto my bedspread. He had grown so much in just a few weeks. Purring, he stomped his way up the comforter toward me, and I reached out to kiss his little triangular head and rub his ears. He collapsed, exhausted, and closed his eyes. I knew how he felt.

In fact, I knew how Mary K. felt as well. I opened my eyes again to see my sister regarding herself in the mirror. I could sense her feelings with more accuracy and immediacy than just sisterly intuition. Mary K. was sad and kind of lost. I frowned, wondering how I could help her. Then she turned around. "I guess I'll go over to Jaycee's. Maybe we can get her sister to take us to the mall. I've still got to get some Christmas presents."

"I'd take you," I said, "but I don't think I can get out of bed."

"Are you coming down with something?" she asked.

Not exactly, but . . . "Probably just a cold." I sniffled experimentally.

"Well, can I get you anything before I leave?"

I thought about food, and my stomach recoiled. "Do we have any ginger ale?"

"Yeah. You want some?"

"Sure."

I was able to keep the ginger ale down. I didn't feel sick, exactly, just drained and fuzzy. Other aftereffects of the brach were apparent as well. It was similar to what I'd felt after my first circle with Cal and Cirrus, but magnified by a factor of ten. My senses seemed even more heightened than they had that time: I could make out distinct threads in the jeans hanging over my desk chair; I saw tiny motes of dust caught in the new paint on my walls. Later in the morning I heard a bizarre crunching sound coming from downstairs, as if a hundred-pound termite was eating the basement. It turned out to be Dagda working on his kibble. I felt my lungs absorbing oxygen from every breath; felt my blood cells flowing through my veins, suspended in plasma; felt how each square inch of my skin interpreted and analyzed air or fabric or whatever touched it.

I felt magick everywhere, flowing around me, flowing out of me, in the air, in anything organic, in the sleeping trees outside, in Dagda, in anything that I touched.

I assumed this hyperawareness would fade gradually. It had better. It was wonderful, but if I were this sensitive all the time, I'd lose my mind.

A golden brownish maple leaf drifted past my window. It came to rest for an instant on the sill, and I gazed meditatively at it, marveling at the complex network of tiny veins that spread across its surface. I almost thought I could make out a face in the intersecting lines—a wide, firm mouth, straight nose, two golden eyes. . . .

Goddess. Cal.

In the next instant the leaf was caught in a gust of wind and danced away.

I lay there in bed, breathing deeply, trying to regain my lost peace. But it was hard, because although after yesterday I no longer feared Cal the way I had, every thought of Cal led to a thought of Selene and to the sure knowledge that she was still searching for me, still plotting to destroy me.

Gradually I became aware of something nagging at the edge of my consciousness. My quest. My search for more knowledge about my birth parents, my heritage. I hadn't done anything about it yet, but now, with the new clarity I had achieved as a result of the brach, I saw how much I needed to. Only then would I be whole; only then would my power be fully accessible to me; only then would it be truly mine. And only then would I have a hope against Selene.

Eventually I struggled to my feet and changed into clean clothes, dismissing a shower as unnecessary. I brushed my hair and my teeth and felt I'd done enough grooming for one day. After I flopped back onto my bed, I sensed Hunter coming up my front walk. I groaned, wanting to see him but knowing I could never make it downstairs to open the door.

"Hunter, just come in," I whispered, sending him a witch message.

Moments later I heard the front door snick open, then Hunter calling, "Morgan?"

"I'm upstairs," I managed to call. "You can come up." I wondered if I now had a spell in the recesses of my brain that would keep my mom from unexpectedly coming home from work.

His footsteps were light on the stairs, and then he was peering around my door. "Is it okay for me to be here?" he asked.

I smiled, pleased that he'd asked. "No one's here but me," I said.

"Right," said Hunter, coming in. "If we feel someone coming home, I'll jump out the window." He stood, tall and lean and newly familiar, and looked down at me. His hair was messy from his hat, and it stood up in pale gold spikes.

"Okay," I said. Cautiously I put out my senses and felt his awareness that I'd done so.

"How are you feeling?" he asked.

"Crappy. Weak. But really, really magicky." I couldn't help grinning.

He groaned theatrically. "Now I'm frightened. Please, please," he said. "I'm begging you. Please do not do anything with your new magick just yet. Do not cast spells. Do not run around town throwing witch fire at anyone. Promise me."

"It's like you don't trust my judgment or something," I said. He came to sit on the end of my bed and put one hand on my comforter-covered leg. I started to feel better.

"Oh," he said, rolling his eyes. "So you actually think you use judgment sometimes?"

I kicked him, and then we were grinning at each other, and I felt much better.

"That was an amazing brach last night," he said. "Very intense."

"It was," I agreed. "How's Alyce? Have you talked to her?"

He nodded. "Sky is with her, and another witch from Starlocket, too. She feels about like you do. She's excited, though. She got a lot from you."

"I got a lot from her," I said slowly. "I haven't begun to process it."

"It will take you a long time," Hunter predicted. Absently he rubbed my leg, below the knee, and I looked at his eyes, wondering how to say what I needed to.

"I'm so sorry about yesterday," I said, and his eyes darkened. I swallowed. "It was just—I couldn't go through that again. The last time—on the cliff—when I thought you were dead, that I had killed you. I just—couldn't go through that. I couldn't have you two fighting—trying to kill each other. Never again."

His face was still, watchful.

"I'm so sorry I put the binding spell on you," I said. "I know how horrible that feels. I've never forgiven Cal for doing it to me. Now I've done it to you. But I just didn't know how else to get out of there and to take you with me. I'm so sorry," I ended miserably.

"Cal needs to come in," Hunter said quietly. "He needs to answer to the council. And because of who I am and where I am, it will be me who has to bring him in."

I nodded, trying to accept that.

Hunter stroked my knee, and I felt a trembly sensation start at his fingertips and move up to the pit of my stomach. He was quiet for a long while, and I reached out and held his hand.

"Yule is tomorrow," he said finally.

"That's right. I lost track of the days. I hope I'll be up to celebrating by then."

"I think you will," he said with a smile.

"There's something else I need to do tomorrow," I said. "If I can move."

"What's that?"

"I need to go to Meshomah Falls." That was the town where my birth parents had briefly lived—and where they had died. "I want to find the place where the barn burned down."

"Why?" he asked.

"To learn," I said. "There's so much I don't know. Who set the fire? Why? I need to find out. I feel like I won't be whole until I do. That's what I learned from the brach."

Hunter looked at me for a long moment. "It's dangerous, you know," he said. "With Cal roaming about and Selene on her way."

I didn't say anything.

Then he nodded. "All right," he said. "I'll pick you up at ten, shall I?"

God, I loved him.

\*       \*       \*

Hunter drove, because I was still a little shaky on Tuesday. He didn't bring up the subject of Cal, except to tell me that he still hadn't been able to locate him. "I wonder if he's got someone helping him," Hunter said, rubbing his chin, and I thought of Selene and felt a flash of dread. Was she here now? No. She couldn't be. I wasn't ready.

Then Hunter took my hand without speaking, and I felt his strength flowing into me, calming me. I am with you, he was saying without words. And I felt suddenly better, lighter.

I'd been to Meshomah Falls once before, and it felt familiar to me now. I directed Hunter to the outskirts of town. There was an old field there, tan and dry from the winter cold. I got out of the car and walked to the middle of it. I still felt weak, drained, as if I were getting over the flu.

Maeve's coven tools were in the trunk of the car, but I left them there. I didn't need them yet. Hunter came to stand next to me.

"Okay. Let's find the old barn site," he said.

I stood still, my arms slightly out by my sides, and shut down all thoughts, all feelings, all expectations. Soon I no longer felt the winter sun on my face or the wind in my hair. But I could see where the barn had been, see what it had looked like and what the site looked like now. I followed it in my mind, tracing how to get there from here. When it was clear, I opened my eyes, feeling vaguely nauseated.

"Okay, I got it," I said, and swallowed. I headed back to the car and the Diet Coke that was waiting there.

"Are you sure you're up to this?" Hunter asked as I swigged soda and held the cold can against my forehead.

"I have to do it," I said. "I just . . . I have to."

He nodded and started the car. "Yes, I think you're right. Tonight at the Yule circle we'll send you some restoring energy."

"Take the next left," I said, already feeling better.

We found it almost fifteen minutes later, after getting lost a couple of times. Like Widow's Vale, this area was hilly and rocky, the narrow roads lined with skeletal trees and bushes. In the springtime it would be beautiful and in the summer unbelievably lush and green. I hoped Maeve had found a small measure of happiness here, at least for a short while.

"There it is," I said, pointing suddenly. I recognized a twisted spruce as one that I'd seen in my mind's eye. "In there."

Hunter pulled the car to the side of the road and peered skeptically past the tree line. We got out, and I quickly jumped the old-fashioned slat fence. Hunter followed. I strode forward through the dead clumps of frozen grass, sending out my senses and looking alertly at everything. There was almost nothing alive around here, no birds, no animals hibernating in nests or trees, no deer or rabbits watching quietly nearby.

"Hmmm," said Hunter, slowing down and scanning the area. "What do you feel?"

I swallowed. "I feel like we're close to something really bad."

I slowed my pace and started looking more closely at the ground. Suddenly I halted, as if an invisible hand had pressed my chest and stopped me cold. I looked closer, focusing sharply on the ground between the clumps of grass. I didn't even know what to look for, but then I saw it: the rippled, broken backbone of a large brick foundation. The barn had once stood here.

I stepped back, as if it were poison ivy. Hunter came up next to me, looking uncomfortable and edgy.

"Now what?" he asked.

"I get my tools," I said.

I made Hunter turn around while I wiggled out of my clothes and put on Maeve's robe. No one but my mother, my sister, and my gynecologist had seen me naked, and I was going to keep it that way. At least for the immediately foreseeable future.

"Okay, I'm ready," I said, and Hunter turned to look at me.

"How do you want to do this?" he said. "I don't have my robe or tools with me."

"I'm thinking meditation," I answered. "Together, the two of us, with my tools."

Hunter thought about it and nodded. By picking our way through the years of overgrowth, we found two walls of the former foundation. Gauging our position from the angle of the crumbling bricks, we sat in what had been the center of the barn. I held Maeve's athame in my left hand, her wand in my right. Between Hunter and me I placed several crystals and two bloodstones. We drew a circle of power around us with a stick and then closed our eyes. I took a deep breath, tried to release tension, and lost myself in nothingness.

*The inside of the barn was dark. Angus and I stood in the middle of the building, hearing running footsteps around the outside. I was muttering spells under my breath, spells I hadn't used in two years. My magick felt dull, blunted, an unhoned blade no longer useful. Beside me I felt Angus's fear, his hopelessness. Why are you wasting energy on feelings? I wanted to scream.*

*My eyes adjusted to the blackness inside the barn. The scents of old hay, animals from long ago, ancient leather filled my nose, and I wanted to sneeze. Still I chanted, drawing power to me:*

"An di allaigh an di aigh . . ." I reached out with my senses, probing, but they recoiled on me. It was as if we were trapped in a cage made of crystal—a cage that reflected our power back at us rather than letting it out to do its work.

The first sharp scent of smoke came to me. Angus gripped my hand tightly, and I shook him off, feeling sudden anger at the way he'd loved me all these years—years when he'd known that I didn't love him. Why hadn't he demanded more from me? Why hadn't he left me? Then maybe he wouldn't be here now, dying with me.

Smoke. I heard the hungry crackling of the fire as it lapped the base of the barn, as it whipped down the sides, hurrying to meet itself, to make a full circle of flames. The barn was old, dry, the wood half rotted: perfect kindling. Ciaran had known.

"Our child." Angus's voice was full of pain.

"She's safe," I said, feeling guilt weighing on me, further weakening my powers. "She will always be safe." The small windows, high on the barn walls, glowed pinkly, and I knew it was from fire, not from dawn. No one would find us. Ciaran's magick would make sure of that. No one would call the fire department until it was much too late. Already the building was filling with smoke, hovering by the ceiling, swirling on itself, thickening.

Maybe it wasn't too late. Maybe I could find a way out. I still had my power, rusty though it might be. "An di allaigh an di aigh . . . ," I began once again.

But at my words, the cage of magick around us seemed to tighten, to contract, glittering as it pressed in on us. I coughed and inhaled smoke. And then I knew there was no hope.

It had come to this. Ciaran was going to be my death. He had shown me what love was, what it could be, and now he would show me my death. I felt sharp regret that Angus would die here, too. I tried to console myself with the fact that it had been his choice. He had always chosen to be with me.

I wondered what Ciaran was doing outside: if he was still watching, making sure we didn't escape; if he was weaving magick all around us, spells of death and binding, panic and fear. I felt panic's claws scraping at my mind, but I refused to let it in. I tried to keep calm, to call power to me. I thought about my baby, my beautiful baby, with her fine, fuzzy infant hair the color of my mother's. Her tilted, brown eyes, so like her father's. The most perfect baby ever born, with a thousand years of Belwicket magick in her veins, in her blood.

She would be safe from this kind of danger. Safe from her heritage. I had made sure of that.

It was hard to breathe, and I dropped to my knees. Angus was coughing, trying to breathe through his shirt, pulled up to cover his nose and mouth. I had mended that shirt this morning, sewed on a button.

Ciaran. Even here, now, I couldn't help remembering how he'd made me feel when we'd first met. It had been so clear we were meant to be together. So clear that we were muìrn beatha dàns. But he was married to another and a father. And I chose Angus. Poor Angus. Then Ciaran chose the darkness, over me.

I felt light-headed. Sweat was beading on my forehead, in my hair; soot was stinging my eyes. Angus was coughing nonstop. I took his hand as I sank into the fine dust on the barn floor, feeling the heat pressing in from all sides. I no longer chanted. It was no use. Ciaran had always been stronger than I—he had gone through the Great Trial.

I had never had a chance.

# 14.
# Bait

November 1981

I'm pregnant. It's a bizarre physiological experience, like being taken over by an alien that I can't control. Every cell in my body is changing. It's thrilling and terrifying: much like being part of Amyranth.

Daniel, of course, is furious. These past six months he's always furious with me, so there's nothing new there. We'd agreed not to have children because our marriage has seemed so rocky. By myself, I decided I wanted to have part of Daniel always, wanted to have something permanent that was partly me and partly him. So I used magick to override his conception block. It was easy.

So Daniel's thrown a fit and hightailed it back to England. I've settled in San Francisco because of the strong Amyranth presence here. What is it about

*England that pulls him back so strongly? This is the third time in three months that he's gone back. For me, my home is where Amyranth is. Daniel's sentimental loyalty seems naïve and misplaced.*

*He'll be back soon. He always comes back. And the mirror shows me that pregnant, I am more beautiful than ever. When he sees me glowing, carrying our child, it will be a new start for us. I can feel it.*

*—SB*

When I opened my eyes, tears were streaming down my face. Hunter was watching me, looking calm and alert. He reached toward me and brushed some tears away with his hand.

"Did you see any of that?" I asked, my throat tight and full of pain.

"Some," he said, helping me stand. We were both chilled through, and I wanted to be gone from this place, far away from these feelings. I looked down at the broken foundations and could still smell the ancient ash, the charred boards. I could hear the snap of the windows as they broke one by one from the heat. The smell of skin and hair, burning. They had been dead by then.

"The images I got were confused," said Hunter. He pulled me to him as we walked back to the car, and by the time I had changed out of my robe and was sitting in the passenger seat, I was crying hard, my hands over my face. Hunter hugged me, his arms around me, his hands stroking my hair.

"It was Ciaran," I finally got out. "The love of my mother's life. He killed her and Angus."

"Why?"

"I don't know," I said, frustrated. "Because he couldn't have her? Because she rejected him when she found out he was married? Because she chose Angus? I don't know."

I rested my head against Hunter's chest, feeling how lean and hard he was through his coat. I knew that he understood pain because of what had happened to his parents. Maybe someday, I'd be able to help Hunter as he was helping me now. Suddenly his fingers stilled against my back and tension entered his body. I raised my head and closed my eyes.

"Selene," I whispered, already throwing up the magick blocks I had learned from Alyce. I quickly erected wall after wall around me, sealing my mind off from outside influences, surrounding myself and Hunter with ward-evil spells, protection spells, spells of concealment and strength. It took only instants, and I felt Selene's increased pressure as she tried to get through, tried to get into my mind. My hand gripped Hunter's, and our powers joined—I felt his strength shoring up mine and was grateful.

Just like that, it was over. I no longer felt any other presence. Slowly Hunter and I let each other go, and I felt a pang of regret at losing that particular closeness.

"She wants you badly," Hunter said grimly, sitting back in his seat. "That's the second time she's tried to get into your mind. She must be closer than I thought. Dammit! We've searched everywhere for her—I scry every day. But I haven't been able to pick up on anything." He thought for a moment, drumming his fingers on the steering wheel. "I'm calling in help from the council." He started the car and turned on the heater.

"Will they really be able to help?" I asked, wrapping my arms around myself. I felt overwhelmed, sad and weary.

"I hope so," Hunter answered me. "Selene is working up to something, and it's going to happen soon. I feel it." He glanced over at me and put his hand on my leg. I was starting to thaw but still felt nauseated. I hoped I wouldn't have to ask Hunter to pull over so I could barf.

"Recline your seat," he suggested as I sipped the rest of my Diet Coke. "Are you sure you should be drinking that? We could stop and get a nice cup of tea somewhere."

"Coke settles your stomach," I said. "Everyone knows that." I put the can in the cup holder, then pulled the lever that reclined my seat.

"Better?" Hunter asked.

"Um," I said. My eyes felt heavy, and I let myself sink into a lovely lack of consciousness where there was no pain. The next thing I knew the car had stopped and Hunter was gently rubbing my shoulder.

"Home again, home again, jiggity jig," he said.

We were parked in front of my house. Through my window I saw that the day had turned ugly, with dark, heavy clouds rolling in from the west. It looked like snow was on the way. My watch said it was four o'clock.

I reached for the handle to straighten my seat but was caught by the expression in Hunter's eyes. All at once he seemed like the most beautiful thing I had ever seen, and I smiled at him. His eyes flared slightly, and he leaned down. I curled my arms around his neck and held him to me as our mouths met. Eagerly I kissed him, wanting to join with him, wanting to show him how I felt about him, how much I appreciated him. His breathing quickened as he held me closer, and it was thrilling to know how much he wanted me, too.

Slowly he pulled back, and our breathing gradually returned to normal.

"We need to talk about what you saw," he said quietly, stroking one finger along my jaw.

I nodded. "Maybe you could come in for a while? We could hang out in the den. My mom will more or less leave us alone in there."

He grinned at me, and we walked up to my front door. Before I could unlock it, it opened, and my mom looked at me kind of wild-eyed.

"Morgan! Thank goodness you're home! Do you know where Mary K. is? Is she with you?" She looked past me as if expecting to see my sister walking up the driveway.

"No," I answered, feeling a jolt of alarm. "I saw her this morning. She said she was going to Jaycee's."

"They haven't seen her all day," my mom said, the lines around her mouth deepening. "I came home early, and there was a message from Jaycee asking why Mary K. had stood her up."

Mom stepped aside and motioned us to come in. I was thinking about possibilities, my brain firing fast, battling the weariness I'd had since Sunday.

"Did she leave a note? What does her room look like?" I asked.

"No note anywhere, and her room is fine, like she just left," said my mom. "Her bicycle is here." Her voice sounded strained. I knew what she was thinking: Bakker.

"Let me call Bakker's house," I said, shrugging out of my coat. I headed for the kitchen, looked up Bakker's number, and dialed it. Maybe his family would know where he had gone. Maybe Mary K., using incredibly bad judgment, was there watching TV or something.

His mother answered, and I asked to speak to Bakker. To my relief, he was home, and soon said a cautious, "Hello?"

"Bakker, it's Morgan Rowlands," I said briskly. "Where's Mary K.?"

"Huh?" he said, instantly defensive. "How would I know?"

"Look, is she there? Just let me talk to her."

"Are you kidding? Thanks to you, she'll never speak to me again. I haven't seen her since school let out."

"It's *your* fault she won't speak to you," I said scathingly. "If I find out she's there and you're lying to me—"

"She's not here. Go screw yourself." Click.

I looked up to see Mom and Hunter watching me. "Apparently she's not with Bakker," I said. I tapped my finger against my lips, thinking. Mary K. had been so different lately. She'd been going to church so often, praying and reading the Bible. I felt a pang of guilt, thinking of all the times I'd tried to talk to her but hadn't pushed her to open up to me. She might be in real trouble now, and maybe I could have prevented it.

"Maybe she just went shopping or something," I said, not believing it. "Or maybe she went to an afternoon service at church. But why would she stand up Jaycee?"

"She wouldn't," said Mom, and I felt her tension, felt how close she was to panicking. "She would never do that. You know how conscientious she is."

I looked at Hunter and saw that he was thinking the

same thing I was: that we should scry to find Mary K., and that we couldn't do it in front of my mom.

"Okay," I said, reaching for my coat. "Tell you what. Hunter and I will go and look at the coffee shop and church, maybe Darcy's house, and some of the shops downtown. We'll call you in an hour with an update, but I'm sure we'll find her. She probably just forgot to leave a note. I'm sure she's okay, and there's a simple explanation."

"Okay," my mom said after a moment. "I'm probably over-reacting. It's just so unlike her to take off like this." She bit her lip. "I already called Dad. He's on his way home. He said he'd take a look around the Taunton mall, see if she's there."

"It'll be okay. We'll call you." Hunter and I went out the front door and started down the walk toward his car. I felt like I'd been in that car all day and didn't want to get back in it. Just as we reached the sidewalk, our next-door neighbor, Mrs. DiNapoli, walked over from her house.

"Hi, Morgan," she said, drawing her coat around her. "Is your mother home?" She smiled and held out a glass meas-uring cup. "I need to borrow—"

"Sugar?" I asked.

"Flour," she said. "Harry's aunt and uncle are coming to dinner, and I'm making a roux. Do you think your folks have any flour?"

"Um, probably," I said as Hunter smiled at Mrs. DiNapoli and opened the driver's side door. "Mom's inside—you can ask her. We were just on our way out."

"Okay." She headed up our driveway as I turned to get in. "That was some car earlier," Mrs. DiNapoli called back. "Whose was it?"

"What do you mean?" I asked.

"That Jaguar Mary K. got into earlier."

I froze. "You saw Mary K. getting into a Jaguar?" I'm so stupid, I thought. Why didn't I ask any of the neighbors if they had seen anything?

Mrs. DiNapoli laughed. "Yes, a beautiful green one."

Selene drove a green Jaguar. I looked at Hunter, and again our thoughts were in accord. He nodded at me briefly, then slid behind the wheel and started the engine.

"I'm not sure whose it was," I said. "How long ago was this?"

Our neighbor shrugged. "Two hours, at least. I'm not sure."

"Okay, thanks, Mrs. DiNapoli." I climbed into the passenger seat and Hunter took off, heading out of town. We knew where we needed to start looking.

Cal's old house.

# 15.
# Trap

April 1982

Be careful what you wish for, they say. Because you may get it.

I've gotten what I wished for, and the Goddess must be laughing. Daniel's come home, after being gone almost three months. The baby is due in June, and I look big and vibrant and fertile, like the Goddess herself. It's been interesting to see how pregnancy affects my magick: I'm more powerful in some ways, but there are some unpredictable side effects. Some spells fall apart, some have unexpected results. Nothing can be counted on. It's funny, for the most part. However, for the last seven months I've haven't been able to do my part for Amyranth. They've been understanding, though—they know I'll soon present them with a perfect Amyranth baby, one literally born to do their work.

*It's hard for me to put the next words down. I've found out the reason Daniel goes to England so much: he has a girlfriend there. He actually told me this himself. I was sure he was joking—what woman, witch or human, can compete with me? But as he droned on and the words started sinking in, I went through being amused, then horrified, then furious. This other woman, whom he won't name, and he have known each other for years and had a childhood romance. But their affair only started six months ago—right after I conceived my baby. I'm shocked beyond words. The idea that Daniel could keep such a secret from me is unbelievable. It means his powers are stronger than I knew, and how is that possible?*

*I'm thinking about what to do next. That this other woman has to be found and eliminated goes without saying. Daniel says their affair is over. Pathetically, he wept when he told me. What a worm! He came back to me for the sake of the baby we're having, but he won't sleep with me and says he won't pretend we're a couple anymore. This won't do at all. He's going to be mine or no one's. I have to break his will, bind him to me. Now I must go—I have research to do and people to consult.*

*—SB*

Hunter pulled over while we were still a mile from Cal's. He cut the engine and turned to me.

"Why are you stopping?" I said urgently. "Let's go! If she has Mary K.—"

"I know, and we'll get there. But first, send Sky and Alyce a witch message," he said. "I'd send it, but yours will be stronger. Tell them to contact the council and get reinforcements to Selene's as fast as they can. It will take a couple of hours at least, but maybe they can get here in time to help us."

"Should I ask Sky and Alyce to meet us there now?" I asked. "We could all join our powers. . . ."

He shook his head. "They aren't equipped for this battle," he said gently. "Neither are you, if it comes to that. But this is about you, about what Selene wants from you."

"I'll be strong enough," I said, not at all sure that was true. "If she's done anything to Mary K.—"

"What's important is that you use your own powers," Hunter said, looking at me intently. "Use your powers, coupled with Alyce's knowledge. Feel the power within you. Know it absolutely. Selene is going to try to use illusion and fear to break you down. Don't let it work."

I looked into his eyes, feeling dread. "All right," I said shakily.

He started the engine. Five minutes later he was turning down the street that led to the huge stone house where Cal and Selene had worked their magick.

Darkness was all around us. It was barely five o'clock but wintertime, and the sun had sunk below the horizon, obscured by ominous-looking clouds. I could feel that soon the sky would open and start dumping snow and ice.

Mary K., I thought as Hunter parked down the street, out of sight of the big house. My sweet sister. Although we shared no blood, I felt we had always been sisters in spirit: destined to be related to each other, to love each other as family. In some ways she was so much savvier than I—she knew what to wear, who to hang out with, how to flirt and be cheerful and charming. But in some ways she was so naive. She trusted most people. She believed that her faith would protect her. She believed that if she was good enough, everything would work out. I knew better than that.

"Pop the trunk," I told Hunter, and he did. I knew I would need every ounce of power I could possibly have: I was still feeling the draining effects of the tàth meànma brach. Without more than a moment's awkward hesitation I stripped off my coat, sweatshirt, and undershirt and put on my mother's robe, the thin emerald green silk instantly warming me in the cold night air. I felt my cheeks heat with a blush as I unsnapped my jeans and pushed them and my underwear down. Of course then I realized I still wore my sneaks and socks and had to kneel and get out of them to get out of my pants.

Then I stood, feeling completely comfortable in the robe and nothing else even though it was winter in upstate New York. Like a Wiccan force field, I thought, picking up Maeve's wand and athame.

"I wish I'd had time to collect my own robe," Hunter said, frowning. He pulled out his athame. Thus armed, we began to move quietly toward the house.

We were immediately aware of a darkness of magick all around. Keeping to the shadows of the hedge that surrounded the property, I cast out my senses and felt a miasma of black magick emanating from the house, from the stones themselves. The green Jaguar sat in the circular driveway, and to my eyes it seemed to glow and pulse, almost as if it were radioactive. I realized that I was terrified and tried to release my fears.

In unspoken agreement we paused, and together we wrapped ourselves in cloaks of illusion, of vagueness, of shadows. With no effort I pulled spells out of Alyce's memory and called them to me, as familiar to me as Dagda. Under any other circumstances I would have felt thrilled with my new ability, but now I merely fretted. To any lesser witch we would certainly be undetectable, but would these spells work on Selene? She was so powerful that I doubted it.

We looked at the house, with its gaping black windows, its air of recent neglect. Dried leaves had blown onto the porch and steps and remained unswept.

"How did she get in?" I whispered. "The house was spelled against her."

"The council did its best," Hunter replied softly. "But Selene has powers and connections we don't fully understand. The question is, how can we get in? The front door will be a trap."

I crouched down for a moment, examining the house. Then an idea came to me, and I stood up. "Come with me."

Without waiting for his response, I strode along the hedge until we reached a break in the tall shrubbery to the right of the house. We crunched across dead grass, around to the back, where a narrow metal staircase led up to the third-floor attic. Cal's old room. I started climbing, my bare feet making hardly any sound.

"We spelled all the entrances," Hunter reminded me quietly.

"I know. But you can break your spells; you made them. And I don't think Selene will expect us to come in this way." The whole time I climbed, I was feeling with my senses, searching for my sister, for Selene's presence, trying to get through the spells of privacy that cloaked the house. I could feel nothing except an aching, bone-deep weariness, the faint edges of nausea around the rim of my consciousness, and the seeping of tendrils of dark magick writhing in the air all around me.

At the top of the narrow staircase was a small wooden door. Cal used to use it to get from his room to the back-yard and to the pool beyond. I stopped for a moment, pressed my hand against my brow, closed my eyes, and concentrated.

It wasn't as if everything suddenly popped out at me in neon colors. But as I thought, willing magick to show itself to me, the layers of the spells on the door slowly and faintly began to glimmer. I was vaguely aware of Hunter, next to me, becoming very still and alert as the sigils and markings of spells shone with a slight sheen around the door frame. I saw the oldest markings, those of Cal himself, spelling the door so that it would open only to his command. I can't say how I knew these spells were his, how I knew what they were and how he had made them. It was more like seeing a daisy and thinking, Daisy. It was clear and instantaneous.

It was also clear that Cal's spells had been mostly obliter-ated, I guessed by the International Council of Witches. Their spells were complicated and gleamed brightly. I didn't know the council members well enough to recognize their handiwork but felt that I saw traces of Hunter's handwriting, his personality in the spells. Again I could never have explained it or proved it. I just knew.

Overlying everything were dark, spiky spells of illusion and repulsion that I recognized as Selene's handiwork. She had used an ancient alphabet and an archaic set of characters, and just seeing the spells written there brought forth a wave of fear that I tried to dismiss. Selene's work glowed the brightest: she had cast these spells recently.

"All right," breathed Hunter next to me. I kept the spells in sight as he began slowly and laboriously dismantling them, layer by layer, saying the words that unknit the spells, dispersing their energy and power. My head was beginning to ache with a sharp, piercing pain at my temples as I strove to concentrate. The cold wind seemed to intensify, and it buffeted us as we stood on that narrow staircase outside the attic of the stone house.

At last the spells were taken apart, and then it was simple for Hunter to magickally undo the mechanical lock of the door. It swung open silently, and with a glance at each other, Hunter and I stepped through.

Inside, Cal's room was as he'd left it that night he'd tried to kill me. With a quick scan I saw he had taken some of his books, and probably some clothes, since his dresser drawers were pulled askew. But it didn't appear that he'd been staying here.

The room was startlingly familiar, and it brought an unwelcome ache to my heart to see the place where Cirrus had had circles, the chair where I'd opened my birthday presents from Cal, the bed where we had lain and kissed for hours.

As noiselessly as possible, we did a quick search of Cal's room. I held my athame before me and on virtually every surface turned up runes, sigils, other markings: the magick Cal had worked in this room. But other than the marks, and some dangerous tools and talismans, we found nothing, no sign of Mary K. or of Cal's or Selene's whereabouts.

"This way," Hunter said, his voice no louder than a whisper, and motioned toward the door that led to the rest of the house. When he opened the door, I almost recoiled. Now I could sense Selene, feel her dark presence. She had been working black magick in this house: its bitter and acrid aura clung to everything. It felt like the very air was contaminated, and I was afraid.

Gently Hunter brushed his hand against my hair, my cheek. "Remember," he whispered. "Fear is one of her weapons. Don't give in to it. Trust your instincts."

My instincts? I thought, panicked. We both knew how reliable *those* had been in the past. But I knew that was the wrong answer, so I just nodded, and we started down the narrow back staircase to the second floor. Maeve's wand felt slim and powerful in my left hand, and the athame felt as protective as a shield. But I still felt vulnerable as I crept downstairs and was glad Hunter was beside me.

Cal's room took up the entire attic, and on the second floor were five bedrooms and four bathrooms. Here, as upstairs, the dusty floors were undisturbed until our feet traced patterns on them. To a rational mind, that meant that no person had walked here since the house had been shut. But witchcraft is not bound by laws of rationality.

Searching as a witch was different than searching as a person. I used my eyes and ears, but more important, I used my senses, my intuition, my Wiccan instinct that warned me when danger was near and what form it would take. Between me, my tools, and Hunter, we made short work of the second floor. None of the rooms looked touched, but more telling, none of the rooms *felt* touched. I didn't detect

Selene's unmistakable aura in any of the bedrooms: she hadn't been to the second floor.

The only time I felt anything at all was when I paused before an open window in the last bedroom. I felt a faint chill there, as if I stood beneath an AC vent, but the window curtains were motionless, and then I picked up on it: Cal. Cal had been here; he'd stood here with a lit candle not long ago. The day Bree, Mary K., and I had come back from Practical Magick and I had seen him. His traces lingered here still.

Hunter came to stand by me. Our eyes met, and he nodded. He felt it, too. Taking my elbow, he led me to the main staircase, the wide, ornately carved steps leading to the first floor. The rich carpet looked dull, dusty, and my nose tickled as our feet stirred motes into the chill, silent air.

Selene's presence felt stronger with every step. In my hand, the hilt of the ancient Belwicket athame seemed to grow warm. Then I knew: Selene was in her library, the hidden library that I had seen only once, a lifetime ago, when I had discovered Maeve's Book of Shadows on Selene's shelves. When Hunter had come here, he hadn't even been able to find the concealed door. In fact, the council witches themselves hadn't been able to break the spells that guarded Selene's secret lair.

Today would be different. Today we would get into the hidden library because today Selene wanted us to. She had taken my sister to try to make me come here. In an instant I saw the whole plan: Selene had been trying to get into my mind and had been thwarted by my ability to block her. Had she then turned to my sister? Mary K. had been withdrawn and sad for weeks—was Selene working on her mind even then?

Since she had first met me, Selene had been courting me, through her son. She had commanded Cal to get close to me, and he had. She had wanted him to make me love him, and he had. She had wanted him to convince me to join their side, to ally my magick and Maeve's coven tools with theirs. This I had refused. Since then she had wanted two things: my compliance or death and Maeve's tools. And now here I was, in her house, at her bidding, just as she had planned.

Today we would finish what had been set in motion the day we met. With a sudden, chilling certainty I knew that Selene intended for only one of us to survive this encounter: her. By the end of the day she wanted me dead and she wanted Maeve's tools. No doubt she also wanted Hunter dead. Mary K. probably didn't matter much to her, but as a witness, she would have to die as well.

I almost sagged against the stair rail as these thoughts flashed like lightning across my mind. If I were a full, initiated witch, I would be quaking in my boots at the idea of facing Selene Belltower. If I had the entire council standing behind me, wands raised, I would still feel a cold and desperate terror. As it was, there was only me and Hunter, and I was just a barefoot, talented amateur from a small town.

I gulped and looked at Hunter, my eyes wide and filling with hopeless tears. Jesus, get me out of this, I thought in panic. Please, God. Hunter watched me, his eyes narrowed, and then he reached out and gripped my shoulder hard, so hard, I winced. "Don't be afraid," he whispered fiercely.

Yeah, right, I wanted to scream. Every cell in my body wanted to turn, run, and get the hell out of here. Only the image of my innocent sister, trustingly getting into Selene's car, kept me in place. I felt nausea rise in the back of my throat, and I wanted to sit down and start crying, right there on the steps.

"Morgan, come." Selene's voice spoke in my mind.

My eyes widened, and I looked at Hunter. His face showed me that he hadn't heard it.

"Selene," I whispered. "She knows I'm here."

Hunter's face hardened. Leaning over, he put his mouth close to mine. "We can do this, love. You can do this."

I tried to focus, but I couldn't stop thinking that I might die today. A deep despair started in the pit of my stomach, as if I had swallowed a cold stone the size of my fist.

But there was nothing to be done. Mary K. was here. She was my sister, and she needed me now. Hunter was by my side as I took a step downward, my bare feet making no sound on the thick carpet. When we reached the bottom of the steps, the parquet floor was cold and dust covered. Here, at last, were signs of disturbance. I saw dim outlines of footprints, swept mostly away by something soft and heavy— the bottom of a cape? A blanket?

I turned and headed down the hallway toward the large kitchen. Halfway down the hall I stopped and looked to my right. The door had to be around here somewhere, I knew. The door to Selene's library.

# 16.
# Selene

June 1982

Praise the Goddess. I finally had my baby boy. He is a big, perfect baby, with fine dark hair like mine and odd, slate-colored eyes that will no doubt change color later. Norris Hathaway and Helen Ford attended as midwives and were absolute lifesavers during labor. Labor! Goddess, I had no idea. I felt I was being rent in two, torn apart, giving birth to an entire world. I tried to be strong but I admit I screamed and cried. Then my son crowned, and Norris reached down to twist out his shoulders. I looked down to see my son emerge into the light, and my tears of pain turned to tears of joy. It was the most incredible magick I've ever made.

His naming ceremony will be next week. I've decided on Calhoun: warrior. His Amyranth name is Sgàth, which means darkness. It's a sweet darkness, like his hair.

*Daniel didn't come to the birth: a sign of his weakness. He slouches around, mooning over England and his whore there, which makes me despise him, though I can't stop wanting him. He seems pleased with his son, less pleased with me. Now that our baby is here, flesh and blood, beautiful and perfect, perhaps Daniel will find happiness with me. It would be best for him if he did.*

*Now that I've had the baby, I'm hungry to get back to work with Amyranth. They were in Wales and then in Germany in the past several months, and I was gnashing my teeth with envy. The Germany trip yielded some ancient books on darkness that I can't wait to see—I can already taste them. It will be intensely fulfilling for me to watch Calhoun grow up within the arms of Amyranth, their son as well as mine. He will be my instrument, my weapon.*

*—SB*

Selene wasn't going to make it *too* easy: it took Hunter and me several minutes to even find the dim outlines of the concealed door. Finally I managed to come up with one of Alyce's revealing spells and, using my athame, detected the barest fingernail-thin line in the hallway wall.

"Ah," Hunter breathed. "Well done."

I stood by, concentrating, lending my power to Hunter while he carefully, slowly, and methodically dismantled the concealment and closure spells. I felt Selene's magick as bursts of pain that needled into every part of my body, but I thought about Mary K., and I tried to ignore them.

It felt like hours later that Hunter passed his hand down the wall and I heard the faint snick of the latch opening. The door, barely taller than Hunter's head, swung open.

The next instant I clamped my mouth shut as darkness and evil surged through the doorway like a flood tide, coming to suck us under and into the room. Instinctively I stepped back, throwing up ward-evil spells and spells of protection on top of the ones Hunter and I had already placed on ourselves. Then I heard the soft, dark velvet of Selene's laughter, from inside the library, and I forced myself to take a step forward, across the threshold, into her lair.

It was dark in the room. The only light present was coming from several black pillar candles on wrought-iron holders taller than me. I remembered the layout from the only other time I had been here: it was a big room, with a high ceiling. Bookshelves lined the walls, connected by brass railings and small ladders on wheels. There was a deep leather couch, several glass display cases, Selene's huge walnut desk, a library table with a globe, and several book stands holding enormous, ancient, crumbling tomes. And everywhere in the room, in every book and cushion and rug, was Selene's magick, her dark magick, her forbidden spells and experiments and concoctions. The needlelike pains intensified as I scanned the room for Mary K.

Hunter moved behind me, coming into the room. I sensed danger coming from him, a deep, controlled anger at Selene's obvious misuse of magick.

"Morgan!" Mary K.'s soft, young voice came from a dark corner of the room. I cast out my senses and detected my sister huddled against the far wall. Sweeping the room for signs of Selene, I walked quickly to Mary K. and knelt down beside her.

"Are you okay?" I murmured, and she leaned forward, pressing her face against me.

"I don't know why I'm here," she said. Her voice was thick, as if she'd just woken from a deep sleep. "I don't know what's going on."

I was ashamed to tell her she had been merely bait, intended to lure me here. I was ashamed to admit that she was in terrible danger because of me and my Wiccan heritage. Instead I said, "It'll be okay. We'll get you out of here. Just hold on, okay?"

She nodded and slumped back down. Just in touching her I had felt that she was spelled—not strongly, but enough to make her lax and docile. Rage sparked deep in my stomach, and I stood. Hunter was still close to the door, and I saw he had prudently wedged a small wooden trunk in its opening.

Where was Selene? I'd heard her laugh. Of course, it could have been an illusion, a glamor. I was panicking: would I be locked in and trapped here? Would Selene set me on fire? Would I burn to death after all? My breathing quickened, and I peered into the darkest shadows of the room.

"Selene will try to scare you," Hunter had said. "Don't be fooled." Easier said than done. I stepped closer to one of the pillar candles and focused on it. Light, I thought. Fire. There were candles in holders on the walls, and around the room were candelabras filled with tall black tapers. One by one I lit them with my mind, sparking them into life, into existence, and the shadows lessened and the room grew brighter.

"Very good," said Selene's voice. "But then, you're a fire fairy. Like Bradhadair."

Bradhadair had been Maeve's Wiccan name, the name given her by her coven. It had been in her Book of Shadows, and probably no one else alive today knew about it. I swung toward the sound of Selene's voice and saw her appear in front of one of the bookcases, stepping out from a deep shadow into the light. She was as beautiful as ever, with her sun-streaked dark hair and strange golden eyes, so like Cal's. This was his mother. She had made him what he was.

Like me, Selene wore only her witch's robe, which was a deep crimson silk embroidered all over with symbols I recognized as the same ancient alphabet she'd used for the door spell. It had been taught to Alyce only so she could recognize it and neutralize it: it was inherently evil, and the letters could only be used for dark magick. Because Alyce had learned it, I knew it, too.

"Morgan, thank you for coming," Selene said. Out of the corner of my eye I saw Hunter circling the room, trying to put Selene between me and him. "I'm truly sorry I had to resort to these means. I assure you I've caused no harm to your sister. But once I realized you wouldn't respond to an ordinary invitation, well, I had to get creative." She gave me a charming, rueful smile and seemed like the most attractive person I'd ever seen. "Please forgive me."

I regarded her. Once I had admired her intensely, envied her knowledge and power and skill. Now I knew better.

"No," I said clearly, and her eyes narrowed.

"It's over, Selene," Hunter said in a voice like ice. "You've had a long run, but your days with Amyranth are done."

Amyranth? What's that? I wondered.

"Morgan?" Selene asked, ignoring Hunter.

"No," I repeated. "I don't forgive you."

"You don't understand," she said patiently. "You don't know enough to realize what you're doing. Hunter here is simply weak and misguided, and who cares? He isn't worth anything to anyone. But you, my dear. You have potential I can't ignore." She smiled again, but it was creepy this time, like a skeleton baring its teeth. "I offer you the chance to be more powerful than you could possibly imagine," she went on. I could hear the sibilant swish of her robe as she moved closer to me. "You are one of the few witches I've met who's worthy of being one of us. You could add to our greatness instead of draining us. You—and your coven tools."

My fists instinctively tightened on my wand and athame, and I tried to release the tension in my body. I had to stay loose and calm, to let the magick flow.

"No," I said again, and my senses picked up the instantaneous flare of anger from Selene. She quickly clamped it down, but the fact that I even felt it meant she wasn't as much in control of herself as she needed to be. I took a deep breath and went against every instinct that I had: I tried to relax, to open myself up, to stop protecting myself. I released anger, fear, distrust, my desire for revenge: I kept thinking, Magick is openness, trust, love. Magick is beauty. Magick is strength and forgiveness. I am made of magick. I thought how I felt after my tàth meànma brach, how I felt that magick was everywhere, in everything, in every molecule. If magick surrounded me, it was mine for the taking. I could access it. I could use it. I had the power of the world at my fingertips if I chose to let it in.

I chose to.

The next moment found me doubled over, gasping, as a wave of searing, biting pain hit me. I gagged, choking on the horrible cramping agony, and then I was on my hands and knees on the floor, sucking in breath and feeling like I was being turned inside out.

"Morgan!" Hunter said, but I was only barely aware of him. Every nerve in my body was being flayed, every sense I had was occupied with the exquisite, soul-consuming torture. My hands, still gripping the tools, clawed into the carpet as an invisible ax cleaved my belly in two. In disbelief I stared at myself, expecting to see guts and blood spewing from my body, but I was whole, unchanged on the outside. And yet I was gasping, writhing on the ground as my insides were eaten by acid.

It was an illusion. I knew it intellectually. But my body didn't know it. Between spasms I glanced up at Selene. She was smiling, a small, secret smile that showed me she enjoyed causing me agony.

"Morgan, you're stronger than that!" Hunter snapped, and his words seeped into my consciousness. "Get up! She can't do this to you!"

She's a playground bully, I thought, my breath coming in fast, shallow pants. When I had bound Cal and Hunter, had knocked them to the ground, I had felt the dark, shameful pleasure of controlling another person. That's what Selene was feeling now.

It was an illusion. Everything in me thought I was dying. But I was more than just my thoughts, more than just my feelings, more than my body. I was Morgan of Kithic and of Belwicket, and I had a thousand years of Woodbane strength inside me.

I feel no pain, I thought. I feel no panic.

Slowly I rose back up to my hands and knees, my mouth parched, sweat popping out on my forehead. My hair dragged on the ground, my hands were claws around my tools. My tools. They were not Maeve's. Not any longer.

I feel no pain, I thought fiercely. I am fine. Everything in my life is perfect, whole, and complete. I am strength. I am power. I am magick.

Then I was standing tall, my back straight, my hands at my sides. I looked calmly at Selene and for one fraction of a second saw disbelief in her eyes. More than disbelief. I saw the barest hint of fear.

Whirling, she turned to face Hunter and threw out her hand. I saw no witch fire, but Hunter immediately raised his hands and drew sigils in the air. His chest heaved as he pulled in breath, and though I couldn't actually see anything, I knew that Selene was trying to do to him what she had done to me and that he was resisting it. I had never seen so much of his power, not even when he was putting the braigh on David Redstone, and it was awesome.

But it wasn't enough for us to resist Selene. We had to actually vanquish her. We had to render her powerless somehow. I searched Alyce's data banks, concealed within my brain, and began to sift through the encyclopedias of knowledge she had acquired in her lifetime.

How do you fight darkness with light? I asked myself. In the same way that sunlight dispels a shadow, came the unhelpful answer. I almost screamed with frustration—I needed something practical, something concrete. Not mumbo jumbo.

The edge of my senses picked up a slight breathing

sound—Mary K. She sat, as motionless as a doll, her open eyes unseeing, in the shadows of the corner. Without thinking, I quickly called up spells of distraction, of turn-away. If Selene looked at Mary K., I wanted her to shift focus slightly, to see nothing, to not remember my sister's presence.

Hunter and Selene were facing each other, and suddenly Hunter surprised me by snatching up a crystal globe from a shelf and humming it at Selene. Her eyes widened and she stepped sideways, but the globe hit her shoulder with an audible thunk. In the next instant she flung out her hand and an athame flew across the room, straight at Hunter. It reminded me too much of that awful night weeks ago, and I flinched, but Hunter deflected the knife easily, and it glanced off a lamp and fell to the ground.

What could I do? I had no experience at things whizzing through the air—I had never practiced controlling physical things like that. In this battle I would need to use magick and magick alone. I would need to use my truth.

I saw Hunter pull out his braigh, the silver chain that was spelled to prevent its wearer from making magick. Coupled with some spells, it was enough to stop most witches.

But Selene merely glanced at Hunter with contempt, dismissing his threat and turning to me. Walking quickly across the room, she said, "Morgan, stop this foolishness. Call off your watchdog. You have it in you to be one of the greatest witches of all time: you are a true Woodbane, pure and ancient. Don't deny your heritage any longer. Join us, my dear."

"No, Selene," I said. Inside me, I consciously opened the door to my magick and with a deep, indrawn breath allowed it to flow. The first strains of a power chant began to thread their way into my mind.

Her beautiful face hardened, and I once again realized what I was up against. Hunter had said that Selene had been wanted by the council for years—that she had been implicated in countless deaths. Clinging to calmness, I nevertheless wished every member of the council would suddenly burst through the open door, capes waving, wands brandished, spells spouting from their lips. Coming here alone had been desperate. It had been crazy. Worse, it had been stupid.

Hunter began moving on Selene. His lips were moving, his eyes intent, and I knew he was starting the binding spells he used as a Seeker. Seeming bored, Selene barely waved a hand at him, and he stopped still, blinking. Then he started forward again, and again she stopped him.

With my mind I reached out, closed my eyes, and tried to see what I felt was there. I saw that Selene was putting up blocks and that Hunter was working through the blocks— but not as quickly as she was able to put them up. I also saw the first thin ribbons of my power spell coming to me, floating toward me on the winds of my heritage. I reached out for them, but Selene interrupted me.

"Morgan, don't you want to know the truth about how your mother died?"

# 17.
# Shift

*Yule, 1982*

    *The house is decorated with yew boughs and holly, wintergreen and mistletoe. Red candles burn and catch Cal's eyes, now golden, like mine. This is his first Yule, and he loves it.*

    *I found out that Daniel's whore in England had a baby, a boy, a month ago. It's Daniel's. She named him Giomanach. Daniel must be shielding her, because I haven't been able to find her, this Fiona, and get rid of her. Now I'm going to ask Amyranth to help me. It's hard to describe the feelings I have. It's so painful to admit to humiliation, despair, fury. If I were truly strong, I would strike Daniel dead. In my fantasies I've done that a thousand times—I've put his head on a spike in my front yard, cut out his heart, and mailed it to dear Fiona. I* would sory to see her opening the box, seeing his heart. I would laugh.

Except that this is Daniel. I don't understand why I feel about him the way I do. Goddess help me, I can't stop loving him. If my love for him could be cut out from me, I would take up an athame and do it. If my need for him could be burned out, I would sear myself with witch fire or candle fire or an athame heated red hot in flame.

The fact that I still love him, despite his betrayal, despite the fact that he had a bastard with another woman, is like a sickness. I asked him how it had happened; were they both such poor witches that they couldn't even weave a contraceptive spell? He snapped at me and said no, the child was an accident, conceived of honest emotion. Unlike Calhoun, who had been my decision alone. He stormed out, into the wet San Francisco fog. He'll be back. It'll be against his will, but he always returns.

The joy in my life right now consists of one being, one perfection who delights me. Cal at six months is surpassing all my hopes and expectations. He has wisdom in his baby eyes, a hunger for knowledge I recognize. He's a beautiful child and easy: calm tempered yet determined, willful yet heartbreakingly sweet. To see his face light up when I come in makes everything else worthwhile. So this Yule is a time of darkness and light, for me as well as the Goddess.

—SB

I blinked and snapped my head to look at Selene. She will use anything against you, I thought. Even your dead mother. This is why you needed to know yourself. And you do.

At once Selene seemed pathetic, like an ant, like an insect, and I felt all-powerful. In my mind the ancient ribbons of power, the crystalline tune that contained the true name of magick itself, intensified.

"I know exactly how my mother died," I answered evenly, and saw her flicker of surprise. "She and Angus were burned to death by Ciaran, her mùirn beatha dàn."

I felt rather than saw Selene sending out fast, dark tendrils of magick, and before they reached me, I put up a block around myself so I remained untouched inside it, free of her anger. I felt the urge to laugh at how easy it was.

But Selene was older than I, much more educated than I, and in the end she knew how to fight better than I did. "You're seeing only what Hunter wants you to see," she said with a frightening intensity. She moved closer to me still, her eyes glowing like a tiger's, lit from within. "He has been controlling you these past weeks. Can't you see that? Look at him."

For some stupid reason I actually did flick a glance toward Hunter. "Don't listen to her!" he gasped, walking toward me with halting movements.

Before my eyes, the Hunter I had come to know changed: the bones of his face grew heavier, his jaw sharper, his mouth more cruel. His eyes sank into shadow. His skin was mottled with odd white striations. His mouth twisted in a hungry leer, and even his teeth seemed sharper, more pointed, more animal-like. He looked like an evil caricature of himself.

In my split second of uncertainty, of dismay, Selene struck.

"An nahl nath rac!" she cried, and shot a bolt of crackly blue lightning toward Hunter. It hit his throat and he gagged, his eyes wide, and sank to his knees.

"Hunter!" I yelled. He still looked different, evil, and I knew Selene was doing it, but I couldn't help feeling repelled. I felt intense guilt and shame. I was supposed to trust myself, my own instincts, but the problem was, my instincts had been wrong before.

Now Selene was muttering dark spells as she advanced on me, and involuntarily I took a step back. All at once panic came crashing down on me: I had screwed up. I had made a good start but had lost it. Now Hunter was down, Mary K. was vulnerable, and I was going to die.

I felt the first prickles of Selene's spells as they flitted around me like biting insects. Tiny stings bit my skin, making me writhe, and gray mist swirled at the edges of my vision. I realized she was going to wrap me in a cloud of pain and smother me. And I couldn't stop her.

"Not my daughter."

I heard the Irish-accented voice clearly in my head, its sweet inflection not hiding the steel underneath the words. I recognized it instantly as Maeve, my birth mother. "Not *my* daughter," she said again in my mind.

I gulped in a breath. I couldn't let Selene win. Hunter was curled on the floor, motionless. I couldn't even see Mary K.; the gray mist had closed in so that I could see only Selene, glowing in front of me as if she contained a fire within her. In my mind I stretched out my hand to seize power, to draw it to me. I tried to forget everything, to concentrate only on my own spells of protection and binding. I am made of magick, I told myself. All of magick is mine for the taking. Again and again I repeated these words until they seemed part of my song, my chant that calls power. Ancient words, recognizable but unknown, came to my lips, and I flung out my arms and twirled in a circle, barely feeling my hair flying out in back of me.

"Menach bis," I muttered, feeling the words coming to me in a voice that I didn't recognize, a man's voice. Could it be Angus? "Allaigh nith rah. Feard, burn, torse, menach bis." I swirled faster in my circle of one, weaving this spell, this one perfect spell that would protect me, stop Selene, help Hunter, and keep Mary K. safe. To me it was like seeing a perfect geometric shape forming in space: the lines of the spell, its forms, its intersections and boundaries and limitations. It was a shape made of light, of energy, of music, and I saw it forming around me in the room, being woven by the words that spilled from my mouth.

And as the shape formed, I saw another shape come into focus in the background, behind Selene. Cal. He stepped through the door, into the library, and Selene's head turned toward him.

"Mother." His voice was clear, strong, but I couldn't read his intentions from his tone. Had he come to help me? Or to help Selene kill me?

No time to stop and ask. I saw myself as if from outside, dressed in Maeve's green silk robe, its hem rippling around my bare ankles like seawater as I turned. Magick crackled all around me, glowing like fireflies, floating in the air: a dandelion flower of magick that had burst and was seeding itself everywhere. Motes of power began to draw themselves around Selene. Inside me was a fierce pride, an exhilaration in my strength and the ecstasy of weaving this spell. With my ancient words I gathered the motes around Selene; I began to encase her in them, as if I were sealing her inside.

Dimly I realized what I was doing. Dimly I recognized the cage of ice and light as I wove it around Selene. It was the same as the cage that had imprisoned Maeve and Angus. But I had no time, no energy to spare for wondering what this meant, where this knowledge had come from. I was caught in the magick. It consumed me.

It was the most beautiful and the most terrifying thing I had ever seen. It was like the beauty of a star's death when it goes nova: exhilarating and devastating. The awe inside me welled up and spilled out of my eyes as tears: purifying salt crystals in and of themselves.

"No!" Selene bellowed suddenly, a horrible, gut-wrenching howl of fury and darkness. "No!" The crystal cage around her shattered, and she loomed within it, dark and malevolent and cloaked with blackness.

I didn't have the experience to duck or swerve or throw up a block. I saw the boiling cloud of dark vapor spinning away from Selene, churning toward me, and I knew that in a moment I would experience the soul being sucked from my body. All I could do was watch.

And then a dark form blocked my sight, and like a high-speed camera, my mind snapped image after image but gave me no time to process what happened. Cal surged forward, his eyes burning and hollow as he blocked Selene's attack on me. I stepped back, eyes wide, mouth open in shock as Cal absorbed the dark vapor; it surrounded him, fell upon him, and then he was sinking to the ground, his eyes already unseeing as his soul left his body.

Now I knew. He had come to help me.

Selene was on him in an instant, screaming, falling onto his chest, beating him, trying to force life back into him as I watched stupidly and without comprehension.

"Sgàth!" she shrieked, barely sounding human. "Sgàth! Come back!" I had never heard a banshee, but that's what she sounded like, an inhuman keening and wailing that seemed to have the agony of the world in it. Her son was dead, and she had killed him.

When Hunter staggered to me and grabbed my hand, I could only stare at him. He looked like himself again, pale and ill, but the Hunter I knew.

"Now," he croaked, his voice sounding charred. "Now."

It all came back to me again, my brain began to function, and Hunter and I took advantage of Selene's grief and joined our powers to bind her.

Feeling cold, I gathered my magick and wove it tightly once more, a beautiful cage. Hunter stepped forward and snapped the silver braigh onto Selene's wrists, catching her unguarded as she held Cal's face and wept over him. She screamed again, the chain already burning her flesh. I shrank back at the horror of it: Cal's dead body, Selene's grief, her endless screaming as she thrashed, trying to get the braigh off.

Then she paused for an instant, her eyes rolling back into her head, and began a deep guttural chant. I saw the silver chain begin to crumble and dissolve. "Morgan!" Hunter yelled, and quickly I dropped my beautiful cage of light and magick over her.

It was like watching a black moth slowly smothering inside a glass. Within a minute Selene's rage was burning out: her screams were quieting, her thrashing had stilled; she lay coiled inside my spell as if trying to hide from the pain.

When I met Hunter's eyes, he looked horrified, shaken, yet there was an acknowledgment on his face that at last he had accomplished his goal. He was breathing hard, sweat beading his pale face, and he met my eyes. "Let's get out of here," he said shakily. "This place is evil."

But I was frozen, staring at Cal. Beautiful Cal, whom I had kissed and loved so much. Kneeling, I reached out to touch his face. Hunter didn't try to stop me.

I shuddered and shrank back—Cal's skin was already cooling. Suddenly racking sobs began to burst through my chest. I wept for Cal: for the brief illusion of love that I'd cherished so deeply, for the way he'd given his own life for mine, for what he could have been if Selene hadn't warped him.

What happened then is hard to explain. Hunter shouted suddenly and I whirled, tears still raining down my cheeks, to see Selene standing, her wrists held in front of her. I could see the blisters, but the silver braigh was gone. Her golden eyes seemed to burn through us. Then she sank down, collapsing on the oriental carpet with her eyes closed. Her mouth opened, and a vaporous stream floated out, like smoke.

Hunter shouted again and threw out his arm to push me back. We watched as the vapor streamed upward and seemed to disappear through the one library window. Then it was gone, and Selene was still and ashen. Hunter stepped quickly to her and put his fingers against her throat. When he looked up, his eyes reflected his shock. "She's dead."

"Goddess," I breathed. I had helped kill Selene—and Cal, too. I was a murderer. How could Hunter and I be standing in a room with two corpses? It was incomprehensible.

"What was that smoke?" My voice was thin and shaky.

"I don't know. I've never seen anything like it before." He looked worried.

"Morgan?" came Mary K.'s voice, and I shook off my paralysis and hurried to her. She was sitting up, blinking, and then she stood to brush off her clothes. She looked around her as if she were waking from a dream, and maybe she was. "What's going on? Where are we?"

"It's all right, Mary K.," said Hunter in his still-raspy voice. He came and took her arm so that we braced her on either side. "Everything's all right now. Let's get you out of here."

By keeping his body close to her, Hunter managed to steer Mary K. out of the room without her seeing Selene's or Cal's bodies. I followed them, forcing myself not to look back. When we were in the hall, Hunter spelled the library door so that it couldn't be shut again. Then we went outside, into the darkness, the biting cold of winter pressing in on us.

As we came down the stone steps, Sky pulled up in her car, followed by a gray sedan. A stout man with graying hair climbed out, and Hunter moved to speak to him: he had to be the closest council member.

I sat on the broad stone steps in my gown. I couldn't think about what had just happened. I couldn't process it. All I could do was hold Mary K.'s hand and start to think up what I would tell my parents. Every version I could think of started with, "It's because I'm a witch."